# A NIGHT TO REMEMBER

Cormac grinned as he unbuckled his sword, tossed it aside, then yanked off his boots. "Would ye belittle the first poetry this poor mon has e'er uttered?"

"Nay," Elspeth whispered, praying that he was not about to give her yet another lesson in the torturous art of being aroused, then left unsatisfied, as she welcomed him into her arms. "Was that what that was?"

He kissed her and she quickly wrapped her arms around him, wondering if this time she could hold him until they were both beyond reason.

"My bonny Elspeth," Cormac murmured against her throat as he unlaced her chemise, "ye should push me away."

"Why? Ye always seem to manage that all on your own."

"Nay, not this time."

"Are ye sure?"

Cormac crouched over her as he eased her thin chemise off her shoulders. "Oh, aye, my green-eyed temptress. This time only ye can stop this."

Seeing the hungry way he stared at her, she threaded her fingers through his hair and gently tugged him closer. "Then there will be nay stopping this time. . . ."

## Books by Hannah Howell

ONLY FOR YOU
MY VALIANT KNIGHT
UNCONQUERED
WILD ROSES
A TASTE OF FIRE
HIGHLAND DESTINY
HIGHLAND HONOR
HIGHLAND PROMISE
A STOCKINGFUL OF JOY
HIGHLAND VOW
HIGHLAND KNIGHT
HIGHLAND HEARTS
HIGHLAND BRIDE
HIGHLAND ANGEL
HIGHLAND GROOM
HIGHLAND WARRIOR
RECKLESS
HIGHLAND CONQUEROR
HIGHLAND CHAMPION

Published by Zebra Books

# HIGHLAND VOW

## Hannah Howell

Zebra Books
Kensington Publishing Corp.
http://www.zebrabooks.com

ZEBRA BOOKS are published by

Kensington Publishing Corp.
850 Third Avenue
New York, NY 10022

All Kensington Titles, Imprints, and Distributed Lines are
available at special quantity discounts for bulk purchases for
sales promotions, premiums, fund-raising, and educational
or institutional use.

Special book excerpts or customized printings can also be
created to fit specific needs. For details, write or phone the
office of the Kensington special sales manager: Kensington
Publishing Corp., 850 Third Avenue, New York, NY 10022,
attn: Special Sales Department, Phone: 1-800-221-2647.

Zebra and the Z logo Reg. U.S. Pat. & TM Off.

First Printing: June 2000

10   9

Printed in the United States of America

# THE MURRAY FAMILY LINEAGE

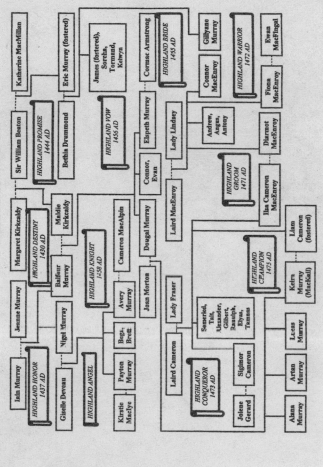

# Prologue

*Scotland—1446*

"Pintle head!"

"Dog droppings!"

Cormac Armstrong almost laughed as the angry childish voices halted his slow, resigned descent into unconciousness. It seemed a cruel jest of fate that he would slowly bleed his young life away to the sharp sounds of bairns taunting each other. The sound filled him with an overwhelming melancholy. It stirred memories of all the times he had quarreled with his brothers, painfully bringing him to the realization that he would never see them again.

"Ye are ugly!"

"Oh, aye? Hah! Weel, I say that ye are ugly, too, and stupid!"

The sound of a small fist hitting a small body was swiftly followed by the raucous sound of children fighting. More young voices cut through the chill, damp morning air as the other children cheered on their selected champions. It sounded as if there was a veritable horde of children on the other side of the thicket he hid behind. Cormac prayed that they would stay where they were, that none of them would cross to his side of the thicket and innocently become involved in his desperate troubles. A heartbeat later, he cursed, for he realized his prayers were to go unanswered.

Huge green eyes and a mass of thick raven curls were the first thing he saw as a small, thin girl wriggled through the thicket and knelt at his side. She was an enchanting child and Cormac desperately wished she would go far away. He did not think his enemies were still following his trail, but he could be wrong, and this fey child would be brutally pushed aside by them, perhaps even killed or injured.

"Go, lassie," he ordered, his voice little more than a hoarse, trembling whisper. "Take all your wee companions and flee this place. Quickly."

"Ye are bleeding," she said after looking him over.

His eyes widened slightly as she began to smooth her tiny, soft hand over his forehead. Her voice was surprisingly deep for such a wee lass, almost sultry. *More voice than girl,* he mused.

"Aye," he agreed, "and I will soon be dead, which isnae a sight for those bonny big eyes."

"Nay, ye willnae die. My mither can heal most any hurt, ye ken. I am Elspeth Murray."

"And I am Cormac Armstrong." He was startled when he found the strength to shake the tiny hand she thrust at him. "Ye must nay tell your mother about me."

"Ye need my mither to make ye stop bleeding."

"Lass, I am bleeding because someone is trying verra hard to kill me."

"Why?"

"They say I am a murderer."

"Are ye?"

"Nay."

"Then my mither can help ye."

Cormac desperately wanted to allow the child to fetch her mother to heal his wounds. He did not want to die. He certainly did not want to die for a crime he had not committed, at least not before he could clear that black stain from his name. It was all so unfair, he thought, then grimaced. He realized that he sounded very much like a child himself.

"Ah, poor laddie," she murmured. "Ye are in pain. Ye need quiet. I will tell the bairns to hush." Before he could protest, she rose and walked back to the edge of the thicket, thrusting herself partway through. "Ye can all just shut your wee mouths," Elspeth yelled in an astoundingly loud, commanding voice. "There is a poor mon bleeding o'er here and he needs some peace. Payton, take your wee thin legs and run. Find Donald or my fither. Get someone, for this laddie sore needs help."

The only thing Cormac could think of to say when she returned to his side was, "I am nay a laddie. I am a mon, a hunted mon." He softly cursed as he watched other children begin to wriggle their way through the thicket.

"How old arc ye?" Elspeth asked as she began to smooth her small hand over his forehead again.

"Seventeen." Cormac wondered how such a tiny hand could be so soothing.

"I am nine today. 'Tis why so many Murrays are gathered together. And ye *are* a lad. My fither says anyone beneath one and twenty years is a lad or a lass and some are ne'er any more, e'en if they grow as old and big as he is. 'Tis what he told my cousin Cordell when he turned sixteen and was boasting of what a fine, grand stallion of a mon he was."

"Aye," agreed an amber-eyed child who was even smaller than Elspeth. She sat down next to him. "Uncle Balfour says a lad needs to gain his spurs, get himself a wife and bairns, and bring honor to both duties ere he can prance about and declare himself a mon. Why is he bleeding, Elspeth?"

"Because he has a few muckle great holes in him, Avery." Elspeth briefly grinned when the other children giggled.

"I can see that. How did he get hurt?"

"Someone is trying to make him pay for a murder he didnae commit."

"Lass"—Cormac glanced around at what was an astonishing array of eleven beautiful children, then fixed his gaze upon Elspeth—"I said I was innocent, but ye cannae be sure I was telling ye the truth."

"Aye, ye are," Elspeth said firmly.

"No one can lie to Elspeth," said a tall, slender boy crouched to the left of Cormac. "I am Ewan, her brother, and 'tis a most troublesome thing, I can tell ye."

Cormac almost smiled, but then fixed a stern gaze on the lad, who looked to be a little older than Elspeth. "Then she will also ken that I speak the truth when I tell her I am naught but trouble—deadly trouble—and that she should just leave me to my fate. Ye should all hie away home ere the danger sniffing at my heels reaches your gates."

The boy opened his mouth to speak, then rapidly closed it. Cormac followed the lad's wide gaze to his sister and his own eyes widened slightly. She was sitting very straight, her beautiful eyes fixed unwaveringly upon her hapless brother. There was a very stern, very adult look upon her small face. Cormac could easily sympathize with the boy's reluctance to argue with that look.

"Ewan, why dinnae ye and the other laddies see if ye can find something to make a litter," Elspeth said. "Oh, and ere ye skip off to do as ye are told, ye can give me that wineskin ye took from Donald."

"I ne'er," the boy began to protest. Then he cursed and handed the wineskin to Elspeth before he and the other boys disappeared.

"There is no real harm in the lad testing his head for wine, lass," Cormac said.

"I ken it and Donald puts a hearty brew in his wineskin, but I am thinking ye will find more use of it. Ewan can test the strength of his innards for this potion some other day."

She revealed a surprising strength as she slipped one thin arm around his shoulders and helped him sit up enough to take a drink. It was not only surprise that made him cough a little, however, as he took a drink. Wine did not burn its way down your throat and spread such warmth throughout your body.

"Avery, ye go and fetch me some water," Elspeth ordered. Then, as soon as her cousin slipped away, she looked at the two remaining girls. "Bega, Morna, one of ye will give me your shift skirt so that I may bind this laddie's wounds. S'truth, I shall need a good piece of both."

"Why dinnae ye use your own?" grumbled the small fair-haired girl. "I will be scolded."

"Nay for helping a mon stop his life's blood from soaking the ground, Bega."

As the two little girls struggled to tear their shifts, Cormac looked at Elspeth. "Lass, this is no chore for a wee child."

"Weel, it willnae be fun, but we cannae be sure how long it will take Payton to bring help, so we had best stop this bleeding if we can. My mither is a healer. I ken a few things. Have some more wine."

"This isnae wine," he murmured, then took another drink. She smiled and he thought, a little dazedly, that she would be a very beautiful woman when she finished growing.

"I ken it. So do most others. But Donald's wife had an evil-tempered drunkard for a father, and she gets most pious when she thinks her mon is drinking the *uisgebeatha*. So he hides it in his wineskin. Now, we all ken that our Donald will ne'er become a drunkard. He doesnae have that weakness in him. But he does like a warming drink now and then or e'en a hearty drink with the other men, so we all ignore his wee lie. I think his wife kens all of that, too, but the wee lie helps her keep her fear from making her be shrewish toward her poor mon."

"If ye have Donald's wineskin, then he cannae be verra far away. Nay, nor would anyone let so many bairns run about unguarded. So, lass, where is Donald?"

"Ah, weel, I fear we were mean to the poor mon. We slipped under his guard. Aye, I think we were too mean, for we have been gone from Donncoill for a verra long time and my fither may come looking for us. That means that soon poor old Donald will hear a question he has come to dread."

"Where are they, Donald?"

Donald shuddered and tried to stand firm before the bellowing laird of Donncoill and his two glaring brothers. Balfour looked ready to beat him senseless and his brothers, Nigel and Eric, looked eager to hold him down while Balfour did so. Donald heartily wished he had not lost his wineskin along with the children, for he could benefit from a long, bracing drink at the moment.

"I dinnae ken," he replied and hastily stepped back from the palpable fury of the Murray brothers. "They were with me one moment and gone the next. I have been searching for them for nearly an hour."

"Our bairns have been out of your sight for an hour?"

Before Donald could think of any reply to that softly hissed question, young Payton trotted up and grabbed his father, Nigel, by the arm, saying, "Ye must come with me now, Papa."

Nigel grasped his young son by his thin shoulders. "Has something happened to the bairns?"

"Nay, we are all hale." He glanced at a pale Donald. "Sorry for slipping away from you."

"Never mind that now, son. Where are the others?" Nigel asked.

"I will show you." Payton started to lead the men back toward Elspeth and the other children. "Elspeth found a bleeding mon and she sent me to find help."

Nigel cast one quick glance at his two frowning brothers. There were a lot of reasons for a man to be lying wounded in the remote corners of Murray lands. Few of those reasons were good ones. Nigel urged his son to hurry as Donald caught the reins of their horses and followed on behind.

"Sorry to have hurt ye, Cormac," Elspeth said as she dampened a scrap of linen and bathed the sweat from his face, "but I think I have eased the bleeding a wee bit."

"Aye, ye did a verra fine job, lass," he struggled to say.

"My mither will have to stitch the wounds on your side and on your leg."

"Lass, I cannae thank ye enough, but will ye nay heed me and go? I cannae be sure I have slipped free of the men hunting me and 'twould sore pain me to see ye hurt if they came here and found me. They would hurt ye and the others."

"I did heed your warning. 'Tis why Avery, Morna, and Bega are keeping a verra close watch."

"Ye are a stubborn lass."

"Aye, I have been scolded for it a time or two. Ye need help and I mean to give it to you."

"I am a hunted—"

"Aye, I ken it. My aunt Gisele, Avery's mither, was hunted, too, and we helped her. She was wrongly accused of a murder, too, so we ken that someone saying ye did it and trying to make ye pay for the crime doesnae make it all true."

Before Cormac could recover from his shock over that revelation and continue the argument, Avery appeared at their side and announced, "Our fithers are coming."

The child had barely finished speaking when Cormac found himself staring up at three hard-faced, well-armed men. He instinctively reached for his sword only to find it gone. Cormac inwardly grimaced when the small boy who had arrived with the men handed his sword over to a tall, amber-eyed man. He knew that he had no strength left to defend himself and that he could have seriously erred by drawing his sword on men who might well help him. Nevertheless, he did not like the fact that he had been so neatly disarmed by a mere child. As if to add insult to injury, his tiny, green-eyed savior collected the knife tucked inside his boot and handed it to the tall, broad-shouldered man with brown hair and brown eyes; then she returned to gently bathing his face.

Balfour Murray looked down at his small daughter. "Ye slipped away from poor Donald."

"Aye, I did," she replied and idly handed a grumbling Donald his wineskin.

"Ye ken that ye shouldnae do that."

"Aye, but I fear the naughtiness o'ertakes me sometimes."

"Weel, the next time the naughtiness starts to o'ertake ye, try to recall that 'twill be followed by a harsh punishment." Balfour looked around, seeing only the four lasses. "Where are the rest?"

"Making a litter for this lad," Elspeth replied.

"Do ye expect me to take him back to Donncoill?"

"Aye."

"Ye are cluttering up my lands with a vast array of the broken and the lame, lass."

"He isnae lame, just bleeding."

Balfour stared down at the youth his daughter was so tenderly caring for. Thick, dark russet hair and clear blue eyes made for a striking combination. The boy's features were well cut and unmarred. His body was long and youthfully lean, but it held the promise that he would become a strong man. If looks carried any weight, Balfour suspected everyone would readily call the lad friend and welcome him. Elspeth might be only nine, but Balfour could not help wondering if, this time, his daughter was acting upon more than her usual tendency to clasp all hurt creatures to her heart. The youth of the lad made Balfour feel inclined to help him without question, but he forced himself to be cautious.

"I am Sir Balfour Murray, laird of Donncoill, and these are my brothers, Sir Nigel and Sir Eric." He nodded first to the man on his left and then to the man on his right. "Who are ye, lad, and why are ye bleeding on this remote part of my lands?" Balfour demanded, not revealing even the smallest hint of mercy.

"I am Cormac Armstrong, sir, and here is where I fell as I tried to reach my kinsmen to the south," Cormac replied.

"Where is your horse?"

"Wandered off when I swooned and fell off his back."

"Who cut ye and why?"

"I am being hunted by the kinsmen of a mon I have been accused of murdering." Cormac sighed when all three men gripped their swords and eyed him with renewed suspicion.

"Did ye do it?"

"Nay."

"And why should I believe ye?" Balfour asked even as he eased his tense, cautious stance a little.

"I can only offer my word of honor." Cormac hoped someone would decide on his fate soon, for he was not sure he could remain conscious much longer. "I am innocent."

"The lads are here with a litter," Nigel announced.

"Weel, best see that it is a sturdy one," Balfour said. "We may yet be dragging the lad back to Donncoill." He looked back at Cormac. 'Who are ye accused of killing?"

"A Douglas mon." Cormac was not surprised to see both Balfour and Eric jerk as they immediately tensed in alarm.

"A Douglas mon, eh? Do ye have the strength to tell the tale?"

"I will try. I was courting a lass. Her family decided to wed her to a Douglas mon. He had more land and coin to offer. Aye, I didnae take the loss weel. I let my tongue clatter too freely and gave too loud a voice to my anger and, aye, to my jealousy. So when the mon turned up dead, with his throat cut, but a six month after the wedding, all eyes turned my way. I didnae do it, but I have no proof that I was elsewhere when he was killed nor do I have anyone else I could turn the suspicion on. So I ran, and I have been running ever since. For two long months."

"And the Douglases chase ye?"

"Some. One of the smaller branches of the clan, but I willnae be welcomed by any Douglas, nor will they who aid me."

" 'Tis a hard choice ye give me, lad. Do I believe ye and risk angering the powerful Douglas clan by keeping ye alive? Or do I leave ye to die, mayhap e'en turn ye o'er to the Douglases e'en though ye might be innocent? Ye ask me to risk a lot on nay more than your word."

"He isnae asking—I am," said Elspeth. "And ye do have one other thing to weigh in his favor, Fither."

"Oh, what is that?"

"From the moment I found him, he has been trying to get me to go away, to just leave him to his fate. He hasnae once ceased to warn me that he could be trouble."

"But ye are a stubborn lass."

"Aye, I am."

Balfour smiled at his daughter, then moved to stand at Cormac's feet. "Come, Eric. Lend us a hand. We will set this young fool on the litter and drag his leaking carcass back to my Maldie so she can mend him."

"Are ye certain about this, Balfour?" asked Eric as he moved to help carry Cormac.

"Not fully, but what murderer, what hunted mon, turns aside an offer of aid because he fears a silly wee lass will be hurt?"

"I am nay silly," Elspeth muttered as she followed her father.

Eric and Balfour briefly exchanged a grin; then Eric said, "None that I ken. Aye, I feel the same as ye do. I just pray we can get this lad healed and away from Donncoill ere the Douglas clan kens what we have done. It sounds cowardly, I ken, but . . ."

"Aye, but. He isnae kin, isnae e'en a friend or the son of a friend." Balfour glanced down at Cormac as he and Eric settled the youth on the litter. "Ye will be mended and made strong again, lad, God willing, but then ye must walk your own path. Do ye understand?" he asked as he studied the youth's gray, sweat-dampened face.

"Aye, I havenae swooned yet," Cormac answered.

"Good. Ye have seen the riches I must protect." Balfour briefly glanced toward the children. "We Murrays are but a small clan. E'en if we call upon all our allies, we are still small—too small to bring the wrath of the Douglas clan down upon our heads." Balfour signaled Donald to attach the litter to his own horse.

"I dinnae think anyone, save the king himself, could pull together enough allies for that battle."

"And mayhap nay e'en him. Ye picked a verra powerful enemy."

"Ah, weel, I have e'er believed that one should strive for the verra best in all things," Cormac whispered, then swooned.

"He hasnae died, has he?" Elspeth asked in a soft, tremulous voice as she touched Cormac's pale cheek.

"Nay, lass." Balfour picked up his daughter, and after Donald and his brothers set the smaller children on the horses, he took his mount by the reins and started to walk back to Donncoill. "The poor lad has just fainted. I believe he will be fine, for he showed a great deal of strength just to stay awake and speak sensibly for so verra long."

"And when he is strong, will ye send him away?"

"I must, lass. 'Twould be fine to raise my sword and defend your poor bloodied laddie, for I feel certain he has been wronged, but the cost would be too dear. It could e'en set us against our king."

"I ken it." Elspeth twined her thin arms around her father's neck and kissed his cheek. "Ye must choose between all of us and a lad ye dinnae ken at all and have no bond with. And I am thinking, in this trouble, 'tis best if he goes on alone. He is the only one who kens where to look for the truth that will free him."

Cormac stood on the steps of the Donncoill keep as his saddled horse was brought over to him. The Murrays had healed him and sheltered him for two months as he had regained his strength. He felt a deep reluctance to leave and not solely because he would have to face the trouble with the Douglases once again. Cormac could not recall ever having stayed at a livelier or more content place. He and his brothers were close, but his own home had never felt so happy. Some of what had pulled him and his brothers together was the unhappiness that had too often darkened the halls of their keep, shadows caused by parents who loathed each other and by too many deadly intrigues.

He inwardly stiffened his spine. He could not hide at Donncoill. He had to clear his name. Turning to face Lady Maldie, he gracefully bowed, then took her small hand in his and touched a kiss to her knuckles. Even as he straightened up to wish her farewell and thank her yet again for her care, a tiny, somewhat dirty hand was stuck in front of his face.

"Elspeth, my love," Maldie said, fighting a grin, "ye must ne'er demand that a mon kiss your hand." She bent a little closer to her tiny daughter. "And I think ye might consider washing a wee bit of the dirt off it first."

"She will be back," Balfour said as he draped his arm around his wife's slim shoulders and watched Elspeth run off. "Ye shall have to play the courtier for her."

"I dinnae mind. 'Tis a painfully small thing to do for the lass," Cormac said. "I would be naught but food for the corbies if she hadnae found me. Truth to tell, I have ne'er understood how she did." He idly patted Elspeth's one-eyed dog Canterbury as the badly scarred wolfhound sat down by his leg.

"Our Elspeth has a true gift for finding the hurt and the troubled," Maldie replied.

Cormac smiled. "And ye are expected to mend them all."

"Aye." Maldie laughed. " 'Tis our good fortune that she has e'er understood that not all wounds can be healed.

Ah, and here she comes"—Maldie bit her lip to stop herself from giggling—"with one verra weel-scrubbed hand."

Elspeth stood in front of Cormac and held out her hand. Cormac struggled not to give in to the urge to glance toward Balfour and Maldie, for their struggle not to laugh was almost tangible and would ruin his own hard-won composure. Little Elspeth was still somewhat dirty, with smudges decorating her face and gown, but the hand she thrust toward him was scrubbed so clean it was a little pink. He dutifully took her tiny hand in his and brushed his lips over her knuckles. After a few moments of reiterating his gratitude, he hurried away, braced for the battle to clear his name.

Balfour picked up his solemn-faced daughter and kissed her cheek. "He is a strong lad. He will be fine."

"Aye, I just felt sad because I think he will be fighting this battle for a verra long time."

# Chapter One

*Scotland—Ten years later*

"My fither will hunt ye down. Aye, and my uncles, my cousins, and all of my clansmen. They will set after ye like a pack of starving, rabid wolves and tear ye into small, bloodied pieces. And I will spit upon your savaged body ere I walk away and leave ye for the carrion birds."

Sir Cormac Armstrong stopped before the heavy door to Sir Colin MacRae's private chambers so abruptly his muscles briefly knotted. It was not the cold threat of vicious retribution that halted him, but the voice of the one who spoke it. That soft, husky voice, one almost too deep for a woman, tore at an old memory—one nearly ten years old, one he had thought he had completely cast from his mind.

Then doubt crept over him. There was no reason for that tiny Murray lass to be in Sir Colin's keep. There was also the fact that he had not had anything to do with the

Murrays since they had so graciously aided him, nothing except to send them word that he had cleared his name, and sent a fine mare for a gift. He could not believe the little girl who had saved his life was not still cherished and protected at Donncoill. His memory could be faulty. And how could Sir Colin have gotten his hands on her? And why?

"Weel, we ken that at least one of your wretched cousins willnae be plaguing us again," drawled Sir Colin. "That fair, impertinent lad who rode with you is surely feeding the corbies as we speak."

"Nay, Payton isnae dead."

Such deep pain, mingled with fervent hope, sounded in those few words that Cormac could almost feel it, and he cursed. It was hard to recall much after so many years, but the name Payton seemed familiar. The name and that voice—a voice that brought forth a very clear memory of a tiny, well-scrubbed hand thrust out for a kiss—finally made Cormac move. He was not sure what he could do, but he needed to know what was going on. This was clearly not a friendly visit, and that could mean that the tiny Murray girl was in danger.

In the week since he had brought his young cousin Mary to Duncaillie for her marriage to Sir Colin's nephew John, Cormac had made an effort to learn every shadowed corner of the keep. He did not like Sir Colin, did not trust the man at all. When his cousin's betrothal had been announced, he had been almost the only one to speak out against it. He had not wanted his family connected by marriage to a man he had learned little good about.

After assuring himself that no one could see him, he slipped into the chamber next to Sir Colin's. No guard had been placed at the connecting door between the two rooms. Sir Colin was either too arrogant to think anyone would dare to spy on him or the man simply did not care.

Cormac pressed himself against the wall next to the door and cautiously eased it open. He glanced quickly around the room he was in, carefully noting several places he could hide in the event that someone noticed the door was cracked open. One thing he had learned, and learned well, in two long years of running from the wrath of the Douglas clan was how to hide, how to use the shadows and the most meager cover to disappear from view. Taking a deep breath to steady himself, he peered into the room.

"That untried lad is of no consequence now," snapped Sir Colin.

"Untried?" The scorn in that husky voice made Cormac flinch. "Even the beardless amongst my brothers and cousins has had more women than ye e'er will."

When Sir Colin bounded out of his heavy oak chair and strode toward his tormentor, Cormac had to tightly clench his fists to stop himself from doing anything rash. To his relief the man halted his advance directly in front of the woman, raising his hand but not delivering the blow he so obviously ached to inflict. Cormac knew he would have lost all restraint if Sir Colin had struck the tiny, slender woman facing him so calmly.

There was no denying what his eyes told him, although Cormac tried to do just that for several minutes. It was hard to believe that Elspeth Murray was standing in Sir Colin's chambers, alone and far from the loving safety of Donncoill. Cormac was not sure he was pleased to see that he had been right all those years ago: Elspeth had definitely grown into a disarmingly beautiful woman.

Thick, wildly tousled hair tumbled down her slim back in heavy waves to stop teasingly at the top of her slim legs. Her hands were tied behind her back and Cormac had to smile. Those hands did not look all that much bigger than they had on the day she had soothed his brow as he had lain bleeding in her father's dirt. Her figure was almost too slender, too delicate, yet just womanly enough to stir an interest in his loins. The way her arms were pulled back clearly revealed the perfect shape of her small breasts. Her waist was temptingly small and her slim hips gracefully rounded. Elspeth's face still seemed to be swamped by her thick hair and wide, brilliant green eyes. There was a childish innocence to her gentle, heart-shaped face, from the small, straight nose to the faintly pointed chin. The long, thick lashes rimming her big eyes and the soft fullness of her mouth bespoke womanhood, however. She was a blood-stirring bundle of contradictions. She was so close to the door he felt he could easily reach out and touch her. Cormac was a little surprised by how hard he had to fight to resist that urge.

Then she spoke in her rich, deep, husky voice, and all hints of the child, all signs of innocence, were torn away. She became a sultry temptress from her wild, unbound hair to her tiny booted feet. Cormac felt the sharp tug of lust. It struck as hard and as fast as a blow to the stomach. Any man who saw her or heard her speak would have to be restrained from kicking down the heavy gates of Donncoill to reach her. If his heart was not already pledged to another, Cormac knew he would be sorely tempted. He wondered if Sir Colin had simply succumbed to her allure.

"What? Ye hesitate to strike a lass?" Elspeth taunted the glowering Sir Colin, her beautiful voice heavily ladened with contempt. "I have long thought that nothing ye could do would e'er surprise me, but mayhap I was wrong."

"Ye do beg to be beaten," Sir Colin said, the faint tremor in his voice all that hinted at his struggle for control.

"Yet ye stand there like a reeking dung heap."

Cormac tensed when Colin wrapped one beefy hand around her long, slender throat and, in a cold voice, drawled, "So that is your game, is it? Ye try to prod me into a blind rage? Nay, my bonny green-eyed bitch, ye are nay the one who will be doing the prodding here." Three of the five men in the room chuckled.

" 'Tis to be rape then, is it? Ye had best be verra sure when ye stick that sad, wee twig of flesh in me that ye are willing to make it your last rut. The moment it touches me, 'twill be a doomed wee laddie."

Sir Colin's hand tightened on her throat. Cormac could see the veins in the man's thick hand bulge. His own hand went to his sword, although he knew it would be madness to interfere. Elspeth made no sound, did not move at all, but kept her gaze fixed steadily upon Sir Colin's flushed face. Cormac noticed her hands clench behind her back until her knuckles whitened. Cormac had to admire her bravery, but he thought it foolhardy to keep goading the man as she was. He could not understand what she thought to gain from the man, save for a quick death. When Cormac decided he was going to have to interfere, no matter how slim the odds of success, Sir Colin finally released her. Elspeth gasped only once and swayed faintly, yet she had to be in pain and starved for breath.

"Some may try to call it rape, but I mean only to bed my wife," Sir Colin said.

"I have already refused you," she replied, her voice a little weaker, a little raspy. "Further discussion of the matter would just be tedious."

"No one refuses me."

"I did and I will."

"Ye will have no more say in this matter." He signaled to the two men flanking her. "Secure her in the west tower." Sir Colin brushed his blunt fingertips over her full mouth and barely snatched them away, out of her reach, before she snapped at them, her even white teeth clicking loudly in the room. "I have a room prepared especially for you."

"I am humbled by your generousity."

"Humbled? Oh, aye, ye too proud wench, ye will soon be verra humbled indeed."

Cormac gently pushed the door shut as far as he dared, stopping just before it latched. A moment later he was in the hall again, using the shadows cast by the torchlight to follow Elspeth and her guards. Only once did someone look back, and that was Elspeth. She stared into the shadows that sheltered him, a frown briefly curving her full lips; then she was tugged along by her guards. Cormac did not think she had seen him, but if she had, she clearly had the wit to say nothing. He followed his prey right to the door of the tower room, all the while struggling to devise some clever plan.

Elspeth stumbled slightly when one of the guards roughly shoved her into the room, but she quickly steadied herself. She swallowed her sigh of relief when the other guard cut the rope binding her wrists. Then she fought the urge to rub them, thus revealing how much they hurt as the blood began to flow to them again. As the heavy door shut behind the two men and she listened to the bolt being dragged across it, she began to rub her chaffed, sore wrists and make a quick but thorough survey of the room.

"It appears that the only way out of this room is if I succumb to the sinful urge to hurl myself from the window and end my poor life," she muttered as she sat down on the huge bed that dominated the room. She frowned and idly bounced up and down on the mattress. "Feathers. The bastard plainly intends to be comfortable as he dishonors me."

Weary, sick with worry over Payton's fate, and knotted with fear, Elspeth curled up on the bed. For just a moment she fought the urge to weep, not wishing to give into that weakness. Then, as the tears began to fall, she shrugged.

She was alone and a good cleansing of her misery could help her maintain her strength, especially later.

After what she feared was a disgracefully prolonged bout of weeping, Elspeth flopped onto her back and stared up at the ceiling. She felt drained, as if some physician had placed leeches all over her—leeches that sucked all the emotion from a body instead of the blood. It was going to take a while to get her strength and wit back—two things she would sorely need in the days ahead.

She thought of Payton and felt as if she could weep all over again if she had had any tears left. Her last sight of her cousin had been that of his bloodied body lying alongside the two men-at-arms who had accompanied them. Elspeth had needed only one look to know that their two guards were dead, but she could not be so certain about Payton. She did not want to be. She wanted to cling to the hope that he was still alive, no matter how small that hope might be. If nothing else, Elspeth could not bear to think upon the pain her uncle Nigel and aunt Gisele would suffer over the loss of their son. Even though her mind told her that it was not her fault, she knew she might never be able to shake free of the guilt she felt, for it had been her rejected suitor who had brought about the tragedy. It struck her as appallingly unfair that the chilling memories and nightmares she had suffered for three long years might finally be pushed aside by the sight of her cousin's murder—an old nightmare replaced by a new one.

Elspeth closed her eyes, deciding it would not hurt to seek the rest her body craved. She would need it to be able to endure what lay ahead. Although she had no doubt that her family would come after her, in force, she also knew they might not arrive in time to save her from all Sir Colin intended. That was in her own hands.

As she felt sleep creep over her, she heard a faint noise at the door. Either someone was bringing her some food and drink or some poor fool had been sent to check to be sure she was still where they had put her. Elspeth resisted the urge to look. She was too tired and too battered to do anything just yet. In truth, she felt almost too tired to even open her eyes. Then someone touched her arm and she tensed, her weariness abruptly shoved aside by alarm even though she felt no real threat from the person she now knew stood next to her bed.

Cautiously, Elspeth opened her eyes just enough to see her visitor through the veil of her still damp lashes. He was a beautiful man. His long, leanly muscular body was bent over her in a strangely protective way. His face was cut in clean lines and unmarred. A high, wide forehead, high-boned cheeks, a long, straight nose, a handsomely firm jaw, and a well-shaped mouth made for a face that easily took a maid's breath away. His creamy skin was almost too pale and fine for a man, although many a woman would envy it, and the healthy warmth of it begged for a touch. It was the perfect complement to his deep auburn hair. His eyes, however, were what truly caught and held her attention. Set beneath neatly arched brows and ringed with long, thick lashes, they were the rich blue of clean, deep water—a color she had seen but once before in her life. They were eyes that had filled many a maidenly dream and some that were very far from maidenly.

"Cormac," she whispered, smiling faintly at the way his beautiful eyes widened slightly in surprise.

"Ye remember me?" he asked softly, a little shaken by the warm look in her rich green eyes and the soft, enticing smile of greeting she gifted him with.

"Ah, ye dinnae remember me. Ye are but tiptoeing through the bedchambers of Duncallie to see if any hold something ye like. I am devastated."

Cormac straightened up and put his hands on his hips. Her drawled taunt had quickly yanked him free of his bemusement better than a sharp slap to the face. She was even more beautiful close to, and for just a moment, as he had stared into her wide, slumberous eyes, he had been seized by the overwhelming urge to crawl onto that bed with her. The way she had whispered his name in her rich, sensuous voice had reached deep inside of him, dragging his tightly controlled lusts to fierce, immediate life. The feeling still lingered, but now he struggled to cool his heated blood.

"Aye, I recall you," he said. "Ye are a wee bit bigger and sharper of tongue, but ye are certainly Elspeth—my tiny, begrimed savior from years past."

Slowly, Elspeth sat up, then knelt on the bed facing him. Some of those not so maidenly dreams she had had about him were crowding her mind, and she fought to push them aside. He had come to rescue her. Elspeth inwardly smiled as she mused that it was a poor time to tell a man that she had loved and lusted after him for ten long years. For all she knew, he was a wedded man with a bairn or two to bounce on his knee. Finding that thought painful, she forced her mind to settle on the matter of rescue.

"And have ye come to be my savior now?" she asked.

"Aye."

Elspeth smiled and abruptly decided to make at least one small dream into a true memory. Cormac could easily think her next action was simply an impulsive expression of relief and gratitude—or be made to think so. She leaned closer and kissed him. His lips were as soft and as delicious as she had always imagined they would be. If he was wed, this stolen kiss would be but a small trespass.

And then it happened. Her mother had warned her. Elspeth wished she had listened more closely, but she had been too young to be comfortable hearing such words as *desire* and *passion* upon her mother's lips.

He trembled faintly and so did she, but she was not

really sure where his shiver ended and hers began. His body tightened and she felt a responsive ache low in her belly. She felt his heat, could almost smell his desire. Cormac gripped her by the shoulders and deepened the kiss. Elspeth readily opened her mouth to welcome the invasion of his tongue. As he caressed the inside of her mouth, she felt as if he stroked her very soul. She wanted to pull him down onto the bed with her, ached to wrap herself around his lean body. Even as that thought passed through her passion-clouded mind, she felt Cormac dredge up some inner strength and start to pull away from her. Elspeth fought the urge to cling to him, to halt his retreat.

Cormac stared at the young woman kneeling in front of him. He fought the urge to vigorously shake his head in an attempt to clear the haze from his mind. It was not easy to cool the fire in his blood as he looked into her wide green eyes, for he was sure he saw passion there. He had to sternly remind himself that Elspeth was a highborn woman—one he owed his life to—and he was not free. He had come to rescue her, not to ravish her.

"Why?" he asked, then hastily cleared his throat to try to banish the huskiness from his voice.

"Why not?" she asked back. "Are ye wed?"

"Nay, but—"

Elspeth did not want to hear the rest, not when her heart still pounded fiercely and she could still taste him. "A rash act, born of my delight to see ye alive and here. I ken that my kinsmen will soon hunt for me, but 'twould be help that would come too late."

"And if we do not move quickly, my aid could also prove worthless."

"Ye have a plan, do ye, my braw knight?" She took careful note of the fact that he had not yet released her, but was moving his strong, long-fingered hands over her upper arms in an idle but telling caress.

"I do. 'Tis why it took me near to an hour to come and fetch you," he replied.

"An hour?" Elspeth muttered, unable to hide her surprise.

"I had to tend to a few matters that will ease our escape ere I could come here."

"I meant no criticism, Sir Cormac. 'Twas just a wee bit disappointing to me to realize I had spent so long wallowing in my misery. I hadnae thought myself such a weakling." She frowned when he chuckled. "Ye find my despair amusing?"

"Nay, lass, merely the indication that ye might e'er consider yourself weak." He took her by the hand and tugged her off the bed. "Ye have ne'er been weak. Nay, not e'en as a wee, muck-smeared bairn of nine."

Elspeth flushed a little with pleasure over his remarks even though they were spoken in a jesting tone. "What is your plan?"

"Ye are to wrap yourself in this cloak and we will walk out of here." He handed her a long, heavy woolen cloak he had set on the bed before trying to wake her.

"That is your plan?" she asked as she donned the cloak.

"Simple is oftentimes the best," he said as he opened the door and dragged her unconcious guard inside.

Elspeth watched as he tied and gagged the man, then tucked him into the bed, pulling the covers up so that only a bit of the man's black hair showed over the blankets. "I dinnae think that will fool them for verra long."

"Long enough for us to escape these walls."

"Are ye truly meaning to just walk out of here with me?"

Cormac tugged the hood of the cape over her head, pulling it forward until it covered her hair and shaded her face. "If any ask what I am about, I shall simply say I am taking my wee cousin Mary for a ride."

"Do ye really have a wee cousin Mary?"

"Aye, and she is here. She is betrothed to Sir Colin's nephew John. I brought her here for her wedding. She stays to her rooms, only coming out to dine in the great hall. The next meal isnae for several hours, so this ruse should work."

As he led her out of the room, then shut and barred the door, she asked, "Would it nay be better to creep away, to keep to the shadows? Mayhap ye ken of a bolt-hole to use."

"All that would be best but then we couldnae take my horse."

Elspeth started to say something, then quickly closed her mouth. His plan was fraught with the chance of failure, but she had none at all. He was also right in thinking it best to take his horse. They would not get very far on foot.

"Do we take your cousin's horse as weel? Or mine?"

"I fear my cousin doesnae have a horse." He grimaced. "She is a timid lass and willnae ride alone. She travels only in a cart or sharing a saddle with another. All here ken it, too. If I suddenly set Mary on a horse 'twould rouse suspicion. To take your horse would also rouse suspicion. I fear we will have to ride two to a saddle."

"Riding is better than walking. Faster."

"Aye, and now I must ask ye to hush."

"Your cousin Mary doesnae talk either?"

He smiled faintly. "Nay much, although she and John seem to have a lot to say to each other when they arenae both trying to hide from Sir Colin. Nay, I think ye must remain silent because of your voice."

"Something is wrong with my voice?"

" 'Tis too distinctive," he replied, but could see by the look on her face that she did not really understand. "Trust me," he said and tugged her hood more closely around her face.

Elspeth nodded and quelled the urge to talk to him.

She threaded her fingers through his, savoring the simple act of holding his hand as they crept through the halls of Duncaillie. It was the only good thing about their walk through the keep, Elspeth thought as she tensely worried about a cry of discovery at every turning. Walking to the stables through the crowded bailey had her stomach knotting with tension so badly it hurt. She stood in the shadows near the door of the stables as Cormac got his horse. She was astounded at the way he spoke so calmly to the men there, as if he did not have a care in the world. He had obviously developed a few interesting skills in the years since she had seen him last.

Cormac set her on his saddle and mounted behind her, still idly jesting with the men. Elspeth fought the urge to hit him and tell him to get moving. When they finally rode out of the bailey, she slumped against him, weak with relief. They were not safe yet, might not be safe for quite a while, but at least they were no longer directly under the gaze of Sir Colin.

"Where do we go now?" she asked. Deciding it felt very good to be so close to him, she made herself more comfortable against his broad chest.

"Since Sir Colin will expect ye to try to get back to Donncoill, I believe we will just continue on in the direction I was planning to go after the wedding."

"Sir Colin could think ye are also trying to get me back to my clan."

"Aye, or to my kinsmen, who live both south and west of here. So that gives the mon two or three ways to search for us. He can have no idea of my true destination. I was to stay for my cousin's wedding, then leave, but I told no one where I would go once the celebrations ended, not even wee Mary."

" 'Tis a good idea, and yet, how then shall I return to my kinsmen? That is where my continued safety lies, isnae

it? Aye, and the means to stop Sir Colin, to make him pay
for kidnapping me, killing two Murray men, and hurting
Payton.''

He noticed that she still refused to consider the possibility her cousin was dead. The Murray clan was obviously
still closely bonded. It would probably be best if she faced
the cold truth that her cousin was either dead or soon
would be, since the cold and a loss of blood would probably
finish what Sir Colin had begun, but he found that he did
not have the heart to steal her hope away.

''The king's court is verra near where I must go. We can
find someone there who can get word to your clan. If we
must, we can set ye under the king's own guard. Your clan
hasnae done anything to hurt your standing with the king,
has it?''

''Nay. That will do. In truth, 'tis near as fine as going
straight to my fither.''

''It should take us near to a fortnight since we should
travel slowly to save our mount's strength. If luck fails us,
and Sir Colin sniffs out our trail, it could take longer.
Can ye endure such a long, rough journey?'' He frowned
slightly as he studied the soft delicacy of the woman in his
arms.

''Oh, aye, I am stronger than I look.''

Elspeth sighed when he made no reply, his doubt so
strong she could almost feel it. She knew she was small
and delicate in appearance, but she was indeed strong. Sir
Cormac Armstrong was going to have to learn that one
should not always make judgments based solely on a person's appearance.

Glancing down at his strong, long-fingered hands upon
the reins, she found herself wondering yet again if he
was betrothed or in love with someone. She needed some
information, needed to know if he was free. By the time
they stopped for the night, Elspeth vowed she would have

it. Then she would have to decide what to do. If he was wedded or betrothed, the next few weeks would be a torment as she tried to hide and even kill all feeling for the man. But if he was free, she had a fortnight to try to make him fall in love with her. That too could prove torturous, ripping her heart and pride to shreds. Fate had been kind enough to give her some time with the man she had adored for so long, but it was obvious that fate had also decided to make her pay dearly for that gift. All she could do was pray that she had what was needed to win the prize.

# Chapter Two

"Four husbands?"

As she spoke, Elspeth peered at Cormac around the horse she was wiping down with a handful of weeds and grass. It had taken some effort on her part, but she had finally pulled from him the name of a woman—Isabel. She had felt her heart break as he had told her of the love he had for this woman, of the deep bond they shared. Then, as he told her more and more about the woman, Elspeth's hurt had begun to change to puzzlement and eventually to anger at Isabel and even some at Cormac for his blind devotion. Isabel's four husbands were a subject he obviously did not want to discuss at length, but she was determined to bleed out of him every morsel of information that she could.

"Aye," Cormac nearly grunted his reply as he built a fire.

"Four *dead* husbands?"

"Aye."

"Four times wed. Four times widowed."

"Aye."

"And such short marriages," she murmured as she walked over and sat down across the fire from him. "Such an ill-fated lot she was married to."

Cormac briefly looked up from the oatmeal he was mixing to glare at her. He knew what she was thinking. Others thought it, too. Four husbands and all dying, strangely and quickly, the longest-surviving one not even marking two full years of marriage. To his shame, even he had found himself wondering, doubting, but he would quickly shove that disloyalty aside. Isabel needed sympathy and support, not suspicions.

"Aye, all weak or foolishly reckless," he snapped, handing her some bread.

*Or as blind as you are,* Elspeth thought as she took a bite of the bread. "No children?"

"Nay."

"So, four weak or reckless and, obviously, seedless husbands. Unless 'tis Isabel. She could be barren." Elspeth heartily hoped the woman was, for although she did not really believe in bad seeds, a child raised by such a woman could easily become as twisted as its mother.

It had struck Cormac as odd that Isabel could share a bed with four men—five if he included himself—and never quicken with child, but he was not about to admit that. He wanted to tell Elspeth to shut up, to stop gnawing at this particular bone. She was doing too good a job of building a case against Isabel, much better than any other had. Others had blatantly accused Isabel and called him a fool for not seeing the truth. Elspeth went at it step by slow step, gently yet persistently, yanking answers from him at every painful step. She was reviving all his doubts and he hated it.

"Who can say?" he muttered.

"Who indeed. Weel, with no bairns to inherit, she must now be quite a rich woman. Wealth can be such a comfort."

There was a definite touch of sarcasm in her voice, but he struggled to ignore it as he handed her a share of the oatmeal and some cheese. "She isnae poor or landless, though she didnae gain it all."

"Of course not," Elspeth murmured as she accepted the rough wooden bowl full of oatmeal. "There were undoubtedly some other males in the late husband's family who would take quite a bit. Lands especially."

"But they always want it all. 'Tis they who have spread such vicious lies about Isabel, trying to make a sad tragedy sound like a crime."

"I see. Did they e'er find the murderer of the mon ye were accused of killing?"

"Once I kenned I was free of pursuit, I fear I gave no thought to it. They must have or I wouldst still be running."

"Or dead. So they must have finally listened to Isabel's claims of your innocence."

Elspeth watched him closely as she spoke. She inwardly sighed when he was suddenly unable to meet her gaze. It was as sad as it was infuriating. Right from the beginning, Cormac had refused to see the truth about dear Isabel. He obviously knew she had done little if anything to help him, yet he found some reason to explain away that betrayal. It was not going to be easy to open his eyes. Elspeth feared he had either ignored the truth or explained it away for so long he would not recognize it if it fell on him. Isabel was a madonna to him, a beautiful victim, a tortured soul used by her kinsmen for their own gain. Elspeth wanted to gag.

What puzzled her was why Isabel kept Cormac so tied to her. He was unquestionably handsome and might be a very good lover. His kisses had certainly lacked for nothing. Nevertheless, the fact that Isabel did all she could to keep Cormac panting at her heels for ten long years seemed to indicate some twisted form of fidelity or caring, and Elspeth refused to believe that Isabel cared for Cormac at all.

The why of what Isabel did to Cormac and why he had allowed it could be discovered later, she decided crossly. What mattered now was that she loved and desired a man who was enslaved, heart and soul, by another woman. Elspeth had no idea of what, if anything, she could do about that. Cormac desired her. She had no doubt about that. She had felt his desire, tasted it. Although thrilling, his longing did not mean all that much, however. Men desired too easily, too shallowly, and sometimes, too fleetingly.

Still, she mused as she helped him clean up after their meager repast, she might be able to use that desire. He clearly had some doubts about his beloved Isabel. Elspeth suspected that Isabel was his first love, perhaps even the first woman he had bedded, and no other woman had been able to break that bond. He might never have given one a chance to try.

There was also the possibility that he pushed aside all attempts by other women to catch and hold his interest. Well, she mused as she spread out their bedding, she always welcomed a true challenge. She was not sure she really had that much of a choice anyway. Her body wanted him and so did her heart. Somehow it seemed a sin not even to try to win him, even though she knew she would break a lot of rules in the attempt.

Nay, she thought as she curled up in a blanket and watched Cormac bank the fire, she was not going to win this man with sweet words, warm looks, and gentle flirtation. She was going to have to be bold and cast aside all restrictions and virginal hesitation. Cormac felt himself bound to another woman. To break that bond, Elspeth knew she would have to give him everything. It was a frightening gamble, for if she lost, she would have shredded her pride, cast aside her chastity, and exposed her heart to a thorough, perhaps everlasting, hurt. But then she thought of what she could have if she won the gamble, and she smiled.

"What are ye grinning about?" Cormac asked as he curled up in his blanket and gave her a crooked half smile.

Seduction was going to be difficult if he never came closer than two feet away, she thought as she replied, "It wasnae a grin. It was an expression of mild amusement."

Cormac laughed. "So what amuses you?"

Since she could not tell him the truth, she shrugged. "I am free."

"For now."

"Are ye concerned that Sir Colin will track us down?"

"Some. We have a good chance of eluding him, but I prefer to remain wary. I learned the worth of that whilst hiding from the Douglases all those years ago."

" 'Tis wise, I suppose," she said, then sighed. "I but dislike the idea of having to constantly glance o'er my shoulder."

" 'Tis nay a good way to walk through life, I confess, but at least one stays alive. After all, if ye are always checking atween your shoulder blades, 'tis verra hard for someone to stick a knife there."

"Now there is a fine, peaceful thought to face the night with."

Cormac chuckled. "Pardon. Dinnae let it shadow your dreams," he added in a far more serious tone. "I ne'er did."

"With the Douglases seeking to end your life, I wonder that ye e'er got any sleep," she said, shivering at the thought of the danger he had been in so long ago.

"Weel, I didnae get too much until I was nearly one and twenty. I was so accustomed to running from any Douglas that it was a while after they decided I was innocent ere I could cease." Cormac wondered why he was speaking so freely of the aching fear he had suffered through while being hunted; then he decided it was the soft intimacy of the night that prompted such honesty.

"That was probably for the best." Elspeth closed her eyes, hoping that would ease the temptation she felt to reach out and touch him, to increase the intimacy they shared to include far more than words. "It may weel have taken a while for all the Douglases to ken that ye were no longer wanted for the murder of a kinsmon. Good news ne'er travels as fast or as far as the bad."

"Aye. Rest now, Elspeth. We must be on our way again by dawn."

Elspeth just muttered an indistinct sound of agreement. She was tired but she knew sleep would be slow to take hold of her. There was too much on her mind. She did, however, wish Cormac to stop talking. His rich, deep voice reached through the shadows to stroke her, make her ache for his touch. Although she did plan to seduce the man or, at least, tempt him into seducing her, tonight was not a good night to begin that game. They were both too tired and wary of pursuit and a little wary of each other as well. After all, she was no longer the child he had known so long ago and he was no longer that bonny, persecuted youth who had stolen her young girl's heart. Instinct told her that he was her mate, her love, but she doubted he felt the same. Since she was also a virgin, she needed a little time to accept her decision to gamble with her chastity.

Cormac forced himself to turn his back on the slight form curled up just feet away. He had never before been so strongly tempted by a woman, other than Isabel. To his dismay, he knew it had been years, if ever, since Isabel had stirred his lusts as swiftly and fiercely as Elspeth did. It could be deprivation causing such a reaction, he told himself. It had been a very long time since he had lain with Isabel or with any woman. Perhaps if he gave into the hunger for a while the sharpness of it would ease.

He cursed under his breath. He often went months, even a year or more, without easing his lusts. The few times he had weakened, he had simply bedded the source of temptation once, sometimes even a few times, and been cured. If it was any other woman causing the twisting ache in his groin, he would do the same now, but he could not do that to Elspeth. He owed her and the Murrays too much to treat Elspeth so callously. The girl was undoubtedly a virgin and he would not rob her of that prize just to assuage an itch, no matter how strong it was. Soon he would see his Isabel again and she would tend to his needs.

It was loneliness really, he told himself as he closed his eyes and reached out for the calming touch of sleep. While he was away from his Isabel, it often cut away at him. It was especially keen when she summoned him to her side as she had done but days ago, for as he rode to her, he was filled with hope and desire, but also a gut-wrenching fear. Too often he was too late, had but a night or two in her arms before she was heartlessly married to another. This time he would win the race, he swore, and finally have Isabel all to himself. Then he would no longer be troubled by the sight of unruly raven hair and beautiful green eyes.

*Payton laughed and Elspeth laughed with him. She turned to share the jest with Robert, one of her uncle Nigel's men-at-arms, and gasped. His rough features were contorted with a chilling mixture of pain and surprise. Even as she reached for him, blood flowed from his mouth and he slid from his horse. Elspeth turned back to Payton and screamed as an arrow slammed into his back, thrusting him from his saddle to sprawl upon the ground. She started to dismount, only faintly aware of the death scream of her*

*other guard and the sound of swiftly approaching horses. She
needed to get to Payton. He was so still, facedown in the dirt, the
dark stain of his life's blood rapidly darkening the back of his
shirt. When she was grabbed from behind and tossed, belly down,
across a saddle, she screamed in fury.*

"Nay, ye bastards, I must help Payton!" She fought
against the hands trying to hold her steady.

"Elspeth, calm yourself."

"Payton! I must help Payton!" She began to weep.
"There is so much blood."

"Sssh, Elspeth. Hush, hush. 'Tis but a dream, a dark
memory come to steal away the peace of sleep."

Slowly Elspeth calmed, realizing that the hands she felt
stroking her, soothing her, did not roughly hold her down.
No horse was beneath her. The deep voice pulling her from
the cold horror of her memory was gentle, sympathetic, not
the harsh, taunting one that had told her her cousin was
dead, food for scavengers. It was another moment before
she was fully aware of where she was and who held her,
but she hesitated to reveal that she had returned to her
senses.

It was pleasant indeed to lie there, enfolded in Cormac's
strong arms. He felt good, safe yet tempting. Although the
memory of Payton lying so still upon the ground, soaked
with blood, twisted her heart with grief, her tears began
to ease. She could sense Cormac's sympathy, his honest
need to ease her pain and sorrow. A moment later, she
smiled faintly against his broad chest. She could also feel
his desire. It was there, just beneath those more gentle-
manly feelings, fighting against the restraints he strove to
keep on it. She nuzzled her face against his throat, heard
him softly catch his breath, and felt his desire rapidly grow
stronger.

Cormac closed his eyes and took a deep breath to steady
himself when he felt Elspeth cuddle closer. The feel of her

slender curves against his body heated his blood, making control almost impossible to maintain. It had been a mistake to get so close yet he knew he could never have ignored her distress.

"Better now?" he asked, not surprised to hear the husky note of desire in his voice, but hoping she did not.

"Aye." She wrapped her arms around him, holding him close when she felt him tense to move away.

"Ye and Payton were close?" Cormac prayed that talking would turn his thoughts away from the passionate fantasies filling his head.

"Aye. In truth, if there is a favorite amongst all of the Murray brats, 'tis Payton. He must certainly be the most beautiful of us all. I refuse to believe that he is dead." She sighed. "I think I could almost wish my old nightmare back rather than keep seeing Payton fall with an arrow in his back."

"Ye had another dark dream that could rob ye of sleep?"

"Aye. Another cousin." She shivered and he held her a little tighter. "Sorcha, my uncle Eric's firstborn. Three years ago she and I were captured by an enemy of his. That mon and two of his minions beat Sorcha and raped her. They made me watch. I was to share that fate, but we were rescued by Eric, my fither, and my uncle Nigel. When Uncle Eric saw what the men had done to his child, his revenge was swift and brutal."

"What happened to Sorcha then?"

"She went to a nunnery. I believe she will soon take her vows."

"Does she truly have the calling or does she hide?"

"I believe that she does have a calling. She was always, weel, more pious than the rest of us. We were all saddened that she left us, though she is near to Donncoill and we all visit whene'er we can, but 'tis easy to see she is happy. Whether 'tis because of a calling or because she feels safe or both, who can say for certain? Her parents have accepted it. They are pleased that she is alive and that the shadows have left her."

"But they did not leave you, did they?"

"Nay. Not until now."

"Whene'er I thought of Donncoill, I recalled only peace and happiness. 'Tis sad to ken that even such havens can be marred by tragedy. 'Tis even sadder that ye were witness to all of it."

"Och, weel, considering how many Murrays there are about, 'twould be a miracle if none were e'er harmed."

Cormac laughed softly. "Aye, there were a lot of you." He gave into the urge to kiss her hair and said quietly, "I pray, for your sake, that your cousin Payton is blessed, that he somehow survives."

"Thank ye," she replied in an equally soft voice. "If any mon can win out o'er such misfortune, 'tis Payton."

"Now that ye have calmed some, I shall return to my own bed."

Elspeth clung just a little tighter, halting his move. She needed to keep him close to her. It occurred to her that Cormac could use the night, the separation of their beds, to fight the desire he felt for her. Each night she could lose any ground gained during the day. There were not many reasons she could give to hold him close at night, not until they became lovers. A lingering fear after a nightmare could serve very well. Although she felt a little guilty for using his sympathy in such a way, she decided the battle she was about to engage in warranted a little subterfuge. Even if she did not win his heart for her own, she might ease Isabel's choking grip on it, and that could only be for the best.

"Could ye nay stay close?" she asked, pleased with the slight waver in her voice.

He could, but he should not, and he could not really

tell her why. "It wouldnae be proper," he muttered, disgusted by that weak excuse.

"I believe propriety was lost the moment Lord Colin grabbed me off my horse. 'Tis just that I fear the dream will return if I am too much alone."

"What happens when ye suffer a nightmare at home?"

"Someone stays with me. I have a verra big bed."

Cormac did not wish to know that. Already images were forming in his mind of a particularly sultry Elspeth sprawled naked on a large bed, reaching for him as he lowered himself on top of her, pressing himself close to the ebony curls between her soft white thighs. . . . He shook his head, grasping desperately for some thought, any thought, that did not include a naked, willing Elspeth.

The problem was, there was no way he could refuse her request. She had watched her cousin and two men-at-arms be murdered, had been kidnapped, threatened with rape, and locked up in a tower room. It was no surprise that she was afraid to be alone. Cormac suspected she was accustomed to being surrounded by loved ones, people she could readily turn to if troubled. Now she had only him and he could not seem to keep his thoughts out of his breeches.

This girl had saved his life, he sternly reminded himself. He also belonged to another, was even now traveling to join her and, God willing, finally marry her. Both things should be enough to control his errant lusts. All Elspeth wanted was to feel safe. He was a grown man. He ought to be able to lie at her side and not sweat with need.

"Aye, I will stay close. Just let me fetch my bedding," he said, hoping his reluctance could not be heard in his voice.

Elspeth let him go, watching him steadily as he moved

his bedding next to hers and made one large bed. He was so tense when he settled down next to her she was surprised he did not creak. It might not be easy to seduce a man so intent on behaving himself. She turned onto her side, her back to him, then reached behind herself, grasped his hand, and tugged his arm around her waist. The man was so stiff it was like trying to cuddle with a rock, she mused and smiled faintly. The strength of his resistance, however, simply proved how strong his desire was, and that gave her hope.

"Thank ye, Cormac," she said, wriggling backward until she was pressed up against him. "I feel safe now."

" 'Tis the least I can do."

Elspeth bit back a giggle. Cormac sounded as if he was choking on something. The part of him twitching impudently against her backside told her it was desire strangling his voice. Surely something that strong would be impossible to fight for long. She could not do so. She already had to wrestle with the urge to turn in his arms, kiss him, and rub her body up against his. Elspeth closed her eyes and hoped his imaginings were as wild and as vivid as her own. After all, if she was going to ache and lose sleep, it was only fair that he did, too.

"Good sleep, Cormac," she said, speaking only a little bit above a whisper.

Cormac inwardly cursed. That soft, husky voice was like a caress. He had not thought his body could swell with desire any more than it had already, and he did not like to be proven wrong. The woman was dangerous, more so because she did not seem to know it. Cormac was surprised Balfour Murray ever let his daughter leave the protective walls of Donncoill; then he decided that a father might not see that his daughter was such a temptation to a man.

"Good sleep to you, Elspeth," he whispered back.

Feeling his desire as she did, Elspeth suspected her dreams would not be restful ones, but they would certainly be interesting.

It was a while before Cormac felt Elspeth relax in sleep. He tried to pull away, but she simply followed him with her lithe body, cuddling up even closer than before. Her shapely backside rubbed against his aching groin and he shuddered.

In a village barely a day's ride away there was a tavern maid who often granted a man her favors for a small fee. He had never answered her smiles before, but perhaps he should do so now. A good rutting would take the edge off a long unsatisfied need, and he would find the temptation of Elspeth easier to resist.

Even as he considered taking the time to dally with the tavern maid, he knew it was foolish. A waste of time and money. Such desperate measures had always failed him before, leaving him empty and unsatisfied. He was cursed with a very single-minded lust. Once fixed upon a woman, no other would do. Cormac knew he could spend a month in the bed of Scotland's most skilled whore, and within moments of seeing Elspeth again, he would be in the same dire state he was now.

What troubled him most was how even thoughts of Isabel, so close and waiting for him, did nothing to cool his ardor. He could not even bring to mind a clear image of Isabel. Elspeth was there, interfering, her green eyes staring out of Isabel's face until that woman disappeared completely and only Elspeth remained. Reminding himself that it had been a very long time since he had seen Isabel did not ease his troubled mind much. Isabel was the woman he had loved and honored for nearly half his life. She should not be so easily pushed out of his thoughts by a tiny, green-eyed girl, even if that girl had a voice that could melt rock.

Elspeth moved against him again in a slow, suggestive way. Cormac groaned, then sighed. It was going to be a very long night. If he remained a gentleman, kept his hands off Elspeth, and continued to honor his bond with Isabel, he deserved nothing less than sainthood.

# Chapter Three

Warmth flooded through Elspeth's veins as she started to wake. It poured into her from the soft lips brushing temptingly over hers. She did not need to open her eyes, did not even need to be awake, to know who held her, who kissed her. It frightened her a little to know that Cormac was already so much a part of her, but she accepted it. She murmured his name and curled her arms around his neck.

"Are ye so accustomed to being kissed awake, my wee angel, that it doesnae startle ye?" Cormac asked as he nibbled lightly on her bottom lip.

It was an insulting question, but Elspeth decided to ignore its implications. Since she so readily accepted and returned his kiss when she was half asleep, it was not surprising that he would wonder about her innocence. She could not tell him she knew him by his smell, by the feel of his desire, or by the fact that her heart already claimed him as its mate. He would either think her mad or trying to entrap him, and he would run, very fast, in the opposite direction. Men, she had discovered at a young age, were not very good about accepting, discussing, or understanding feelings.

"I kenned it was you." She threaded her fingers through his thick hair and pressed her body even closer to his. "After all, I fell asleep with ye at my side. 'Tis no great surprise that I would expect to see ye there when I woke."

"Someone could have cut my throat in the night and taken my place."

"I believe I might have noticed that."

He grinned briefly, then kissed her. That led to another, deeper kiss. Cormac told himself that the kisses meant nothing—they were merely idle pleasures, easily stolen and just as easily forgotten. It was clear that Elspeth felt the same.

It did not explain how she made him feel, however. His blood was pounding in his veins. He wanted to crawl inside her and stay there. Never had one kiss stirred his desire so swiftly or so fiercely. Here was danger, he thought, but he could not find the will to pull free. He needed her and he could not make himself believe it was because of a lengthy celibacy.

Elspeth clung to him, tasting his growing desire and letting herself be swept away by it. She tilted her head back at the first touch of his lips on her throat. A small part of her was afraid of the strength of the passions flowing between them, of the ferocity of them, but she ruthlessly quelled the fear. This was what she wanted, what she needed, what her heart had longed for before she was even old enough to understand.

When she felt his warm, lightly callused palm cover her breast, she realized he had managed to half undress her and she had not even noticed. No man had ever touched her there and she felt it was both strange and beautiful.

He rubbed his thumb over her nipple and the feeling that ripped through her was so sudden and so powerful she flinched, pulling away slightly. One look at his face told her that she had managed to break the spell they were under and she inwardly cursed.

Cormac yanked himself away from her and staggered to his feet. His groin pulsed with eagerness to continue and his hands shook slightly. He stared at tiny Elspeth in a mixture of wonder and dismay as she calmly fixed her bodice.

"Jesu," he groaned. "What did ye do to me?"

"Me?" Elspeth got up and started to roll up her blankets. "I believe I was sound asleep when all this began."

She was not going to let him get away with blaming her for the madness that had seized them, nor with making any other excuses. He wanted her. Denying it as he might, excusing it as he so obviously wanted to, or trying to ignore it would not work. She would not let it.

"Weel, nay completely asleep." He ran his fingers through his hair as he tried to clear his head. "Ye are a weelborn lass, a maid, and a woman I owe a great debt to. 'Twas verra wrong of me to try to take advantage of our situation."

"Ye fret too much. Did ye hear me screaming a protest?"

"Ye should have."

Elspeth shrugged and moved to start a fire. "Mayhap. And I may be a maid, and weelborn, but I am no child. I am nearly twenty, far past marrying age. I believe I am old enough to worry about my own chastity."

"Ye didnae seem to be worrying verra hard."

"How verra tactless of ye to point that out."

"I dinnae understand ye." He frowned and rubbed his hand over his chin. "And what do ye mean ye *may* be a maid?"

So like a man to hear that and little else, she thought crossly. " 'Twas just an ill choice of words. Why are ye so upset?"

Cormac did not really know, but he quickly found a suitable answer for her. "Because I am nay free to dally."

"Dally, is it?" Elspeth murmured, briefly contemplating the pleasure of hurling the small iron pot she held at his head. "And just how are ye not free? Ye said ye werenae betrothed and werenae married. Thus ye are free."

"True, I may be neither wed nor betrothed, but I have exchanged vows with a woman. We did so when I was but a lad and she a year younger. Those bonds still hold true."

"How touching and honorable."

Elspeth decided it was time to get away from him before she lost her temper. She handed him the little pot, proud of herself for not cracking him over the head with it, and marched off into the shelter of the surrounding trees. A little time to calm herself was what she needed. She could still feel his kisses, his touch, and she needed to shake free of the emotions he had stirred up inside of her. The last vestiges of the fierce passion they had so briefly shared had to be conquered before she could hear him talk of vows spoken or make any more excuses.

After seeing to her personal needs, then washing up in the icy water of the small brook wending its way through the trees, Elspeth felt better. Her sense of purpose was restored. It had just been disappointing to discover that Cormac was not going to be won over easily. He was going to be a hard nut to crack, especially since he had made some sort of vow to the wretched Isabel and was too honorable a man to cast it aside too quickly. Well, she would make a vow, too: She was going to do everything in her power to make him forswear his.

\* \* \*

Cormac shivered as the icy water he splashed on his face trickled down inside his shirt. It was not as good as a cold bath, but it had taken some of the edge off his aching need. Still a little dazed, he moved to the fire to make some porridge to break their fast. The mundane chore was not enough to stop him from thinking, however.

He did not understand what had just happened. Although he had not been completely faithful to Isabel, his dalliances had been few and far between. There was the occasional temptation he had given into, the women he had bedded during the bursts of jealousy he suffered each time Isabel had married and the few times his need had grown far too great to ignore. In none of those brief interludes, however, had he ever lost control or all sense of guilt. He had not even thought of Isabel until Elspeth had suddenly tensed beneath his touch and brought him back to his senses. None of the other women had been the virginal daughter of a laird, either.

It was pure madness, he decided. Ellpeth's voice was enough to make him rock hard. He could still taste the sweetness of her lips and could not stop himself from wondering if the rest of her tasted as sweet. His palm still tingled from the feel of her full, silken breast, the tip hard and taunting. He could easily, willingly, drown himself in the taste and feel of her, and that deeply troubled him.

A too-long celibacy had to be the cause. Cormac did not want to even consider anything else. The answer was simple. They would pause in the next village to get a few more supplies, and he would find that willing tavern maid, take her to bed, and rut this insanity out of his blood. Then he and Elspeth could continue their journey and begin acting like sensible people.

There was only one catch in his plan. How did he slip

away for this much needed rutting without Elspeth guessing what he was doing? Then he saw her walking back from the wood. The mere sight of her lithe shape made him ache. Cormac decided he owed her no explanations. His only concern should be getting her back, safely, into the hands of her family. If she found out what he was doing in the village, it was just too bad.

"Ye could at least feign a pleasant humor," Elspeth said as she sat by the fire and helped herself to some bread and cheese while she waited for the porridge to finish cooking.

"I dinnae usually begin my mornings by trying to ravish virginal maids I owe a great debt to," he drawled. "I beg your pardon if I seem a little disturbed by my own behavior."

"Cormac, I have seven brothers and more male cousins than any sensible person would want. Do ye really think ye could ravish me without spilling at least a little of your own blood?"

"I am a great deal bigger and stronger than ye are."

"As are most men, which is why I was taught every weak point a mon has. I wasnae taught just how to hurt a mon, either, but how to slip free of nearly any hold ye can think of and to use specific pains to ease those holds. If the men who had attacked Sorcha and me hadnae been so numerous and hadnae grabbed Sorcha thus distracting me, I may have e'en slipped free of that horror. Sadly, no one had e'er taught Sorcha what they taught me. She ne'er asked and she was e'er more a lady than I was."

"Ye didnae do anything to me."

"Nay, I didnae, did I?" she said in a soft calm voice, holding his gaze.

Elspeth saw exactly when he understood the meaning behind her words. His expression was an intriguing mix of desire, shock, and alarm. Then he looked angry. That hint of desire and alarm told her clearly that he desired her, but did not want to. The shock was easy to understand, for she doubted he had had many wellborn virgins declare their desire for him so bluntly. It was the anger she was not sure of. Did her boldness annoy him or was he angry because she had just made it clear that she would do nothing to help him resist temptation?

"Ye are mad."

"I hadnae realized that honesty had sunk so low in people's esteem that it was now considered part of insanity," she murmured.

"Eat."

She ate, deciding it did no good to goad him. Anger might well give him the strength he sought. Elspeth would have liked to say more, but she had made herself clear about what she wanted. That would have to be enough for now.

They finished their meager meal in silence. Together they broke camp. When silence continued to reign after she swung herself up behind Cormac on his horse, she decided he was obviously going to sulk. It seemed she was going to be punished in a small way for being so ill mannered as to stir his desire. Cormac was definitely going to be a hard nut to crack.

"Just how stupid does the mon think I am?" Elspeth muttered as she glared at the front of the inn and tavern Cormac had disappeared into.

As they had purchased some supplies, Cormac had stolen a moment to speak privately with one of the merchants. He had tugged the rotund man far enough away from her to destroy all chance that she might overhear what they said. All she caught were the words *tavern, Annie,* and *skilled lass.* Those words added to the quick, amused, yet knowing looks of the merchant told Elspeth more than she really wanted to know. Cormac was looking for a whore.

It hurt, and that enraged her. The very thought of Cormac kissing and touching another woman twisted her innards with jealousy and the sharp craving to do violence. There she stood, ready, willing, and able—or at least soon to be taught how to be able if Cormac would just give her a chance. She was also afraid that a hearty tussle beneath the sheets with this Annie could actually succeed in giving Cormac the strength to ignore her.

For a moment she considered marching into the tavern and letting Cormac know just how furious she was. Then she heard the sounds coming out of the tavern. It was obviously filled with men, many of them already deep into their drinking if the sounds of loud revelry were any indication. If she went in there now, she could easily find herself neck deep in trouble before she even found Cormac.

Then she recalled that there had to be a kitchen door. She could slip inside unseen and then find Cormac. Although she suspected it would feel as if her heart was being cut from her chest with a dull knife if she caught him with a woman, she was not going to stand there and just wait until he strolled out adjusting his clothes. Maybe if she thoroughly embarrassed him or shamed him, he would give up the notion that he could fight the passion that flared between them by spending himself in another woman. It chilled her to think she might have to suffer this at every tavern or inn between here and the king's court.

Preparing herself for the distasteful deed was useless, so Elspeth just took a deep breath and started around the side of the building toward the back. She was almost there when she collided with a buxom young woman hurrying from the privy in the back of the yard toward the same door. Elspeth took one look at her and inwardly cursed.

If she could not divert the woman, Cormac certainly would not be turning her down.

"Are ye Annie?" she asked, shifting to block the woman's way through the door.

"Aye. Do I ken ye?" Annie's blue eyes narrowed and she impatiently pushed a lock of golden hair off her pretty face. "I really cannae stay here and talk. Old George told me there is a fine looking young gentlemon asking for me."

"I ken it, and if ye answer that call, I can make it so that no one will wish your company again."

Elspeth felt a twinge of guilt when her cold, hard threat made the woman turn pale, her eyes widening so much that it had to be painful. It was not Annie who deserved the brunt of Elspeth's anger and hurt. Since she and Cormac had exchanged no vows, she supposed he did not, either. On the other hand, it was insulting that he would run from what she offered and go to another. Elspeth supposed she could excuse her anger that way if pressed.

"Are ye his wife?" Annie surreptitiously looked around, obviously seeking a clear route of escape.

"I intend to be. He is coming to ye because he wants me and feels 'twould be dishonorable to bed a virgin."

Annie winced, then smiled sadly. "I have had me a few of those. They speak sweetly to me, then call out for the one they truly want when their lust grows hot enough to close their eyes."

"That is terrible." Elspeth shook her head. "Men can be such incredible swine. My cousin Payton—"

"Payton? Nay Sir Payton Murray, son of Sir Nigel and Lady Gisele?"

"Ye ken my cousin?" Payton might just be getting a little too free with his favors, Elspeth mused.

"Oh, he has ne'er been with me." Annie's sigh was heavy with regret; then she brightened. "But ye can tell me a few things about that gentle, fair knight others wouldnae ken, cannae ye?"

"Weel aye, mayhaps," Elspeth mumbled, struggling to adjust to Payton being spoken of in such reverent terms.

"Wait. I will get us each an ale. We can sit on the bench o'er there."

Elspeth was still too surprised over the woman's reaction to Payton's name to stop her from darting away and going inside. She cursed when she realized it could all be a ploy. Just as she decided Annie had tricked her, the woman reappeared with a tray of bread and cheese and two tankards of ale. Elspeth just shook her head and followed Annie over to the bench. She had wanted the tryst Cormac sought to be stopped. It was churlish to fret over how that had been accomplished.

"I had a wee peek at your mon," Annie said as she sat down. "I can see why ye are so possessive."

After taking a sip of ale, Elspeth admitted, "I have to be. He is fighting me hard and I only have a fortnight or so to win him over. He believes himself in love with and bound to another woman. We are traveling to her now."

"And yet he still seeks me out?"

"I ken it doesnae sound verra good of him, but the lady Isabel doesnae deserve faithfulness and I havenae earned the right to ask for it yet."

"Lady Isabel Douglas?" Annie muttered a curse when Elspeth nodded. "When one sees a woman like that, one wonders how anyone can think they have the right to call me a whore."

"True. *Wheesht,* do ye ken everyone in Scotland?" Elspeth asked and laughed softly. "I am Elspeth Murray of Donncoill."

"Ah, the daughter of the healer. I hear ye are becoming near as weel kenned for your skills as she is."

"Thank ye. Forgive me, but *how* do ye ken so much?"

"The tavern and the inn lie on a verra busy road to the king's court when he holds it. I hear a great deal, especially since many think naught of speaking freely in front of a tavern slut. 'Tis truth that many pay no heed, but I do. Ye ne'er can tell when such information could turn in my favor. I have earned a coin or two for it, and 'tis a fact, I would rather fatten my purse that way for all I have the freedom to choose what mon I play the whore for."

"I was thinking that ye have a verra understanding master, verra lenient."

"Oh, he isnae my master. Old George is my cousin. I own a wee piece of all this, ye ken. Nay enough to keep my purse full, but it means I dinnae have to grovel for a ha'penny every day." She gave Elspeth a decidedly wicked wink. "I like a good tussle now and then. Soon decided I may as weel get a coin or two whilst I was enjoying myself. Now are ye close to that good knight, Sir Payton? I heard a dark rumor that he may be dead."

Elspeth took a large drink of ale to still the unease she felt hearing that the rumor of Payton's death was already spreading. "I dinnae think he is, although I myself saw him felled with an arrow in his back."

"Oh, that such a bonny lad should be cut down by a cowardly attack from behind."

After nodding a hearty agreement, Elspeth frowned. "Just how is it that my cousin is so weel kenned and spoken of?"

"M'lady, he is a bonny, bonny young mon. He but walks by and he rips a sigh of longing from the heart of every woman who sees him, young or old. And there is a sweetness, a kindness, in him. True, he rarely beds down with lasses such as I, but he doesnae scorn us, either. 'Tis already weel kenned that, if ye are playing the whore just to feed your bairns, Sir Payton has an open, generous hand." Annie gave a sot snort of disgust as she chewed on a piece of bread. "Jane, a dirty slut who works at an inn in the next village, borrows her sister's bairns and puts herself in Sir Payton's way as he travels to and from court."

"I will be certain to tell him." She studied Annie closely and saw the sharp wit behind the woman's eyes. "I shall also tell my kinsmen about your ability to gather information. Such things can be verra useful and weel worth a coin or two."

"Can ye tell me a thing or two about Sir Payton now? I should love to have a tale or two about him that no one else kens." Annie winced and scratched at her arm.

"What ails ye?" Elspeth asked even as she took Annie's hand in hers and pushed up the sleeve of her bodice. "An ugly rash. Is it everywhere on your body?"

"Just on my arms and a wee bit on my chest. It comes and goes. 'Tis naught."

Elspeth studied it closely even as she set her bag on the table. "Ye didnae catch it from anyone?"

"Nay. As I said, I choose my men most carefully. And this used to trouble me when I was a child, too, ere I ever kenned a mon."

"Ah." Elspeth took out a salve. " 'Tis something ye are eating or touching that your body doesnae like. Watch what ye eat, when the rash appears, and ye will soon discover what food is doing this to ye. If nay a food, something ye dinnae use each day. Just keep an eye on when it comes and goes and all that happens at that time or, rather, a wee bit before. Now I will tell ye a tale or two about Payton as I mix ye a salve for those spots." With a smile, Elspeth began to relate a few humorous stories concerning Payton.

It was as Elspeth spread a little of her salve on Annie's arms that she knew Cormac was there watching her. Annie glanced toward the kitchen door, then gave Elspeth a look full of laughter. Elspeth chanced a glance at Cormac and had to bite back a grin. He stood in the rear door of the inn, staring at her in dismay and anger, his fists on his hips. She wondered if he would have the audacity to try to fulfill his plans and almost wanted to dare him to try. Elspeth knew it would serve no purpose, would even make her road harder, but she ached to have a confrontation with him. She turned her attention back to Annie, suggesting yet again that she watch her reaction to things, particularly to several foods that Elspeth knew other people had problems with.

Cormac cursed and ran his fingers through his hair as he watched Elspeth chat amiably with the tavern maid he had intended to make use of. After the man called Old George had assured him that Annie would soon join him, he had sat drinking his ale and convincing himself, yet again, that this was what he wanted and needed. A quick sighting of the fair-haired, fulsome maid had encouraged Cormac. He felt sure he would have no trouble bedding her. When the woman disappeared and did not return, Cormac's patience had waned. He could not leave Elspeth waiting for hours. Ignoring Old George's sputtered protests, Cormac had decided to look for the maid. Never had he thought he would find her visiting with the very woman who tormented him so. It was enough to make a grown man want to scream and bang his head against a hard wall until the confusion passed.

For a brief moment, Cormac contemplated marching over there, grabbing the buxom Annie by the hand, and dragging her off. He even imagined himself haughtily telling Elspeth to wait. If he found an hour or two was not enough, she could get herself a room and he would see her in the morning. It would serve the woman right for daring to interfere in a man's business, and he felt sure that she had interfered. She might even feel it was such a slap in the face that she would no longer look at him in that longing way that set his blood afire and scattered his wits.

Then he sighed and slumped against the wall. He could not do it. It had felt awkward enough to leave her waiting outside of the tavern with weak, muttered excuses about needing some ale and the tavern being no place for a woman. Cormac had been able to see in her expression that Elspeth had not believed a word he had said. Discretion had not eased his odd sense of guilt and hesitation. He doubted bluntness would, either. And despite the sharp ache in his loins, he really did not want to argue over his right to bed a tavern maid.

Resigning himself to aching with a constantly inspired but never satisfied lust, he straightened up and walked over to Elspeth. There would be other tavern maids between here and the king's court. But now that he had dragged his wits out of his breeches long enough to think clearly, he recognized that it had been careless to leave Elspeth alone. There had been no sign of Sir Colin, but that did not mean that the man was not pursuing them. Two, possibly three, men had already died because of Sir Colin's lust for Elspeth. Cormac sincerely doubted that the man had given up.

"Shall we go?" he asked, glancing briefly at the rash on the maid that Elspeth was gently treating and wondering if he had actually been saved by Elspeth's interference.

"All done drinking your ale?" Elspeth asked sweetly as she placed the pot of salve in Annie's hand and gathered up the rest of her things.

"Aye." Cormac did not believe her pose of sweet innocence at all.

"Weel, I am ready to ride on if ye are," she said, but Cormac was already walking away. *"Wheesht,* he isnae going to be verra cheerful company for a while," she muttered, then smiled crookedly when Annie laughed.

"True," agreed Annie, "but he will be easier to woo into your arms, m'lady. I dinnae think I have e'er seen a mon strung so taut or lusting so bad for a lass."

"He will have to get o'er his sulk first. I will tell my kinsmen about what a keen eye and ear ye have, Annie, and I think ye will see one soon."

"Send Sir Payton."

"Elspeth!" bellowed Cormac.

Although she shook her head and muttered about domineering men, making Annie giggle again, Elspeth hurried to follow Cormac. She had accomplished what she had set out to do. Cormac had not given away what she considered hers. She just wished she could find an easy, painless way to make Cormac see what she did: They were mates. However, if she had to tie up and hide away every whore and less than virtuous woman between them and the court to ensure his fidelity to her until he saw that truth, she would. Isabel was enough of a force to overcome. She needed no other impediments.

# Chapter Four

Elspeth rolled her eyes as a grim-faced Cormac strode off to go hunting, and then she grabbed up her clothes. For two days she had endured Cormac's strange moods and she was weary of them. She would wake up in the morning in his arms, the heat and need between them nearly blinding. He would kiss her and move his strong hands over her all too willing body. Then he would touch a part of her he had not touched before. She would start slightly, mostly from the power of the feeling that would surge through her. That would be just enough to make him shake his head as if to clear it; then he would pull away from her with an alacrity that was positively insulting. And he would stay as far away from her as he could for the rest of the day. She was surprised he still allowed her plea of fearing her nightmares to keep him curled up beside her at night.

It could not go on much longer, she mused as she got a piece of soap out of her bag. There were no more new places for him to touch. All she had to do was try to control her reactions to his intimate touches, to temper them, at least until there was no longer any chance of turning back. If he kept sending her into a fever and then stopping, it would not be him trying to drag some stranger to bed in the next village they reached. It was her maidenhead that truly held him back and she was beginning to think she was going to have to find someone to rid her of it. It was either that or slip into a madness born of continuous aching unfulfillment.

The little brook they had camped by twisted its way through the moors and forest on its slow journey to the next village. Elspeth followed it until she found a sheltered spot where the shrubs and trees gave her some covering to soothe her modesty, but allowed enough of a view that she should be able to see any danger if it approached. The water was probably cold, but she was in dire need of a bath. She also needed to wash most of her clothes.

After a final look around to be sure she was in private, she shed her clothes. The late summer sun was lovely and warm, but it only took one toe dipped into the water to tell her it would not be so pleasant. Elspeth grabbed her soap and one of her stockings to use as a cloth and plunged into the water. Her teeth clenched against a shocked screech as the cold water slapped her warm skin. She kept them clenched to keep them from chattering. Even as she washed her hair, then scrubbed herself, she did not think she had ever taken so swift a bath.

Once out of the unwelcoming water, Elspeth used her clothes to rub her hair dry enough so that it ceased to drip and rubbed her body dry with enough vigor to restore the flow of blood. Slipping on her chemise, she knelt by the water and washed out her clothes, letting the sun finish the work of warming and drying her. By the time she needed her clothes again they would be dry and, if she was very careful, not too badly wrinkled.

They would reach another village on the morrow, Elspeth thought, then cursed. There would probably be an inn or a tavern and another willing maid she would have to threaten. Yesterday had proven even a village was not needed, just a cottage with a lusty widow. That woman had required the glimpse of a knife to keep her roving eye and welcoming smile away from Cormac. It was turning into a strange game. He looked interested, she took away the source of his interest, and they moved on. She knew he was aware that she was doing or saying something to the women, and although he clearly did not like it, they never mentioned the matter.

It was also a hurtful game. There she was, warm and welcoming, all too embarrassingly eager to share his passion, yet he kept shoving her aside. Even though she understood what he was doing and why when he gave those women a warm smile, it was painful to watch. Elspeth knew that, at the moment, her greatest fear was that he would give his passion to some other woman before she had even had a chance to taste it.


Cormac stared blindly around the campsite and dropped the two rabbits he had caught and prepared on the ground. Elspeth was gone, but that was not what caused him to feel so panicked. There were many reasons for her to have wandered away from the camp. Her bag was gone as well, however.

Had she finally walked away, decided she would do better on her own? He would not blame her if she had. Traveling with a man who tried to ravish her every morning, then snapped at her or ignored her all day had to be driving her mad. It was certainly doing that to him. She could also have decided that she had had enough of seeing him sniffing after every other woman they met. Being knotted up with lust and unable to sate himself on the one who stirred it up was turning him into a blind, rutting beast. A tavern maid, a milkmaid, a widow—any woman other than a well-bred virgin who gave him the least hint of welcome. Such behavior had to have given Elspeth a complete disgust of him. In fact, the way he seemed so eager to bed down with any woman probably had her believing that the passion he had revealed to her was just common lust. She might even be ashamed of herself for responding to him as she did.

None of that was important, however. At least not as important as the fact that Sir Colin was after her, was even willing to kill to get his hands on her. It was not only Elspeth's chastity at stake or the threat of a forced marriage to a man she loathed. The moment Sir Colin succeeded in wedding and bedding her against her will, the Murrays would be gathering men and arms. They might already be doing so. Her family and their allies would all be endangered as they fought to rescue her and avenge her as well as the men Sir Colin had murdered. Cormac knew how such a happening could devastate Elspeth, and because of what he owed her and her family, he had to do all in his power to stop it. That meant keeping Elspeth safe and close by his side until Sir Colin gave up or died.

Cormac mentally checked that all of his weapons were where they should be as he located Elspeth's trail and followed it into the forest. He was not sure what he could do if she was determined to flee him. An apology for his behavior would probably help, but it would not be easy. What could he say? That he did not usually allow himself to be led around by his staff? That he did not usually act like a rutting swine willing to make a wellborn lass wait outside the door while he eased the ache in his groin on any woman willing to lie down for him?

And just what kept happening to those women? he wondered yet again. One minute they were smiling and swishing their hips in blatant invitation; the next they were like ice and a little frightened. Elspeth was doing something to make the women rescind their avid welcomes. Cormac did not like to think Elspeth was threatening the women. Yet one minute, that widow had been so eager she nearly had his breeches off him before he finished greeting her. Then, after he had gone off for a moment of privacy, he came back to utter rejection. Elspeth's look of innocence might have been convincing if the widow had not kept glancing her way as if she expected to be murdered in her lonely bed. Just perhaps Elspeth owed him an apology as well. Reprehensible as his actions might be, she had no right to interfere.

When he finally saw Elspeth, he stopped short, then took several slow, very deep breaths to calm an instinctive flare of rage. He was out looking for her, worrying about her, and she was sunning herself on the riverbank. A quick glance at the array of clothing carefully hung from the branches told Cormac that she had not planned to flee, had just come to wash her clothes. The recollection of the panic he had felt troubled him. The fact that there had been no need for it annoyed him.

As he stepped closer to her, all his plans for scolding her about her recklessness and thoughlessness fled his mind. She lay on her back, her beautiful thick hair spread out around her to dry in the sun. Her lithe frame was clothed only in a thin linen chemise that reached to just below her knees. Despite his efforts to control himself, his gaze slid from her full breasts to her tiny waist. He paused to stare hungrily at the faintly visible shadow between her long slim legs. Even her feet were pretty, he thought dazedly as he silently knelt by her side.

Elspeth slowly opened her eyes and smiled at him and Cormac knew he had reached the end of his tether. "Ye look like a beautiful nymph who has crawled from the chill depths of the river to honor the sun with her presence."

Her heart skipped alarmingly at the husky flattery, and she tried to dim the allure of the words by saying, " 'Tis barely a brook."

Cormac grinned as he unbuckled his sword, tossed it aside, then yanked off his boots. "Would ye belittle the first poetry this poor mon has e'er uttered?"

"Nay," Elspeth whispered, praying that he was not about to give her yet another lesson in the torturous art of being aroused, then left unsatisfied as she welcomed him into her arms. "Was that what that was?"

"Aye, but I think ye may be the potion that can make this mon trill words as bonny as any minstrel has."

He kissed her and she quickly wrapped her arms around him, wondering if this time she could hold him until they were both beyond reason. His kiss was slow and thorough yet there was a strong hint of desperation behind it. If he left her too soon this time, she was sure she would just roll over and weep.

"My bonny Elspeth," he murmured against her throat as he unlaced her chemise, "ye should push me away."

"Why? Ye always seem to manage that all on your own."

"Nay, not this time."

"Are ye sure?"

Cormac crouched over her as he eased her thin chemise off her shoulders and tugged it down to her waist. The sight of her full breasts, the rose-hued tips hard and beckoning, had him fighting to catch his breath. Her skin was smooth, unblemished cream and he licked his lips in anticipation of the taste of it. When he curved his hands around her breasts and lightly stroked the puckered nipples with his thumbs, she shuddered, her beautiful eyes darkening with her need.

"Oh, aye my green eyed temptress. This time only ye can stop this."

Seeing the hungry way he stared at her breasts as he continued to taunt the aching tips with his fingers, she threaded her fingers through his hair and gently tugged him closer. "Then there will be nay stopping this time."

He groaned with a mixture of resignation and delight as he dragged his tongue over her taut nipple and she caressed his ears with a soft gasp of pleasure. She tasted as sweet as he had known she would. When he drew that tip deep into his mouth and suckled, she cried out and clung to him. Cormac felt her passionate response in his very bones and wondered if he would have the strength to go slowly.

Elspeth was nearly desperate to touch him, to be rid of the clothes that hid his flesh from her hands and lips. She cursed her fingers, which proved strangely clumsy as she struggled to unlace his doublet. A soft sound of relief and encouragement escaped her when Cormac paused in his delicious assault on her breasts to help her.

With so many males in her family, Elspeth was no stranger to what a man's body looked like. When Cormac shed the last of his clothes, she studied him with eyes gone wide with admiration. He was all lean, hard muscle. Broad shoulders, a flat, hard stomach, trim hips, and long, well-formed legs—all warranted her attention and admiration. His skin was smooth and glowed with health, a creamy, lightly golden tone that begged for her touch. A thin arrow of reddish brown hair began just below his navel, blossomed around his rather impressive endowments, and lightly dusted his strong legs. It was no wonder Isabel clung to him so tenaciously, she thought, shifting her body so that he could finish removing her chemise.

"Ye are so beautiful," she whispered, reaching out to trail her fingers down his chest and over his stomach.

"Strange lass," he said, the wonder in his voice making the words an endearment. " 'Tis ye who are beautiful."

As he stared down at the slim beauty exposed to his view, Cormac wondered why he had not yet flung himself on top of her as every muscle in his body demanded. Her waist was so tiny he was not surprised to see that he could nearly span it with his hands. Her hips had a womanly flare to them despite her slender build. Her legs looked surprisingly long with a space at the top of her thighs that begged for a man. Her beautiful skin continued right on down to her adorable little toes. Cormac was not surprised to see his hand shake slightly as he reached out to gently caress the tidy vee of ebony curls that decorated her womanly secrets.

Slowly, he eased his body down on top of hers, echoing the faint shudder that rippled through her as their flesh met. Delight swept through him with such force he rested his forehead against hers as he battled the urge to immediately spill his seed.

"Oh, oh, my," Elspeth gasped. "That feels so good."

"Ah, lass, somehow the words are just inadequate. There simply are none to describe this pleasure."

He slid his hand between her thighs and after just a few strokes of his long fingers, Elspeth doubted she could have found any words at all, even to describe the simplest of things. Cormac kissed her, thrusting his tongue into her mouth even as he slid his finger inside of her body. Elspeth shivered and arched greedily into his hand.

"Cormac," she said, her voice so thick and husky she was not sure her words were clear. "I ache."

"Aye, angel, I ken the feeling weel," he muttered against the hollow at the base of her throat.

"Then why are ye waiting?" She could feel her insides tighten as he continued to stroke her so intimately.

"Ye need to be ready. 'Tis your first time."

"Jesu," she gasped as she felt the hint of some intense feeling ripple through her. "How ready need I be?"

Then, suddenly, that hint was followed by wave after wave of a rich, blinding pleasure. Elspeth clutched frantically at Cormac, alternately trying to twist away from his hand and arching into it, trying to flee the ferocity of her own passion and to add to it. She was still dazed and panting from the force of it all when she felt him lift her trembling legs and wrap them around his waist. Grabbing hold of his arms, she tried to regain her scattered wits and concentrate on what was about to happen. She met his gaze and read the passion there, as well as an intensity, a need, she did not fully understand.

"Now, lass. Now ye are ready," he said, and gritting his teeth, he plunged into her body, ruthlessly battering his way past her maidenhead before he stopped.

Something tickled at the back of his mind, but Cormac had no time for it. He had heard her gasp of pain, felt her slight body briefly recoil from him. It took every ounce of will he possessed to hold still. Cormac looked at her, frowning when he saw that she was a little pale and tears glittered in her eyes. That proof of the pain he had caused her helped him hold on to his control.

"I have hurt ye," he said, gently stroking her breasts and praying he could restir at least some of the passion he had killed with his rough possession of her.

"Nay too badly," she said, taking slow deep breaths and forcing herself to relax.

It had hurt rather more than she had expected it to, but she would not admit that. His possession had been swift and fierce, her maidenhead rather abruptly destroy-ed. Elspeth was not sure slower would have been any better, and since complaint of any kind could easily be mistaken for criticism, she decided to say nothing. What she found curious was the look of astonishment, then confusion, that had crossed his face when he had charged through the proof of her innocence and sensed the pain he had inflicted. It was as if he had never bedded a virgin before.

Deciding that now was not the time to consider such things, she fought to relax, knowing it was the surest way to ease the discomfort she felt. She shifted her legs a little higher up his body and found that helped her to accept his invasion of her body with a little more ease. The soft kisses he covered her breasts with stirred her desire again and that too helped. Sighing with an increasing pleasure as she began to savor the way their bodies were joined, Elspeth smoothed her hands over his strong back.

"The pain has eased," she said, stroking his hard but-tocks and feeling him tremble.

"Thank God," he whispered and began to move.

What little pain had remained swiftly dissipated as Els-peth felt the intimate stroking of his body. The realization that no two people could ever be physically closer than this only added to her rapidly reviving desire. With her hands and her body she tried to pull him even deeper inside of her. His movements grew fiercer, his thrusts harder, more demanding. Elspeth greedily met each one. Then he slipped his hand between them, touching her close to where their bodies thrusted and parried. One touch of his long finger made her tense with anticipation. The second made her shatter.

Cormac felt her arch and cry out as her release tore through her. He savored each fevered twist of her lithe body and then he lost the last thin threads of his control. The tremors within her, the convulsive tightening of the wet heat engulfing him, soon dragged him to passion's heights along with her. He cried out her name, plunged deep, and shuddered as his seed flowed into her body. Reckless, a voice whispered in his head, but he allowed the voice of common sense to be drowned out by the heady delight he felt as he collapsed, sated and happy, into Elspeth's slim arms.

A cool breeze sweeping over his backside recalled Cormac to his senses. As he eased the intimacy of their embrace, he fought to hide the increasing dismay he felt from Elspeth. It would hurt her. She did not deserve to suffer the brunt of his conflicting emotions. He brushed a kiss over her lips, yanked a square of linen from his doublet, and went to dampen it in the brook.

After washing her blood from his groin, Cormac rinsed out the cloth and returned to Elspeth's side. Ignoring her blushes and muttered protests, he cleaned her off as well. That little voice he had heard as he had shattered Elspeth's innocence returned and demanded to be heeded. There had been no shield to batter down when he had first bedded down with Isabel, no blood upon his thighs or upon hers. Isabel had winced sweetly and sniffled a little, but he now knew her little display of pain had been false. She had sworn that she was a virgin, that she was giving him her innocence out of love, a gift her husband did not deserve. Isabel had lied to him. She had stared into his eyes and lied. Someone had been there before him.

Unable to decide what he felt or thought about that revelation, Cormac pushed it all aside and smiled at Elspeth. She *had* been a virgin and it would require all of his attention and skill to see them through this awkward moment with no embarrassment or confusion and hurt feelings. And no promises he could not keep, he thought to himself.

"Come, angel, it grows chill," Cormac said as he handed her her clothes, then began to tug on his own.

"Aye, it does," she murmured as she began to dress, and she was not referring to the slight bite to the evening air.

Something had changed, she thought, watching Cormac closely as they dressed. One moment he had been lying sated and content in her arms, and she had no doubt about his contentment. Then he had begun to withdraw from her. What she now saw was little more than a polite mask. He was doing his utmost to get them dressed and back to camp without serious conversation, embarrassment, or any real display of feeling.

There was a part of her that wanted to scream at him. She was sure he had been with her in body and spirit as they had climbed passion's dizzying heights. Yet this wall he now built between them made her doubt her senses. She asked for no vows or words of love, even though she ached to hear them. He could, however, give her something beside this cool gentleness he now showed her. Even a few empty flatteries would be acceptable. She felt irrevocably changed. Something wondrous had happened between them, but for all the depth of feeling he was showing, she could have simply scraped her knee.

It was not easy but she caged her riotous emotions. She equaled his air of friendly calm interspersed with light banter as she gathered her clean clothes and followed him back to their camp. The quickest way to lose him now would be to push too hard. Elspeth knew she had to be patient and understanding. She even had to swallow some of her pride. She also knew it was probably going to be one of the hardest things she had ever done.

\*　\*　\*

Cormac frowned, glancing at Elspeth's slim, blanket-shrouded form as he banked the fire. She had not made any demands, cried any tears, or forced him to discuss what had happened between them. He should be pleased that she was so calm, so indefatigably reasonable, but he was not. She had just lost her chastity on a riverbank to a man who gave her no words of love or promises of marriage, yet she acted as if she was quite accustomed to having a lover. He decided the reason he was troubled by that was because it was confusing. She was confusing.

The passion he had just shared with her also left him troubled. It was the best, the sweetest, the fiercest he had ever known. Better than he had ever enjoyed with Isabel. That not only dismayed him—it frightened him. Worse, he was not cured of wanting Elspeth. Despite having been utterly sated only a few hours ago, he was aching to love her again.

Guilt also pinched at him. Guilt for having betrayed Isabel, for enjoying lovemaking with Elspeth so much, and for wanting to do it again and again until he could not walk. And guilt for taking Elspeth's maidenhead when he knew he could not offer her more than a brief affair. The worst was the guilt he felt for losing control so completely he had spilled his seed inside of her—something he had rarely done with Isabel. He had the chilling feeling that, if he made love to Elspeth again, the same thing would happen. She was some madness in his blood and he did not know what to do about it.

As he moved to stand near their rough bed, he thought about separating himself from her. He sighed, for he could not do it. Elspeth still suffered from bad dreams, still needed the comfort of someone close at hand. Now that they had made love, there was no longer any reason to keep himself apart. And if he tried to sleep apart from her now, he knew he would hurt her feelings and he could not do that, either.

When he slid in beside her, she turned and cuddled up next to him. His body immediately tightened with need and he inwardly cursed himself. Once he could try to excuse as an unthinking moment of blind passion, but if he continued to make love to her, he would be silently promising her more than he had to give. She began to caress his chest and he quickly stopped her by catching her hand firmly in his. At least tonight he could push her away with good reason—one that would not insult or hurt her or even hint at his own emotional turmoil.

"Nay, lass," he said and brushed a kiss over her forehead. "Ye are sore and must needs heal."

"Aye, there is a wee bit of tenderness," she agreed. "I probably should have sat in the water for a while to ease it."

"Oh, aye, turning your sweet parts into ice is a sure cure."

She giggled, not only at his words, but at the glimpse of the old Cormac that slipped through the strange shield he had put between them. "Ye regret it, dinnae ye?"

He sighed and combed his fingers through her hair as he groped for a way to be truthful yet kind. "Aye, but nay because it was with you. I wanted you and 'twas the sweetest I have e'er tasted, but I should ne'er have tasted it. I should have resisted temptation, for I cannae give ye any more than that."

That hurt, but Elspeth told herself to be sensible. One tussle on a riverbank was not enough to break Isabel's grip on him. "I dinnae believe I asked ye to give me more."

"Ye should. A weelborn lass like ye should be demanding more. Ye should have saved that gift for your husband."

"I am nearly twenty and havenae met any mon I wanted for a husband or a lover. Ye make me burn. Mayhap I decided that, e'en though ye say ye can give me no more than a brief love affair, I had waited long enough for that more ye speak of. Now I would just take what I wanted."

"For a lass like ye such recklessness can have serious consequences.

"That is my trouble to face, nay yours."

"Elspeth . . ."

She brushed her lips over his, stopping his words. "Nay more. I have both the wit and the will to say nay to a mon. I didnae want to say it to ye. Just accept that and cast aside your guilt for ye havenae earned it. I am a woman grown, nay a child ye need to protect or decide things for. Let it lie, Cormac. Talking on it too much will have us saying things neither of us wants to hear." She made herself comfortable in his arms. "Rest. 'Tis what I intend to do."

He stared up at the stars and wished he could see things so clearly. She offered him passion without fetters and he ached to accept it. Yet instinct told him it was already far from that simple.

# Chapter Five

As the door shut behind Cormac, Elspeth cursed and looked around the room for something she could throw. When she had fallen asleep in his arms last night she had thought that everything was settled, that she had eased his concerns. He did not know that she had been lying through her teeth when she had offered him passion without demands. Yet when she had opened her eyes this morning, Cormac had donned an extraordinarily thick emotional armor. He had decided that he needed to protect her from herself, from him, and from her own passions. He had been kind, courteous, and distant all day. And now, the *coup de grâce:* He had gotten them separate rooms at the inn.

Deciding it was too late to gain any satisfaction from throwing something at the door since Cormac was now too far away to hear it, Elspeth flung herself down on the bed. Now that her maidenhead was gone, she felt that Cormac would no longer feel a need to restrain his desire.

Through the passion they shared, she had intended to try to reach his heart, to break Isabel's grip on him. That would be impossible if Cormac intended to cloak himself in the mantle of chivalry. The fact that he thought he had to protect her from the error of her own judgment was also extremely insulting. It was a common tendency among men and one of their most annoying.

A soft rap at the door reminded Elspeth that she had ordered a bath. She quickly let the maids in and waited impatiently for them to fill her tub. The moment she latched the door behind them, she stripped off her clothes. It had been too long since she had enjoyed such a luxury, and she suspected she might have a very long wait before she could enjoy it again. She sighed with pleasure as she lowered her body into the hot water, the soft scent of the herbs she had hastily sprinkled in the bath quickly soothing her. There was nothing like a long soak in a hot bath to help one think. There had to be a solution to her problem with Cormac, and before the water cooled, she intended to find it.

Cormac sank into the hot water of his bath and prayed it would help ease the tension in his body. One of the maids who had brought the water had given him a pretty, welcoming smile, but he had not returned it. He now knew that he would not find any respite from his longing in another woman's arms. His lust was firmly fixed on Elspeth, and that one wild moment of indescribable passion they had shared had only made it worse.

"What in God's sweet name will happen when I finally meet with Isabel?" he asked his knee, then grimaced. Now he was talking to himself. "Nay, I worry o'er naught. 'Twill all be set right when I see Isabel again."

He began to scrub himself clean. During the night he

had decided he could not allow himself to be lured back into Elspeth's arms. Unfortunately, his memory of the pleasure he had found there constantly made his resolve waver. The fact that she was willing to be his lover, to share her passion freely, and to ask for nothing but an equal return made the temptation almost impossible to resist. It had been very hard to maintain his decision to act as a gentleman should when he felt her lithe body pressed close against his back all day long as they rode.

"I need another horse."

After considering his meager purse for a moment, he was not sure he could afford one, certainly not one as good as his own. Since, at some point, they might have to flee Sir Colin, a second horse was also practical. Elspeth was small, but even her added weight would slow his horse down if they had to gallop for any great distance. If it was possible to get a second horse, Cormac felt the practical reasons would keep Elspeth from guessing why he had even considered it in the first place. He certainly could not tell her that he had done it because, if he felt her breasts rubbing against his back just one more time, he would have her on her back on the ground before she could blink.

Determined now, he hurriedly finished his bath. If he was lucky he could buy a decent horse without completely emptying his purse and be back in time to meet Elspeth for the evening meal. If he was very lucky indeed, he mused ruefully, he could accomplish his task and still have enough to pay for that meal.

Elspeth frowned as she sniffed the small pot of scent the shop woman held out. It was pleasant, a gentle scent of lavender, one she had always preferred. Her own supply had been one of the many victims of her kidnapping, lost along with the lovely gowns she had intended to wear during her friend's wedding celebration. Once she was safe again, she would have to send Bridgit a lovely gift and a very long letter of explanation.

"Is it too strong, m'lady?" the woman asked.

"Nay, 'tis lovely. My favorite in truth." She smiled faintly. "I had thought to try something different, something a mon might find verra alluring."

"Ah, a mon." The shop woman picked up one of the little pots Elspeth had tried, hesitated over, and set aside. "Some ladies say this scent draws a mon and stirs his passions."

Elspeth sniffed it again, then sighed. "I just dinnae think it suits me for all it is pleasing to the nose." She returned to the lavender. "I believe I will stay with what I ken mixes weel with my own scent."

"Verra wise. Do ye wish some soap as weel?"

"Aye." Elspeth carefully counted out the money for her purchases, smiling a little nervously when she caught the woman studying her intently. "Is something wrong?"

"Weel, I am nay sure how to say this, but if 'tis a mon's desire ye seek to stir, I may have something for ye."

"Dinnae fear insulting me. I am in the midst of a fierce battle for a mon's heart. I will consider any weapon." She gasped with pleasure when the woman spread a beautiful night rail out on the smooth wooden table. " 'Tis lovely."

Elspeth's eyes widened when she slid her fingers beneath the soft cloth and realized how thin it was. It would not hide much at all. Closer inspection revealed that most of the bodice was made of a fine lace, thick in just the right places to hide the tips of her breasts yet thin everywhere else. The only things that would hold the gown on a woman's body were the delicate ribbons at the top of each sleeve. It would certainly be a sensuous garment. Elspeth was just not sure she was daring enough to wear it or, if she was, if she had enough coin to buy it.

"A verra fine weapon indeed," Elspeth said, "but it may be too costly for me." She winced when the woman named the price, for it would leave her with barely enough to buy an ale. "Mayhap some of the cost can be taken in trade. Do ye have any ailments, mistress? I am a healer, and I have learned a great deal from my mother, Lady Maldie Murray."

"Oh, I have heard of her. E'en the Douglases have sought her out. I do have trouble with my hands," the woman said, holding them out for Elspeth to look at. "They can ache something fierce from time to time and it hinders my work."

"Ah, a troublesome thing." Elspeth set her herb bag on the table and searched for a certain salve she was sure would help. " 'Tisnae curable, ye ken, mistress, but the ache can be eased. Dinnae let your hands get chilled and try nay to get them wet when the air cools." She held out a small pot of salve. "Rub this on when the aching starts, but nay too thickly." She took out a scrap of parchment and a lump of charcoal with a knife-honed point and wrote out the recipe for the salve. "This will allow ye to make more as ye need it. Best ye get it copied in proper ink as soon as ye can, for this will smudge easily. Ye can read?"

The woman nodded, shyly admitting to a skill good enough to understand the recipes for her scents and soaps. She and Elspeth bartered for a little while. By the time Elspeth left the tiny shop, she had purchased the night rail for half its cost and gotten a few hints on what men liked. It seemed that, once women learned she was fighting for a man's heart, they not only excused a great deal that would otherwise shock them, but were eager to offer advice. It was the romance of it, Elspeth supposed.

Near the inn she met an old woman selling ribbons.

Even though she had already bought two, Elspeth stopped to look over the woman's wares. Hiding behind the elder lady's skirts was a small, big-eyed girl. Both were ragged and looked hungry. Even as Elspeth talked to the child, she knew she would be parting with a little more of her coin. Finally, after buying two ribbons she did not need for far more than the old woman asked, she started on her way to the inn only to find that way blocked by three large men. They were eyeing her in a way that made her blood chill.

"If ye would excuse me, sirs," she said pleasantly, attempting to step around them only to have them move to block her path again.

"A bonny wee lass ye are," said the darkest of the three.

"Thank ye kindly. Now if ye would just let me pass."

"And all alone."

"My mon waits for me at the inn."

"Oh, aye? No mon would let a lass what looks like ye and sounds like ye to run about unguarded."

Elspeth surreptitiously adjusted her bag so that her hands were free. She knew she had no chance of winning against three burly men, but if they attacked, she might be able to delay being captured and dragged off long enough for help to come. She also intended to scream, to make a great deal of noise, in the hope that someone would come to her aid. Since she was not sure if Cormac was still at the inn, she could not count on his rescue.

"I will be sure to tell him of your advice," she said. "Sir Cormac will be most grateful," she added, heavily stressing the word *sir*, but only the shortest one of the three men seemed to find mention of a knight of any interest.

It happened too quickly for her to react completely. Two of the three men lunged at her. The third, who had frowned at the mention of a knight, hesitated, then turned and fled, ignoring the taunts of his companions. Elspeth managed to get out several earsplitting screams before the dark man got one filthy hand clamped over her mouth. She struggled fiercely and was gratified to hear grunts of pain and curses, but she was still being dragged away.

Then, suddenly, she was free. The men not only released her, but she was shoved aside so roughly she ended up sprawled in the street. As she stumbled to her feet she saw people watching her. They had obviously seen what was happening, but had not been moved to help her. Sending them a look of pure disgust, she turned to find Cormac standing between her and her attackers, his sword pointing at the dark man's soft belly. Cormac looked as if he ached to kill her attackers, and they looked as if they desperately wished they had followed the companion they had so loudly taunted about his cowardice. Elspeth waited tensely to see what would happen, torn between wanting the men to pay dearly for the brutality they had intended to inflict upon her and not wanting to see Cormac cut down two unarmed men sweating with fear.

Cormac stared at the two men he faced. They were so terrified he was sure they had soiled themselves. When he had seen them dragging off a fiercely struggling Elspeth, his rage had been swift and blinding. As he had drawn his sword, his only thought had been to kill them. They must have seen that murderous intent in his face, for they had not only immediately released Elspeth, but they had also thrown her away. They had not been quick enough to escape him, however, and he had them pinned between him and the wattle and daub walls of the cooper's shop. Seeing that Elspeth was unharmed, his rage had eased enough for him to see that he faced two complete cowards. They had not even attempted to draw the knives he could see sticking out of their boots. Although he felt that men who forced themselves upon women deserved death, he could not bring himself to cut them down as they stood there trembling.

"Are ye hurt, Elspeth?" Cormac asked.

"Nay, I am fine, Cormac," she replied.

"Get their knives." He pressed his sword to the dark man's belly. "Dinnae try anything, either of ye, for I can cut this mon open in a blinking."

Cormac's voice was so cold it even made Elspeth shiver as she quickly collected the men's knives. "Done, Cormac."

"Leave," he told the men. "I should slaughter ye like the swine ye are, but I havenae the stomach to cut down men so afeared that they have pissed themselves. But heed me: Dinnae e'er let me set eyes on ye again. Go."

They went. Elspeth was astounded at just how fast the men could run. A squeak of surprise escaped her when Cormac roughly grabbed her by the arm and started to drag her toward the inn. One glance at his face told her that his anger was now fixed on her.

"I cannae believe ye were fool enough to go out wandering about all on your own," Cormac snapped.

"'Tis nay dark yet and I stayed within the bounds of the village," she protested.

"And ye saw just how safe that was."

"It shouldnae be unsafe. I but went to buy a few ribbons. A simple common chore hundreds of lasses do each day. Then three fools corner me, talking foolishness about how a lass who looks and sounds like me shouldnae be allowed to roam about alone. And what, pray tell, does how I sound matter? And how dare ye growl at me just because some fools try to steal what they werenae offered and have no right to?"

He stopped just inside the tavern, took a quick look around to make sure it would be safe to leave her alone for a moment, then stared at her. She had looked pale when he had first faced her after the attack. Now she was flushed with anger. He supposed she had good reason for that anger and was right to say that she did not deserve his fury. She had done nothing wrong. She simply did not understand what she could do to a man with her lithe beauty and that sensual voice. It was not something he could easily explain, either.

There was still Sir Colin as a threat, however, and he decided to use that to make her understand the danger of going off alone. "What if they had been Sir Coilin's men?"

Elspeth bit her bottom lip in consternation, for she realized she had forgotten all about that looming threat. "I dinnae think they were."

"Nay, but they could have been. The next men might be. I havenae yet seen any signs of the mon, but I ken he is searching for you. He has killed to get ye once, so we ken there is nothing he willnae do to get ye back."

"If he can find me," she felt compelled to protest. "That willnae be easy."

"True, but it isnae impossible, either, and ye arenae the only one who forgot that." He glanced back at the few men in the tavern, scowling when he caught them all staring at Elspeth. "Weel, 'tis plain that ye cannae be left alone. Fate clearly doesnae want me to veer an inch from the torturous path she has set me on," he muttered. "Wait here." After sending the men in the tavern one sweeping glare as a warning to stay away from Elspeth, he went in search of the innkeeper.

The incident with the village bullies had shown Cormac that he could not leave Elspeth alone, could not separate himself from the temptation of her and protect her at the same time. He felt torn as he informed the innkeeper that he now wished to share the room with his *wife*. Part of him was quite obviously pleased at the prospect of sharing a bed with Elspeth, of sharing that glorious passion that flared so easily between them, but another part of him was disgusted by his own weakness. In the end he would be using Elspeth, sating his body with hers while holding all else for another. Despite her apparent acceptance of that, he knew she deserved so much more.

It was not until she was back in her room, watching a grim-faced Cormac bring in his things, that Elspeth realized what had happened. They would no longer have separate rooms. She washed up in preparation for the meal they would soon share and fought hard to hide her delight over the arrangements. She easily excused the way Cormac looked as if he was facing the gallows. No man would be pleased to have his strenuous attempts to be chivalrous all ruined. Recalling the desire she had felt in him, that passion that had so readily equaled her own, made it easier to endure his black mood. After all, he would not be so upset if he was confident he could resist her.

Her understanding was severely strained as they shared a hearty meal. Cormac responded so abysmally to her attempts at conversation that she finally gave up. She began to think the night was not going to be the wondrous passionate time she had hoped for. Surely a man sunk so deeply into a black mood, as Cormac now was, could not feel amorous.

Trying to convince herself that there was still a chance to continue her plan, Elspeth excused herself and went to the room they were going to share. She washed up, donned her scandalous night rail, and dabbed her new scent in what she hoped were all the appropriate spots. Then, instinct telling her it would not be wise to face Cormac so boldly until he had released some of the blackness weighing him down, she wrapped herself in a blanket. Praying that he would not stay in the tavern drinking himself into a stupor, she curled up in a hard chair near the small fire and waited. When Cormac finally joined her, he looked neither drunk nor quite as black humored as he had earlier. He did, however, look chagrined that she was still awake. After giving her an absent smile, he sat down on the edge of the bed and took off his boots. Elspeth decided that she could lose little by trying to find out what ailed the man.

"Ye look as if someone has died," she said, moving to stand in front of him.

Cormac noticed she was barefoot and sighed. She really did have pretty, little feet. Elspeth had none of the attributes poets and minstrels praised. She was not fair of hair or blue of eye or sweet, modest, and retiring. Nor was she fulsome, although her slender body held all the curves any man could want. And yet he thought she had to be one of the most beautiful women he had ever seen, in face, in body, and in spirit. He supposed most men would excuse him for wanting her so much and probably think him completely mad for his reluctance to take what she offered him so freely.

"l find I am not the honorable mon I thought I was," he said, finally meeting her searching gaze.

"Why? Because ye didnae hold firm to your vows?" she asked.

He had not even considered that, but was loath to admit it, so he simply ignored her question. "I have let my lusts rule me. I have bedded a virgin maid, and sweet Jesu, I want to do so again. Yet I am not free. I travel to a woman I have been bound to for ten years and this time I may weel be able to save her from further ill use by her family. After all these years, I may weel be able to fulfill the vow I once made and marry her." He hesitated and dragged his fingers through his hair.

Elspeth prayed he would cease speaking of Isabel, for she was tempted to scream at him to open his cursed eyes and actually look at the woman he was wasting his life on. "As I have told ye before, ye fret too much."

"Angel, I want you. I dinnae think there is a part of me that doesnae ache for you. And now that I ken what we can share together, that hunger only grows stronger. 'Tisnae right, for I can offer ye naught but my passion. Ye deserve more. If I give into this hunger, I will just be using ye to slack it, for I ken I cannae give ye any more and I ken that it must end. That is wrong, Elspeth, and yet I am ashamed to confess that I am verra eager to be wrong."

"Ah, poor Cormac, how ye do love to torment yourself. I have said that I want ye. I have told ye that I burn for you. Ye have told me the truth: Ye cannae offer me any more than passion. I prefer to think of what we can share as a pleasant thing, a joyous sharing. If ye wish to think of it as using me, then, fine, use me." She let go of the blanket.

Cormac watched the blanket slide down her body and pool at her feet. He lifted his gaze back to her and drew his breath in so sharply he nearly choked himself. The night rail she wore somehow both concealed and revealed. It was so thin he could see the outline of her slender body yet cleverly placed lace kept certain intimate areas almost modestly concealed. He tore his gaze from her body and looked at her face just as she smiled. It was a smile of sensual invitation that heated his blood yet there was the hint of mischievousness there as well. She knew exactly what she was doing to him. The knowledge of what he could do to her as well was all that kept that from pinching his pride.

"Where did ye get that?" he asked as he quickly shed his doublet and shirt.

"From a wee shop in the town. Do ye like it?"

" 'Tis the devil's own creation made to tempt a mon into lustful sin."

"I should hope so, for I paid a fair price for it."

"Wretched lass," he murmured, his voice trembling with laughter as he finished shedding his clothes.

The way Elspeth stared at him made him feel both weak with desire and not just a little vain. She made no attempt to hide how much she appreciated the look of him. He found himself thinking it was just how Isabel looked at him and then frowned, for he suddenly knew that was not true. There was always a measuring quality in Isabel's gaze, as if she compared him to someone. That thought so disturbed him that he quickly banished it and turned his full attention back to Elspeth. Although he could offer her no future, he vowed that, for whatever time they would have together, he would be solely hers in body and in mind.

"My maiden dreams ne'er came near to matching the beauty of you," she said, reaching out to boldly stroke his hardened staff.

"Ye had maidenly dreams about me?" Cormac clenched his hands at his sides as he fought for enough control to enjoy her touch for a while.

"Oh, aye. Ye were my knight. I found ye wounded, being hunted by men who wished ye dead for a crime ye didnae commit, and ye were such a bonny lad e'en then. Aye, and then ye kissed my hand in parting." She took a step closer to him so that she could caress him with more ease, delighted at the pleasure he so obviously received from her touch. "At first they were sweet, childish dreams of heroic rescues, but then I grew older and learned something about the ways of men and women. Then those dreams were nay longer so sweet, but hot. Verra, verra hot."

Her soft husky voice stroked him almost as well as her long slender fingers. The thought of being the man in her dreams for years was a heady one. It could also mean that it was not simply desire that drove Elspeth into his arms, that her feelings ran a great deal deeper than she admitted.

It would explain a lot. It would also mean that it would be most unkind of him to indulge in a brief affair with her, then cast her aside once he was reunited with Isabel.

He was just about to ask her, as bluntly as he dared, what she did feel for him when she suddenly went down on her knees in front of him and ran her tongue along his aching length. His whole body swayed from the force of the delight that rushed through him. Cormac tugged on the ribbons at the sleeves of her gown and watched it slide off her body. With his hands on her shoulders, he struggled to contain his passion long enough to savor the way she loved him with her mouth. She followed his hoarse requests with a sweet willingness that made him dizzy.

Finally, knowing he could endure no more, he pulled her to her feet and nearly threw her on the bed. Despite the crippling need he felt to be inside her, he held back, wanting to be sure she was ready for him. When he slid his fingers through the tight curls at the juncture of her thighs and found her already damp with invitation, he lost the last shreds of his control. With a soft cry he plunged into her. It was a wild, frantic ride, and when she cried out in release, he was right there with her.

It was a long time before Cormac regained the wit to recall just how fierce his loving had been and he cautiously raised himself up on his forearms to look at her. The faint smile on her lightly flushed face was one of pure female satisfaction. Cormac did not think she knew what a wonder she was.

"Did I hurt ye, lass?" he still felt compelled to ask.

"Nay," she replied, then grinned. "But the headboard of this bed was a wee bit hard."

He laughed as he eased the intimacy of their embrace. After cleaning them both off, he quickly rejoined her in bed, lying on his back and tugging her into his arms until she was sprawled on top of him. He was in it now, knee deep and sinking fast, but Cormac decided he would worry about it all later.

Elspeth felt him harden against her and her eyes widened. "Again?"

"Ah, angel, now that we have begun this affair, I mean for it to be the wildest, most passionate, and most exhausting one there has e'er been."

That suited Elspeth just fine. It meant he would not be pushing her away again. And just maybe, he would find beneath that wildness and that passion the spark of love. And if not, if she lost her gamble for his heart, once the pain eased she would have a lot of sweet memories.

# Chapter Six

*v*

While she waited for Cormac to finish stabling their horses, Elspeth wandered to the doors of the warm, and a little too fragrant, stable to take a deep breath of fresh air. It had troubled her a little to find that Cormac had gotten her her own horse, but she had firmly told herself not to be so foolish. The need for one was easy to see and she could not put their lives at risk just because she liked to be close to Cormac. He was no longer trying to push her away. She did not have to greedily cling to every small opportunity to be near him.

Although their affair was only two days old, he was certainly living up to his promise to make it a wild, passionate, and exhausting one. If they kept spending so much time indulging their passion and so little time traveling, it would be Michaelmas before they reached the king's court. That suited her just fine, for at court waited Isabel. Elspeth found a small reason to hope in the fact that Cormac was not rushing to his lady's side.

A strange shriek, one of pain and fear, caught her attention. She stepped outside of the doorway and looked around. When she heard it again, she realized it was a cat. Then she heard the laughter of boys. Without another thought, she started toward the sounds, which were coming from an alley just across the rutted, muddy road.

She had fully expected to find boys tormenting some poor animal, but Elspeth was still shocked at the cruelty she saw. Four youths had cornered a large cat at the back of the alley between the butcher's shop and a small candlemaker's shop. They were taking turns poking the animal with sharpened sticks, laughing heartily as it howled and tried to defend itself. Already its fur was matted with blood, so much so that even the mud on its coat could not hide it. They were torturing the animal to death and finding humor in its valiant struggle to stay alive.

Elspeth marched right up to the closest boy, soundly boxed his ears, and grabbed his stick when he dropped it. She then found herself facing four scowling boys, who, although younger than her, were all a lot bigger. And now they were angry.

"Such men ye are to torture a wee animal to death," she sneered at them.

" 'Tis just a cat," grumbled the one she had struck. He glared at her as he rubbed his abused ears.

" 'Tis smaller than ye and ye have it trapped. 'Tis but one cat and there are four of you. 'Tis naught but cowardly, cruel torture, and ye should all be ashamed of yourselves."

"Is it yours?" asked the smallest of the four, who had already tossed aside his stick.

"Nay, but that doesnae mean I will allow ye to continue this sickening game," Elspeth said.

"And ye think ye can stop it?" said the biggest youth. "There are four of us and nay too much of ye, lass."

The arrogance of the boy made Elspeth ache to slap

him numb. He could not be much older than four and ten, for there was only the hint of future hair on his narrow face. The sneering way he said the word *lass* and the contempt on his face told her that he already had a very low opinion of women. She suspected his father, if he had one about, was a swinish brute. The way the other three youths looked at him told her they recognized him as the leader of the pack, admired for his maturity and strength. That only made her all the more eager to set him in his place, for he would eventually corrupt the others. Glancing at the poor cat, she wondered if he had not already accomplished that.

"I have seven brothers and a vast horde of male cousins," she said, keeping her voice hard and fixing her gaze firmly on him. "Ye dinnae frighten me, laddie. Any *mon* who needs three others just to corner and torment a wee cat is naught but a cowardly, wee worm who needs the pain of those weaker and smaller to make himself look big."

"Ye black-haired bitch," he snarled and charged at her.

Elspeth let him come, and just as he reached for her, she darted to the side. He stumbled past her and she kicked him in the backside. Cursing with an amazing fluency, he sprawled facedown in the dirt, his stick flying out of his hand. Elspeth quickly kicked it out of his reach and tossed hers after it. When he staggered to his feet, she faced him, her fists clenched and ready. He looked surprised for a moment, then sneered, assuming he would now have the upper hand. He clearly had paid no heed to her talk of her brothers and cousins. Elspeth had no trouble fighting a lad, even one a little bigger than she was. Recalling what he had called her just before he had charged, she decided she was also going to enjoy it.

"Ye must be mad," he scoffed, putting up his fists. "Ye willnae be so bonny soon."

His fists were a lot bigger than hers, but Elspeth was still not worried. A youth like him would not have any true skill, for he had simply not had the time to learn it. She was undoubtedly quicker. He was facing her squarely, confident of his superiority. She knew how to stay out of the way of those fists. Elspeth smiled. She also had no qualms about cheating.

He swung, oblivious to the soft protests of his friends, who obviously felt he should not be fighting with a lady. Elspeth ducked and hit him hard in the stomach. His friends grew silent. The boy cursed and swung again. Elspeth ducked and popped back up to punch him in the nose. He howled and put a hand over his bleeding nose. She reached out, grabbed his little finger, and began to bend it backward. For a brief moment she was afraid he would hold firm until it broke; then he yielded, allowing her to urge him down on his knees. When he tried to grab at her with his other hand, she caught hold of the little finger of that hand as well, but did not have to bend it far before he became still. She had the little bully completely at her mercy now. All she had to do was think of the right things to say, something that might actually spark a hint of wisdom in his head.

"Do ye need any help, angel?" drawled an all too familiar voice.

Cormac had seen Elspeth disappear from the front of the stables and cursed. After settling with the stablemaster, he hurried after her. He had thought that he had made her understand the danger she was in. By the time he got outside the stables, all he saw of her was a flash of skirt as she disappeared into an alley across the street. Her impulsiveness was going to get her killed, he thought angrily as he went after her, pausing only long enough to make sure no one was around who might trap them both in the alley.

He arrived just in time to see her kick the older youth

in the backside. Although he stayed to the shadows, he was ready to move in quickly. Cormac gaped along with the boys when she readied herself to fight it out with the young bully who had cursed her. The boy was right. She was mad. The boy was younger but he was bigger and stronger. And, Cormac thought crossly, well-bred young ladies were not supposed to indulge in brawls.

Even as Cormac moved closer, intending to put a quick stop to this foolishness, the youth threw the first punch. Cormac stopped, impressed by how quickly Elspeth moved. Someone had taught her well. She was too small and delicate to trade punch for punch, but she was obviously very good at ducking, then darting in to strike hard and fast before skipping out of reach again. He was very interested in the way she brought the young bully to his knees.

*And all for a cat,* he mused, one look at the animal enough to tell him that she had caught the boys in the midst of torturing the animal. Only Elspeth would find that something to fight about. Cormac moved out of the shadows and almost smiled at the way the friends of Elspeth's foe looked at him in horror. One thing that struck him as odd was that the cat had not run away. It sat there, steadily watching Elspeth with its big yellow eyes. When Elspeth routed the bully, Cormac could have sworn the cat smiled; then he told himself not to be such a fanciful idiot. It was just a trick of the dim light in the alley. He turned his attention to Elspeth and spoke to let her know he was there.

Elspeth almost cursed when she saw Cormac standing there, but she struggled to act as if there was nothing unusual about a well-bred lass thrashing a young man. "Nay, thank ye, Sir Cormac. I believe I have everything weel in hand."

"Oh, aye, I believe ye do. Argued a lot with your brothers and cousins, did ye?"

She decided he expected no reply to his nonsense, so she turned her attention on the boy. "Ye are a wretched child," she scolded the youth. "I dinnae ken if ye have the wit to understand this, but try to heed me. This sort of behavior does ye no honor. Ye belittle yourself when ye prey upon the weaker, the smaller. Mayhap ye should recite and recall a few old but verra wise sayings. Make friends, nay enemies, and ye will live longer. Ye can catch more flies with honey than with vinegar. Honor lost is forever gone. Do unto others as ye would have them do unto you."

"Enough!" the youth cried.

"Tormented by proverbs," murmured Cormac. "An unusual yet obviously effective torture."

Elspeth decided that, as soon as she was done with the boy, she would hit Cormac. "Laddie, if ye build a name as a bully, if ye gain your strength only by tormenting the weak, ye will sorely regret it. Ye will be constantly challenged, and one day, someone bigger and stronger than ye will repay all your wee cruelties with some of his own." She released him and watched him stagger to his feet. "If ye gain followers through fear, once ye yourself are conquered by someone stronger, faster, and crueler than you, none of those who bowed to you will come to your defense. Now go ere I think of a few more words of wisdom to deafen ye with."

She did not even bother to see if the boys did as she told them to, but turned to the cat. Cormac was there. He would watch her back. Murmuring gentling words, Elspeth slowly approached the wounded animal. It seemed somewhat strange that it just sat there, apparently unafraid, and watched her. She prayed that the calm acceptance she sensed in the animal was because it instinctively trusted her and not because it was so close to death it had no more strength to fight.

Cormac watched the boys until he was sure they were

gone and had no intention of retaliating. Then he turned back to watch Elspeth. "Ye shouldnae get so close. He could be maddened with pain and hurt you."

" 'Tis just a cat," she said, still keeping her voice low and calm as she held her hand out, palm up, for the cat to study and sniff as it pleased. "It may give me a few nasty scratches, but it cannae kill me. Nay like a dog could."

"That beast is near as big as a dog. Mayhap I should just put it out of its misery."

"The poor laddie is miserable, but I dinnae think he is so bad he must be killed." She flashed Cormac a brief happy smile when the cat licked her fingers and then stuck his big head under her palm so that she could scratch his battered ears.

"What is that noise?"

" 'Tis the cat. He purrs." She took a cloth out of her herb bag and gently wrapped it around the cat before picking it up. "Ah, my poor, sad laddie. Be at ease. I will tend all your hurts," she murmured as she stood with the cat in her arms.

"Elspeth, please tell me that ye arenae intending to keep that brute." Cormac sighed when she just stared at him as if she expected him to understand. " 'Tis but a cat, Elspeth."

"He likes me. I have to get him somewhere I can clean him and tend to his wounds. The poor wee thing has dozens of them. Are we to stay at the inn?"

"Aye, I sent the stable boy to secure us a room." He sighed again when he saw that she was not going to release the foolish cat and gently nudged her ahead of him out of the alley. "He willnae stay, especially if ye try to clean him."

Elspeth allowed Cormac to escort her to the inn. She knew Cormac would not understand why she had to keep the cat. She already knew it would break her heart to lose the animal, and the cat seemed to have decided that she was his. The animal should have fled the moment the boys had turned their attention to her, but it had not. It had sat there quietly, watching her discipline its tormentors and waiting for her to claim him.

The moment they stepped into the inn, Cormac was hailed by two men. Their abrupt greeting startled her and she felt Cormac tense at her side. The cat also tensed, pressing itself closer to her chest. Elspeth suspected it would be a long time before the cat accepted men. Its experience in the alley, and probably elsewhere, had taught it that the males of the world were not to be easily trusted.

"Cormac, good to see ye, old friend," said a tall blond man as he lightly slapped Cormac on the back.

"Aye," agreed a plumper, shorter, and much darker man. "We hadnae thought to find ye until we got to court." After vigorously shaking Cormac's hand, he turned to smile at Elspeth. "Introduce us, Cormac."

Cormac was glad to see his friends. They were good men. He had fought alongside Sir Owen MacDunn and Sir Paul MacLennon several times. He was not, however, glad to introduce them to Elspeth. They were looking at her too intently and seemed too pleased to be doing so. Reluctantly, he made the introductions, scowling when, because she was holding the cat, she offered the two men her cheek to kiss in greeting.

"I didnae ken ye were wed now, Cormac," said Sir Owen, absently brushing a lock of his fair hair off his face.

"Or betrothed, either," said Sir Paul as he cautiously reached out one slightly plump hand to pat the cat, his hazel eyes widening at the huge purr that erupted from the animal.

"He isnae either," Elspeth said, blushing faintly, but determined to tell the truth, if only to stop Cormac from doing so in a way that could easily be a little too blunt and painful for her taste. "We travel together to the court." She was a little surprised at the depth of the disappointment that briefly showed in their expressions.

"Wait here," Cormac told them. "I will go and see about our room, Elspeth."

"He is still running after that cursed bitch Isabel," snapped Paul after Cormac walked away.

Somewhat stunned at the hard anger in the very amiable-looking man's voice, Elspeth said quietly, "I fear so. Although, at the moment, I have succeeded in slowing his pace a great deal." When both men looked at her and smiled with blatant approval, she smiled back. "For now, he seems to have forgotten his urgent need to get to her before she is married again."

"Do ye believe she is simply ill used and ill fated?" Owen asked.

"I believe her to be a coldhearted, murderous woman who has buried four ill-fated husbands and toys with Cormac like some spoiled, vain child. I believe she could have kept the Douglases off his back ten years ago, but couldnae be troubled to do so or, mayhap, e'en set them there to protect herself."

"Ah, so ye have met the woman then," drawled Owen. He grinned when Elspeth giggled, but then he sighed. "I just thought, when we saw him with ye, a weelborn lass . . ." He stumbled to a halt and colored slightly when he realized he could not continue without saying something indelicate, perhaps even insulting.

"Cormac will explain why I am here, traveling alone with him. As for the rest, I pray ye will look kindly upon my sins. I intend to win him away from Isabel but have little time in which to do so. Virtue and maidenly modesty are not what will defeat that woman or break her grip. 'Tis a fierce battle I fight now and I pray ye will view my sins as but necessary tactics or weapons." She waited a little tensely for their reaction to those words, breathing a healthy sigh of relief when they both slowly grinned.

"Clever lass," murmured Owen. "Do ye think ye can win?"

"I think so, but 'tis hard to say," replied Elspeth. "I have weakened her grip. Of that much I am sure. But she has held him for ten years or more. Her talons have sunk deep. The few weeks I have may not be enough to extract them."

"If he doesnae choose you, m'lady, he deserves to be thrashed within an inch of his miserable life."

"If he doesnae choose me, I give ye leave to do just that."

Cormac frowned when he returned to find his friends laughing companionably with Elspeth. "A lad waits at the stairs to show ye to our room," he told Elspeth. "Do ye think ye can fix the cat enough so that he will be able to fend for himself again?"

"Oh, aye, I can fix him," she said, refusing to respond to his implication that she would have to let the cat go. "Shall I see ye both at the evening meal?" she asked Cormac's two friends, and when they both nodded, she went to find her room.

"I think she means to keep that cat, Cormac," Paul said, watching Elspeth follow a boy up the stairs.

"I think she does, too," Cormac said, sighing with resignation.

"Just what is wrong with it?"

As Cormac nudged them toward a table and ordered them each an ale, he told them the whole story. Cormac relaxed a little because his friends were both amused and astonished by Elspeth's actions. He knew just when the amiable conversation was going to turn serious, however, could see it in their expressions, but he could not think of a way to avoid it. As quickly as he could, he told them what had happened to Elspeth, the danger she was in, but he could see that it was not enough to divert them, either.

"Ye should marry that lass," Owen said in his usual blunt manner. "Ye dishonor her otherwise."

"I think 'twould take far more than I could ever do to tarnish Elspeth's honor," Cormac said carefully. "And I cannae marry her, though she would make a fine wife. I am not free." He ignored their muttered curses, hardened to the disapproval of his friends and kinsmen. "I have made that verra clear to Elspeth, but she says it doesnae matter."

"And ye believe her. Ye believe that a lady, who has held firm to her chastity for nearly twenty years, will then toss it all aside for the bonny smile of a mon chasing after another woman, just because of a simple lusting?"

"Nay," Cormac admitted reluctantly, "though it took a wee while for that truth to sink in. I was a wee bit too muddled to think clearly. And I am nay really the villain here. True, I am weak, too weak to resist temptation, but I was sorely pressed. She may look a sweet angel, but she is a determined lass when she decides she wants something." He flushed a little under the looks of amused scorn his friends sent him. "Tell me, if a lass like that freely offered herself to ye, making no demands and asking no promises, how long do ye think ye would hold out?"

"About one heartbeat," said Owen and Paul nodded a firm agreement.

"Weel, to the reason why we have been looking for ye: to give ye a warning," Paul said. "And now we ken why it is needed."

"A warning about what?" asked Cormac.

"A certain Sir Colin is hard on your heels. He searches for ye and the lass. Claims ye stole her and she is his betrothed."

" 'Tis a lie. As I said, Elspeth refused to wed him and he kidnapped her to try to force her to it."

Paul nodded. "We felt there had to be a good reason for ye to disappear with the lass."

"I had hoped that we had shaken free of the mon, that he wouldnae be able to guess which way we went. Too many other choices for him to make."

"He does complain vigorously about the ineptitude of his men and how long it took them to find your trail. But he is on it now, and ye and Elspeth are the sort most folk recall verra clearly."

Cormac cursed, finished his ale, and called for another. " 'Tis time to start running now, I suppose. Aye, and to take a winding trail. 'Twill cost me days, but fewer people will see us. That will make our trail less clear and, mayhap, slow him down." He looked toward the stairs. "Elspeth will be disappointed. Surprised, too. I dinnae think she believes or understands how much the mon wants her."

"Nay, I dinnae think she does," murmured Owen, and Cormac had the distinct feeling that his friend was not referring to Sir Colin.

Elspeth stroked the cat as it greedily lapped up the cream she had fetched it. It had also quickly and efficiently cleaned a small plate of chicken scraps. Despite its size, it was obviously very hungry. She felt it deserved a fine treat, however, after allowing her to clean all the mud and blood off its thick gray fur and tend its wounds. Although it had hunched its shoulders in distaste, it had also allowed her to wipe it down with an herbal wash to rid it of fleas.

She was still not sure why she felt so compelled to keep the cat. It was not pretty, being big, broad faced, and well scarred, but she felt bonded to it in some odd way. The way the cat allowed her to do anything she chose to it made her wonder if it felt the same or if it was just clever enough to know a soft heart when it saw one. Cormac was not going to be pleased.

"I shall call ye Muddy," she said and giggled when the cat cast her a faintly disgruntled look as it finished the cream. "If ye have something ye prefer, ye best say so now. I didnae think so."

Muddy began to wash his face.

"Now I must leave ye for a wee while," she said as she rinsed out the shallow bowl that had held the cream and filled it with water. "There is your box of sand the maid so kindly fetched for ye. Ye need to heal ere ye can slip outside to do your business. Although once we are traveling again, ye will have no box of sand. I do hope ye like to travel."

The cat walked over to the bed, jumped up, and settled itself comfortably at the foot of it.

"Enjoy that while ye can. Once Cormac and I slip beneath the covers it willnae be such a peaceful place to sleep for a while." She patted the cat again, smiling at its thunderous purr, and then left to rejoin Cormac and his friends.

It was comforting to know that Cormac's friends did not see Isabel in the same blind way Cormac did. Despite the fact that she was behaving shamelessly, both men were more than willing to overlook that if it got their friend out of Isabel's grasp. Elspeth had to admire Cormac's loyalty, the way he clung to his belief in Isabel when it was apparent no one else he knew liked or trusted the woman. She had a feeling, however, that a lot of that loyalty was now inspired by pure stubbornness. The more others disapproved, the tighter he clung to his convictions. If she had a chance, she would try to advise his friends of her suspicions. Perhaps if the harsh criticism of Isabel lessened, Cormac would relax in his constant defense of her just enough to start seeing what others did.

As she approached the table where Cormac and his friends sat, they all turned to look at her. Something in their expressions sent a chill of alarm down her spine. They looked too grim and just a little uneasy. She hurriedly sat in the seat Cormac held out for her, then grasped his hand as he returned to his seat by her side.

"What is wrong?" she asked.

"Now, angel, why do ye think anything is wrong?" Cormac knew he was going to have to tell her about Sir Colin, but he was reluctant to do so.

" 'Tis a feeling I got as I joined ye."

"Ah. And speaking of feelings, how is the cat?"

The fact that he was trying so hard to distract her made Elspeth even more nervous, but since a maid was setting the food on the table, she decided to let him get away with it for a little while. "He is fine. I have named him Muddy."

"I dinnae think he needs a name to roam the streets of this village."

Again, Elspeth simply ignored his assumption, which was something of a subtle command to leave the cat behind. "I have washed him, tended all of his wounds, and fed him some cream and chicken scraps. I e'en wiped him down with some herbs to kill any fleas he might have and he smells quite nice. I left him sleeping on the bed."

"Ye arenae going to leave him behind, are ye?"

She gave Cormac a smile that was almost apologetic. "Nay. I cannae."

"We may have to travel rough and fast."

"I think he will be fine settled in a roomy bag as a carrier. He is a verra complacent beast."

"He kens he has just landed in clover," said Owen, grinning faintly. "A keen eye for a too soft heart."

Elspeth grimaced, then laughed softly. "I did wonder

on that myself." She tested the slabs of roast on the plate set before her and decided the meat was passably good. "He tolerated being washed clean far too sweetly for a cat, as if he tolerated me doing such things because he kenned that I would then treat him far too weel." She turned her gaze on Cormac the moment the maid left their table. "Now, what is wrong?"

"Ye sure ye dinnae want to wait until we eat?" Cormac asked.

"Ye are so reluctant to tell me whate'er it is that I begin to grow verra nervous. That willnae make the food set easy in my belly."

"Sir Colin has found our trail."

It was hard, but Elspeth restrained herself from cursing virulently. Not only was she dismayed by Sir Colin's persistance, but it meant that the journey would now become rough and fast, just as Cormac had hinted it would. It was going to be difficult to carry on a love affair or try to win Cormac's heart while running for her life. And his, she suddenly thought.

"Then mayhap 'tis time for us to go our separate ways," she said quietly.

"Dinnae be an idiot."

And that, she decided, was that, as Cormac and his friends began to discuss what needed to be done to keep Elspeth out of Sir Colin's grasp. They had taken up her cause and would not be disuaded now. Elspeth did not want anyone to risk his life for her, but she knew that none of these men would listen. All she could do was promise herself that she would do everything in her power to keep Cormac safe. If it came to a choice between Cormac's life and allowing herself to be taken back to Sir Colin, she would choose the latter without hesitation.

# Chapter Seven

"I cannae believe any friend of mine can be such a blind fool," grumbled Paul as he sat down by the fire.

Tearing her gaze from where Cormac had just disappeared into the woods, obviously in as much of a sour temper as Paul, Elspeth sighed. She idly stroked Muddy, who was sprawled gracelessly on her lap. The two men had clearly just exchanged some harsh words and she suspected the tense conversation had had to do with her or Isabel or both.

For three days Cormac's friends had ridden with them. It was good to have the added protection of two skilled swordsmen. Most of the time they were pleasant company. There had been no sign of Sir Colin or his men, however, and Elspeth began to think it might be better if Owen and Paul left. She and Cormac had no privacy, no time alone, and if he was suffering as much as she was over that lack, it was no wonder that tempers were growing so short.

The other problem was that Owen and Paul could not

seem to resist mentioning Isabel. Elspeth knew that they meant well, that they were trying to help turn Cormac her way, but their interference could easily prove disastrous. They could not hide their feelings about Isabel, which only reminded Cormac how persecuted he felt the woman was. In fact, simply reminding Cormac of Isabel was not helpful, if only because it recalled him to the fact that he had been running to the woman's side before he had stumbled into this tangle with Sir Colin. *And before I yanked him into my bed*, Elspeth thought with another sigh.

"Paul," she began, glancing at Owen to make sure he was listening as well, "ye do ken that every time ye belittle Isabel ye strengthen Cormac's need to protect her, dinnae ye?" She nodded when he grimaced. "Obviously a lot of people have tried to talk to Cormac, tried to make him see what that woman really is, and it hasnae worked at all, has it? Truth tell, I believe his stubbornness now keeps this game going. Believe me when I say there is naught more guaranteed to make a stubborn person cling firmly to an idea, no matter how foolish, than for everyone to tell him that it is foolish and wrong. I recognize the symptoms. I have been kenned to suffer from them myself from time to time. And then, of course, one must recall that he is a mon." She ignored the way Paul and Owen eyed her warily. "Most men would rather cut off their right toe than admit that they are wrong."

Owen laughed. "Come. It isnae that bad."

"Oh, aye, it is. E'en when a mon finally kens that he is wrong, he is apt to stand by his error until he can figure out a way to change his stance without actually admitting he is wrong." She smiled at the two men, who were laughing even as they tried to argue with her opinion.

"But, lass, I thought ye were trying to get Cormac to see that he is wrong," said Paul after he stopped laughing.

"Weel, aye, but I would ne'er tell him flat out that he

was wrong. Not unless there was nay longer anything to gain from being silent. My plan is mostly aimed at making him no longer want Isabel. I thought it might be easier to make him cast aside an old vow than to admit that he had been wrong."

"Arenae ye worried that, if he gets to court and Isabel is free, he will then marry her as he has sworn to do?"

Just the mention of such a possibility stabbed Elspeth to the heart, but she replied calmly, "A wee bit, but I dinnae think that will e'er happen." She raised her hand to halt Owen's protests. "Oh, he might weel ask her, but Isabel willnae want to marry him. If we are all right about her, then Isabel has had every chance to marry Cormac. I believe there is some prize to be had at the end of this macabre succession of murdered husbands and Cormac isnae the one who holds it."

"Jesu," muttered Owen. "I ne'er thought of that. And 'tis something a Douglas has, for she keeps marrying Douglases."

"What did ye think she was doing?"

"I thought she just wanted the money or was mad."

"If she was mad, I think Cormac would be dead by now, for her victims are all men who have been intimate with her. It matters not at the moment, however. I do wish that ye would take more care not to mention that woman, if ye please. She looms as a verra determined obstacle as it is. 'Tis best for me if Cormac thinks of her as little as possible."

"Fair enough," agreed Owen and Paul nodded. Then Owen eyed Elspeth uneasily as she stood up with a still sleepy Muddy in her arms. "I hope ye arenae thinking of putting that thing on me."

"Muddy is *nay* a thing." She ignored Owen's scowl and soft curse as she set Muddy in his lap. "He but needs to be warm and he will keep ye verra warm, too," she said, watching as the cat settled down with a heavy sigh and then began to purr. "He likes you."

"How nice. Now my life has a purpose."

Elspeth laughed and kissed his cheek, then went in search of Cormac. She really hated to go near Cormac when there was any chance at all that he was thinking of Isabel, but it was also a very good time to bring herself to his notice. She knew she could not allow herself to be pushed aside by Isabel in his thoughts, especially when, for now, she was not able to replace Isabel in his arms. There was so little time for her to carve herself a niche in his heart and mind, she could not waste a moment of it.

She found him not far from the campsite, leaning against a gnarled tree and staring off toward the moors. He had obviously heard her approach, for he held his hand out for her without even turning to look her way. Elspeth put her hand in his, then gave a little squeak of surprise as he swiftly pulled her into his arms.

"I just thought I would come and see where ye liked to sulk," she said.

Cormac looked down at her, his lips twitching into a smile when he saw her impish expression. "Wretch. I am nay sulking."

"Of course not."

"I just thought it was better if I came out here to think rather than punch a dear friend in the nose."

"Oh, aye, infinitely better."

"No one is with you?"

"Nay, Paul obviously has the sense to ken how to protect his nose, and when I came to look for you, Muddy was still a wee bit sleepy, so I put him in Owen's lap." She grinned when Cormac laughed. "Muddy likes Owen."

"How fortunate Owen must feel. We may yet need their swords," he muttered.

Elspeth smiled against his chest. Just as she had done

several times over the last three days, Cormac was convincing himself that it would be foolish to dismiss the help of his friends. She could feel the hunger in him and it stirred her own, although it had never been fully at rest. Cormac might have left the camp because of something said about Isabel, but it was she he was thinking of now, she he wanted so badly he could not stop himself from caressing her.

"Curse Sir Colin," he said in a husky voice even as he slid his hands down over her backside and pulled her closer to him.

"He isnae here now, either," she whispered, standing on tiptoe to kiss the underside of his chin.

"True." He slowly rubbed himself against her and wondered why he was torturing himself so.

"And neither are your friends."

Cormac put his hand under her chin and tilted her face up to his. Her eyes were lit with the same need that had him aching so badly he could barely sleep at night. He could almost feel the pulse of it in her slim body. The passion she could stir within him was a wildness in his blood, one he knew she shared. In the past, a few bouts of lovemaking had been enough to sate him with every other woman save Isabel. With Elspeth, each time he made love to her, it simply added to his need for her. Three days without touching her had been pure torture.

He glanced around. She was right. They were completely alone. Cormac saw no signs of danger, although he was so choked with lust he would not be surprised if it hampered his vision. He looked back at Elspeth just as she wet her lips with her tongue. Cormac groaned and kissed her.

*A conflagration,* Elspeth thought dazedly as the passion she and Cormac had struggled to tame raged into life. His hands were everywhere and she feverishly tried to match his every caress. She prayed no one came along, for she doubted any interruption would be heeded now. They were too starved for each other, too frantic in their need to be cautious.

Suddenly, Elspeth found herself turned so that her back was against the tree. Cormac tugged her bodice down and feasted on her breasts. When the warmth of his mouth left them, she muttered a protest, then tensed slightly as he fell to his knees in front of her. The thin linen breeches that she wore beneath her skirts to protect herself from chaffing while riding astride, and from the occasional chill breeze that slipped beneath her petticoats, were suddenly gone. She murmured another protest when he pushed up her skirts, for she felt too exposed. Then he touched his lips to the soft heat between her legs and she nearly screamed. With a stroke of his tongue he banished all of her resistance. Elspeth threaded her fingers into his thick hair but she was not sure if it was to hold him there or to hold herself upright.

Even as her release began to shiver through her and she called to him, Cormac stood up. With one arm curled around her to support her, Cormac wrapped her legs around his trim waist. He kissed her, and as he slid his tongue into her mouth, he entered her body. It took only a few thrusts before she cried out to him, wanting him with her as she flew, and he plunged deep inside her, soaring to the heights but a heartbeat later. She clung tight to him as he slumped against her, pressing her hard against the tree. It was a while before they ceased to tremble with a lingering pleasure, their breathing slowing to a more normal pace.

"Ye drive a mon to madness, angel," he said softly, brushing a wrenchingly tender kiss over her mouth before easing out of her and setting her back on her feet.

" 'Tis a pleasant madness," she murmured, blushing fiercely as she tugged on her little breeches and smoothed down her skirts.

Seeing her blushes and a hint of nervousness in her movements, Cormac quickly straightened his clothes. He moved to stand in front of her, halting her somewhat agitated tidying of her bodice by grasping her hands in his. Then he waited patiently for her to look at him, smiling when she finally peered at him through the thick shield of her long lashes.

"We have done naught to regret, have we?" he asked, touching a kiss to the tip of her nose.

"I sometimes find my own wantonness a wee bit unsettling," she replied in a soft voice. "I mean, to do, weel, *that* in the full light of day."

"Ye loved me in that way."

She shrugged. "I had heard that men liked that and I found it a pleasure myself."

"I rather thought ye liked it, too. My returning the pleasure, I mean."

"Oh, aye," she admitted, unable to look at him as she did, however. " 'Tis just the thought of how ye were seeing so much of me. 'Twill take a wee bit of getting used to, I suppose."

"I like looking at you. Ye are verra beautiful. Wet," he murmured against her cheek as he kissed it. "Hot. And delicious."

Blushing fiercely again, yet also excited by his words, Elspeth looked up at him, thinking to lightly scold him for his brazen talk. Over his shoulder she caught sight of something that made her tense with fear. Five armed men were swiftly approaching across the moor. She binked in the vain hope of making the vision fade, but on they came.

"Oh, sweet Jesu," she cried out in horror as she realized the danger Cormac was now in.

"Weel, I didnae think it was so perverse." Cormac wondered why she should be so shocked by something she had so obviously enjoyed.

"Nay, fool, not that!" She pulled free of his hold and pointed at the men, who were getting far too close for comfort. "Look there! Sir Colin's men?"

"Probably." He drew his sword, grabbed her hand with his free one, and started to run back toward their camp. "But I dinnae think the who or the why matters too much right now."

Elspeth, fighting to keep pace with him, her skirts held up in one hand, knew he was right. All that mattered now was that five men were swiftly getting closer and the swords in their hands heralded their deadly intentions. Cormac had his sword at the ready in case one of the men drew dangerously close, but there really was not much chance of him thwarting this attack without the help of Paul and Owen. Now was the time to prove that their presence was worth all the frustration she and Cormac had suffered for three days.

It was an eerily silent pursuit and once Elspeth chanced to look behind her to make certain the men were still there. They were close enough to see that they were sweating. The lack of any hoots, of taunts and jeers, or even of commands to halt made the men seem all the more dangerous to her. If these were Sir Colin's men, he had finally found himself some with a little skill and determination.

"Owen! Paul! 'Ware, attack!" Cormac bellowed and one of the men at their heels cursed viciously.

Elspeth nearly screamed when a large knife slammed into a tree just ahead of them and to the left. Someone behind them had made an attempt to cut off Cormac's warning to his friends. She really did not need to see such chilling proof that her troubles had put Cormac and anyone else who helped her into deadly danger. And she knew these men would not give her the chance to graciously surrender herself to save the lives of Cormac, Paul,

and Owen. Elspeth prayed that Cormac and his friends
were good in a fight—very, very good.

As they ran into camp, Elspeth saw that Owen and Paul
were ready to meet what followed them. Cormac nearly
threw her to the far side of the camp. Elspeth knew her
part now was to sit quietly and pray, to stay completely out
of the way of the battle, and not to distract the men now
trying to protect her. She had always found that galling.
It was one reason she had tried to learn as much about
fighting as possible. In a sword fight, however, she had
finally had to concede that she lacked the strength to
endure for very long. She also knew that, if she jumped
into the fray now because she needed to prove herself, she
would undoubtedly do no more than get her friends killed,
quickly.

The sharp clash of swords that came within a breath of
the attackers reaching the camp made Elspeth flinch. She
crouched at the far edge of the camp, her knife in her
hand, and Muddy hiding behind her back. Cormac and
his friends were in a tight little circle, swords and daggers
slashing at the men who surrounded them. Elspeth cautiously inched back into the undergrowth. If one of the
five men facing Cormac and the others decided to look
around, she did not want to catch his eye.

One man screamed, staggered back, and fell to the
ground a few feet away from her. Elspeth took a look at
the wounds in his chest and stomach and felt bile sting
the back of her throat. She prayed the wound to his chest
had killed him or would do so quickly. The slash to his
belly would make him linger in torturous pain for a long
time. When he made no other sound and did not move,
she said a brief prayer for his soul and turned her full
attention back to the fight.

Her gallant defenders were not unscathed, but her
knowledgeable gaze found no cause for alarm yet. Another

of the attackers fell and the three remaining men stood back just a little. A subtle crackle of underbrush behind her caught her attention, but intent upon watching Cormac, she shrugged it aside as unimportant. Muddy was probably exploring, she thought absently, and then winced as Paul took a shallow cut on his arm.

Just as Cormac killed the man he faced, Elspeth found herself grabbed from behind. She had the wild thought that Muddy was a very poor watch cat; then she gathered enough wit to hide her dagger in a pocket secreted in the folds of her skirts. The man wrapped his arms around her, lifting her slightly off the ground, and took a few steps toward the men still fighting.

"Best ye stop now," said the man holding her.

Even as he spoke, Paul killed the man he faced. The only one of the attackers left still standing staggered over to the man holding her. Elspeth saw the looks of dismay on the faces of Cormac, Owen, and Paul and watched as they quickly turned to ones of cold, hard fury. At least there were not enough men left to kill Cormac and his friends. The two who now held her would only be interested in fleeing and all they needed to do to halt any possible pursuit was to steal the horses. Knowing that, this time, no one had died trying to protect her was almost enough to make Elspeth face her captivity with calm resignation. Almost. She drummed the back of her heels against her captor's shins and savored his curses.

"Cease that, ye little bitch," the man snapped.

"Let me go." She managed to bend her pinioned arms just enough to drive them back into his ribs.

"I am warning ye," he growled as he tightened his hold on her until it hurt.

"Ye cannae kill me. Sir Colin wouldnae like it."

"Nay, I cannae kill ye, but I can put ye into a verra hard sleep."

That was true and Elspeth was not sure she would gain enough from her struggles to make them worth that promised pain. She had at least confirmed that these were Sir Colin's hirelings. It was more than she could understand when she realized that four men had just died so that Sir Colin could have her. She sincerely doubted that those four men really wanted to die for such a reason, but they had to obey their laird. Sir Colin obviously had no respect for life. It would be nothing short of pure torture to be touched by such a man.

"Let the lass go," demanded Cormac, fighting to control the rage he felt as he watched Elspeth being handled so roughly by Sir Colin's man.

"After all it has cost me to catch her?" The man holding Elspeth laughed, the sound filled with scorn and anger. "Nay. Sir Colin wants the wee bitch. He wants ye dead as weel, but he will have to wait for that treat."

"If ye hand her o'er to that bastard, I will hunt ye down. Ye will ne'er ken another moment of peace until I give it to ye at the point of my sword. I will make it my quest."

"Oh, aye? And if I dinnae get her back to Sir Colin, I will ken that peace e'en sooner at the tip of his sword."

"This is enough to bring the Murrays and all their kinsmen to your gates screaming for your blood. Ye are sowing the seeds of a long, killing feud with this foul act."

"Not my gates. I give this wench to Sir Colin, collect my purse, and leave. Ye are spitting into the wind, laddie. Ye have lost. Accept it."

Cormac inwardly cursed. The man was a mercenary; a man like him had no clan loyalty. All a feud would mean to him was more opportunities to gain coin for the use of his sword. It was also clear that he did not really care that capturing Elspeth had cost him the lives of four men. That just meant that his share of the purse would be greater. It also meant that there was nothing short of killing the man that would make him release Elspeth.

"Now," the man continued, "ye and your friends will just toss your swords aside. Will here will collect them and then we will be taking your horses."

"Dinnae kill them," Elspeth said, hoping her words sounded more like a command than the plea they really were.

"No coin offered for their deaths, lass. Sir Colin badly wants your laddie dead and gutted, but he hasnae offered to pay for it yet."

Even as Cormac tossed his weapons down, his friends quickly doing the same, he tried to think of some way to stop this. If the man got away with Elspeth, the horses, and their weapons, it would be a long time before he could give chase. Long enough for Sir Colin to hurt Elspeth and to get her secured behind the walls of his keep, where it could prove impossible to rescue her a second time. Reading that knowledge in Elspeth's wide eyes, he felt an urge to beg her forgiveness.

Will was just stepping over to collect the weapons when something fell out of the tree directly over the mercenary and landed on his head. It took a second before Cormac realized that something was Muddy. The mercenary screamed and let go of Elspeth, who had the good sense to quickly scramble away. Cormac was not sure if the cat was flailing around in an attempt to hurt the mercenary as much as possible or if it was simply trying not to be flung off. As he made a hasty wish that the animal did not get badly hurt, Cormac rushed to retrieve his sword.

Still winded from being thrown to the ground, Elspeth paused in her clumsy escape only when she felt she had put enough distance between herself and her captor, and then she looked to see what had made him scream. She gaped, unable to believe the hissing, growling, scratching mass of gray fur on the man's head was her cat. Blood was streaming down the man's face and she dazedly wondered if she should rethink her opinion that a cat could do one no real harm. Elspeth cried out in alarm when the man finally yanked Muddy off his head and, ignoring the way those sharp claws and teeth were slashing at his hands and arms, held the cat only long enough to fling it away. If Cormac had not been in her way fighting with the man named Will, she knew she would have heedlessly run to her cat, who now lay at the far edge of the camp. Instead, she sat praying that Cormac would win and that Muddy was only knocked out.

Cormac killed Will even as Owen and Paul finished collecting their weapons. All three of them then turned to face the man who had briefly held Elspeth. Although Cormac suspected a lot of the blood on the man's face was from scratches on his scalp, the sort that always bled freely, he still looked painfully savaged. There might even have been some damage done to one or both of his eyes. When the man drew his sword, Cormac cursed. He did not really want to fight a man who probably could not see clearly. In truth, now that Elspeth was safe, he simply did not want to fight anymore. Five men lay dead and he really did not want to make it six.

"Give it up, mon," Cormac said as the mercenary swiped his sleeve across his face in a vain attempt to clear the blood away.

"Is it dead?" the man asked.

"What?" Out of the corner of his eye, Cormac saw Elspeth start to edge across the camp and, with one slashing movement of his hand, silently ordered her to stay put.

"Is that hellborn beast dead?"

"The cat?" It was hard to understand how or why, when facing three armed men and certain death, the mercenary would concern himself with the fate of the cat. "He willnae be leaping on ye again, if that is what worries ye. I think ye should give more thought to the fact that three swords face your one and none of us has blood streaming into his eyes.''

The mercenary stared at them for a long moment and Cormac wondered if he was waiting for his vision or his wits to clear. Then, suddenly, the man threw both his sword and his dagger. Cormac and his friends dodged the weapons, which landed in the dirt right where Cormac had been standing a moment before. The man wasted no time in running off, disappearing into the shadow of the trees.

"Should we run him down?" asked Owen.

"Nay." Cormac wiped his sword clean on Will's jupon and resheathed it, feeling a little sickened as he grimly noted the toll Sir Colin's lust for Elspeth had taken. " 'Tis done.''

"He could get back to Sir Colin and set the mon on your trail.''

"Possibly, although he implied that Sir Colin is treating failure verra harshly. Also, he is bleeding, unarmed, and, I suspect, on foot, so he willnae reach Sir Colin too quickly even if he decides to face the mon.'' He glanced at his friends and smiled crookedly. "And none of us is in the condition needed to hunt a mon down.''

"Aye, true enough." Owen winced and lifted his shirt high enough to study a cut low on his right side.

"Jesu, Owen, that nearly gutted ye," muttered Paul and he shook his head. "Best have Elspeth look close at that.''

Cormac looked toward where he had last seen Elspeth, but she was not there. He then saw her running across the camp just behind them. Her steps faltered a little as she neared Muddy's body until she was almost creeping toward the cat. His two friends followed his gaze and sighed.

Later Cormac knew he would find some amusement in

it all, but he was too concerned about Elspeth and too weary of fighting to do so now. Yet he almost smiled at the way he and his friends stood, unable to move and exchanging wary glances. They were battle-hardened soldiers. They had just fought and killed five men. Each one of them stood with blood trickling from several minor wounds. Yet each one of them hesitated now, afraid to face a tiny, green-eyed woman who might be about to discover that her ugly cat was dead. Cormac took a deep breath to steady himself and started toward Elspeth, faintly aware of his friends reluctantly shuffling along behind him.

Elspeth knelt by her cat. It was impossible to tell if he was breathing, but she knew that did not mean he was dead. She could see no blood, could see nothing twisted or broken. After clenching her hands tightly for a moment, she then tentatively reached out one hand. She sensed the three men gathered behind her, sensed their taut air of watchfulness, and was touched by their concern, even if it was probably more for her than for the cat. Taking a deep breath, terrified that the body beneath her hand would be cold, she stroked her cat.

# Chapter Eight

Muddy purred.

Elspeth felt tears sting her eyes as she more thoroughly checked the cat for any injury. The three heavy sighs of relief from behind her almost made her smile. She endured the three heavy pats on the head she got before the men moved away. When Muddy staggered to his feet and shook his head, swaying a little, she sat down and coaxed him onto her lap.

As she stroked the cat, idly using her hands to check yet again for any serious wound, Elspeth watched the men remove the bodies from the camp. Five deaths. She could not comprehend it. There was a touch of sadness in her heart for the dead men themselves, but not too much, for they would have killed Cormac, Owen, and Paul without hesitation or guilt. What she struggled and failed to understand was why Sir Colin would send men to kill or be killed just to drag her into his bed. He would find no delight there, for she did not want him and had made that very plain. And he had to know that she would spend every hour of her life fighting to be free of him.

When Cormac and his friends sat around the fire, Elspeth realized that they had wounds that needed tending. Carrying Muddy over to the fire, she set him on a blanket Owen hastily put down, then fetched her herb bag. For what felt like hours, she cleaned wounds—small ones that needed only salve and larger ones that required a few stitches. Weary and feeling utterly depressed in spirit, she gathered up Muddy and sat down next to Cormac, settling the cat on her lap.

"Is the brute hurt at all?" Cormac asked, wondering at the sadness in her eyes.

"Oh, nay." She stroked the cat, letting his rythmic purr soothe her tattered feelings a little. "He is but weary."

Cormac laughed as did Paul and Owen. "That cat does little else but sleep, Elspeth."

"He likes a good sleep," she said and was able to briefly return the men's smiles. "Cats do. And mayhap because he has had such a rough life until now, he wasnae able to enjoy it like this."

Suddenly noticing the blood on Muddy's claws, she shivered and quickly tugged a cloth from her herb bag to wipe it off. It struck her as odd that, after seeing five men die, and cleaning the wounds of three men, she should find the sight of a man's blood on her pet so gruesome. Dampening the cloth with a little water, she quickly removed it.

"I ne'er thought a cat would try to protect anyone," said Owen.

"Weel, 'tis nay their usual way and they arenae really made to be verra good at it, are they?" She tossed aside the cloth and resumed petting the cat. "My mither was helped once by a wee cat, so wee it didnae e'en have a mew, just a squeak. Followed my mither everywhere. Just before my mither was supposed to go to her childbed with my youngest brother, she went out looking for some herbs she would need. She fell and wrenched her ankle so badly she couldnae walk, and that is when the child decided 'twas time for it to come into the world.''

Elspeth saw how eagerly all three men listened and realized they were as anxious to forget about the deaths they had just seen as she was. "There she was, out all alone, and too far away to call for help and be heeded. Mither said it was some odd madness that made her tell that wee cat to fetch my fither. Wee Amber—which is what we called her because she was all that color, eyes and fur—went trotting off. It took her a while but she got all the way back to the great hall, climbed up my fither's leg, batted him on the cheeks, then jumped down and trotted away. He didnae follow, so she did it again, then again, until my fither got up and followed her. Said he felt foolish trailing after a tiny yellow cat as if she was some fine hunting dog, but he couldnae ignore the way she was acting. Wee Amber took him right to my mither. Oh, she was a verra, verra spoiled cat for the rest of her life and has a tidy little grave in the verra fine pet graveyard.''

"The verra fine pet graveyard?" asked Paul.

"Aye, 'tis the place where we laid to rest those animals we felt true affection for. Consecrated ground, too.''

For a while, as they picked at their simple meal, they exchanged stories of their childhoods. At least, Elspeth noticed, she, Owen, and Paul did. Cormac had very little to say. Elspeth wondered if his childhood had really been that barren or if he was one of those men who found it difficult to talk freely of personal things like his family. She hoped it was the latter, for she hated to think of him having had a sad childhood.

"I think we must send word to your family now, Elspeth," Cormac said abruptly.

" 'Twould be wonderful to let them ken how I fare and''—she took a deep breath to steady herself—''to find out how Payton fares. Sir Payton Murray,'' she clarified for Owen and Paul when they frowned slightly. ''My cousin.''

"Sir Payton, of course,'' muttered Owen. "The bonny brave knight who makes even sensible, pure women swoon with longing.''

"What do ye mean?''

Owen blushed, realizing that he had been complaining and sarcastic about her kinsman—one who might well have died protecting her. "Weel, Sir Payton Murray is much honored. I have ne'er met him himself, glimpsed him in passing only, but many speak weel of him. Minstrels have sung about him.''

"About Payton?'' Elspeth laughed. "Oh, wait until I tell the others. Minstrels have sung about him? Truly?'' She laughed even harder when Owen nodded. "Oh, pardon, Muddy,'' she said when the cat gave her a disgusted look, left her lap, and sprawled across Owen's. " 'Tis just all this talk of Payton as if he is some Charlemagne.'' She shook her head. "Minstrels singing about him. Jesu.''

"He isnae like that?''

"Weel, he is bonny, but why shouldnae he be? His parents are bonny. And he does have a verra good heart. But he is my cousin. I have grown up with him. I have seen him all gangly and spotty. I have suffered through him, my brothers, and my cousins all seeing who could belch the loudest and the longest. Oh, and contests of other rude noises as weel, I am ashamed to say. I have kenned him when he was still of an age to have glorious tantrums and his mother felt compelled to dump a bucket of water o'er his head. 'Tis just hard to think of the lad who boasted of writing his name in the snow better than my brother Connor could as one some minstrels trill about.'' She blushed when all three men grinned, telling her they knew exactly what the boys had used for quill and ink. "Aye, especially when that boast had the two of the fools drinking ale and water until they sloshed so that that boast could be proven true or false." She shivered, all her humor vanished as she suddenly recalled, all too clearly, her last sight of Payton.

Cormac took her hand in his, easily guessing her thoughts. "As ye once told me, if anyone can elude ill fate, 'tis he."

"Aye, of course."

"And I do believe 'tis best if we send word to your kinsmen. Owen and Paul can go and tell them of your troubles. They can also tell them where ye are going so that someone can come for you."

That hurt, but Elspeth firmly told herself now was not the time to fret over the fact that Cormac still foresaw no future for them. "Considering what has just happened, do ye think it wise to send away two skilled swordsmen?"

"Aye, Cormac," said Paul. "I was just thinking the same."

"I have decided that Elspeth and I should return to surrounding ourselves with others. On the morrow we can rejoin one of the main routes to the king's court. At this time of the year, many people travel to the king's court, either to attend the court or to sell their wares to the crowd that gathers there. A large assault as we suffered through tonight will be impossible there. In truth, I believe I erred in thinking back ways and winding trails were the best route. Even with you two at our side"—he smiled briefly at his friends, silently thanking them for their aid—"we are too much alone."

"None of her kinsmen will be able to reach ye to help until ye finish your journey or e'en later."

"Nay, but they can get to court to meet us. If Sir Colin hasnae quit or died by then, Elspeth will need all the help she can get. We all ken how easily a laird and his men can slip through the crowds at the king's court. And if we dinnae reach the court, the Murrays will be ready and armed to come to her aid."

"Weel, it doesnae sound any more dangerous than this plan proved to be. I am surprised ye havenae already sent word to her kinsmen."

"I couldnae find anyone I trusted enough. That message could easily have been ferreted out by Sir Colin and brought him right to us."

Elspeth stood up, weary and still stinging from Cormac's blithe mention of their coming separation. "I am sure ye dinnae really need me to sort it all out. I am to bed."

"But, angel, do ye agree with my plan?" asked Cormac.

"I have ne'er been hunted before. Ye have. I am willing to follow your lead in this."

Elspeth slipped away for a moment of privacy, then spread out her rough bed a short distance away from the men. As she wrapped herself up in a blanket and settled herself with her back to the men, she could hear their murmurs as they made plans, and it soothed her. A moment later she felt Muddy settle himself against her back and his deep purr plus the warmth of him helped to relax her.

The bone-deep weariness she felt would help her sleep and she was glad of it. Her heart felt too much like a heavy, cold stone in her chest. Men were dying because some man lusted after her and could not tolerate being told nay. She could not completely stop herself from feeling guilty, from wondering sadly if there had been something, anything at all, that she could have done to prevent all of this.

And then there was Cormac—the love of her life, her soul, her heart, her mate. The man who could so easily know when she had just recalled what fate might have befallen Payton and offer her a comforting touch plus a few encouraging words. The man who could make love to her as if he was starved for the feel of her, could not survive another moment without feeling her in his arms. The man who spoke so calmly of setting her aside once they reached the king's court.

A few more days was all she had left with Cormac. Could it possibly be enough? She knew she had reached him in some ways, knew it deep in her heart with a confidence that refused to be shaken. But it was clear that she had not yet gained a hold deep enough to pry him loose from Isabel. Oh, Elspeth loathed that woman so much that she wondered if it might be wise to worry a little less about what Cormac was planning to do when they reached the court and a little more about what she herself might do. There was the sour taste of jealousy within her, but Elspeth knew it was mostly fury she felt toward Lady Isabel Douglas. The woman was heartlessly tripping along, destroying one life after another and Elspeth knew that, given half a chance, Isabel would blithely destroy hers, too.

Breathing slowly and deeply, Elspeth fought to calm herself, to clear her mind of all worry and questions that had no easy answers. If she let her thoughts continue down the path they were going, she would grow sad, fretful, and angry. Those were not emotions conducive to seducing a man into loving her. And she had only a few days left to produce that miracle. She would need a clear head and lots of rest to conduct the final battle for the man she loved.

As she cleared up after the sparse morning meal, Elspeth kept a close watch on Paul and Owen. They moved a little stiffly, but after checking their wounds in the clear light of day, she felt they could ride to her family without seriously risking their own health. When Cormac left his friends to seek a moment of privacy, she hurried over to the men, smiling at the way Owen had paused in his preparations to stroke Muddy.

"Elspeth, if perchance this laddie produces a litter," Owen said, coloring faintly, "and one looks as ugly as he does . . ."

"I will see that ye get it as soon as it is weaned," she promised, then handed him a small, beautifully etched silver ring. "Show this to my kinsmen to let them ken for certain that ye come to them with my knowledge and blessings."

"Do ye think it may be needed?"

"We cannae be certain what they have heard or been told. They may be verra wary at the moment, especially if Payton is . . ." She stumbled to a halt, still unable to voice the possibility of Payton dying.

Owen patted her on the shoulder in an endearing, if slightly awkward, attempt to soothe her and offer a silent encouragement. "Should we say anything about Cormac and ye? They may ask some awkward questions."

"They may, and although I shouldnae really ask ye to lie, I would much rather they heard about him from me. If I win my gamble, then they can all celebrate the fact that I have finally selected a mate, something I think they begin to fear I shall ne'er do. If I lose"—she shrugged—"weel, what I do tell them shall have to be far less than the truth anyway. 'Tis best if ye try to stand clear of that morass."

Paul stepped forward and kissed her cheek. "Ye will win, Elspeth. What ye offer our thick-witted friend is far more than Isabel e'er has or e'er will. I have to believe that Cormac will see that. Just be patient if he takes a wee while in seeing that for himself."

"I pray ye are right, but then as ye say, your friend can be a wee bit thick-witted."

Cormac tried not to feel jealous when he returned to find his friends sharing a jest with Elspeth, all three of them laughing companionably. He could not claim Elspeth, not once he was reunited with Isabel. He was bound by a vow and a lengthy, if troubled, history with that woman. Guiltily, he admitted to himself that he really had no right to share anything at all with Elspeth, but he would continue to do so for as long as he could. After their time together was ended, however, she would be free to belong to another. Elspeth was not a woman who should ever live alone. Owen and Paul were good men and they obviously liked Elspeth. Perhaps one of them could give her what she needed and deserved.

The thought had barely finished forming in his mind when he felt the punch of anger and denial in his gut. He could not bear the thought of her sharing anything with another man. If she married Owen or Paul, Cormac would have to see her with whichever friend she chose and he would have to hear about her. He knew it would be intolerable, and he was galled by his own selfish possessiveness. He could not keep her, but it was painfully clear that he did not want anyone else to have her, either. It was fortunate that, once she went away, he could stay far away from her for a while. It might give him the time and distance needed to rid himself of this unwarranted possessiveness.

"Ye two take care," he said, briefly clasping each man's hand before they mounted, then fighting not to pull Elspeth to his side when she gave each man a friendly kiss of farewell.

"We will," replied Owen, "though 'tis the two of ye who court the most danger. Are ye certain about this plan of yours, Cormac?"

"Nay, but 'tis a good plan all the same. Sir Colin will take time to recover from this defeat. Unless he is charging about Scotland with his entire garrison at his back, the loss of five men will badly hurt him. The fact that these men were mercenaries makes me think the mon left most of his clansmen guarding his lands in case the Murrays came clamoring at his gates. And there is still the chance it will be a long time, if ever, before he kens what happened here last night. Enough time for me and Elspeth to get to court. There is where protection will be needed if Sir Colin persists, if only because there will be a multitude of men there hungry for a coin or two and willing to do most anything to get it. He may e'en have some influence with the king and could get the mon to believe his tale of a kidnapped betrothed. So bring me some Murrays."

"Trust us," Paul said even as he and Owen spurred their mounts, quickly disappearing into the morning mists.

"They should be safe, shouldnae they?" asked Elspeth.

Turning to look at her, and almost smiling at the way the cat sitting by her feet was watching him as if it also waited for his assurances, Cormac replied, "Aye, they are skilled at fighting and verra skilled at running and hiding when the odds are heavily against them."

"Verra good skills to have."

"They are. Sir Colin doesnae want them, either,"

"Nay, just me." She shivered and huddled against him when he pulled her into his arms. "I just dinnae understand this, no matter how hard I try. 'Tis madness, I think."

"The mon wants ye. Mayhap he believes he loves you or thinks ye are what he needs to fulfill some dream."

"He ne'er revealed such a depth of passion when he courted me. Nay, no passion at all, until I told him nay."

"Angel, there are men who find a nay a verra great challenge and some who see it as a grave insult and even some who find it a spur to a deep passion, e'en love. And mayhap he is just a wee bit mad."

"A great deal mad."

She felt him move against her, the hard proof of his

desire shifting against her belly in a strange mixture of
almost absentminded desire and need. It was pleasing to
know that he could not stop himself from wanting her,
that his desire for her was already such a part of him it
needed no conscious effort on his part to be stirred to life.
It would be even more pleasing if that need and wanting
was firmly set a little higher, she thought wryly.

"We are alone now," he said.

Elspeth glanced up to meet his gaze and saw that the
message his body was sending him had finally reached his
brain. "Muddy is here."

"Muddy is a clever cat. He will be able to tell that 'tis
time to go and do a little hunting."

As he talked, he started walking. Since he was still holding her in his arms, that required Elspeth to walk backward.
She laughed softly when she stumbled and he simply lifted
her up slightly until he was carrying her along.

"Shouldnae we be hastening to leave this place?"

"Aye, we probably should," he said, stopping at the edge
of his crude bed of blankets. "But 'tis still early yet and
the next place we shall pause for the night isnae e'en a
full day's ride from here."

"I was thinking more of the threat of Sir Colin," she
murmured as he set her on her feet and began to take off
her clothes.

"E'en he wouldnae be so cruel as to deny us an hour
or two of delight."

"An hour or two?"

Cormac tossd the last of her clothing aside and stared
at her. "Weel, maybe not that long."

She was blushing deeply but did not attempt to hide
herself from his gaze, although he noticed that her hands
were tightly clenched at her sides and he smiled faintly.
The sight of her affected him as powerfully as touching
her or tasting her did. She was silken, creamy perfection

from her slim neck all the way to her delicate feet. Looking at her and knowing he would soon touch and possess that perfection were anticipation at its keenest. Even if they had a long future ahead of them, instead of mere days, he doubted the pleasure of just looking at her would ever lessen.

He took a deep breath to steady himself as he shed his clothes. His desire for her was always strong, but the thought of how she would soon leave, would soon find another, made it all the sharper. For the first time since he had met Isabel, since he had begun that long, troubled relationship, he had met a woman he would sorely regret parting with. He felt a need to glut himself on her, to make as many sweet memories as he could. For the first time since he had sworn himself to Isabel, he felt regret for that vow and his inability to break it.

Even as Elspeth reached for him, he reached for her. He gently eased her down on the blankets, crouching over her. He prayed for the strength to go slowly. Cormac wanted to savor every delicate, soft inch of her. He wanted to kiss her everywhere, starting at her full, tempting mouth and going all the way down to her cute little toes, then kissing his way all the way back up again. Even as he touched his mouth to hers, he conceded that he might find the willpower to make the trip down—once. As he kissed the hollow at the base of her throat and she stroked his legs with her feet, he was no longer sure he would even make it to her knees.

Elspeth cried out with pleasure when his taunting mouth finally closed around the aching tip of her breast. She thrust her fingers in his thick hair and held him close even as she rubbed her body against his. He was going too slow. She could feel the taut control he exerted over his passion and she was determined to break it.

"Ah, angel," he groaned against her ribs, "ye arenae helping me. I want to go slow."

"I ken it. I am just nay sure I can bear it right now," she said, not surprised at the unsteadiness of her voice, for she was trembling with the strength of her need for him.

When he kissed the dark curls adorning her womanhood, she was shocked over such intimacy in the bright light of day, but only for the length of a heartbeat or two. Then she lost herself to the pleasure of his intimate kiss, all modesty vanquished with a stroke of his tongue. She cried out to him as her passion crested, but he paid her no heed. Nor did he give her any time to recoup her senses, instead quickly driving her to the brink all over again. When she felt herself rushing toward yet another peak, she threatened him with dire consequences if he did not join her on that heady ride.

Cormac laughed and, kneeling between her legs, held her firmly by her slim hips and plunged into her. He groaned, and teeth gritted against the fierce urge to move, he held still. She was so tight, so wet with welcome, and so hot. The pleasure of it went all the way to the marrow of his bones. Then she squirmed against him, wrapping her slender legs tightly around his waist and pulling him in as deep as he could go. All control vanished, and with a soft growl, Cormac proceeded to drive them both to the heights they so hungered for. A shaft of pure satisfaction briefly cut through his blind desire when they found that peak at the same time, relinquishing themselves to the power of their releases as one.

It was a long time before Cormac had the strength or wit to do more than sprawl on top of Elspeth and idly toy with her breasts. As they drew closer to court, Cormac realized that his regrets about having to leave Elspeth were beginning to outweigh his guilt. He did not want to give her up, but he had to. Because he had pledged himself to another, all Elspeth could ever be was his mistress. Cormac knew that would slowly destroy her, even destroy all they shared. He could not treat her or Isabel with such a callous disregard for their feelings, either.

"Now I think we had best set our wee minds back on the problem of eluding Sir Colin," he said, lightly kissing her as he ended the intimacy of their embrace.

The moment he left her arms, Elspeth sat up and reached for her clothes. "The mention of that mon is as good as a bucket of icy water. Steals all the lovely warmth away."

"Aye, but better that than risking the chance that the fool might actually get his hands on you."

Elspeth shivered at the mere thought of that possibility and hurried to finish dressing. In no time at all, they had completed the breaking up of their camp, doing their best to clear away all signs of their presence. Muddy returned just in time to be set in his carrier, licking his lips in a way that told her he had found something to eat.

Cormac looked at the cat idly cleaning himself and showing no qualms about being set in a bag on the back of a horse. "Ye would think he was born to this," he said and shook his head as he mounted. "He seems to ken everything about traveling."

"Maybe he was traveling with someone and he got separated from him somehow," Elspeth said as she swung herself up on her horse and tried to adjust her skirts a little more modestly. "I did notice that he requires no training, yet I think some should have been required."

"And mayhap he has enough wit to do just what is needed to have ye keep him at your side."

She laughed softly and scratched the cat's head. "That, too, is a possibility. And now he is a hero. A brave wee laddie who risked his own fair neck just to save me." She exchanged a grin with Cormac over the cat's loud purring.

"That isnae a wee laddie. 'Tis a monstrous great cat." He reached out across the small space separating their horses and lightly scratched the cat's head. "And a clever brute who kens how to make himself indispensible."

As Cormac nudged his mount into a gentle trot, Elspeth quickly followed suit. She agreed with Cormac's feeling that it would probably be a while before Sir Colin would be able to trouble them again, but she also felt a small urge to hurry. The attack last night had come too close to costing Cormac and his friends their lives and losing her her freedom. She did not want to go to the king's court because Isabel was there. However, it could bring her and Cormac some measure of safety. It was now a choice between the risk of losing Cormac to Isabel or watching him die at Sir Colin's hands. And that, she thought sadly, was no choice at all. It would tear her heart out to lose Cormac to Isabel, but she would rather have that happen than live without him, than live knowing that her troubles with an insane rejected suitor had cost Cormac his life. Far better he was lost to Isabel than lost forever in death's cold embrace.

# Chapter Nine

"Alive?"

Owen and Paul stood facing three scowling Murray lairds and tried not to tremble. They were tired, hungry, and dirty, but they had no intention of recalling Sir Balfour Murray to the rules of hospitality until they had satisfactorily answered his questions. Although he had spoken that one word softly, it seemed to have cut through the tense air in the great hall of Donncoill as well as an enraged bellow. His brothers, Sir Nigel and Sir Eric, did not look any less threatening. Neither Owen nor Paul had the courage to look at Elspeth's mother Lady Maldie, or her aunts Gisele and Bethia. They had the sinking feeling that those women would be looking far more fierce than their husbands.

"Aye, Elspeth is alive," Owen said and hurriedly produced the small ring she had given him. "She sent this with us. She said it would tell ye that she kens we are coming to ye and approves." He almost stepped back when Sir Balfour walked over to snatch the ring from his hand.

"Balfour?" called Lady Maldie, who looked so much like Elspeth it had startled Owen a little.

Sir Balfour walked over to the woman and enfolded her in his arms, saying hoarsely, "Our bairn is alive, Maldie."

"Does that mean we arenae going to be able to kill that bastard Sir Colin?" asked Sir Nigel, his amber eyes hard with anger.

"Oh, nay," said Balfour. "It just means we have a chance to bring Elspeth safely home before we kill the mon."

"Weel, while ye all decide how, when, and in what ways ye will kill that bastard," Lady Maldie said as she tugged free of her husband's embrace, "we ladies shall see to the care of these poor lads."

"I have a lot of questions I must ask them," protested Balfour even as his wife, Gisele, and Bethia started to lead Owen and Paul out of the great hall.

"Ye can ask them after they have bathed, rested a wee bit, and set some food in their bellies."

It was time for the evening meal before Paul and Owen felt ready to face the rigorous questioning they knew the Murrays would put them through. Owen grimaced as they were led straight to the head table, where waited the three Murray lairds, their wives, Sir Payton, and Elspeth's brother Connor. Owen briefly scowled at Paul when that man neatly manuvered the seating so that Owen was closest to the Murrays, thus in the direct line of attack.

"My wife told me what little else ye have had to say about my daughter whilst ye bathed and dined," said Balfour, fixing a stern dark gaze on Owen even as he filled his plate with food. "She is alive, Sir Colin is still on her trail, Sir Cormac saved her, and the two of them are making their way to the king's court."

"Aye, sir." Owen also filled his plate, pleased by the

quality and quantity of the food, yet not sure he was going to be able to relax enough to enjoy it. "She and Cormac were safe enough until Sir Colin sniffed out the direction they were headed in. There was one fierce attack and it cost Sir Colin five mercenaries. 'Tis then that Cormac decided to return to the more crowded roads and sent us to tell ye where he and Elspeth are headed. He feels that, if Sir Colin persists, and if Cormac doesnae get the chance to kill him, there could be danger even at the king's court."

"And do ye ken how Sir Colin justifies stealing my lass and then hunting her down?"

"He is telling all who will listen that Elspeth is his betrothed wife and that Cormac has stolen her."

Balfour cursed. "And not one Murray about to contest that vile lie."

"Young Cormac does have a true skill for being accused of crimes he hasnae committed," said Lady Maldie.

"Aye, he does that, m'lady," replied Owen. "He also kens that, if Sir Colin gets to the king, he may whisper that lie into our liege lord's ear and be believed. I think that may be another reason he decided it was now even more important to try to reach some of her kinsmen." Realizing that the Murrays were probably not going to ask too many questions about what might be happening between Cormac and Elspeth, Owen relaxed and began to enjoy his meal.

"I will go to court to fetch Elspeth," said Payton.

"Nay," cried his mother, Gisele. "Ye are barely healed from your wound."

Owen ate as he listened to the argument that ensued. Sir Payton's mother took a lot of convincing and extracted several promises before reluctantly agreeing. It was clear that Payton felt a need to redeem himself, for it was while Elspeth was in his care that she had been abducted. By the time Owen and Paul were ready to seek their beds it was decided that Sir Payton and a small force of men would rest and prepare on the morrow, then leave for the king's court at dawn the next day. Owen regretted the fact that he and Paul could not go along with them, but they were already late in responding to a summons from Paul's father. He was not surprised, however, when Payton caught up with him and Paul just outside of the bedchamber they had been given to use.

"There are things ye didnae tell the elders," said Payton, crossing his arms over his chest as he leaned against the wall and watched the two men closely.

"I believe we gave your kinsmen all the information needed," replied Owen.

"Aye, all that was needed, but nay the full truth."

"And what do ye think I have lied about?"

"Oh, nay, dinnae act as if I insult ye. I dinnae speak of lies. I speak of things left unsaid, truths left untold."

"If things were left unsaid, mayhap that is what all concerned wished," Paul said quietly.

"All or just your friend Cormac?" Payton asked.

"All."

Payton smiled faintly. "I dinnae ken why, but Elspeth and I have always been close. Dinnae fear for your friend. I ken weel how my cousin feels about the fool and just what she might do with what she would see as a perfect chance to fulfill a dream. Sadly, I also ken that her bonny knight is nay a free mon, that that whore Lady Isabel Douglas holds him tight in her murderous little fist. I would but like a hint of what I might find when I reach my cousin."

Owen and Paul looked at each other for a moment before Paul said, " 'Tis hoped that ye will find that Cormac has saved her from Sir Colin and that the bastard is dead. 'Tis also hoped that ye will find that Elspeth has saved our friend."

\* \* \*

"Muddy, where are ye going?" cried Elspeth as her cat suddenly leaped from his carrier.

Cormac reined in beside Elspeth even as she began to dismount. "Mayhap he just had a sudden need for a patch of dirt."

"Oh." She hesitated, frowning in the direction her cat had gone, then she shook her head. "Nay, something is wrong."

"Elspeth," Cormac said, but he could not fully repress a smile, " 'tis just a cat."

"l ken it, but my instinct tells me to follow him."

Sighing in resignation, Cormac dismounted when she started after her cat. "Foolish beast," he muttered and began to tether the horses. "It probably just saw something that looked like food, but I must now follow them on this fool's errand. She has gone off alone."

He hurried after her, softly cursing her impulsiveness. It was an endearing part of her nature, except when there was a madman at her heels. Cormac had thought she had finally understood the danger. When he reached her and found her kneeling by something on the ground, he prayed she was not about to collect some other poor beast.

Elspeth saw Muddy sitting by what looked like a bundle of rags. She frowned a little at the way the cat stared so intently at that bundle; then she noticed that the tiny clump of rags had a plump little arm and was waving it around even as it gurgled happily. It took a moment before she could shake free of her astonishment. Then Elspeth moved closer to peer at the baby. A quick look around revealed no supplies, nothing more than the ragged swaddling around the baby, and the only other person near at hand was the scowling man marching up to her.

"Oh, ye poor wee thing," she crooned as she removed the infant's rags and found no sign of injury. "Ye have been cast aside, havenae ye?" After rewrapping the child, she picked it up in her arms.

"Oh, nay, not a bairn," Cormac complained as he reached her side.

"Someone has just left him here, Cormac," Elspeth said, her outrage trembling in her voice. "Just tossed the poor, wee lad aside as if he is nay more than a bundle of soiled rushes."

"Why are ye staring at me like that?" he demanded when he lifted his gaze from the child.

"I was waiting for ye to tell me that I am wrong or foolish, naught but a suspicious fool. That no one would just toss this poor bairn away."

Cormac sighed and dragged his fingers through his hair. Elspeth looked appalled and hurt. The shock he could easily understand, but not the hurt. It was as if this callous act had struck her to the heart. It was as if she was feeling all the pain of rejection the baby was too young to feel for himself.

"Mayhap the mother or father has but slipped away for a moment." It was a pathetic attempt to disguise the ugly truth, but Cormac felt strangely proud of himself when Elspeth gave him a wide smile of gratitude and kissed his cheek.

"Ye are sweet, Cormac," she said, then grew solemn again. "But now that my shock has faded, I ken the truth. Someone has thrown her bairn away, left him here to die. Such cruelty. Why not leave the bairn at the church? It may give a lad such as this a hard life, but 'tis life all the same. Far better that than becoming some beastie's meal."

" 'Tis strange for a lad to be cast aside. 'Tis often the

lasses who get abandoned if a family has too many mouths to feed." He sighed. "Elspeth, we cannae take the bairn with us."

"Weel, we cannae leave the poor wee laddie here."

"Oh, nay, and I wasnae meaning that we should. 'Tis just that we are running from a killer. It may not be safe for the bairn. He isnae a cat ye can stuff in a carrier, but which will take care of itself for the most part."

"The bairn obviously comes from that village." Elspeth nodded toward the small cluster of buildings just beyond the foot of the small knoll she and Cormac stood on.

"Aye, I suspect he does. A bastard, mayhap. Some lass's dark secret."

"This bairn is no newborn, Cormac. Aye, a lass may be able to hide the fact that she is carrying some mon's bastard, but 'tis near impossible to hide the infant once it arrives. Bairns tend to be verra noisy creatures." She looked back at the village. "Someone down there will ken where he comes from. If that isnae any help, surely someone will be willing to foster a healthy male child."

Cormac was relieved to hear her speak of finding the child a home. "Are ye sure he is healthy?"

"Aye, I looked beneath the rags. The lad is perfect. Plump, healthy color, and of a good temper, I think. Oh, and he has the cutest wee birthmark low on his round little belly. It looks just like a star."

As he stared into the infant's bright black eyes, Cormac began to feel uneasy. A plump, healthy male child should not have been cast aside. Unfair as it might be, male children were considered of far greater worth than girl children. Elspeth was right to think that someone would take the boy in, yet why had no one done so yet?

Hiding his sudden doubts, Cormac helped her walk back to the horses. He held the baby while Elspeth settled the cat in its carrier, then mounted. As he handed her the baby, he had the sinking feeling that their entourage had just grown by one—one completely helpless, demanding bairn.

Elspeth frowned as they rode into the village. At first everyone seemed friendly enough. Then the person who had just greeted them would see the cooing child she held and become silent and wary. They would look at her as if she had committed some grave sin by bringing the child she carried into their peaceful village. It was as if they feared the helpless baby she held, yet that made no sense at all. What person with any wit could fear a tiny child?

While Cormac stabled the horses, Elspeth set about trying to discover who had borne the child. She knew she would not be able to give the baby back into the arms of the woman who could abandon her own child, but she did want to ask the woman why she had done such an appalling thing. After several people took one look at the baby, then rudely walked away before she could speak to them, Elspeth cornered a well-dresssed woman of middle years.

"Dinnae ye dare walk away from me," Elspeth snapped, halting the woman's attempts to get around her. "I but need to ask a fcw questions and yet ye all flee from me as if I am covered in plague sores."

"Weel, what do ye expect when ye bring that devil child here?" the woman said, hastily making the sign of the cross when she saw that the baby was looking at her.

"Devil child? What foolishness is this? 'Tis but a wee bairn and I seek its mother."

"The bairn's mother was hanged, then burned as a witch only a few days ago."

"Sweet Jesu," Elspeth whispered. "So 'twas one of ye who set the child out to die?"

"Aye. We cannae keep such a child with us. He carries the devil's mark."

"That wee star upon his belly?"

The woman nodded. 'Tis the devil's mark. His mother consorted with the devil. Oh, aye, she tried to claim it was some lordling who wandered through on his way to see the king. She wanted us to believe he seduced her and left her with child, but she was e'er wild and sharp of tongue, and had no morals at all. When this appeared with its black hair and black eyes, we all kenned the truth. His mother was as fair as fair can be, yet look at the thing she pushed out of her womb. Dark as Satan the bairn is and kissed by the devil. Nary a one in the village wanted to curse themselves with such a misbegotten child, so we set it on the hill."

"To die. Ye left a wee bairn on a hill to die, to be savaged by animals or starve or die of cold."

"We left Satan's heir to his care or God's judgment."

Elspeth dearly wanted to beat the woman. "Go away."

"Eh? Ye are the one who demanded I stand here, close to that wee demon, and risk my soul being tainted, just to answer a few questions. Now ye snarl at me and tell me to go away."

"Aye, and if ye have any scrap of wit in that head, which I doubt, ye will leave verra, verra quickly."

It did not surprise Elspeth when the woman turned pale and looked frightened. Her voice had been so hard and cold, thrumming with fury, that it had even made her shiver. Holding the baby close and stroking his thick raven curls, she watched the woman hurry away. The spite and the superstitious nonsense that had come out of that woman's mouth made Elspeth feel ill. She thanked God that the child she held was too small to understand any of the woman's hateful words.

There had always been some belief in witches. Because of their healing skills, her mother and she had inspired not just a few whispers. But Elspeth had never confronted such a depth of belief before, the sort of belief that would cause people to brutally kill one of their own or put a tiny baby on a hill to die. She was shaking with the strength of her anger and disgust. There was absolutely no way she would ever leave this child in this village. Cormac would just have to understand that.

Cormac watched an older woman practically run away from Elspeth. She had almost the same expression on her round face as the widow had had after he had left her alone with Elspeth for a few moments. He looked back at Elspeth and frowned. It was hard to believe someone that sweet of face and that delicate of body could do or say anything that would so frighten someone. Yet it was obvious that Elspeth could and did.

As he drew nearer to Elspeth he noticed that she was standing tensely. By the time he reached her side, he could see that she was trembling faintly. Worried, he put his arm around her and studied her too pale face. When she met his gaze he realized she was furious. He also realized that she still held the child.

"Ye havenae found out who the mother is yet?" he asked.

"Oh, I ken now, after I forced someone to talk to me."

"Aye, I saw her. 'Tis clear the conversation wasnae pleasant. She wasnae the mother, was she?"

"Nay, she was probably one of the ones who lit the fire beneath the woman who was though. It seems the laddie's mother was tried, convicted, and burned as a witch only a few days ago. I suppose one should be pleased that they were all merciful enough to hang the woman first. I but pray it killed her or so nearly did so that she wasnae sensible when they set her alight. Then they set this wee bairn out to die."

"Jesu." Cormac looked at the child and sighed. "What made them think that the woman was a witch?"

"Oh, a lot of things. She must have been beautiful from the way that evil woman described her. Verra fair. It seems she had the sin of a sharp tongue as weel. She claimed she had been seduced and left with child by a lordling who passed through here on his way to the king's court, but she was always wild and immoral, so the righteous women of the village didnae believe that. Then she had this verra dark child with that birthmark. There is your proof that she consorted with the devil. She had to die so that the good women of this village could continue to be good women. And once the witch was dead, this spawn of the devil was set upon the hill so that he, too, would die. In my foolishness I have brought this great evil back into their village and threatened their pure, wee souls."

He reached out and gently ruffled the child's dark curls. "So I gather we add another stray to our number."

"E'en if someone would take him, I cannae leave him here, Cormac. I cannae."

"Nay, of course not. Come along. I have gotten us a room at the inn."

"They may not let us in, carrying all this potent evil, for fear their milk will curdle in the jug."

"In the temper ye are in, I dinnae think they will dare to refuse us," Cormac drawled as he took her by the arm and started toward the inn, a place clearly established to serve those who were traveling to and from the court.

Although the innkeeper, his wife, and the maids did not refuse them, they crossed themselves whenever they drew near to the child. Elspeth had to bite her tongue to keep herself from threatening to break their fingers. When she and Cormac settled into their room, Elspeth fed the child some milky oatmeal and goat's milk from a bladder a terrified maid had brought them. She used the time spent tending to the child's needs to try to calm herself, and not solely because her mood could upset the child. Her anger was too great and was already making her head ache and her stomach churn. There was no one she could vent it on, so she needed to conquer it.

Cormac sat before a small fire, sipping his ale and watching Elspeth closely. This business had deeply upset her. He did not think it was because she had been so sheltered she did not realize such injustices occurred. It was, he suspected, hearing the murder of the child's mother and even the attempted murder of the child justified so coldly by that woman. Since her mother and she were healers, they might have faced this sort of threat from time to time, which would add a chillingly personal touch to the sad tale. Fortunately, she and her mother had obviously not met such prejudices and superstition in this deadly a form.

He looked at the child again as Elspeth put clean changing cloths on the baby. A lordling on his way to the king's court, the mother had claimed the father to be. Although that could include several hundred men, Cormac doubted many were so dark. Then again the lordling could easily have been some lowly apprentice in borrowed finery blessed with a clever tongue.

Reluctantly, Cormac decided a concentrated search for the father would be foolish. He would recall all the important facts about the baby's story, get a better, more fixed time of conception, and a more detailed description of the mother. All that, together with the child's strikingly dark looks, would be enough. Anytime he came upon a man who had the look of the child he would relate the tale. If the child's father was alive, he might eventually stumble across the man. If not, Cormac thought as he watched Elspeth cuddle the child, murmuring sweet nonsense to the boy, the lad had found himself a safe, loving haven.

"Did the woman give the child a name?" Cormac asked.

"Nay, yet the woman who bore him must have given

him one so that he could be christened," said Elspeth; then she sighed. "If he e'er was christened. The feelings against the mother may already have been too strong."

" 'Tis easy enough to discover." Cormac finished his ale and stood up. "And there is still time left in the day to do so."

"Mayhap we shouldnae stir things up, shouldnae remind these fools that the bairn is still alive and here with us."

"Angel, do ye really think that fool woman ye threatened is hiding under her wee bed, silent and trembling? Mayhap trembling, but ne'er silent."

"And who said I had threatened her?"

"Her face said it. It was just like the look upon that randy widow's face." He grinned when she blushed and refused to look at him. "And ye with such a sweet face." He tsked and chuckled when she glared at him. "I think ye need to rest and I will go and ask a few hard questions." Cormac kissed her on the forehead. "Ye are looking a wee bit pale."

"I suspect I am," Elspeth said as she settled herself on her back on the bed, placing the child securely at her side. Muddy curled up on the other side of the child. " 'Twas the anger. It was so great I have given myself a headache and set my insides to churning. Each vile word that foolish woman said only added to it. I wanted to rip her tongue out for saying such evil things about a wee bairn."

"Such a fierce defender of the weak ye are, my love. 'Tis strange the way Muddy found him and how he seems quite attached to the bairn already."

"Weel, I think we have already had more than enough proof that Muddy isnae like most cats."

"Aye." He brushed a few stray wisps of hair off her face with his fingers and gently kissed her again. "Rest." He winked. "Ye will need it, for I mean to take fierce advantage of having ye in a proper bed again."

"There is a thought to sweeten my dreams. Just what do ye think to learn and why do ye wish to learn it?"

"We need to ken a name for the bairn and find out if he was christened. And I want a name and a better description of his mother. The time of his birth would also be helpful, for 'twould set a clearer time of conception, of when his sire did wander through the area."

"Ye think a search should be made for his father."

"Nay a hard search. The laddie has a home, hasnae he?"

"Aye," Elspeth said, lightly stroking the child's thick hair.

"But an eye should be kept open for the father. A wary eye. The wee lad has suffered enough. 'Tis good that he is too young to ken it. He does have a father, though, and he may be a good mon. There may e'en be a good reason he ne'er came back here. All I seek is the truth, and if we e'er see a mon who could be the lad's father, then we can decide if the tale should be told to him."

Elspeth nodded. "I understand. And if the lad comes of age and no one has yet stumbled upon his father, he may wish to search for him himself. Then we shall have something that could help him find the mon's trail. My uncle Eric was set upon a hillside to die when he was but a newborn, and he was a youth of thirteen ere he kenned the full truth of his birth and a mon grown ere he was reunited with his mother's kinsmen." She smiled faintly at Cormac's shock. "Aye, he isnae blood family, but he was raised a Murray until the truth was discovered, and he chose to stay a Murray. This lad will be a Murray, too. And unless he chooses elsewise, he can stay one. Go on then. I will rest, for I have an urge to take fierce advantage of ye in a bed as weel."

Cormac laughed and kissed her before he left. Elspeth sighed and closed her eyes. She wondered if Cormac was aware of how often he had said *we* when he spoke of keeping an eye out for the child's father. Elspeth did not let herself find too much reason to hope in what could be a mere slip of the tongue. It could also mean, however, that a part of Cormac already saw and accepted them as a pair, could see a future for them despite Lady Isabel. If that was true, Elspeth prayed that part of Cormac would hurry up and possess the whole of him, for Lady Isabel was not very far away.

She idly rubbed the child's back as she waited for sleep to overtake her. It would be nice if the child had a father out there, somewhere, who would welcome him, love him, and see that he had a good life. She also knew how rarely that happened for a bastard. It pleased her that Cormac was not even suggesting a swift, intense search for that man. Such haste could lead to mistakes and misjudgments. If, at some time in the years ahead, the boy's father was found, Elspeth wanted to be very sure he was a good man before she entrusted him with the life of this child.

Just as she started to fall asleep, Elspeth sensed she was being watched. It was so strong a feeling, it jerked her back into full awareness with an almost painful skip of her heart. Slowly, she opened her eyes and, for the first time in her life, almost fainted. Standing there by her bed, smiling coldly, was Sir Colin MacRae.

# Chapter Ten

Cormac understood Elspeth's anger even more now that he had spoken to some of the townspeople. To hear such viciousness spat out against a child of only a few months of age made the bile sting the back of his throat. Anne Seaton had been the bairn's mother and she had obviously not made much effort to win the love and admiration of the people in the village. Beautiful and vain, she had definitely bedded one too many husbands. There may have been a fool or two who believed her a witch, who truly thought a dark babe born to such a fair mother was proof of evil. What most of the people had clearly decided was that it was a good way to be rid of someone they did not like, at least at first.

By the time they had lashed the woman to the pyre, Cormac suspected a large number of the villagers had begun to believe the talk of witchcraft. In their frenzy of fear and hate they had tried to rid the village of the child as well. They certainly were not going to claim elsewise now, not after killing the woman. Burning a witch was righteous justice. Murdering a woman who had been unlikable, killing her in such a brutal way, just because she could not keep her legs or her mouth closed or you wanted her gone, was not. Anne's death was wrong, but at least it was now explained.

For the attempted murder of a tiny baby, however, there was no explanation. A child that young was incapable of evil. Some fools had even used the child's sweet temper as proof of the devil's stain. The young priest had gone along with the killing of Anne, and Cormac strongly suspected that was because the fool had lusted after her, but he had never openly agreed with what had been done to the child. Unfortunately, he was a coward and had not had the backbone to stand up to the villagers.

Only one person had seen the lordling Anne had claimed to be the babe's father. A man as dark as the child, big, and very forbidding. Of course, the one who had seen him had been the poor fool caught rutting with Anne by this intimidating lordling. If the man had not been drinking heavily, Cormac doubted he would have confessed so much. The man had also been weighted down with guilt, for he had been away from the village when Anne was accused, then murdered, and his wife had been one of the ones screaming the loudest for Anne's blood. Cormac suspected the man's life was a living hell at the moment.

Stepping into the inn, Cormac frowned. There was a great deal of noise coming from upstairs, and a small crowd of the curious had gathered at the bottom. Recalling how everyone felt about the waif Elspeth had taken in, Cormac suddenly feared the noise was coming from his bedchamber. He pushed the onlookers out of the way and bolted up the stairs.

"What is going on here?" he demanded of the innkeeper, his wife, and the two maids standing in and near the open door of his and Elspeth's room.

"Dorcas came to feed the bairn," said the innkeeper, "and that beast wouldnae let her touch it."

Cormac glanced at the plump, softly weeping maid, who held a hand over a badly scratched arm. "Why should she be coming to attend the bairn?"

"It was crying and your wife wasnae quieting it. It appears she has deserted you."

A chill went down Cormac's spine and he pushed his way into his room. Muddy stood next to the sniffling child on the bed. His fur was standing up, his battered ears were flattened, and he was growling, low and deep. There was no sign of Elspeth.

For just one moment, Cormac feared that the innkeeper was right, that Elspeth had deserted him. Then he shook his head, pushing away that illogical and disloyal thought. Elspeth would never leave the child or the cat. Her things were still in the room. The bed was badly mussed and a stool was tipped over. The window was wide open and he walked over to it. He glanced down but saw nothing, so he closed the window. While he had been out gathering a few answers, Sir Colin had stolen Elspeth.

"Did any of ye see who took my wife? Or were ye all too busy trying to protect your wee sad souls from a bairn to notice that one of your guests was being stolen away?" Cormac cautiously approached a still tensed Muddy.

"We saw no one," snapped the innkeeper and his too plump wife nodded vigorously in agreement. "She has left you."

"Nay, she was taken." Gently stroking the cat, Cormac finally got it to calm down. "Elspeth would ne'er leave the child or her cat. E'en if I judge her wrong and she could do both, she would ne'er leave all of her things behind.

There are also signs of a small struggle. Dorcas, ye were ready to tend to the child?"

"Aye, sir," the maid answered, "but the cat wouldnae let me near him."

"He will now. He had been frightened by what happened here. Come, Dorcas."

"The cat doesnae like me, sir."

"I swear to ye, he will now. He is calm and I shall introduce ye, marking ye as safe."

It took several moments before he could coax Dorcas into patting Muddy. He ached to set out after Elspeth, but he knew he had to settle the care of the child first. After several more tries, he got Dorcas to touch the baby. She relaxed when Muddy just sat and watched her. The baby calmed under her touch and Cormac stood up, allowing her more room to tend to the child.

"Ye arenae afraid of this great, monstrous demon, are ye?" Cormac asked as Dorcas efficiently changed the baby's rags.

" 'Tis just a wee bairn," Dorcas replied softly, casting a nervous glance at the three people still lurking in the doorway. " 'Twas terrible what they tried to do, but I was too much of a coward to stop it or help."

" 'There wasnae much one lass could do against so many crying out for blood. When did the bairn start to cry?"

"An hour ago, mayhap less."

"That was when Elspeth was taken then. I want ye to stay with the bairn."

"Ye arenae going to run off and leave that devil's spawn here," said the innkeeper, his last word ending on a high squeak as Cormac grabbed him by the front of his jupon and lifted him slightly off his feet.

"I have had my fill of such foolish talk. 'Tis a bairn. A wee bairn." He released the short, squat man so abruptly he stumbled back into his wife, nearly sending her sprawling onto the floor. "Dorcas will stay here and care for the child. If anything happens to him, I will hunt ye down and gut ye."

"What if ye dinnae come back?" the innkeeper demanded, although his tone was more respectful. "We willnae take it."

"I wouldnae think of giving him to ye or leaving him in this madhouse." He tossed a few coins on the tiny table by the bed, glad now that he had swallowed his pride enough to ask Owen for a small loan. "If neither I nor my wife return, send the cat and the bairn to Sir Balfour Murray and Lady Maldie at Donncoill. Tell them Elspeth wished the bairn fostered." He strode toward them, nudging all three back into the hall and shutting the door behind him. "I am sure ye have work to do. Ye are nay longer needed here. I would advise ye to make sure Dorcas has all she needs."

The moment they were gone, he hurried out of the inn and went to study the ground beneath Elspeth's window. It was easy to see that she had been taken out of the room that way. Cormac could not see anything to mark Elspeth's passing, but the footprints leading away from the window sank deeper than the ones leading to it, telling Cormac that the man had left there carrying something, and that something was probably Elspeth. He hurried away to get his horse, praying that Sir Colin continued to leave such a clear trail and that the light of the fading day remained strong enough for him to follow Sir Colin to where he would camp for the night.

"I cannae believe ye would threaten a bairn," Elspeth said as Sir Colin dragged her off his horse and pushed her inside a small cottage. "And a cat!"

What Elspeth could not really believe was that, after all

the running, the fighting, and the killing, Sir Colin had simply slipped into her room through a window and carried her off. She had just lain there, too stupid with shock and weariness to do any more than gape as his man had held a knife on the baby and a hissing Muddy. That stupidity had allowed him time to deliver one clean punch to her jaw, knocking her out cold. She had made it so easy for him, she thought crossly as she rubbed her throbbing jaw.

"It worked. Ye are here," he said coldly as he lit a fire in the small fireplace.

"Cormac will come for me," she said, sounding far more confident than she felt.

"Let him. I ache to kill the bastard."

"Why are ye doing this?"

"Ye are mine." He stood up and glared at her. "No woman tells me nay. Did ye really think I would just slink away like some whipped cur without avenging that insult?"

"What insult? Ye asked me to wed with you. I said nay and most pleasantly and kindly if I recall."

"And just who do ye think ye are to tell me nay? Ye are almost twenty and still unwed. Ye come from a verra small clan. Ye have a wee dowry. Your mother is naught but some whore's get. I honored ye by asking ye to be my wife."

"Dinnae ye speak of my mither that way or I will gut ye like the pig ye are."

Elspeth was not surprised when her cold insult earned her a brutal slap that caused her to fall on her backside. She had always sensed the cruelty in the man. It would be wise to guard her tongue, but she doubted she would be able to. It was hard to believe that all the deaths and turmoil were caused because this man was too vain to accept a nay. Considering all the insulting things he had just said about her and her family, she had to wonder why he had even asked her in the first place.

Cormac had to have discovered that she was gone by now, she thought as she considered her next move. She hoped he did not think that she had just deserted him. She also hoped that he would know that she had been taken from him and by whom. The questions were, would he come after her, and if he did, had Sir Colin left him a clear enough trail to follow? Then she sternly told herself not to be an idiot. Cormac would try his best to save her. He had vowed to keep her safe. Sadly, she knew just how tenaciously Cormac clung to any vow he had made. She could only pray that honoring this one would not get him killed.

"I suppose young Cormac has had you," Sir Colin said, his voice almost pleasant. "Even though he seems to spend his life running after that whore Lady Isabel, ye would be too sweet for him to resist. So has he had your maidenhead?"

Despite the almost friendly tone of his voice, instinct warned Elspeth that the truth would utterly enrage the man. There was a taut, waiting quality about him. He had leashed some emotion and she strongly suspected it was fury.

Standing up and brushing off her skirts, Elspeth replied haughtily, "I dinnae believe that is a proper question for a gentlemon to be asking a lady."

"Oh, ye are good, wench." Sir Colin briefly smiled, but his eyes remained hard and cold. "Ye can tell what a person thinks or feels, cannae ye? 'Tis one reason I want you. Such a skill would be invaluable to a mon seeking power, as I do."

"I cannae tell such things," she protested. "I but have a sense of strong emotions in a person. So do many people if they would but heed it."

"What matter if it is a gift or just a good eye for a telltale twitch? Ye can tell right now that I am angry, verra, verra angry."

"That takes no strange skill. Ye fair stink of it."

Elspeth inwardly cursed when his faint smile told her her words had merely confirmed his belief. In a way, he was right. She could sense many things about people. Rarely could anyone successfully lie to her. Elspeth was not sure how she was able to tell such things, why she seemed so sensitive to the feelings of others no matter how well hidden they were, but she had accepted the strange skill a long time ago. She would not, however, allow Sir Colin to twist it to his own ill use.

"And why do ye suppose I am angry?" he asked almost idly. "Could it possibly be because my betrothed wife has been merrily rutting her way across the countryside with Sir Cormac Armstrong? An Armstrong, my love? And one of those particular Armstrongs?" He shook his head. "Rogues and thieves, the lot of them. And this particular Armstrong must be the saddest of that sad lot. Why, he is so ensorcelled by Lady Isabel, I doubt he can e'en get his rod stiff for another woman."

"I would not ken a thing about that." It was plain that Sir Colin was not believing her pose of a haughty innocent, but Elspeth decided it was far too late to change the game now.

"Of course not, but ye have tried to test it, havenae ye? After all, Sir Cormac is the braw knight of your maidenly dreams. The bonny laddie ye would think of in the dark of night to make yourself wet with longing."

"How verra crude ye are. I am appalled at your utter lack of good manners."

What truly appalled Elspeth was that he even knew that dark little secret, knew that she had longed for Cormac for years. Very few people knew about those dreams. There was obviously a weakness in Donncoill, some soft spot he had found and used to ferret out all kinds of information. It was probably one of the maids, seduced and thinking herself in love. Elspeth could sympathize, but as soon as she could, she would warn her family that someone at Donncoill was either foolishly free with the clan's secrets or disloyal. And since this time it was one of her most closely guarded secrets, it was probably someone close to her, which made her both sad and angry.

"We shall make a fine pair, ye and I." Sir Colin moved toward her. "Ye have a keen wit, lass. I shall only have to teach ye a few things."

Elspeth tried to stay out of his reach without looking as if she was running away from him. "Oh, aye, things like lying, murder, theft, and how to smile sweetly as I slip a knife between a mon's ribs."

"Aye. I believe ye will prove to be most adept."

His calm answer to her insult startled Elspeth so much she stumbled over a low stool. Colin was on her in an instant. The man was far more clever than she had thought him to be. He had seen how she tried to use his tendency to fly into a blind rage against him, and so he had unraveled that net, even managing to turn her game back on her.

Elspeth hit the floor so hard all the breath was knocked out of her. Despite that, she struggled to keep Sir Colin from pinning her down too completely. She also fought against being weakened by the knowledge that she could only delay him, not conquer him.

"Get off me, ye great fool," she snapped, refusing to let the man know just how afraid she really was.

"Ye are going to give me what ye have been giving Armstrong," he said, slapping her hard when she managed to get one hand free and punch him in the side of his head. "Ye willnae get away from me this time, so why not sit back and enjoy it?"

"Enjoy rape? Ye are mad. If ye do this, there will be so

many trying to kill ye, ye willnae be able to find a hole deep enough in all of Scotland to hide in. Aye, and I will be at the head of that line.''

Even as she cursed him and threatened him, Elspeth fought him with all of her strength. Each trick she tried, however, was only partially successful. She got her leg between his and brought her knee up, but he shifted just in time and took the blow on the leg not in the groin. She got a hand free and tried to gouge at his eyes, but he turned his head and she got his cheek instead. It quickly became clear to her that Sir Colin was no novice in the raping of women. She began to doubt that she had any trick or move that he did not already know, that he could not anticipate and avoid the worst of.

She tried to concentrate only on the fight, to ignore the fact that he was relentlessly tearing her clothes off. ''Cormac will cut ye into tiny pieces and feed ye to the corbies.''

''Cormac willnae get within ten yards of this place. Four men wait outside, eager and ready to kill him.'' Sir Colin finally got her bodice open, leaving only her thin linen chemise protecting her breasts. ''Ah, such beauties they are. Ye will be a fine ride.''

When he started to bend his head to her breast, there was one brief moment when his head was close to hers, and Elspeth took quick advantage of that. She slammed her head into his. He howled and released his grasp enough for her to shove him off her. Dizzy from the blow, which she thought might have hurt her as much as it had him, Elspeth could not get to her feet, so she had to crawl away from him. She cursed when she felt him grab at her skirts, tearing them.

Elspeth flipped on her back and kicked him in the face, knocking him away again. This time she managed to get to her feet, but took only a few steps before he tackled her to the floor yet again. Weakened and groggy, Elspeth was unable to stop him from pinning her firmly beneath him this time. His triumphant smile told her he knew he was winning and she ached to slap it off his face.

There was still a small chance of getting away, she told herself in an attempt to hold back the waves of defeat and despair threatening to completely flood her heart and mind. He would have to move a little in order to position himself properly, perhaps even loosen his grip on her wrists and legs, and then she would start fighting again. The moment she tried to shift her position, however, he slapped her, hard. He started yanking at her skirts and petticoats, and she tried to move again. He slapped her again. By the time she recovered from that blow, she wore little more than her chemise and stockings. Elspeth realized that Sir Colin intended to keep her dazed until it was too late for her to protect herself.

She started to pray. Elspeth prayed she would be given one more chance to escape—one that had some chance of being successful. She prayed that, if she failed to escape violation at Sir Colin's hands, it would not hurt too badly, would not leave her so scarred in mind and heart that she became cold at the mere touch of a man. She prayed that Sir Colin had lied about the four men outside waiting to kill Cormac.

Cormac stared at the little cottage as he crouched in the underbrush. He had been so intent on trying to follow Sir Colin's trail, he had almost ridden right up to the door. The sound of a loud sneeze cutting through the air was all that had stopped him, giving him time to tether his horse and creep up to a sheltered spot within sight of the cottage.

Although he was desperate to race to the cottage and

save Elspeth, Cormac forced himself to wait. Sir Colin had not gone very far after stealing Elspeth away, barely a mile from the village. He could have ridden for a few more hours. Cormac had the sinking feeling that Sir Colin had stopped here because he could no longer wait to possess Elspeth. The thought of that man touching her sorely threatened his control. Cormac wanted to do something, something more than crouch in the shadows, watching the four armed men who stood between him and Elspeth. He waited, continually reminding himself that a blind rush now would just get him killed and leave Elspeth completely at Sir Colin's mercy.

He tensed when one of the men strolled off into the surrounding wood just to his left. Silently, Cormac tracked him. He caught the man in the midst of relieving himself against a tree. Slipping up behind him, he clamped his hand over the man's mouth even as he rammed his knife up between the man's ribs. As he lowered the body to the ground, he felt no real satisfaction. He found such killing distasteful, but had learned long ago that it was necessary sometimes. The reminder that this man would not have hesitated to do the same to him eased the pang of guilt he felt. So did the knowledge that the man had been willing to stand guard over Elspeth's rape. For a few coins he had become a willing partner in the destruction of a woman.

Returning to his hiding place, Cormac waited for another chance. Three guards were still too many for him to confront openly. If one would just be foolish enough to go after his friend, that would be enough. He had taken down two men before with a dagger and a sword.

The wait became excruciating and Cormac was trying to think of ways he could quickly cut down three men and still make it into the cottage alive when, after a brief conference with his companions, another man slipped into the woods. Cormac caught him as he bent over the body of the other man. He let this body fall next to the other one.

As he silently made his way back to the cottage, making full use of the deepening shadows of late evening, he readied his knife and his sword. Although he had never thought he would be grateful for all those years of running and hiding from the Douglases, he had to admit he had learned a lot. Those hard lessons in stealth were proving their worth now. He hated the killing, but he was glad he had learned how to do it quickly and quietly.

When he got near enough to see the two remaining guards, he would have smiled if he had not been forced into the position of killing them. They stood together, obviously discussing what might have happened to the other two and trying to decide how best to protect themselves. They were going to make it easy for him.

Taking a deep breath to steady himself, Cormac started toward the cottage at a steady lope. The moment the men saw him, Cormac threw his knife, catching one man in the throat. The other was ready for him, sword in hand and braced for a fight by the time he drew near. Cormac cursed as their swords clashed. This one would not be a quiet kill. All he could do was pray that it was a quick one—quick enough so that, even if Sir Colin was warned by the sound, he would not have enough time to flee or prepare an adequate defense.

"Ah, so ye are awake again. Good."

Elspeth blinked and stared at Sir Colin. He had obviously slapped her one time too often and too hard. She was so dazed with pain she was not sure when or why she had lost consciousness.

Her head cleared quickly when she realized that she was no longer on a floor and that she could not move her hands or her feet. Ice flowed through her veins as she looked down at herself. She was lashed by the wrists and ankles to the four rough-hewn posts of a large bed. What horrified her the most, however, was that she was naked. There would be no more chances to escape. She inwardly cringed when Sir Colin reached out to touch the curve of one breast with his fingers.

This was going to destroy her, she decided. Fighting to the last yet still losing, still being taken against her will, somehow did not seem as appalling as this. She would have at least had the comfort of knowing she had fought her fate, had perhaps inflicted some damage upon her defiler. This left her totally helpless. She was laid out like some ancient human sacrifice. He would not have to hit her at all, which meant she would be completely aware throughout her own degradation. Suddenly, she felt utterly terrified, but she fought to hide it, not wanting to give Sir Colin the satisfaction.

"Sadly, aye, it appears I am indeed awake, although I would be forgiven if I believed myself caught in the verra worst of nightmares," she said, pleased with the chill calm in her voice.

"Helpless and naked and yet ye still try to spit at me," Sir Colin said, a glimmer of amusement in his expression. "We will breed some fine sons, men worthy of ruling Scotland."

"I believe there is already a king on the throne and a dynasty set."

"At the birth of our first son, I shall begin to destroy it. Do ye ken whose house this is?"

It took Elspeth a moment to understand him, his change of subject was so abrupt. "Nay. Should I?"

"Ye took in the witch's bairn, didnae ye?" Sir Colin sat down on the edge of the bed and took off his boots.

"Ye cannae be the lordling who seduced her and left

her with child." Elspeth grasped at the topic of discussion a little desperately, needing a distraction, for she knew exactly why Sir Colin was starting to remove his clothes. "Ye arenae dark enough."

"Nay, I left no bairn in her." He chuckled. "Claimed she was seduced, did she? The villagers probably killed her simply for the telling of such a huge lie and, worse, thinking all of them were fool enough to believe it. Nay, that lass was born a whore. Most of the men in the area and many of those who made regular journeys to court kenned all about her." He glanced around the tidy little cottage with approval as he unlaced his heavily padded jupon. "She was beautiful enough to do verra weel for herself."

"But nay enough for any of those who enjoyed her favors to put a halt to that murder."

"Of course not. She was a whore and an ill-tempered one at that. And mayhap she wasnae really a witch, but she had certainly done enough to warrant a good hanging. Did ye think that wee, black-eyed devil was the only bairn she ever carried? Nay, she didnae want bairns, but was cursed fertile. Cleaned most of them from her body once she kenned that they were there. When she was too late to do that safely, she birthed them, then got rid of them. Killed two, mayhap more. They are buried out back of this bonny, little cottage along with a mon or two who had angered her. Nay, not the father," he replied to the unspoken question Elspeth could not hide. "My wee cousin was a hard woman."

"Of course, I should have kenned it, being that ye are so much alike. What a lovely chat we are having. Just like old friends, we are. Mayhap ye should untie me and I will fetch us both an ale."

Sir Colin laughed as he tossed aside his jupon and began to unlace his shirt. Then he suddenly tensed. "What was that?"

Elspeth heard it, too. The distinct sound of sword-on-sword fighting now shattered the peace just outside the cottage door. Anything could be happening out there, even an argument amongst the guards Sir Colin had out there. She preferred to think that it was Cormac. She laughed softly as Sir Colin scrambled to get his sword even as the door to the cottage was kicked open so fiercely it cracked.

"Ah, Sir Colin, I fear your death has just come to the door."

# Chapter Eleven

The sight that greeted Cormac's eyes when he kicked the door open to the cottage nearly made him roar with fury. All that kept him from acting too swiftly and too blindly, endangering himself and Elspeth with the recklessness of rage, was Elspeth herself. Her almost cheerful words nearly made him laugh. And she was smiling at him. She was tied naked to a bed and covered in livid bruises, yet she smiled.

"I dinnae ken who is madder, lass, ye or I," Cormac said, keeping most of his attention on a coldly furious Sir Colin, who, Cormac noted with relief, was still mostly dressed.

"Ye, of course. I dinnae go about kicking in people's doors," she replied, almost giddy with the relief of seeing him alive and ready to put an end to Sir Colin's insanity. "I dinnae suppose ye will have time to cut my bonds ere ye have to fight with this fool."

"If I dance close by ye whilst blinding this madmon with my skill and grace, I will be sure to see to it."

"Thank ye. Weel, go on then. Kill him."

"Bloodthirsty wench."

"Now that the two of ye have greeted each other," Sir Colin snapped, "mayhap we can get on with the business of my killing you, Armstrong."

"Oh, aye? Do ye think ye can do any better than your hired churls?"

"Killed them all, did ye?" Sir Colin shook his head and tsked. "Your lover is quite bloodthirsty, isnae he, Elspeth?"

"I didnae give ye leave to speak to me with such familiarity," she said.

"Verra sharp of tongue for a lass tied naked to a bed," murmured Sir Colin and then he smiled, almost sweetly, at Cormac. "Ye did happen to notice that she was naked, didnae ye? Verra fine skin the lass has. Soft. Verra soft. Bruises a wee bit too easily though. Ah, but so sweet to the taste. Like honey on the tongue."

It was not hard to guess Sir Colin's game. Cormac struggled against the fury the man's words stirred to life inside of him. Fighting had to be done coldly, logically. Some emotion was acceptable, giving one the incentive to continue despite any pain and to kill if necessary. A little caution and care for one's own life was also a good thing. Rage was not. Rage caused one to be careless, to blind one to everything but the need to wound or kill. Rage could steal away a man's skill.

Cormac knew all that, repeated the lessons he had learned over and over. It did not help much. Every poisonous word that dripped from Sir Colin's tongue fed his anger. The mere thought of Sir Colin looking upon Elspeth's beauty made him ache to kill the man. The thought that the man might have touched her, tasted her soft skin, made him shake with the urge to cut him into small pieces slowly.

Elspeth could see the struggle Cormac was caught in. His anger was winning, and that was just what Sir Colin wanted. A part of her was thrilled that Cormac could be so enraged at the idea that some other man had touched her, but she had watched enough lessons in the art of fighting to understand the risk of such uncontroled emotion. A clear head and a cold heart, Payton had always said, and he well understood the value of those words, for he had struggled long and hard to learn the lesson. Somehow, she had to dim the power of Sir Colin's venom. She had to break the spell the man was so cleverly weaving.

"Oh, do be quiet, Sir Colin," she scolded, her tone one of pure irritation. "Ye boast of false conquests like some untried lad who spewed on the sheets when faced with his first woman."

The look of astonishment on Sir Colin's face almost made Cormac laugh. His anger was still there, but Elspeth's tart and somewhat crude words had brought him back to his senses. She would not be helped if he got himself killed while lashing out in a jealous rage. This was his chance to end the threat to her and he would not fail her.

Sir Colin lunged and Cormac easily deflected the blow. And then Cormac was so caught up in the fight, he had no time to think of the insults inflicted upon Elspeth. At one point in the battle he found a moment to cut the ropes binding one of her wrists to the bed. Then, hoping she could now free herself, he pressed Sir Colin as hard as he could until the man was far away from the bed.

Ignoring the aches and pains in her body, Elspeth struggled to loosen the ropes on her other wrist. She fought against the need to watch Sir Colin and Cormac fight each other, the need to see that Cormac remained unharmed. The clang of the swords, the grunts and curses of the men,

made for a distressing background as she slowly undid her
bonds. Her arms and legs ached, her bruises throbbed,
and her wrists and ankles stung from the rub of the tight
rope, but Elspeth ignored it all. When she was finally free,
she found her chemise on the floor, where Sir Colin had
dropped it, and tugged it on. Sitting on the bed, she looked
at the two men who appeared evenly matched, and she
wondered if there was something, anything, she could do
to help Cormac.

She clapped her hands over her mouth to keep from
crying out when Sir Colin's sword slashed across Cormac's
right arm. It was a shallow wound running from his shoulder nearly to his elbow, but it bled freely. Elspeth knew
all too well how that loss of blood could weaken a man.
Even if it did not completely weaken Cormac, it would
soon steal the strength from his sword arm, giving Sir Colin
a deadly advantage.

Even as that concern passed through her mind, Cormac
shifted his sword to his left hand and kept fighting with
no evident loss of skill. She nearly laughed at the look of
astonishment on Sir Colin's sweat-drenched face. Elspeth
knew it was too soon to stop worrying, however. Cormac
was still bleeding freely from his wound.

Her eyes began to hurt from watching Cormac so steadily, blinking as little as possible for fear of missing something. Then she saw what she had dreaded—a slight falter
in Cormac's step, a faint loss of the deadly grace he had
shown until now. Sir Colin saw it, too, for he smiled. Before
she could do anything to help Cormac, Sir Colin slashed
his leg. A scream was caught chokingly in her throat as
Cormac stumbled and fell. Sir Colin hurried closer, eager
to deliver the death stroke, but Cormac rolled out of the
way. Sir Colin cursed and lunged again, seeing Cormac as
already defeated, for he lay on his side, obviously struggling
to move out of harm's way. That proved to be a mistake.

He raised his sword for the deathblow and then Cormac moved so swiftly even Elspeth gasped. He flipped over and sat up in one swift, clean move, plunging his sword deep into Sir Colin's exposed chest.

Elspeth felt as if everything stopped along with her ability to breath. For one horrifying moment, Sir Colin stood there, his sword still raised to strike, staring in amazement at the sword piercing his body. Then his sword tumbled from his lax hands, and he fell. Cormac barely got his sword free of the man's flesh before he was pulled along in Sir Colin's descent.

"Cormac," she cried, racing to his side as he slumped back down onto the floor.

When she knelt next to him, Cormac grasped her hand. Groggy, weak from loss of blood, and becoming all too aware of the burning pain of his wounds, he was still interested in only one thing. Everything else could wait until he had the reassurances he needed from Elspeth's own lips.

"Was I too late?" he asked.

"Nay," she replied. "For all I was splayed out like a gutted salmon, Sir Colin did nay more than fondle me a wee bit. It was quite disgusting, but I shall recover. He was too busy gloating and then he gave me one slap too many. Unconsciousness didnae appeal to him."

"Thank God." He closed his eyes. "I believe I will rest now."

"Do ye think ye could get to the bed ere ye faint?"

"Help me." He barely stifled a groan as she put her arms around him and helped him to his feet. "And I said rest."

"Of course." Staggering a little beneath his weight, she got him over to the bed and barely escaped falling on top of him when he collapsed on top of it. "There, now ye may *rest* and I will tend to these wounds."

It was not until he opened his eyes to find Elspeth wrapping a linen cloth around the cleaned and stitched wound on his leg that Cormac realized he had passed out. He took note of the fact that he was naked and clean and also that he had a bandage on his arm. It was clear that he had been insensible for a lot longer than he had thought he was. A quick look around the room revealed the blanket-shrouded body of Sir Colin.

"Ah, good," he murmured. "I won."

Tucking a clean blanket around him, Elspeth shook her head. "I grow verra weary of trying to keep the blood in your body, Cormac. I begin to think ye are trying to see how much ye have by spilling it all out upon the ground."

He smiled faintly and lifted his left hand to gently stroke her bruised cheek. "Ye fought hard, didnae ye, angel mine?"

"Of course." She sighed as she sat down on the edge of the bed. "I kenned I couldnae win, but, aye, I fought him. 'Tis why he kept hitting me. Once he hit me too hard, and when I regained my senses, I realized he had taken quick, ruthless advantage of my unconsciousness. When I found myself trussed up and naked," she shivered, "I felt so helpless. I realized that, although I thought I had resigned myself to being raped, most of my calm came from the fact that I was fighting him. I dinnae understand why, but I kenned that, if he raped me whilst I was so helpless, it could easily destroy me. He robbed me of all chance to comfort myself with the fact that dishonoring me had not been easy for him."

"Mayhap by fighting to the bitter end, ye wouldnae feel as if ye had lost all your honor. He could ne'er have taken that from ye, Elspeth, no matter how much he violated you." He returned her somewhat tremulous smile. "Did he e'er say why?"

" 'Twas all because I refused him. He felt he was doing

me the greatest of honors by asking me to be his wife, and I spit on it. He told me what a poor choice I was and he obviously felt the sacrifice he had made by even thinking of wedding me deserved my most humble gratitude. My refusal was an insult he couldnae bear. He also thought I had some special gift."

"A gift?"

"Aye." She grimaced. "I do seem to be able to, weel, sense what people feel. 'Tis why I could almost always tell when someone lied to me. Still can. With Sir Colin I could sense when I was enraging him despite how pleasantly he spoke and how sweetly he smiled. 'Tis difficult to explain."

"I ken what ye try to say. Ye feel more keenly than others. Or see. Or smell. What matter? Ye can see behind the masks. 'Tis a fine gift."

"Oh, aye. 'Tis a gift from my mother, although she says mine is much keener than hers. It has helped my family elude a trap or two. It sometimes helps me in my healing work, for although pain isnae an emotion, I can sometimes sense where it is. Sadly, I can also sense when a person or an animal is dying. There is a look in the eyes, a smell, a feel to the skin, something that tells me that, even if the person is fighting with everything they have, they cannae win. They are soon to die. I try not to let too many people ken about that part of it. But Sir Colin kenned most of what I can do and he wanted it for his own, wanted to use it to gain power and riches."

Cormac nodded. "I can see how it might help a mon do that." He struggled to sit up only to have Elspeth hold him down, and the ease with which she could do so was dismaying. "We must hie back to the village. I left all of our belongings, the bairn, and the cat there. Aye, and your horse."

"How far are we from the village?" Elspeth asked as she rose to mix him a very mild sleeping potion.

"A mile, mayhap less. I was verra surprised that he stayed so close."

"Then I will go and get everything."

"Nay, we cannae stay here. Unless ... Did Sir Colin murder the poor soul who lived here?"

"Nay, the villagers did that. This is the witch's home."

"Her name was Anne Seaton. So 'tis probably the bairn's now."

"Aye, and we shall use it until ye are strong enough to travel." She slipped an arm around his shoulders, helping him sit up enough to drink the potion she had made for him. "Sir MacRae camped here so that he could be more comfortable as he committed his crimes. It seems Mistress Anne was a cousin of his."

"Blood will tell. She wasnae a good woman, lass, though she didnae deserve the death she was served with."

"Weel, I am nay so sure she didnae. Sir Colin said there are bodies buried here. That wee bairn was surely meant to be. His mother cleaned her womb of a few bairns, and if 'twas too late for that, she killed them ere they lived long enough to be seen. Sir Colin implied that there is a mon or two buried here as weel. For some reason she wanted this bairn to live. Drink this."

"What is this foul brew?"

"Something to ease your pain."

He drank it, grimacing at its bitter taste. "She kept this bairn to torment his father. She didnae christen the lad because, as she told the priest, bairns often die and she wanted the father to ken that his son had died unnamed and unshriven."

As she made him more comfortable in the bed, she shivered at his words. "Nay, not a good woman at all."

"Are ye going to tell the villagers?"

"I do hate to give them cause to think that what they did was just, but, aye, I will. If there is a mon or two buried behind this cottage, he or they may have a family who worry o'er what happened to him, who hunger to ken their fate, be it good or bad."

Cormac began to feel very groggy. "That brew wasnae just for the pain, was it?"

"Nay, 'twill make ye sleep for a wee while," she replied, smiling a little when he almost immediately went to sleep, and then she hurried to get dressed.

Elspeth decided to get rid of the bodies first. Using the blanket she had covered Sir Colin with, she dragged him and then the two guards into the woods. Despite what they had tried to do to her, she was sorry she did not have the strength to bury them. If her tale of bodies buried at Anne Seaton's cottage brought any of the men in the village out to investigate, she would have them see to it.

In her search for Cormac's horse, she found the other two guards and sighed. Her troubles had put a lot of blood on Cormac's hands. She tried to console herself with the knowledge that it had been self-defense, a battle for life and honor. The men had been mercenaries, and the worst of their breed, the sort who cared only about the coin. No man with any honor left would have joined with Sir Colin. She was glad that he had used such men and not dragged his own clansmen into it.

The ride to the village took all of her courage. It was more night than day and she had to fight against seeing danger in every shadow. As she walked into the inn, she almost smiled at the way the innkeeper and his wife gaped at her. She knew she looked appalling with her tattered dress and bruised face, but she calmly settled the account and went up to collect her things, the baby, and Muddy.

"Oh, m'lady," cried Dorcas as Elspeth stepped into the room. "What happened to ye and where is your bonny mon?"

"A long and troubled tale, I fear, Dorcas. I was taken

and Sir Cormac rescued me. He has a wound or two and so I have come to get our things, the bairn, and the cat." Elspeth smiled as she stepped up to the bed and a loudly purring Muddy demanded her attention. "Ye are a good cat," she told him as she scratched his head. "Ye tried to protect the bairn, didnae ye?"

"He did that." Dorcas showed Elspeth the scratches on her arm. "E'en from me."

"I am sorry."

"Nay, he meant no harm and your mon soothed him quick enough."

"Ye are a good soul to care for the bairn as ye have."

"He is just a wee bairn, isnae he? Black as the devil hisself, true enough, but just a bairn. It was wrong what they did."

"To the bairn, aye. I begin to think his mother was long o'erdue for a hanging. 'Tis just a shame it was done for all the wrong reasons. Could ye fetch me your priest, Dorcas? I have a few things I must tell him."

By the time Dorcas returned with the young priest, Elspeth was packed and very ready to leave. As she told him all she had learned of Anne Seaton, and all that had happened to her and Cormac, she was a little afraid he would swoon. It was clear he had never thought to deal with such dark events in such a tiny village. He told her he would come to the cottage in the morning with a few men and, perhaps, someone from the laird who held most of the land in the area. She then got him to christen the baby, whom she called Alan, naming her cousins Payton and Sorcha as godparents. Elspeth thanked Dorcas, gave the priest some money, and headed back to the cottage, battling exhaustion every step of the way.

"Where have ye been?" demanded Cormac as she stumbled into the cottage, carrying Alan and the cat.

Elspeth blinked and stared at Cormac, who had managed to sit up and was obviously thinking of getting out of bed. "Ye didnae sleep verra long at all," she said, setting Muddy down and handing Cormac the child. "Let me see to our things and the horses ere ye begin to scold me."

Feeling dizzy and weak from struggling to sit up, Cormac feared he would drop the child. He cautiously lay back down, settling the baby against his chest. When Muddy got on the bed to sprawl purring loudly at his side, he smiled. It was strange, but despite the pain of his wounds, he felt content, as if all was now as it should be and he could rest.

As soon as Elspeth finished unpacking, seeing to the horses, settling Alan in his bed, and checking Cormac's wounds, she stripped down to her thin chemise and crawled into bed next to Cormac. There did not seem to be any part of her that did not ache. She was glad that, despite the lurid bruises and ugly marks left by her bonds, she had no wounds that needed tending. She was simply too tired to do it. Taking hold of Cormac's hand, she told him everything she had done while in the village.

"Alan. A good name," Cormac said as he tugged his hand free, slid his arm around her shoulders, and tucked her up against his side. "Poor lass." He pressed a kiss to the top of her head. "And poor me. I had such lovely plans for this night."

Elspeth laughed softly then yawned. "So did I. E'en if I didnae ache all over, I am just too tired."

"And I would probably bleed all over you."

"Aye, ye would." She kissed his chest, then rubbed her cheek against his warm skin, reveling in the fact that he was alive and by her side. " 'Tis over."

Cormac rested his cheek against her hair. "Aye, ye are safe now."

"Ye dinnae think his heir or his clansmen will seek revenge?"

"Nay. His heir is the lad my cousin Mary is probably

wed to by now. He seemed a fair-minded lad. And although I wasnae there for verra long, I didnae get the feeling that his clan will be weeping much o'er Sir Colin's grave. 'Twas no secret amongst them what he had done to ye and intended to do. They willnae be surprised that he was killed because of it. Get some rest, angel. It sounds as if ye will be busy on the morrow. I fear I may not be of much help, either."

"Ye should be able to talk weel enough. If anyone needs to have some questions answered, I shall send them to you."

"Fair enough. Are ye going to tell Alan about his mother when he is old enough to ask about her?"

Elspeth sighed. "I dinnae ken. 'Tisnae a tale anyone would wish to hear about their mother. Then again, everyone here will ken the truth, so what will be gained by hiding it? I think I am just too weary to e'en worry about it just now. Good sleep, Cormac."

"Good sleep, angel."

Cormac stared up at the ceiling, smiling faintly at how quickly Elspeth fell asleep in his arms. His life had become very complicated since meeting her. When he had seen her tied to the bed, naked and helpless, he had known what Sir Colin had intended or what he had already accomplished, and his rage had been nearly blinding. It was not only Elspeth's troubles he had gotten himself deeply tangled up in, but Elspeth herself as well. He dared not even look into his heart. He was not free to do so. Yet he knew even now it was going to hurt when she left.

A part of him wanted to give up on his vow and run off with Elspeth. He could barely recall the emotions that had prompted the vow to Isabel years ago. Yet he could not do it. His parents continuously did all they could to blacken their name and that stain spread to their children. They gambled, whored, bred children, and cast them aside, nearly beggared their people, and were widely known as liars and cheats. Cormac had long ago decided that he would show the world that not all of his family were so lacking in honor, and had done his best to make his siblings understand the value of keeping one's word. He had given his word to stand by Isabel, vowed to love and honor her. She counted on him to keep his word. He could not fail her. He could not fail himself, either. Although he was deeply confused about his feelings at the moment, he was sure of one thing. He had made a vow and he would stand by it. He could only pray that he did not destroy them all by doing so.

It took more than one day to sort everything out. At times, Elspeth felt a strong urge to tell everyone to just go away, but she knew Anne Seaton's crimes needed to be confirmed, and so did the story she and Cormac told of how Sir Colin had died. The bodies of two men and three babies were found buried in Anne Seaton's kitchen garden. Elspeth's heart ached for them all, but mostly it ached for little Alan. He would have to know the truth about his mother someday and it would be a hard truth for anyone to accept. She was going to have to make sure that he was deeply loved. It might soften the blow and make it easier for him to understand that his mother's sins were hers alone, that there was no fault in him and no taint to be passed on to his children.

The laird's man produced the papers needed to show that the cottage and its lands now belonged to Alan. It was not much, but it was more than many another bastard held. She tried to get a father's name and gained no new information. The laird's man refused to tell her who had bought the cottage and the land for Anne Seaton, for he would not break a confidence. Elspeth compromised by telling the man that, if he ever felt he could give her the name, he was to send the information to Donncoill. She briefly considered leaving word that the man might have a son, but decided she needed to meet with and come to know any man who might try to claim the child. Alan's mother had left him with enough of a burden to bear. Elspeth had no intention of letting anyone take the boy unless she approved of him and felt certain that Alan would be loved.

Five days had come and gone before she and Cormac finally found themselves alone again. Although they had not made love, Elspeth felt they were closer than they had been before. When they were not dealing with the villagers, the laird's man, or the priest, they talked. Elspeth finally began to learn more about Cormac and about his past. Although Isabel's name occasionally slipped into the conversation, she appeared only as part of a tale about something else, hastily mentioned and hastily forgotten.

When Elspeth returned from fetching water on the sixth day and found Cormac fully dressed and on his feet, she knew that their time in the cottage was at an end. He was unsteady and needed to clutch the bedpost to stay upright, but she knew he would insist that he was strong enough to travel the last few miles to the king's court, and thus to Isabel. For a moment she tried to convince herself that he was in a hurry to reach the king's court because that was where he had told her family to find her, but she could not make herself believe it. She had hoped he would linger at the cottage until he was well enough for them to make love at least once more before confronting the problem of Isabel, but it was evident that that was not going to happen, either.

"Ye are going to fall flat on your face," she said as she put the bucket of water down on the table.

"I am nay that weak." He grimaced as he sat back down

on the bed. "I can ride. We dinnae have that far left to go."

"Why not wait another day or two? That wound to your leg was deep and ye lost a lot of blood. Aye, ye have some of your strength back, but if ye try to ride now, ye could easily use it all up."

"Then I will rest when I get there." He sighed and dragged his fingers through his hair. "Paul and Owen have certainly delivered our message to your family by now. Your family could already be looking for you. If ye arenae at court as we said ye would be, they could easily ride to Sir Colin's lands hot for blood. Ye have to be there when they come for ye, or that feud we may have avoided could begin in earnest. Ye dinnae want that, do ye?"

"Nay, of course not. So we leave on the morrow?"

"Aye. At first light."

As she crawled into bed beside him that night, Elspeth clung to him and fought to still her fears. She loved him so much she could not believe he could not love her back. A passion as fierce as the one they shared had to be born of love. Elspeth just prayed it was enough to make him finally walk away from Isabel, but she could not be sure it would be.

In all their talks, Elspeth had learned one very disturbing thing: Cormac's parents were little more than whores, thieves, and liars. She felt sympathy for Cormac and his siblings, unloved and shamed by their notorious parents, but he had obviously survived that harsh childhood. What troubled her was that Cormac seemed to feel the burden of restoring the family honor rested squarely upon his broad shoulders.

All good men held their honor dear, but Cormac held it dearer than most, so dear he could not even consider breaking his word. It was not just his own integrity he desperately needed to perserve, but that of his siblings.

His parents had made sure that the honor of their clan was little more than a jest, and Cormac was blindly determined to change that. To him, any wavering was akin to starting down the path his parents walked, and he could never do it. There was no gray for Cormac, only black and white. One either kept one's word, and thus one's honor, or one broke them both.

Which meant, she thought as she fought the urge to cry, his vow to Isabel was as good as chiseled in stone.

# Chapter Twelve

"I told ye it was foolish to climb back on a horse so soon," Elspeth scolded as she helped a pale, sweating Cormac into his bed.

They had barely made it to the inn Cormac always stayed at when coming to the king's court. For every foot of the last two miles Elspeth had expected Cormac to tumble off his horse and sprawl facedown in the dirt. She had bit her tongue against complaints and fretting so much she was surprised there was still one in her mouth. All she had been able to do was keep a close eye out for any new bleeding from his wounds.

"It may not have been the wisest thing I have ever done," Cormac conceded, smiling faintly as a muttering Elspeth took his clothes off. "Ye can scold me in a clear voice, Elspeth. I believe I am mon enough to endure it."

She just shook her head as she changed his bandages, cleaning and putting salve on his wounds, before covering them again with clean strips of linen. His eyes were closed by the time she was done, but his color was better. She tugged the blankets over him, annoyed at his stubbornness yet deeply relieved that he had not caused himself any serious harm.

Elspeth turned her attention to unpacking and tending to little Alan's needs. She knew some of her anger at Cormac came from the fact that she could not be sure why he had risked his health to get here. He claimed it was to meet with her family, to ensure that they were given no reason to ride against Sir Colin's clan. And yet, this was where he was headed when they had first joined forces, racing to answer Isabel's call. Elspeth knew she had slowed him down, made him hesitate, but she was not sure she had stopped him from returning to the woman.

When Cormac slept through the meal the maid brought, as well as the bath Elspeth indulged in, she was pleased even though she felt a little abandoned. As she crawled into bed beside him, he muttered her name as he slid his good arm around her and pulled her up next to his side. Then, with a sigh that sounded very much like satisfaction, he grew quiet again. *He reaches for me in his dreams,* she thought and tried to find some glimmer of hope in that.

Cormac winced because the bright sunlight hurt his eyes. It took him a moment to adjust to the light, but then he looked around, recognizing the inn he had so often stayed in. Elspeth was dressed in a pretty green gown and was just finishing a rather intricate braiding of her hair. Alan lay in the cradle they had brought with them from the cottage, murmuring to himself as he played with his toes. Muddy was sprawled on his back in the sun at the foot of the bed, looking big and disreputable. Cormac smiled. They were an odd little group, but the sight of them made him feel content.

"Ah, ye are awake at last," Elspeth said, smiling at him as she walked to the side of his bed.

"Nay, let me try to sit up without any help." There were several twinges as he did so, but Cormac felt stronger than he had in days. "Just how long have I been asleep?"

"Weel, ye went to sleep shortly after we got here. Then ye woke up yesterday to eat and have a lad help ye see to your needs. And all through last night. 'Tis now noon of the second day."

"Good God." He shook his head. "Nay wonder I am near to starving."

"The lad should be here soon with some food, and if ye wish, he will help ye clean up a bit."

"Aye, that would be welcome." He frowned when she donned her cape. "Where are ye going?"

"To the court. I think that is the best place to leave word for my kinsmen, dinnae ye?"

"Oh, aye." Cormac inwardly scolded himself for feeling as if she were deserting him and looking a little too eager to do so. "Just make sure that the ones ye tell plan to linger here for a while. E'en better would be someone who kens your family. A kinsmon perhaps." He frowned as he thought of Elspeth wandering alone amongst all those lusty courtiers. "Mayhap ye should wait until I can take ye there."

Elspeth laughed softly and kissed his cheek. "I will be fine. If ye wish, the lad can watch Alan, although the bairn should soon be asleep and I dinnae intend to be gone too long."

Even as Elspeth went out, the innkeeper's young son Robbie came in, carrying a large tray of food. Cormac put aside his concerns as he saw to his personal needs, filled his empty belly, and then got himself as thoroughly washed as one could without actually getting in a tub. He only felt slightly tired by all that activity and that pleased him. A long, uninterrupted sleep had obviously been just what he had needed. With Robbie's help, he walked around the room a few times until he knew he was leaning more on the boy than he was actually walking.

After washing off the sweat those exertions had raised, Cormac climbed back into bed, weary but content. It would be a few more days before he could walk very far, if only because he needed to build up his strength, but he was healing at an acceptable speed. After a short rest, he knew there was one thing he was certainly recovered enough to indulge in. It had been far too long since he and Elspeth had made love and he ached for her. The wound on his arm was healed enough that Elspeth could already remove the stitches she had put in. She had said that they were mostly used to try to reduce the size of the scar he would have. It was his leg that would cause some awkwardness, but then he grinned. Elspeth would just have to do most of the work.

As Robbie started to leave, Cormac glanced at the boy's fair hair and was suddenly, sharply, reminded of why he had been planning to come to this place. *Isabel.* He sighed and asked the boy to bring him a quill, ink, and parchment. Within moments he had written a short message to Isabel and sent the boy to deliver it to her. He then lay in bed, staring at the ceiling and wondering why he felt as if he had just betrayed Elspeth.

Elspeth frowned as she wove her way through the crowd of people who seemed to be everywhere in the bailey, the halls, and the chambers of the king's court. Just as she began to think that she had wasted her time, that there was no one in this pack of well-dressed beggars she could leave a message with, she spotted her foster cousin James Drummond. She roughly made her way through the crowd, breathing a sigh of relief when she reached him even as he started to leave with two other men.

"James," she cried, stumbling forward and grabbing him by the arm.

"God's teeth, Elspeth!" He laughed as he hugged her and kissed her on each cheek. "I have heard some dire tales about you—so dire that I was soon to ride to Donncoill and see what was wrong." He glanced at his two companions. "I willnae be going with ye, lads. Mayhap we will meet up later."

After watching the two young men walk away, Elspeth looked at her handsome cousin and smiled faintly. "Ye didnae introduce me to your friends, James." Her smile widened when he blushed faintly and looked a little uneasy. "Lecherous?"

James sighed and nodded. "Good friends and I would trust them to guard my back weel in a fight."

"But ye arenae sure ye would trust them near any of the lasses in your family." She laughed when he reluctantly nodded, then grew serious as she braced herself and asked, "Have ye heard any news of Payton?"

"Weel, I have heard a few whispers that he is dead, which caused far too many women to start weeping, if ye ask me, but I dinnae believe it."

"I dinnae want to believe it, either, but I saw him felled by an arrow." She gave James a very brief accounting of her troubles with Sir Colin and welcomed his comforting hug.

"Everyone kens I am here, Elspeth. If Payton were dead or still lost, I would have heard something."

"Ye hadnae heard about me."

"Ah, weel, I suspect that is because they kenned exactly what happened to ye, and e'en though they may think ye are still with Sir Colin, they ken that ye are alive. As soon as it was decided what needed to be done, I would have been sent for. Just as I would have been sent for if Payton were dead or a hunt was on to find him."

"Of course. Thank ye. I admit that my hope for him was fading a wee bit. But ye are exactly right. Had Payton been killed or was still lost, our family wouldnae have left ye here to play with your lecherous friends."

"Lechery can be very hard work, lass." James chuckled when she gave him a disgusted look. "Now I must needs find ye a place to stay. I dinnae think there are any rooms free here, but it willnae take long to find out."

"I have a room, James," she said quietly, and waited patiently for him to think things through.

"Elspeth, ye cannae share a room at an inn with that mon," James said, keeping his voice low and watching the people around them to make sure no one came close enough to hear him. "Ye must ken what people will think."

"Aye." She shrugged, glancing around at the crowd and frowning when she saw a rather voluptuous blond woman staring at her somewhat intently. "They can say all they wish, talk until their foolish tongues fall from their mouths. I dinnae care. I will stay with Cormac."

For a long time James stared at her; then he cursed. "He is the one, isnae he?"

She smiled a little sadly as she nodded. "He is."

"But he is—weel, 'tis said that he is verra deeply involved with a woman. Has been for years, though God alone kens why."

"I ken it. Lady Isabel Douglas, she of the four dead husbands. He bound himself to her with a vow whilst still a lad, but youthful folly or nay, Cormac deeply believes in holding to a vow." She shook her head. "I understand it all—I truly do—and good sense should have told me to stay faraway from such a tangle."

"But ye couldnae find any good sense."

"Oh, it was there. I just ignored it. I love him. I think

I have loved him since I was a child. This may be the biggest and most foolish risk I have e'er taken, but I had to try. Can ye understand that, James?"

"Aye, I can understand. I just wish ye had chosen to gamble in something where ye had a better chance of winning. Any mon would be a fool to turn ye aside for a woman like Lady Isabel, but, sweeting, I do think ye may have given your heart to a fool."

"Weel, there are a few things I have learned since I began this, which if I had kenned them at the start might have made me hesitate." She frowned, then shook her head. "Nay. I still would have thrown the dice. I just might have prayed o'er them a little harder." She saw young Robbie wend his way through the crowd and hand the fulsome blonde a message. "Who is that woman? The one the fair-haired lad is standing with?"

"That is the notorious Lady Isabel. Elspeth, are ye ill? Ye have gone quite pale."

That did not surprise her. Elspeth felt quite ill. She knew, deep in her suddenly aching heart, that Cormac had sent Isabel a message. He had not given up on the woman. Elspeth wanted to believe that he was simply doing the honorable thing, that he would have to see Isabel in order to end their long, tangled affair, but she dared not nurse that hope.

"I think I am but tired." She kissed James's cheek and could tell by the sympathetic look in his eyes that he knew what really ailed her. "I am sure we will see each other again whilst we are both wandering about this place. Just let the family ken that all is weel if they arrive and find ye ere I find them."

"Agreed. Elspeth, take care. Isabel isnae a woman to cross swords with. Most people believe she has killed at least one, if not all, of her husbands. She is a whore, but a clever one. She has bedded nearly every powerful mon at court and doesnae hesitate to use them to her own advantage. The woman could destroy you."

"I ken it. And in truth, she could be able to order the king himself about and it wouldnae matter. She only has to do one thing."

"Ah, bed your bonny knight."

"Weel, aye, that might do it." The mere thought of Isabel and Cormac in a passionate embrace made bile sting the back of her throat. "Actually, I was thinking that all she has to do is hold Cormac to his vow." She saw Robbie start to leave. "I will see ye later, James. Dinnae worry about me."

"Easier said than done," he muttered as he watched Elspeth leave and noticed how closely Lady Isabel watched her.

Elspeth collapsed against the cool stone wall of the inn and tried to get her riotous emotions under control. She had caught Robbie, and since none had sworn him to secrecy, he had quickly told her that Cormac had indeed sent a note to Isabel and what Isabel had said in reply. Without prompting, he threw in a few well-chosen pieces of gossip about the woman that made Elspeth wonder at Cormac's blindness. When even beardless boys knew what Isabel was, it was past time for the man to pay attention. Although the boy had no idea what Cormac had said, Isabel's answer had been enough to give Elspeth a very good idea. Cormac had told Isabel that he was here, had answered her summons, and was ready to meet with her. Isabel had told him that he was not to come to her; she would send for him. A few small coins had been enough to get Robbie to swear he would not tell Cormac about their little chat.

Not a very romantic exchange, she thought, but still a

threat. It was hard to conquer her hurt and anger, however. She could not face Cormac until she did. There was still a chance for her to win. Instinct told her that Isabel would never let go of Cormac, but he might be prepared to end their long relationship. Despite his beliefs, could he really cling to a vow that had brought him so little after ten long years?

Elspeth straightened up and took a deep breath to steady herself. She still had a chance. Until he actually chose Isabel, it was foolish to give up. She had known that he was coming here to see Isabel, that the woman had sent for him. It was foolish to believe that one small exchange of messages meant she had already lost her gamble. Elspeth headed toward the door of the inn. She had one night, maybe more, to make her mark. Even if she was about to be cast aside for an old mistress and an old vow, she would not waste what little time she might have left with Cormac wallowing in fear and regret. Isabel was not in his bed yet and Elspeth planned to fill it so completely that Isabel would find it very crowded even if Cormac did choose her.

When she entered the room, she found Cormac staring at the ceiling and frowning. Isabel's message had evidently not pleased him. Good. Perhaps, in her arrogance, the woman would err. Any man would find it galling to be sent for and then told to wait. Elspeth inwardly shook her head. She would not hope, would not try to see a promise that was not there. She would take it one hour at a time. The ax might be about to fall, but until it did, she would ignore how it hung over her head.

Cormac watched Elspeth shed her cloak, then move to check on a sleeping Alan. Now that he had contacted Isabel, he could see his path more clearly. Elspeth was fever in his blood, but Isabel was the woman he had loved for ten years. He had feelings for Elspeth that he could not deny. He was undoubtedly infatuaded with the girl, but that could not be allowed to make him break his word to Isabel. It all sounded so reasonable, yet it did little to settle his sudden unease.

As Elspeth told him about meeting her cousin James at court, Cormac relaxed. The rest of the day passed in pleasant conversation, play with Alan, and a fine meal. As Elspeth settled the baby in his bed, however, Cormac felt his uncertainties return. He felt as if he stood on the edge of some great precipice with a dangerously strong wind pushing at his back.

He had just arranged a future meeting with a woman he had been involved with for ten years, a woman who was free and whom he had vowed to wed. Yet as he watched Elspeth undress, he knew he would continue with his plan to indulge in a long, lust-filled night with her. He reminded himself that Elspeth had set herself in his bed and asked for no promises. She shared the passion that ate at him and never pressed for more. She also knew all about Isabel, about the vow he had made. Despite that stern lecture, when Elspeth slipped into bed beside him and he took her into his arms, he had the gnawing feeling that he was betraying someone. But who? Isabel because he felt such a need for Elspeth and had actually considered breaking his word for her sake? Or Elspeth because he bedded her even though he knew he would soon have to set her aside?

"Ye look troubled, Cormac," Elspeth said as she snuggled up close to his warmth.

"Do I? Mayhap that is because I ache, but I am nay sure I have the strength or ability to satisfy that hunger," he said, sliding his hands down her back and gently caressing her taut little buttocks.

Elspeth smoothed her hand down over his stomach, smiling faintly at the way he trembled gently beneath her touch. She found him hard and eager for her. Almost idly, she stroked him, loving the way he murmured his pleasure, the way his breathing grew unsteady, and the sound of his heartbeat growing faster beneath her ear.

There was no doubt about his desire for her. Elspeth decided her last toss of the dice would be to use that passion to its fullest, to revel in it, and force Cormac to do the same. She was going to leave him so sated, so filled with heated, delicious memories that he would never be free of her, no matter how far away he might send her.

Cormac groaned as Elspeth covered his stomach with soft kisses and teasing strokes of her tongue. When she took her kisses lower, he shuddered. Raising himself up on his uninjured arm, he watched her love him with her mouth. He threaded his fingers through her hair and held it out of the way so that he could see her tongue stroke him and watch as he slipped in and out of her mouth. He could not think of anything that had given him as much pleasure in his life, and he fought for the strength to enjoy it for as long as he could.

Finally, unable to endure any more, he tugged her up his body. They both gasped with pleasure when she lowered herself onto him. Cormac pulled her face down to his and kissed her—a slow, thorough kiss that revealed his hunger and made her share it.

His hands on her slim hips, he urged her to move, but she just smiled. "Do ye mean to drive me mad, angel mine?"

"Aye, mayhap I do." She caressed his broad chest with her hands and moved ever so slightly. " 'Tis always so quick. I always wish it to last so much longer. I just wish to be still and feel."

"Feel what, love?"

He watched her close her eyes. Her head was tilted back slightly, her long hair brushing against his thighs. There was such a look of pleasure on her face, a beautiful expression of innocent yet sensual delight, it was almost enough to finish him.

"To feel ye inside me," she whispered. "To feel how ye fill me."

The rich huskiness of her voice only added to his desperate need for her, and not at all surprised to hear his voice tremble, he said, "Elspeth, my sweet angel, if ye have even the smallest wish that we take this journey together, ye best move. Now."

Elspeth moved. At first it was slow and easy, as they both fought to cling to the knife's edge for as long as possible. Then their hunger consumed them. She needed no urging from Cormac, knew instinctively when it was time to cease playing with each other. His words of encouragement as she rode him were unnecessary, but she loved the sound of them. Even as her release tore through her body, he gripped her tightly by the hips and held her still as he plunged deep inside of her to spill his seed. Still trembling faintly from the power of it, Elspeth collapsed in his arms.

"Ah, love, ye will age me before my time," Cormac said, brushing a kiss over her forehead. "All things considered, I believe I must reconsider the number of times we can enjoy this dance tonight."

"Oh? How many times were ye planning on *dancing*?"

"Fifteen." He laughed at her look of shock, then kissed her when she scowled at him even as her eyes sparkled with laughter.

"We wouldnae be able to walk for a month," she said as she slipped out of bed and fetched a damp cloth to clean them off with. "I think six at the most."

He laughed again, and after they had washed themselves, he watched her sidle up the bed a little to place the cloth in a bowl of water at the side of the bed. As she turned back to him, he caught her around the waist and pulled her close. Her beautiful breasts were level with his mouth and he took quick advantage of that.

Elspeth combed her fingers through his hair as he feasted on her breasts. She murmured with a mixture of pleasure and regret when he moved his kisses to dance them along her ribs. Pleasure tumbled through her as he covered her stomach with tender nips and heated strokes of his tongue. It was not until he hooked her leg over his shoulder that she realized what he planned to do. She suddenly became all too aware of how they were positioned, how much he could see, how bright the candles shone, and she tensed.

"Nay, angel, nay," he murmured, licking the inside of her thigh. "Let me pleasure ye. Let me taste your sweetness."

It was to be a night to remember, for him as well as for her, she reminded herself. There was no place for shyness or hesitation. She was in a fight for her very heart. Closing her eyes, she willed herself to relax and think not of what he could see, only of what he could make her feel. Silently, she gave him permission to do as he pleased.

He proceeded to drive her mad. Several times she reached out for the sharp pleasure of release, only to have him somehow hold her back. He teased and taunted her with that rich prize until she was nearly begging him and then he let her soar. Even as she was still trembling from that delight, he started all over again. A second time. A third. Until Elspeth collapsed, almost senseless. When she recovered, she paid him back in kind.

They dozed, then made love again. Elspeth was a little astounded at how often they reached for each other. They were like greedy children gorging on sweets. She sensed the same desperate need in Cormac that drove her. Dawn was lighting the sky as they again soared to the heights together. She collapsed in his arms, certain she could not even move a finger.

"How is your leg?" she finally asked, then yawned as she slid off him and curled up at his side.

"The left one is fine. The right one aches a wee bit. The middle one will need a splint."

Elspeth laughed and lazily swatted him. "Wretch. Ye cannae blame me. I believe I was sleeping peacefully when ye ravished me awake." She thought idly that, after the night they had just indulged in, if she had one tiny scrap of modesty left it would be a miracle.

"Ravished ye awake, hmmm? I like the sound of that." He yawned even as he said, "Alan is humming."

Hearing the soft drone coming from Alan's cradle, she smiled and closed her eyes. "That is fine. He will do that for a wee while, sleep another hour or two, then start again. I have time for a nice nap."

"Ye can sleep through that?" He slid his hand down her back and brought it to rest on the soft curve of her backside.

" 'Tis a happy sound."

"Mayhap he wants some attention." Cormac did not think he had ever felt so completely exhausted or content.

"Aye, but if I give it to him, he will expect it every morn at this hour."

"Ah, weel, ignore him then." He smiled when he heard her sleepy giggle. "Have your rest then, angel. I promise to leave ye unravished. In truth, I dinnae think I have another ravish left in me anyway."

A few hours later Cormac woke to the sound of Alan humming and sucking on his fingers. At the same time, Elspeth's fingers and tongue were bringing Cormac swiftly to the point of aching need. He reached down, grabbed her by the ankle, and swung her around so that he could return the compliment. He gave her her first release quickly, then settled back for a long, leisurely enjoyment, knowing that this time they had the will to slowly savor what they could make each other feel. Then Elspeth did something very clever and exciting with her tongue and Cormac decided he might just be wrong about his powers of endurance.

Elspeth grimaced a little as she left the sleeping Cormac's lax hold and slipped out of bed to get dressed, for she ached in some very interesting places. She washed and quickly put her clothes on, for there was a slightly chilly bite to the air. As she fed Alan, she watched Cormac sleep. She felt oddly proud of having so thoroughly exhausted him, yet a little embarrassed about some of the things she had done to put him in that state.

She shook away her doubts. If the man did not remember the night they had just spent with fondness and a return of the passion they had shared, he did not deserve another one like it. She had done her best and, Elspeth smiled, she had enjoyed every wild, sweaty minute of it.

Now, she thought as she settled Alan back in his cradle, it was time to leave Cormac alone. After some of the things she had done and allowed him to do, she was not sure she wanted to face him right away anyway. A little time away to calm herself and accept her own behavior would probably be for the best. The important thing, however, was to give Cormac some time alone to think. He had not had much of that since he had led her out of Sir Colin's tower room. They had been together constantly, battling Sir Colin and their own passions. As she crept out of their room, intent on finding herself something to eat, she prayed that whatever thinking Cormac did, it led him down the path she wanted and needed him to go down.

# Chapter Thirteen

Even though her body still ached, Elspeth smiled faintly as she left the inn and began to walk to the court. They were the pleasant aches caused by vigorous lovemaking and she savored the memories provoked by each one. Her skin still felt flushed from the kisses and sweet words Cormac had brushed against her flesh. Elspeth felt sure that she had finally reached his heart, that she had at last stirred far more than his base lusts. Surely no man could speak such intoxicating words to a woman or make love to her so sweetly unless he loved. The three little words she ached to hear would soon follow. Cormac just needed time to think about everything and see the truth and she would idle the whole day away if needed to give him that time.

"So ye are alive," drawled a deep voice from directly behind her.

Elspeth squeaked with fright, whirled around, and then

squealed with joy when she saw who stood there. "Payton! Thanks be to God!" She flung herself into his arms and covered his face with kisses. "I feared that foul mon had murdered you."

" 'Twas a near thing, lass. They did kill those two lads with us. Ere I bled to death, however, I was found by a shepherd and nursed, and word was sent to Donncoill." Payton glanced around, took Elspeth by the arm, and dragged her over to sit on a bench in front of a tavern. He quietly urged the four men with him to go have an ale, then turned to face Elspeth. "Did Sir Colin hurt you?"

"Nay. He had no time ere Cormac rescued me," Elspeth replied, clutching Payton's hand in hers, almost afraid to believe that he was really there, still a little pale, but alive and well.

"So his friends said. But why bring ye here? Why not ride to us?"

"Cormac felt this was the shortest and safest way to come. And this was where he was headed ere I joined him."

"Aye, to see the fair Isabel."

There was a hard, almost sneering tone to his voice, and she frowned. "Do ye ken the lady?"

"Some."

The way Payton said that one word and would not meet her gaze told Elspeth a great deal. "Ye have bedded her."

"Once."

"Only once?"

" 'Twas enough." Payton sighed and ran a hand through his thick red-gold hair. "I dinnae ken how to explain it to ye, lass. She devours a mon. I dinnae think I was supposed to be aware enough to see, but there was this look in her eye that stole all the delight away. I have ne'er believed in such creatures, but if there is such a demon as a succubus, she would be one."

"Ah, poor Cormac," she murmured.

"How can ye feel sorry for the fool? The way ye say his name tells me that ye feel something for him, yet how can ye feel pity for him when he chases after a whore like Isabel?"

"How can I not? And 'tis not pity, truly—just sympathy. Aye, I care for him. I love the poor, blind fool. I think he may love me, but he doesnae see it yet. Ten years of loyalty to Isabel makes him blind to all else. And he has made a vow to her. 'Twould take too long to explain, but trust me, it could weel take more than I can do or give him to make him break a vow. I think I have begun to make him see the truth, but I am nay so sure I wish to put it to the test just yet. Sadly, I dinnae believe I have any more time to play this game. Ye are here and I believe I just saw that succubus slinking toward the inn where I left Cormac, abed and unprotected." Elspeth frowned as she quickly stood up. "In truth, that black-hearted sorceress shouldnae be going near him at all. She said she would send for him, not come and find him."

"Have ye met her?" Payton asked, idly watching the come-hither sway of Isabel's hips as she walked toward the inn.

"Aye." Elspeth poked him in the arm to gain his attention and frowned at his unrepentant grin.

"No harm in looking at the beauty, lass." He grew serious again. "She has seen ye as a threat."

"Me?" Elspeth found that almost laughable, for in her eyes, Isabel was all that men claimed to crave.

"Aye, ye." He smiled faintly and kissed her on the cheek. "Ye are a beautiful woman, Elspeth."

"But she—"

"I ken it. She is beautiful in ways the poets and minstrels trill about. That doesnae change the fact that ye, too, are beautiful. And Isabel is verra ugly inside, lass. She kens it and she also sees that your beauty goes to the bone."

"Cormac hasnae been completely faithful to her for these past ten years."

"Aye, but I would wager there were none like you. You are no tavern slut or common wench. Ye are someone he could marry, someone who could take the heart that bitch has kept clutched in her fist for so long. She goes now to tighten her grip, to recall him to that love he has sworn for her."

"Oh. And remind him of his vow. That is somewhat distressing," she murmured, but her mind and heart were screaming at her to move, to race to the inn and try to stop what Isabel was going to do.

"I will wait here for you."

Elspeth sighed, not surprised that Payton had guessed her feelings, but not sure she liked it. "I am nay sure it is wise to run o'er there. I may be tempted to try to make him break his vow and that would nay serve me weel in the end. And I cannae be his strength either, e'en if he was looking for some to fight her allure."

"And why not? The mon has given her ten years of his life. When the rest of us lads were romping freely through lust's fields, he was following her, believing her a poor martyr to her kinsmen's greed. Just because he continues on that path doesnae mean he likes it still, doesnae mean he has no doubts, that the bond hasnae been weakened or e'en broken. No one likes to think that he has wasted ten years, that for all his sacrifice and hurt, he has no more than he had at the start of the ordeal."

"Let us just say that he has finally thought of some way to break his vow and hold on to his honor. All ye have just said should give him the strength he needs to cast her aside."

"Aye and nay. He may wish to do it, but if he does, he admits that he has wasted ten years. The mon may weel need a strong nudge to do that. Go, lass. Let him see what he could have. Let him see the worth of what he now holds compared to what he continues to reach for. Ye dinnae and ye will e'er wonder if it would have helped."

"I dinnae wish to actually see and hear how badly I have lost my gamble," she whispered.

"Because ye gave all that any lass can give a mon?"

"How could ye ken that?" Elspeth worried that there was some look she carried that told Payton she was no longer chaste.

"I ken how ye think, lass, for we have e'er thought alike. Ye want the mon—a mon who feels tied to another. I suspect ye looked at the problem of Isabel, gathered what knowledge ye could, and quickly saw the bitch for what she is. Since there was no need to respect the woman's claim on Cormac, ye decided to turn him your way. And how to do that, how to catch and hold a mon who believes himself in love with another? By giving him everything, by holding him close and warm, by seeping into his blood and heart, and by feeding his want until that too belongs to you."

"Ye think ye are so verra clever, dinnae ye?" she grumbled.

"Weel, aye, I am." He met her look of disgust with a wide grin. " 'Tis what I would do, lass. I would try to make my lover see only my face, crave only my touch. If my lover wavered, undecided, I would want to be sure I have left enough need and joy in heart and mind so that, if I had to leave, my memory would refuse to be shaken off. Aye, and mayhap the change of heart I sought in my lover would come once I was gone."

"I am a coward."

Payton laughed softly and hugged her. "Nay, just reluctant to be hurt. Only a fool wouldnae hesitate to have her heart broken. Ye are no fool. I wish I could assure ye that there will be no hurt dealt, but I havenae seen ye and that fool together. I cannae judge. All I can do is tell ye to stiffen that bonny backbone and face it, put yourself in his sight to remind him he now has a choice. If he is too much the fool to take it, if he cannae see that a vow made to a whore isnae one that should be kept, I will be right here, lass, ready to take ye home."

She leaned back and eyed him sternly. "And ye willnae go and *speak* to him if he does prove to be a fool."

"Cannae I?"

"Nay, ye cannae. This is all my doing. I saw what I wanted and I reached for it. If I get my hand slapped away, 'tis my fault. I didnae e'en stop when I realized there was far more to fight than another woman, that there was this tangle of vows and honor and Cormac's need to clean away the stain his parents have soaked their names in. I dinnae need my kinsmen rushing in to repay some imagined insult with their fists or their swords. The decision was mine and mine alone. In truth, the mon was verra hard to seduce." She smiled faintly when Payton laughed.

"A gentlemon, eh?"

"Verra much so and all knotted up with thoughts of all he owed me and the Murrays."

"But ye overcame all of that."

"Aye." She blushed faintly. "I discovered that what my mither told me was true. I am like her. I felt what he felt. I kenned that he desired me. 'Twas odd, and a bit of a shock, when he first kissed me."

"I have always wondered on the truth of that," said Payton, his beautiful eyes alight with interest. "I fear I scoffed at such things. I felt it all carried the taint of magic, of some romantic imagining."

Elspeth nodded. "So did I. Aye, and I was most embarrassed to hear my own mither speak of such things. But I swear to ye, Payton 'tis the truth. I felt his desire. It fed my own, intertwined with it, and I think, in some small way, he felt the same. 'Tis verra difficult to explain, for I am nay sure I understand it.''

"It may be born of the same thing that helps ye tell when someone is lying.''

"Ah, aye, some odd gift that aids me in feeling what others feel. 'Twould explain a lot.''

"So ye should feel more sure of yourself, more able to confront Cormac, for ye must ken what he feels.''

"Some, aye. The desire, the gentleness, e'en a caring. But I also feel his confusion, his doubt. Aye, and his pain. I ken that I have made him happy, and if not for Isabel and a vow made, he would be mine without question. But there is an Isabel and there is a vow, and the conflicts I have raised in him concerning that woman, and mayhap his own honor, have made him verra unhappy. I fear I didnae have enough time to turn him completely, and I also fear he hasnae had enough time to decide what he wants or what he really needs. Yet ye are right: I must face it.'' She pulled free of his light embrace and took a deep breath to steady herself. "The moment of truth is upon me and I cannae stay here hiding from it.''

"I pray ye will find the truth ye need.'' Payton kissed her on the cheek.

"I pray I do as weel, but be prepared to leave this place. If I find that he is still caught tightly in Isabel's web, that he cannae e'en consider that there may be a way to end the tight bond of his youthful vow, I willnae wish to stay here.''

"Not e'en to fight for him?''

"I have done that since escaping Sir Colin's hold. If all I have done isnae enough to make him at least hesitate to return to Isabel, then I shallnae linger at his side.'' She started to walk toward the inn. "I just pray that, if he chooses to cling to that bitch, I can control my hurt and anger enough to depart with some scrap of dignity.''

* * *

"Isabel," Cormac cried in surprise as the woman stepped quietly into the room. "Ye said ye would send for me."

He eased himself up into more of a seated position against the bed pillows. The walking he had just done may indeed have strengthened his legs, but for the moment, it left him as weak as a babe and he cursed the ill timing of her visit. Cormac would have liked to face her clear-headed and steady on his feet. He realized that he also wished she had not come to him in the room he shared with Elspeth. What puzzled him was that he did not feel embarrassed to have Isabel see him sprawled on the bed he shared with his lover, but he did feel that he was betraying Elspeth in some way.

"I couldnae wait to see you, my dearest love," Isabel said as she hurried to his side of the bed and took his hand in hers.

"Nay? 'Twas ye who said I must wait to see you."

She tensed as she heard the distinct sound of a small child babbling. Her gaze lit upon the large basket and the small child contentedly playing with its toes. She grimaced with distaste at the sight of it as well as the huge gray cat scated next to the child, watching her with what she felt was a steady, malevolent look in its yellow eyes.

"Yours?" she asked.

"Oh, nay, Elspeth rescued them. The bairn was cast aside to die and the cat was being tormented."

Isabel studied him through narrowed eyes, hoping he saw the look as a flirtatious one cast from beneath lowered lashes, and not the wary perusal it was. Matters were worse than she had realized. Cormac had not yet kissed her, had not even made an attempt to do so. She could see none of that desperate hunger in his gaze that she had become so accustomed to. The little Murray bitch was obviously keeping him well satisfied. But should she display a jealous anger, or should she be hurt and tearful, or should she just simply pretend that the Murray woman did not even exist?

She decided to get angry first. If he reacted badly, she could always resort to tears after that, pretending the anger was bred of her pain. Cormac always weakened when she cried. When he attempted to soothe her, while his sympathy was strong, she had always been able to steer him in the direction she wished him to go. At the moment, that was as far away from skinny Elspeth Murray as she could push him. She would try to do it without revealing her secret, but if forced to it, she had one very strong weapon to use—something that would surely pull Cormac back to her side and keep him there.

Cormac was hers. She had taken his innocence, and although she suspected he had not been completely faithful to her, she felt sure that he had strayed only a few times. He saw her as a sweet innocent, a victim ill used by her family and her husbands. Isabel found that both amusing and enchanting. Cormac was also handsome, young, strong, and virile. Perhaps a little too virile, she mused, for three times she had tried to rid herself of his child. He was her creation and the one true constant in her life. He gave her love, more faithfulness than any other, honor, and gallantry, and she knew she deserved none of it. She had no intention of losing all that, however, and certainly not to some little woman from a clan whose only claim to reknown seemed to be their skill at breeding.

"Are ye afraid your lover will catch us together?" she said, her voice holding a tempered sharpness.

"Isabel," Cormac began. Then he paused to fight a strong sense of resentment, for he knew now that Isabel had been no virgin when they had first lain together. So, too, had she bedded down with four husbands and, if rumor was to believed, a few lovers as well. She had no right to condemn him, especially when they were more often apart than together.

Then he sought for the understanding he had always felt before. Isabel had not chosen any of her husbands and he had no proof that she had taken any lovers. The trials they had suffered through were not of her making. Cormac could sympathize, but suddenly, he knew that he would not allow her to sharpen her tongue on Elspeth, nor demean what he and Elspeth shared. It was, perhaps, time for Isabel to return a little of the vast amount of understanding he had always shown her.

"Elspeth isnae your concern," he said cooly, but stroked the back of her hand a gentle caress intended to soften the harshness of his words.

"How can ye say that, my love?"

He shrugged. "I doubt I can make ye understand. Elspeth has saved my life not once, but twice. I owe her and her clan more than I can e'er repay. She and I are friends." He was a little surprised to realize that he meant that wholeheartedly. " 'Tis all ye need to ken."

*Friends?* Isabel thought. She had the feeling Cormac would never call her a friend. That meant that Elspeth already held a part of Cormac she herself had never reached, and that enraged Isabel. He was slipping away from her. She could feel it, hear it in the coolness of his voice. Isabel convulsively tightened her grip upon his hand, ignoring the frown he sent her way.

"I am sorry," she said with what she prayed was an appropriate contriteness. "I fear her presence at your side has preyed upon my mind. E'er since I saw her, I have feared that she would take ye away from me. 'Tis why I pushed ye away at first, thought to make ye wait. 'Twas naught but jealousy speaking."

Her evident unhappiness plucked at his guilt, although

it was neither as strong nor as swift to arrive as he felt it ought to be. This was the woman he had pledged himself to, the woman he might well be marrying very soon. There should be no secrets between them and yet he felt no urge to confess or apologize.

He hugged her closer, wrapping his arm around her shoulders as she sat down on the bed and gently pressed herself against his chest. Despite not having held her for almost a year, he felt not even the faintest flicker of lust. He told himself it was because she was unhappy, needed soothing not seducing, but he did not really believe himself.

"Ye have no cause to be jealous," he lied, another first with Isabel that did not cause him as much unease as it ought to.

"I could not bear to lose you, Cormac."

"That can ne'er happen, Isabel. We are pledged."

"I ken that I have no right to hold fast to you. I should release ye from that vow we made when we were nay more than bairns. Selfishly, I dinnae, and I force ye to be alone. 'Tis just that I need ye so. Ye are the only good thing in my sad life, my only source of joy. Without your love to keep me strong, I would simply wither and die. But I must nay condemn ye to sharing my misery."

Her words were spoken in a soft, tremulous voice, her sadness clear to hear. Cormac knew he should immediately swear his devotion, repeat his pledge, and then make love to her. Yet he suddenly felt as if they were acting out some strange, almost morbid play. He grew and changed, Isabel grew and changed, husbands and lovers came and went, yet this remained the same. Isabel bemoaned her selfishness and hinted at setting him free, and he assured her that he wished only to be with her. At the moment, he felt no inclination to do that, and that both astonished and dismayed him.

For ten long years he had faithfully uttered the words she now waited for. They should come easily yet they remained locked inside of him. He felt angry over her demands. Had he not proven his devotion time and time again over the last ten years? Was he not here, having raced to her side yet again? And despite Elspeth's place in his life, had he not immediately sent word to Isabel that he had arrived and meekly accepted her demand that he wait to be called? How much more assurance could the woman need?

Something was seriously wrong. Something had changed. Cormac felt none of the biting hunger he had always felt upon seeing Isabel. He could not even feel that the lack of lust was due solely to having spent himself in Elspeth's arms but hours ago, yet it made a reasonable excuse and he clutched at it. A little voice in his head was advising him to look more closely, to open his eyes and see that he was free of Isabel, even hinting that there were ways to break his pledge yet keep his honor, but he ruthlessly silenced it.

Cormac refused to accept that he had wasted ten years of his life or, far worse, had played the faithful fool for that long. He did not want to think that he had mistakenly locked himself into a vow he could not, would not break, but would always regret. It was just that he was tired, that he had thoroughly sated himself in Elspeth's soft arms. The infatuation he suffered needed time to fade. Soon all of the old feelings Isabel had always stirred in him would return. It would all be all right soon. He just had to wait a little while.

"Cormac?" Isabel pressed when he continued to sit there, silent and brooding.

She kissed the hollow near his ear, something she knew he really liked. Isabel was stunned when she felt him tense beneath the touch of her lips. He did not actually move away, but she felt him retreat in some way. Matters were far, far worse than she had thought. Then she heard a faint noise near the door, the soft rustle of a skirt across a rush-strewn floor. It could be a maid, but instinct told Isabel that it was Elspeth Murray. She might have trouble pulling Cormac back to her side, but it could be done in time. It could be done a lot quicker if little Elspeth Murray was gone, and that was something Isabel felt she could do. All she needed was a few minutes before Cormac saw that Elspeth had returned. She placed her hands on Cormac's cheeks and pulled his mouth down to hers, hiding the fury she felt when he was slow to return her fierce kiss.

"Ah, Cormac, my love," she whispered, though loud enough to be heard by the person near the door, "how I have longed for you." Keeping her hands on his cheeks, she held him facing her, although she noticed that his gaze wandered a little. "There is still a fire between us."

He had felt none, but heard himself say, "Aye, Isabel. There has e'er been that." Cormac told himself it was not a complete lie, for once he was himself again, he felt sure that fire would return.

Knowing it was going to be difficult to pull ardent confessions from him at the moment, Isabel struggled to turn their discussion in the direction she needed it to go. If she asked just the right questions or phrased her words in just the right way, she could pull free words that could easily sound ardent and full of love. Cormac did not actually have to declare his heart was hers and hers alone, but Isabel felt sure she could make it sound very much as if he did. She fought the urge to turn and assure herself that the one she wished to overhear all of this was actually standing there.

"After so many years, so many shared nights, surely ye cannae cast me aside like some weel-gnawed bone?" she said.

"Nay, of course not," Cormac began, irritated that he

would have to remind her yet again that he was not a man to break his word.

"Oh, ye have made me so happy. I was so afraid, Cormac."

"There is nay a need to fear, sweeting," Cormac said as he stroked her hair. "I am here for ye, as always. Just as I promised."

"I can always depend upon your love, cannae I?"

"Of course."

Cormac spoke absently, mostly out of habit. This was what he always did. This was what he had come here for. He paid little attention to what she said, however, for his thoughts were on the kiss they had just shared. It had been pleasant, but little else, and he began to think the cause was far more than weariness and well-sated passion. He had also found himself worrying that he could be caught kissing Isabel, that Elspeth could discover them together. In fact, he wanted Isabel to go away, and since he had been dreaming of this reunion for months, that made no sense at all. He decided to obey that urge, however. He would tell her whatever was needed to soothe her and get her to leave. Then he would be able to do some clear thinking.

"I am so glad ye came to see me again, my love," Isabel said, brushing her lips over his. "I believe that there is hope for us this time, that finally we may be able to be together as we have always wished to be. Are ye nay happy?"

"Of course, Isabel. How could I not be? Is it nay what I have sought for ten long years?" So why did he suddenly feel so trapped? he asked himself and found no answer. "But mayhap ye should leave here ere we are discovered."

"Oh, I care not," she declared with what she felt was an admirable display of passion. "I am done with hiding how I feel about you, how we feel about each other. 'Tis past time we grabbed hold of what we crave and cast aside all propriety and fear of danger. We should herald our love from the North Sea to the Thames."

Cormac barely stopped himself from shouting, *God nay!* He should be ecstatic that Isabel was finally brave enough to freely proclaim her love, but all he could think of was that Elspeth would hear and be hurt. Yet again he thought that something strange was happening and he desperately needed to be alone to figure it all out.

"I am glad, Isabel, and often have I wished we could do just that. Howbeit, I believe a little caution would be wise just now," he said gently. Then he noticed that she looked ready to weep and hurriedly kissed her. "We are older now, too wise to indulge in such headiness, such rash actions. Let us proceed with just a little discretion."

"Ah, ye need to speak with your whore. I understand and will wait. But nay for long, my love."

Before Cormac could reprimand her for her harsh words about Elspeth, a chillingly familiar, husky voice drawled, "Why wait? Let us clear the board here and now." And Cormac felt as if something inside him needed to scream aloud in panic and frustration.

# Chapter Fourteen

Elspeth felt as if she would shatter. Pain throbbed through her body with each beat of her heart. She was not exactly sure what caused her the most pain: the sight of Cormac and Isabel embracing or Cormac's words. Elspeth decided it was probably the latter, for there rang the death knell for all of her hopes and dreams. She had lost her gamble.

The need for some act of violence, however small, was so strong that Elspeth trembled with it. She wanted to yank Isabel away from Cormac. She wanted to slap the woman numb for robbing her and Cormac of any chance of happiness. She wanted to beat Cormac black-and-blue, preferably with a large blunt object, for being such a blind fool. It would do no good, however. Elspeth knew that, and so she stood clutching the edge of the door until the urge had all but passed.

"Elspeth," Cormac began, easing free of Isabel's hold,

but he could think of nothing to say. "How long have ye been there?"

"Long enough," Elspeth replied.

*Too long,* Cormac thought. The pale, tight look on her face told him that she had probably heard everything he and Isabel had said to each other. He had the urge to rush to her side and loudly declare it all lies, to try to take back every word he had just said. Anything to take the look of pain from her beautiful eyes. He could not do that to Isabel, however. She did not deserve to be hurt any more than Elspeth did. And just now, he was not exactly sure that he had lied to Isabel. He needed time to search his own heart and he could see that he was not going to be given that luxury.

"Elspeth, we need to talk," he said, glancing only briefly at Isabel as she stood up.

"I dinnae believe we have anything to say to each other," Elspeth said.

"Of course ye do, child," Isabel said, taking a moment to smooth her gown, silently implying that she and Cormac had been ardent enough to require such fussy tidying. "I will leave ye to talk." She touched a kiss to Cormac's mouth, inwardly cursing his blatant distraction. "Send me word later, my love. When ye are free. Then we can meet again."

It was not easy, but Elspeth resisted the temptation to trip Isabel as the woman swept by her. The look of smug triumph upon Isabel's perfect features made Elspeth want to scream. Isabel had won. They both knew it. She did not need to gloat.

And just what had Isabel won? Elspeth thought as she looked back at Cormac. Anger surged to the fore in her heart, briefly pushing aside her hurt, and she clung to it. He was a blind fool. She was willing to give him everything, all that any mon could want, and yet he clung to a woman who only toyed with him. He clung to his vow out of a sense of honor, and Isabel used it to keep him captive. Elspeth wondered when she had become a fool, too. It was the only explanation for her trying so hard to win a man who could not see beyond a pretty face, for her loving a man who would probably still believe Isabel a sweet victim even if he caught her standing over her husband's body, a bloodied dagger in her soft white hand. And it was his blindness that made him honor a vow to a woman who would not know honor it fell on her.

Cormac cursed his weakness as he swung his legs over the side of the bed only to discover he could not stand up without wavering slightly. He should not have pushed himself by walking after having exerted himself so delightfully last night. It would be better if he could stand firm now, could move quickly, and if needed, could hold firmly to Elspeth. Instead, he was going to have to depend upon the strength of his words and he had little confidence in his ability to soothe her fury. He was distracted from planning his first statements when Elspeth began to gather up her things.

"What are ye doing?" he demanded.

"Leaving," she replied as she shoved her few possessions into her small sack.

"We need to talk, Elspeth."

"About what?"

"About what ye saw or heard here."

"I saw and heard two old lovers renewing their affair. I saw that ye cannae break a vow, no matter how old and no matter how much matters have changed for both of ye. What else was I supposed to see?"

He dragged his fingers through his hair. "I wasnae renewing the affair with Isabel."

"Nay?" Elspeth shoved the last of her things in her bag, then tied it shut, very tightly, as she envisioned the top of her bag as Cormac's neck. "She had her tongue down your throat because she was so glad ye were saying fare-thee-weel, did she?"

"Ye kenned that I was coming here to meet with her."

"Aye, I did. 'Tis clear that I am a great fool for thinking what happened between us might have caused a wee change or two in your plans. Weel, it appears your lady love is right and 'tis time to say fareweel to your whore."

"Isabel spoke unkindly," he began.

"Dinnae apologize for her. Aye, she spoke unkindly, but dinnae try to say that she didnae mean it. She did."

"She ne'er would have spoken so crudely if she had kenned that ye might hear it."

Elspeth wondered how an otherwise intelligent man could be so utterly stupid. "She kenned I would hear it, for she kenned that I was standing there." She settled Alan in his sling, then coaxed Muddy into his bag.

"Nay." He stopped when she looked at him with disgust. "Elspeth, ye must try to understand. I am pledged to her. Isabel has had a verra hard, unhappy life. She needs me."

It happened before she could grasp control of herself. Elspeth hit him with her bag—twice. For a moment she was horrified that she had struck a wounded man. Then he straightened up, rubbed his head, and glared at her. When she saw that she had not really hurt him, she had to forcibly quell the urge to do it again. She wanted to hurt him, and since she could not do it emotionally, she ached to do it physically. It was past time to leave. Denied its usual release, the violence she felt found its way into the angry words she began to spit out at him.

"Aye, poor, wee, tormented Isabel," she sneered. "Fine. Run to her as ye have done for so long, though curse me if I can see what ye have gained for your ten years of martyrdom. Most men would have considered the vows made no longer valid after her first marriage, let alone her fourth."

"Marriages that were forced upon her. 'Tisnae her fault that we must be apart so often. I am sorry if ye feel that I have used ye unfairly."

"Of course ye have."

"Weel, I didnae notice ye crying nay too verra often," he snapped, furious at himself for making such a mess of things and at her for the sharp words that cut him to the bone.

"And I wasnae referring to all the rutting we have been indulging in. The unfairness comes from the fact that ye ne'er once considered changing your course. Ye ne'er even tried to take more from me than lust or to give me more than that. I was ne'er more than a pair of conveniently spread thighs and ye ne'er gave me the chance to be more."

"I ne'er thought ye would wish to be more," he whispered, and he knew that was not the complete truth.

"Then ye are an even greater fool than I thought ye were. Or a liar." She knew her smile had a nasty twist to it when she saw him flush. "Aye, for a while I do believe I was as great a fool as ye are. I chased after something I could ne'er have. My only consolation is that, unlike yourself, I have the wit to see that I but waste my time."

Cormac stood up and reached for her. "Stay awhile, Elspeth, at least long enough to regain some calm."

"Dinnae touch me," she snapped, slapping his hand away. "Stay? I think not. I havenae the stomach to watch ye try to decide what to do with me whilst ye trail after Isabel. Ye may not think it, but I do have some pride. I willnae allow ye to trample it any more than ye already have. I ken I said ye need make me no promises, but that doesnae mean ye need nay respect me, either. Ye have made your choice."

"Ye cannae expect a mon to cast aside ten years with a

woman in but a day or two. Nay, not when there is a pledge that was made.''

"Nay? I *loved* ye. I gave ye all a woman can give a mon. I tossed my pride, my chastity, and my heart at your feet, and I was willing, nay, eager to give ye whate'er else I could if ye had but asked.'' Her anger grew as she spoke and her pain began to slowly break free of the tight bonds she had placed upon it, adding a soft agony to her voice. "But I wonder if ye ken what love is? *I* would ne'er have left ye. *I* would have had to be dragged, chained and screaming, to stand before the altar with another mon. *I* would have been at your side whilst ye fled the Douglases and would have turned o'er every rock to find the real killer. *I* would have cried your innocence loudly from one end of Scotland to the other. Love is like that. 'Tis nay meekly going from one husband to another nor summoning ye only when trouble brews.

"Fine. Ye have chosen the bed ye wish to lie in. Ye will have your precious honor. For all I ache and rage, I pray that we are all wrong about Isabel, that she is indeed the poor, sweet madonna ye think she is. But I believe ye will find it a rocky bed. Mayhap ye will think on me, on all I offered ye, and all ye treated so callously, all ye tossed aside. For tossed it aside ye have, and 'twill take more than ye may have to offer to e'er pick it up again. Aye, heed this, my bonny lover: If ye decide in my favor after I am gone, 'twill take more than pretty smiles and fair words to make me want to risk this agony a second time. If ye do decide 'tis me ye want, ye are going to have to crawl—just as ye have crawled to Isabel for ten, long, wasted years.''

She noticed he looked stunned, his eyes wide and his face pale. Elspeth shook her head and left, quietly shutting the door behind her. The click of the latch sounded so final she felt it deep in her soul. Forcing herself to be calm, she left the inn. It did not surprise her to find Isabel waiting for her just outside of the inn door.

"Ye didnae go far," Elspeth said, trying to hide her intense dislike of the woman.

"I just wanted to see that ye do—go far, that is." Isabel smiled faintly.

"Ye do like to gloat when ye win, dinnae ye? 'Tis most unbecoming."

Isabel straightened up and glared at her. "Aye, I have won. 'Tis glad I am that ye have the sense to see that and leave. Some women might try to fight for the mon they wanted."

"And ye think I havenae? I have fought verra hard indeed. Still, 'tis difficult to o'ercome ten years of enslavement. Ten years of believing oneself in love with a woman who ne'er really existed. Ten years of honoring a vow he ne'er should have made in the first place. Aye, ye may smile. Ye have won the right to keep toying with the poor, blind fool. For how long though? Ye play a vicious and chancy game, mistress. Cormac is the only one who thinks ye naught but some poor, sweet lass forced to bow to her greedy family's will. At the moment, I believe his wretched sense of honor is all that holds him to you. His kinsmen see ye for what ye are. So do his friends. So does most everyone else. Ye dinnae hide what ye are before others and one day ye willnae be able to hide what ye are before Cormac, either."

"And ye think he will then run back to you?"

Elspeth shrugged. "He may. It matters not. He will run from ye and ye best hope he does, too. After all, he may just decide to make ye pay for your deceits and I surely dinnae envy ye facing a mon who kens ye have made a complete fool out of him for most of his adult life."

"Cormac loves me. He has always loved me. Ye couldnae take that away and it eats at ye, doesnae it?"

"Mayhap. Although I think ye already wonder if 'tis still love or merely a mon unable to break his word. And although it appears that he has chosen you, I willnae disappear as completely as ye wish. Nay, mistress, I am in his blood, in his memory, and a wee bit in his heart. Oh, aye, I ken weel that he will remember me and ye will ne'er be sure when my memory intrudes or why or if he is comparing ye with me."

Isabel's laugh was short and cold. "And ye think ye could possibly win in such a comparison?"

"Aye, for ye see, I gave him the one thing ye ne'er have, the one thing ye probably cannae give anyone."

"If ye think Cormac and I have loved chastely, then ye are indeed a fool."

"I speak not of passion, mistress, but of love. I loved him completely, without demands, without restraint. He kens I loved him, for I told him so. And there is where ye will fail to conquer me, for ye have ne'er loved him. For ten years ye have spat on a gift many women would kill for. Ye have abused his honor and his love. And that, mistress, is why I despise ye and always will. That is why I believe ye are an even greater fool than poor Cormac." Elspeth could tell by the cold, scornful look upon Isabel's face that the woman simply did not understand.

"A verra pretty speech," drawled Isabel, her blue eyes narrowed in dislike, "but I believe ye were just leaving?"

"Aye, Payton waits for me. I believe ye ken my cousin, Sir Payton Murray?"

It was undoubtedly a little mean-spirited of her, but Elspeth took great delight in the way Isabel's eyes widened and the woman paled slightly. Isabel spread her charms so far and wide, Elspeth was very surprised that Cormac had not been deafened by the whispers of what a whore the woman was. But, she thought sadly, he probably ignored or denied them as he did so much else about the woman.

Elspeth knew the moment the woman realized that her little indiscretion was not going to be whispered into Cormac's ear, and she nearly rolled her eyes in disgust when Isabel began to look decidedly eager.

"Is Payton staying at court?" Isabel asked, then gave Elspeth a smug look. "He is a verra good lover."

"Tsk, Isabel. Ye truly should be a wee bit more discreet, a wee bit less sexually gluttonous. If ye dinnae start keeping your white thighs pressed together more often, there isnae going to be a mon left in Scotland whom Cormac can look in the eyes."

Ignoring Isabel's hissed curse, Elspeth walked away. Losing to such a woman made her feel ill, but she fought to walk away straight and proud. Although she did not possess the skill to hide her pain from Isabel's keen eyes, she wanted to leave the woman with the impression that Elspeth Murray would not suffer for long.

As she approached Payton, he stood up, took one long look at her, and then held out his arms. Elspeth did not hesitate to accept his hug, but she only allowed herself a small taste of his sympathy. Too much and she would be weeping as loud as a milk-starved bairn.

"I am ready to return to Donncoill," she said as she stepped out of his embrace.

Glancing at her two companions, Payton half smiled. "It should nay surprise me that we willnae be returning without a stray or two." He reached out to ruffle the child's thick, dark curls, then scratched the cat's chin.

"Someone left the bairn by the road to die and no one in the nearest village would claim him. I call him Alan. The cat was being sadly tortured by some wretched children. He wouldnae leave after I rescued him and tended his wounds. His name is Muddy." She smiled faintly as she stroked the big cat's head and the animal purred loud enough to make Payton laugh.

"Ye are leaving the fool then?"

"Aye, he has made his choice."

"And ye dinnae wish to stay and try to change his wee mind?"

"Nay. I did all I kenned how to do just that and none of it worked. Unless he sees that Isabel but uses his honor against him and isnae worthy of it, he will cling to his pledge to her."

"Do ye think he will regret his choice and seek ye out?"

Elspeth shrugged as Payton helped her secure her bags on one of his horses. "I didnae tell him I would wait."

" 'Twas probably wise."

She mounted, then sighed and looked down at Payton, who watched her with some concern. "I fear I didnae hold my temper. I said things." She shook her head. "I told him that I might consider taking him back if he crawled to me as he has crawled to Isabel for ten long years." She was not surprised to see Payton wince. "I dinnae think he will see any promise or welcome in that, do ye?"

"Nay, lass. Weel, we shall return to Donncoill. Mayhap some time, some distance," he began, then just patted her leg and went to gather his men.

Since they had a late start, they rode for only a few hours before camping for the night. It was a quiet, somber group that shared bread, cheese, and wine around a small fire. Elspeth suspected she was responsible for the mood of the men, but she had no idea of how to fix it or any real inclination to do so. It took all of her wit and strength to keep herself from falling into a sodden, weeping lump of pain.

Caring for Alan helped some, although even he was unusually quiet. Muddy disappeared to find his own food, returning shortly after Alan fell asleep and curling up next to the child's basket. Elspeth helped clean up after the meal, then spread her bedding out next to Payton's and prayed for sleep as she curled up in her blanket.

It did not come. She listened to the men bank the fire and decide who would take which watch. She listened to them settle down on their beds, some murmuring a shy good sleep to Alan. The familiar rumble of Muddy's purr told her that some had even paused to stroke the cat. One man even complimented the animal for protecting little Alan so well.

By the time Payton sought his bed, she knew she would find little sleep this night. She listened as he stretched out. Then he shifted around several times as he sought a comfortable spot. Then he scratched himself for a little while. Then he yawned. Finally, he was quiet, but she knew he watched her, and she refused to look his way.

For a little while she stared up at the stars. Then she studied the moon. She smoothed the wrinkles from her blanket. She studied the stars again. It was obviously going to be a very long night.

What she wanted to do was cry. She wanted to weep, to howl out her pain and grief. Her chest ached with the need. Her throat felt so tight and full she was surprised she was not strangling. Elspeth could not display such wretched emotion before the men, however. It would embarrass all of them. She also feared that, once she began, once she let that sadness loose, she would be weeping and wailing all the way to Donncoill.

"No one will fault ye for crying, Elspeth," Payton said.

"I ken it, but I willnae do it," she vowed.

"Because he isnae worth it?"

"Weel, mayhap he isnae, but all we could have shared together, all he tossed away, certainly is. And, Jesu, how can ye condemn a mon for wishing to honor a vow?"

Payton reached out and tugged her closer. He wrapped one strong arm around her waist and held her, her back against his chest. She felt as taut as a bowstring and it worried him. Elspeth was a woman who was free with her emotions, hiding little or nothing. This control was unlike her and he cursed Sir Cormac for teaching it to her.

"Ye are young, Elspeth," he said. "Ye will heal. Oft-said words, and nay verra comforting just now, but still true."

"I ken it. Yet I dinnae think I will e'er love anyone as much as I loved him," she whispered. " 'Tis odd, but although I am verra angry and verra hurt, I still feel sorry for him. I e'en find myself hoping that he finds some happiness, that he doesnae pay too high a price for choosing honor o'er me. I e'en find myself wondering, if I did go back, could I still save him from Isabel?" She released a shaky laugh. "Such a contrary lass I am. I want to hurt him as he has hurt me, but I dinnae want him to be hurt by another."

"Understandable. Ye love him. I have ne'er been in love myself, but I do believe that this will pass, that ye will heal. I believe love is an emotion that must be returned, must be nurtured, or 'twill wither and die." He hesitated a moment and then cleared his throat. "What if he has left ye with child, Elspeth?"

Elspeth felt her heart contract with both fear and hope. If she was carrying Cormac's child it would cause so many problems it made her head spin to think of them. It would also hurt and disappoint her family, at least for a while. She had no fear of losing their love, however, and she knew, without doubt, that they would all love her child. Cormac, however, would have to avoid all of her kinsmen as avidly as he had avoided the Douglases for years, she mused. She knew she could get her whole family to swear not to kill or seriously injure him, but she suspected they could find other ways to make his life a misery.

The joy and hope came from the thought that she would have a part of Cormac to love. There would be sadness, too. A child would give her someone to spend her hopeless love on, but it would also prevent her from ever completely forgetting Cormac. Memories would be stirred each time she looked at the child they had created together. She could only hope that those memories would soon be more sweet than painful.

"I willnae ken if I am with child for a while yet," she said. "If I am—weel, that will be both joyous and sad, but I will deal with it."

" 'Twill probably end all chance of ye marrying anyone."

"I think I have done that anyway." She felt tears sting her eyes and tried to fight them back. "I kenned weel what I might lose when I decided to love Cormac and to try to make him love me. I really had no choice. I think I have loved him since I first set eyes on him, although I was but a child. Even then I must have sensed that he was the other half of me, but I did ken it for certain the first time his lips touched mine. In my arrogance, or mayhap my naivete, I thought he would ken it, too. All I had to do was make him look close enough to see." She started to quietly weep and decided it might be a good thing to release a little of the grief knotting her insides. "I could have made him verra happy, Payton."

Payton held her a little closer and kissed the top of her head. "Aye, lass, ye could have, and I think his tossing aside that precious gift for a whore like Isabel is truly what makes the mon a fool."

"They must have rutted all night," Isabel snapped. "The room stank of it."

Sir Kenneth Douglas watched his lover pace their bed-chamber with some interest as he half sat, half sprawled on their bed. "A smell ye are most familiar with."

Isabel glared at him. At the moment, she was unmoved

by the sight of his naked and obviously aroused body. Since her first marriage to his cousin they had been bound tightly by lust and the blood on their hands. Neither of them was faithful to the other, each of them taking lovers when they pleased, yet in a strange way, they were as good as married. Their scheme to become rich and powerful through her husbands kept them together as did their fierce, insatiable lust for each other. Kenneth was the one man she had never been able to control. With his black hair, black eyes, and swarthy skin, he looked more like some Spaniard than a Scot. He also looked hard, cold, and dangerous—all things that made her pulse leap. To her utter disgust, the way he constantly reminded her of what she was, disparaging her with softly spoken insults, also excited her.

"Weel, the threat she posed is gone now," Isabel said. "She wasnae so difficult to rout."

"Are ye sure?"

"I watched her ride away with Sir Payton carrying her bag, some brat, and a monstrous cat. She is gone."

"In body, mayhap, but in spirit?" He shrugged. " 'Twill be a while ere ye can be certain her memory doesnae linger with him. If it does, he may no longer be the complacent, adoring fool he has been up until now. She may have opened his eyes."

"And ye think that could make him dangerous?"

"He kens a lot about ye, Isabel. Too much. Until now, his blind devotion, his belief that ye are a poor, much wronged innocent, and his strange adherence to a vow many men would have cast aside long ago have kept him from seeing too clearly. If his eyes have now been cleared of the great wonder of ye," he drawled, his sarcastic tone so sharp she frowned, "he may weel start to think more deeply on all he has seen, and he may no longer be so blind that he cannae understand the importance of it all."

Isabel sighed with a swiftly passing regret then sat down

on the bed. "Ye want to be rid of him." She reached out
and curled her long, slender fingers around his erection.

"It may be for the best, but we willnae waste such a
sacrifice. Unless he forces us to act sooner than we might
like, we shall wait until we make good use of him. He can
die protecting you. That should please his little chivalrous
soul."

"I dinnae wish to talk on that now." She bent over him,
replacing her stroking fingers with her tongue.

"Regrets? Shall ye miss the fool?"

Kenneth was not the only one who could wield a soft,
yet bitter, insult or taunt. "He had a few fine qualities"—
she lightly squeezed his manhood—"that I will dearly
miss." In some ways she spoke the truth, but she purred
with victorious delight as her lover took up the challenge
she had thrown out.

# Chapter Fifteen

Cormac swore and stood up. For three days, sleep had been elusive. For three long days, every time he closed his eyes, he saw the look on Elspeth's face, heard the pain in her voice, remembered every word she had said. For three torturous days, he had done little else but think and try desperately to convince himself that he was not the fool she had called him. Hour after slowly passing hour, he fought to ignore the emptiness he felt, the pain barely held in check by doubt and denial. The only things that grew stronger were his body and the sense that he had made the biggest mistake of his life when he had not stopped Elspeth from leaving him.

He stood by the window and stared into the street, waiting for the fourth day to begin. Nights were wasted on him at the moment. They were passed in hours of groping, unproductive, confusing thought. The few times he managed to grasp at a little sleep, that respite would be cruelly ended when he would wake in a state of sweating need only to find himself clutching nothing but a pillow—a pillow that still carried the faint scent of lavender, her scent. Then he had to fight that overwhelming sense of loss and emptiness all over again. He found he even missed that cursed cat.

Even more troubling than his confused feelings was the complete lack of word or sight of the woman who had instigated this emotional chaos, this wretched, unending soul-searching. Isabel had swept in, demanded her due, cajoled words of love from him, then left. While still deep in shock over the painful scene with Elspeth, he had dutifully sent word to Isabel that his lover was gone. Isabel had responded with absence and complete silence.

That Isabel would so thoroughly ignore him after she had gained what she obviously wanted only added to the doubts tearing him apart. He did not want to think she had used and deceived him for ten years, but the thought was creeping through his heart and mind like poison through his blood. Had his love become no more than a sick habit? Had she been using his sense of honor and the vows made by a lovesick youth to hold him in thrall? Was he truly blind to what she really was? Every rumor and accusation he had heard whispered about her ruthlessly plagued him now. Had she never truly loved him? She should be here to help him, to soothe away his doubts and ease the odd emptiness Elspeth had cursed him with.

He needed answers and he was not finding them trapped alone in his room with only his own confused thoughts for company. Cormac slammed his fist against the wall, almost welcoming the stinging pain in his hand. Enough was enough. He was not going to sit there like some foolish lapdog waiting for his mistress to dole him out tiny scraps of affection.

The time it took to wash and dress did not ease his determination to see Isabel. Nor did the time it took to get some food to break his fast. It did make the morning pass a little more quickly, however. It was midmorning before he set out to see Isabel. For once he was not concerned about anyone seeing him go to her or about breaking his promise to wait until she came to him or summoned him to her side.

As he entered the castle, however, and made his way to Isabel's rooms, Cormac felt uneasy. Isabel was, through her marriages, firmly part of the powerful Douglas clan. It was not a clan to anger, he well knew. That did not seem to be a great part of his sudden unease, though, and he was puzzled. Some instinct was telling him that he should not do this, that he was not going to like the results, but he forced his hesitation aside. It was far past time for a confrontation. After ten years, Isabel owed him something, if only a few honest answers.

What he found outside Isabel's rooms caused him to falter. Four men stood there, their faces grim. Two stood with their ears pressed to the door while the other two stood guard. Cormac felt his stomach knot with tension and a hint of fear when he saw that they were Douglases. None of them made a move to threaten him or halt his approach, however, so he walked up to them.

"So, Armstrong, ye actually come to her now, do ye?" drawled a tall, broad-shouldered man, his voice pitched low so as not to carry.

"I have come to speak to Isabel, aye," he replied. "What are ye doing here?"

"We are listening to a most interesting conversation, or so it promises to be when it begins again. Care to join us?"

"Ye ken who I am, but I dinnae recognize any of you," he said even as he stepped closer to the door.

"I am Sir Ranald," replied the tall man. "The mon with his ear still pressed against the door is my brother James. The mon to your right is Ian, to the left is Wallace. Douglases all." He smiled coldly. "I am your lover's new betrothed."

Cormac stared at the man, feeling the sharp stab of betrayal. Isabel had said nothing about a new marriage being arranged, yet she had to have known even as she was reminding him of his pledge to her. Again she pulled him to her side when she was not free to do so. This time he felt no pain or sorrow, only a cold, hard fury.

"When?" he asked.

"It was all settled a fortnight ago," replied Ranald, watching Cormac very closely.

Here was proof that Isabel had indeed known what was being arranged for her even as she had sent for him. "Congratulations."

"Ah, now what have I done that ye would curse me so?"

"Ye are about to marry a verra beautiful, wealthy woman. Ye think that is a curse?"

"When that woman has put four of my kinsmen in the ground, aye." He looked at James, who still listened at the door. "Are they done yet?"

"Soon, if I judge the sounds right," said James.

"When they cry out in satisfaction, crack open the door. We will have to be most silent then, but at least we shall hear what is said more clearly." Ranald looked back at Cormac. "Ah, ye didnae really think her faithful, did ye?"

He had, save for her brief marriages, but Cormac decided he would rather cut out his tongue with a spoon then admit it to this cold-eyed man. "Is all this just to prove her faithless so that ye might end the betrothal?"

"I hope to gain far more than that, but if we fail to hear all we wish—aye, that would suit me for now."

Reluctantly, Cormac moved to the door and pressed his ear against it. The door not being of thick oak, but of a lighter wood, the muffled sounds he heard came through clear enough for him to recognize them, and he inwardly winced. If that was Isabel in there, she was definitely enjoying a lusty bout of lovemaking. Cormac frowned and stepped back, wondering why he felt no flare of jealousy. He should want to kick the door down so that he could see with his own eyes that Isabel was no more than the whore so many called her. Instead, he was ready to wait, prepared to see the Douglas men play their game through to the end. The only emotions he did feel were sharp annoyance and a deep disappointment in himself as well as in Isabel.

"Could be her maid," Cormac felt compelled to say and just shrugged when all four men briefly looked at him as if he was completely witless. He was starting to get accustomed to that look.

"Now that would disappoint me, but I ken exactly who so loudly ruts behind this thankfully thin door. 'Tis my betrothed and my cousin Kenneth. We have kept a close watch on the both of them since they came to court and long before that. I believe that the pair have long been lovers and a great deal more."

Before Cormac could ask Ranald exactly what that more was, James signaled them all to be silent. The last of the couple's cries resounded clearly through the now cracked door. Cormac felt himself blush faintly beneath Sir Ranald's steady gaze, for he recognized the woman's cries as Isabel's. She had led him to believe he was the only one who had ever heard them. Clearly that was a lie. He wondered how many other lies she had told him.

"Ah, Kenneth, my love, ye just get better and better," said Isabel as she rubbed her feet up and down his strong calves.

"Your skills improve as weel, my sweet." Kenneth eased their bodies apart and moved to sit on the side of the bed. " 'Tis a wonder, considering your taste for sweet lads."

"Cormac isnae a lad. He is but a few years younger than ye are."

"Since he has probably kenned verra few women besides your sweet self, I consider him a lad."

*This could become very embarrassing,* Cormac mused, but he did not move away. The truth was worth a little humiliation. All his other emotions were now buried beneath a deep, gnawing need to find out who Isabel really was. He had the sick feeling that the woman he thought a wronged innocent for so long, the woman he had pledged his life to, was nothing but the scheming whore everyone said she was.

"I have taught him all I know," Isabel said.

"Ah, weel, then he must be a veritable stallion of a lover," Kenneth drawled.

"Are ye jealous, lover?"

"Of some toy from your childhood ye are unwilling to cast aside? I think not."

Cormac winced, his discomfort added to by the looks of sympathy the other four men sent him. If he had been as wrong about Isabel as everyone said he was, he supposed he deserved their pity. If they knew what he had given up for this woman, they would probably weep for him. There was a good chance he would weep for himself if the truth about Isabel proved to be as ugly as everyone said it was.

"If ye arenae jealous of Cormac, why did ye allow him to take the blame for my first husband's death?"

"He was there and he was easily made to look guilty. Ye would rather have set my kinsmen on our trail?"

"Nay. They gave Cormac little rest till ye gave them that fool Donald." Isabel's chuckle was soft yet sharply cold. "To think that fool Donald thought he could trick us, rule us with our secrets. He deserved to hang for that conceit alone. Where are my stockings?"

"I tossed them o'er by the wall."

"Ah, I see them. Do ye still believe that Donald's sacrifice worked?"

"It has been near to ten years, love, and none have looked our way. We succeeded there. Dinnae worry on it. If ye feel the need to brood and quake, worry on the other three fools ye wed. Some still puzzle o'er those deaths. I think we erred in trying to make them look like accidents," Kenneth murmured. "Stupidity, recklessness, illness. That leaves those who cared about the fools no one to blame but God, and few accept that verra weel. 'Tis easier and ends all wondering if there is someone to hang for the death. The thirst for vengeance is quenched and the mon soon forgotten."

"There is some wisdom in that. Still, must it be Cormac again?"

"Feeling some tenderness toward the fool?" Kenneth asked, a thread of anger in his cold voice. "E'en after he tossed ye aside for the wee Murray lass?"

"He didnae toss me aside," Isabel snapped. "I am here and she isnae, is she?"

"Isnae she? I think ye ken, as I do, that she lingers in his mind. Ye have lost your grip there, love. He stays because he pledged himself to you and ye can depend upon Sir Cormac to honor a pledge as surely as ye can depend upon his parents to break one. Dinnae be too vain to accept the truth and the danger of that. Ye have played with that puppet far too long. The strings grow brittle. They didnae break with this lass, but they may with the next. Aye, for all we ken, he begins to think he has erred in choosing ye o'er the Murray lass. Those strings could already be frayed near to breaking. Our plan has no room for sentimentality."

" 'Twas nay sentimentality," Isabel grumbled. "Mayhap I but grow weary of being rutted on so that ye can fill your pockets and gain lands. Mayhap I think I have buried one too many husbands. I am nay the only one whose hands are stained with the blood of four men. Ye are as soaked in it as I am, yet 'tis me they watch, me they suspect.''

"But 'tis best this way. I am nay a beautiful woman who can steal a mon's wits with sweet words and a honeyed mouth,'' Kenneth said, a hint of sarcasm in his soft voice. " 'Tis men who will judge and hang us, and ye are far more capable of seducing away their suspicions than I am. This will be the last one.''

"Are ye certain?''

"Aye. Whilst ye weep o'er the grave of poor cousin Ranald, I shall be made laird of his lands. He is the last one to stand between me and all I covet.''

"Except for his father.''

"An old mon who will die ere his son does.''

"And ye willnae change your mind about putting the blame for Ranald's death upon Cormac?''

"Nay. 'Tis time he left us and he shows no sign of doing that on his own.''

"If we must,'' Isabel said, no hint of reluctance in her voice. "How long must I stay wed this time?''

"Nay too long. Cousin Ranald can be such a reckless young mon. I am sure we will think of a suitable way to end his life ere ye grow too tired of him. Ye may e'en enjoy yourself. 'Tis said that he is a skilled lover.''

"I wouldnae ken. He has shown no inclination to take advantage of our betrothal.''

"Poor Isabel. A mon who can resist your many charms. There is a wonder. Weel, come here and let me soothe your bruised vanity.''

"We have just finished dressing,'' Isabel protested.

"All ye need to do is unlace my breeches.''

Cormac watched Ranald signal sharply with his hand, stopping his men from interrupting the lovers. It took him a moment to see the advantage of letting Isabel and

Kenneth become amorous again. Kenneth would certainly be caught at a disadvantage, unable to react quickly enough to defend himself. Isabel and Kenneth would also be set off balance by the interruption, unable to deny that they were lovers. Since Isabel was betrothed, it was almost adultery. Sir Ranald could kill them both for that alone and suffer little for the act.

Cormac felt numb. Everyone had been right about her. She was a murderous, deceitful whore. He had lost ten years of his life to her. He had lost Elspeth. He was surprised his friends and family had stayed loyal to such a complete idiot. It did not require much thought, even by a witless fool like himself, he thought sourly, to know what Kenneth was asking of Isabel. Cormac had no doubt that Isabel would soon oblige the man. She had always displayed both skill and enjoyment in the task. It was not something he wished to see, but he would force himself to see this through to the bitter end. Although he did not think he was fool enough to let her talk her way out of this, even if she yet again tried to play upon his sense of honor by reminding him of vows made, a stark image or two to enhance all he had just heard might not be amiss.

"And pleasuring you is what will soothe my vanity, is it?" she asked.

"I ken ye weel, lover. Ye adore having a mon at your mercy. Here I am, willing to be tempted and tortured by your skillful mouth. Enslave me. There's the lass. See what ye do to a mon? Make a meal of me," he coaxed.

"A meal? 'Tis a feast."

The noises Kenneth began to make told Cormac and the Douglas men that the couple were now fully occupied. As James eased open the door, Cormac stepped up beside Ranald. The scene that met his eyes brought no real pain, just disgust. Kenneth was sprawled in a chair, his head thrown back, and his eyes closed. Isabel knelt between his

legs, loudly pleasuring him. If he ever again doubted that
Isabel was little better than a base whore, Cormac knew
he would only have to recall this scene to put a swift end
to that madness.

The four Douglas men silently encircled the couple.
Cormac stood next to Sir Ranald as that man touched the
point of his sword to Kenneth's throat. At the same time,
James grabbed hold of Isabel's hair and yanked her away
from Kenneth. The noise made as she was forced to release
her lover only added to the sordidness of the scene. The
looks on the faces of the lovers—a mixture of guilt, horror,
and fear—gave Cormac some small satisfaction.

"Ye look surprised, Cousin," drawled Sir Ranald. "It
seems your own pleasure deafened you to our arrival."

"Would ye kill a kinsmon o'er this whore?" asked Kenneth.

Isabel gasped, then after giving Kenneth a look full of
loathing, turned a soft, beseeching gaze upon Sir Ranald.
"He seduced me, Sir Ranald. 'Twas but a moment of weakness ere we were betrothed and he has used my guilt o'er
that to force me to remain his lover."

"Aye, we all heard your virulent protests," said Ranald,
"and saw how fiercely he held ye upon your knees. I suppose your mouth was too full to call for aid." He smiled
coldly when Isabel flushed, the color in her cheeks so
obviously due to fury rather than shame or embarrassment.
"Ah, woe, how my heart is broken."

"Enough jesting, Cousin," said Kenneth. "Let me leave
so that ye may deal as ye wish with the woman. Surely ye
cannae kill a mon for taking what was so freely and vigorously offered? 'Tis nay as if I deflowered your virgin bride.
Ye have heard all the rumors about her. 'Twas such talk
that made ye reluctant to accept the betrothal. Weel, I
have given ye a good, sound reason to end it. E'en your

father, who pressed for the match, willnae fault ye for casting her aside after this."

"True, but he would flay me alive if I allowed a murderer of our kinsmen to slip free of weel-earned justice."

"Do ye truly believe she killed her husbands?"

The look of surprise and horror on Kenneth's handsome face astonished Cormac with its perfection. He knew he should not be surprised that, once caught, Isabel and Kenneth would turn against each other. These two had murdered four innocent men for the basest motive—greed. They now calmly plotted to kill another and blame Cormac for the deed. Like so many others, Kenneth had allowed Isabel's allure to lead him into danger. If he had had the strength to resist that temptation, he would be a free man now, free to continue eliminating those of his kinsmen who stood in the way of what he craved. Cormac suspected the man's continued success in his plotting had made him too arrogant to be cautious.

"Ah, Cousin, ye are good," murmured Sir Ranald. "So innocent ye look with your monhood displayed for all to see and that proud piece still wet from my betrothed's tender attentions."

A faint gleam of sweat on Kenneth's forehead was all that revealed his growing agitation. "She is but a whore."

"That she is, and I willnae have ye thinking I am such a fool that I would spill Douglas blood over such a faithless bitch. Nay, I willnae be seeing ye dead because of her."

"Then why does your sword still rest against my throat?"

"I but ponder my choices. Do I kill ye now? Or do I take ye to our laird and let him decide how to make ye pay for the deaths of four of our own?"

"I dinnae ken what ye mean."

"Did ye really think we had but now arrived? Nay, Cousin. We were here ere ye began your first bout of rutting." He nodded when both Isabel and Kenneth grew deathly pale.

"No one will heed ye," Kenneth said, only the faintest of tremors in his voice to reveal his fear. "They will think ye spout naught but lies born of jealousy."

"I think not. I have four other witnessess to your confessions. And hers."

"Four?" Isabel looked at the Douglas men, then at Cormac, her lovely blue eyes widening. "Ye would betray me, my love?"

Cormac watched her eyes fill with tears. Her expression was one of deep sorrow and pain. She was as skilled as Kenneth, he realized. He wondered if anything she did or said was real. Cormac supposed that, one day, he might find some comfort in the fact that he had been fooled by the most adept deceiver he had ever had the misfortune to know. At the moment, however, he was finding it increasingly difficult to resist the urge to slap that perfect face.

"Aye, Isabel, I would have the world ken the whole ugly truth about you," he replied.

"How can ye say such a thing after all we have meant to each other, all we have endured together?"

"Together? I endured like the witless fool I am. Ye did nay more than keep another stallion in your stable." He shook his head. "Four deaths, Isabel? Four murders? And for what? This fool who turns on ye in a blinking just to try to save his own worthless hide? For money and lands? Ye had plenty of both. Nay, Isabel, we had nothing. At first, I was just too blinded by your beauty and my lust to ken it. And just lately, I was too desperate to prove I had the honor my parents lacked by clinging to a pledge made years ago—a pledge I should have considered finished at least by the time ye wed your second husband. Honor. I cannae believe I wasted it on such a whore.

"Cease weeping," he snapped. "I will nay longer be

deceived by such ploys. Nay, especially not when I have just witnessed ye supping greedily and noisily upon another mon's staff. Ye forget. I have also just heard ye and your lover plot yet another murder and talk of how ye would set the blame upon me again."

Isabel's expression changed swiftly from sorrow to narrow-eyed fury. "Ye are just angry because ye blame me for the loss of that little Murray whore."

"Aye, ye are to blame, but so am I. And," he added in a cold, hard voice, "if ye wish to keep your bonny looks ye will ne'er speak of Elspeth like that again. Ye are nay fit to e'en speak her name, and whilst I may have the excuse of being a complete fool enslaved by a bonny face and a whore's skills, ye have none at all."

"These men will see me dead!"

Cormac did feel a pang at that thought, a genuine touch of sorrow. This woman had been a big part of his life, intertwined somehow with every move he had made in the last ten years. Despite the lies and betrayals, it was not easy to think of her impending death. He forced himself to look away, to remember that she was guilty of the death of four men—five if one included the hapless Donald the lovers had spoken of so callously. And it could have been six, for she had done nothing to stop her lover from tossing Cormac to the wolves. She would have let him die for her crimes if the unfortunate Donald had not come along.

"As ye were willing to see me dead once. Aye, and again after ye killed Sir Ranald."

"Ye had best think again, Cormac," she said, her voice hard. "Ye make a mistake in turning your back on me now."

He stared at her in surprise. "Do ye threaten me?"

"I but tell ye that ye could lose a great deal if ye cast me aside, if ye leave me to these men."

"Ye make no sense, woman. I have already lost a great deal because of you. What more harm can ye do me?"

"Shut the bitch up, James," ordered Sir Ranald. "This game grows tiresome."

"Cormac, ye best heed me," Isabel began, but despite her struggles, James soon had her bound and gagged.

Sir Ranald, who was busy helping the other two men secure Sir Kenneth, looked at Cormac. "She but tries to play with ye a bit more. The bitch can feel the sting of the hemp upon her fine throat and seeks to save herself."

"I ken it," Cormac said, then grimaced. "Still, 'tis hard to break such an old habit. I but need a wee bit of time to accept that what I believed for so verra long was all a lie and that this ugliness is the truth."

"Ye will stay to act witness?"

"Aye. Do ye really think ye will need it?"

"Mayhap. There are those who havenae yet seen the truth and Kenneth has a few powerful allies. 'Tis hard to say if they are loyal, thus may try to save them, or if they will now slink away, afeared of being touched by all of this. And Isabel isnae without allies, either. She has e'er kenned which men to bed to gain her the most advantage. Then again, some of them may be more than willing to see her hang for playing games with them."

"Considering how swiftly those two turned upon each other, ye may find yourself weighted down with ones eager to reveal more of their perfidy."

"True. Weel, ye need nay linger here and witness this. They will be weel secured and I will send word if I need ye or if all is done and ye may leave. Aye, and mayhap chase down the wee Murray lass."

"Do ye ken Elspeth?" Cormac asked in some surprise.

"A wee bit. She and her mother came to my father's keep to help when some illness struck us hard. Verra skilled at healing, as her mother is. And verra bonny indeed. Her clan is small but rich, and nay without influence when they choose to use it. 'Twould be a good match. Odd that she didnae tell ye about her cousin and Isabel if ye were so, er, close.''

"Do ye mean Sir Payton?"

"Aye. Bonny laddie. Brave and honorable." Sir Ranald laughed softly and shook his head. "When he heard I was to wed Isabel, he came to me. Faced me calmly and told me what he believed was the truth about my betrothed. Hit close to the mark, he did. Also told me he had bedded down with her once."

"Brave indeed." *Young Payton, too,* Cormac mused and inwardly shook his head in disgust. "Elspeth said naught, either because she didnae ken it or she didnae think I would heed her words."

"But ye would now?"

"Aye, but I fear it is far too late to do me any good," he said, not really referring to any confession about Payton, sadness and regret weighting each word.

# Chapter Sixteen

"Are ye trying to drink dry every barrel in town?"

Cormac blinked, recognizing the voice even in his drunken haze. He glanced up from the tankard of ale he had been blindly staring into and looked at his brother William. He blinked again slowly, trying to make William's face clearer and steadier. Cormac wondered what time it was. He had returned to the inn after the disaster in Isabel's rooms and then decided to get drunk. That plan had succeeded. He was very drunk indeed, but he had not yet reached that sodden oblivion he reached for. The arrival of his brother and a few more of his family was not wholly welcome, but at least it meant he would have some help finding his bed.

"Hello, Will, and to ye, too, Alaister." He nodded at his other brother, then squinted. "Be those others our cousins Malcolm and David?"

"Aye, ye sodden fool," William said as he and the others sat down at the table and he signaled the maid to bring over another jug of ale and four tankards. "We have been searching for ye for a fortnight or more."

"Oh, aye? What for?"

"Weel, ye are probably too drunk to understand, but our parents are dead."

"Did they finally kill each other?"

"Nay. Thieves did it. They were traveling home from enjoying a week of debauchery with their friends and their carriage was robbed. Still drunk, they decided to fight to save what few coins they had and were quickly cut down. Old Patrick and his son saw it all. They wisely surrendered. They brought the bodies back for us to bury."

Cormac knew that, beneath the ocean of ale he had consumed, lurked a flicker of grief. His parents had been good at making children, but had cared little or nothing for their progeny. They had not cared for each other much, either, constantly filling the halls of the keep with angry words, recriminations, and insults. The only things either of them had shared an interest in were drinking themselves numb and bedding others—as many others as possible. Half of the ones he called cousin were actually his half brothers and half sisters, bastards bred and forgotten by his mother and his father. Nonetheless, they had given him life, and for that reason alone he owed them some measure of grief. He was just too drunk to do it now.

"Ye are the laird of Aigballa now, Cormac," Alaister said, his green-brown eyes dark with concern.

"Jesu, so I am," Cormac muttered, then took a long drink.

"So ye must come home."

"Cannae. Have to stay to see Isabel hanged." He grinned as all four young men choked on their ale, then helped each other calm down. It was rare that he could so utterly shock his kinsmen and he hoped he would be able to recall this moment when he finally emerged from the drunken stupor he was sinking into. "I am a witness."

"To what?" demanded William, his voice still hoarse from choking on his ale.

"Her perfidy." Cormac had the feeling that the oblivion he sought was swiftly creeping up on him. "Confession made afore me and four Douglases. Heard her. Saw her, too. She didnae look quite so bonny with Sir Kenneth's rod halfway down her greedy throat. Jesu, I dinnae ken what troubles me more: that she deceived me, that I could be such a fool, that she has spat upon my honor for so long and I didnae ken it, or that all of ye can now say I told ye so." He could not keep his eyes open any longer. "Ah, Elspeth, my angel, I am so sorry," he whispered and fell forward.

William winced in sympathetic pain when Cormac's head hit the scarred, filthy table with a loud crack. "We will have to carry the fool to bed."

"What made him drink so deeply?" asked Alaister. "He rarely does this."

"Something to do with Isabel, the Douglases, a certain Sir Kenneth's staff, and someone named Elspeth. I think the poor fool has finally seen Isabel for what she is. Howbeit, the truth will have to wait until his head clears. Considering how much he has drunk, that may take a few days."

"I am nay sure it is a good sign that him seeing the truth about that whore has made him drink like this."

"What would ye do if ye just found out that ye had wasted ten years of your life on a murderous bitch?" William nodded when his younger brother and their cousins all grimaced. "I am thinking that isnae all of it, though. Nay, my gut tells me this Elspeth is what prods this wallow. Weel, no sense in trying to guess. We will take him to his bed and pray he wakes up sensible enough to talk in the morning."

* * *

Cormac held himself perfectly still and wondered if he should, or even could, open his eyes. He felt the effects of the vast quantity of ale he had drunk in every vein, every muscle, even deep in his very bones. The problem was that he had to relieve himself so desperately that it, too, was painful. That meant that he had to move, and although his experience with such heavy drinking was slight, he knew it was going to cost him dearly.

"Do ye need the piss pot?" asked a familiar voice.

Easing his eyes open slowly, Cormac felt the light in the room burn its way into his brain. "That you, Will?"

"Aye. Let me help ye sit up. Alaister's gone to fix ye a potion."

Even as Will helped him sit up, Cormac opened his eyes a little wider. It was a struggle to do what he needed to do, for his head felt as if it would shatter and his stomach roiled. Muttering his thanks to Will for helping him, he eased his body back down on the bed. A moment later he was half lifted and someone made him drink a foul-tasting potion. As he was settled flat yet again, someone else slapped a very cold, very wet cloth upon his forehead.

"Ye should be better in an hour or two," Will said, "and then we can talk."

It took almost three hours before Cormac could open his eyes, before he felt capable of doing anything more than groan with pain. He looked at his brothers and cousins and marveled at their patience. Although he could recall very little past the moment he left Isabel, he had obviously said enough to rouse their curiosity.

"Did I hear ye say our parents were dead?" he asked.

"Aye," replied Will. "Thieves killed them and ye are now our laird. Have some bread," he said as he shoved a chunk of fresh bread into Cormac's hand. " 'Twill soak up the poison and help ye talk sense. I have a whole loaf."

"I said something last eve? Something that interested you?" Cormac slowly ate the bread, finding that he was recovered enough for it to actually help him.

"Ye told us ye had to stay here to watch Isabel hang. I admit that roused my curiousity some."

"Ah, aye, that." Cormac kept filling his belly with the bread Will handed him as he told them all he had heard and seen. "Sir Ranald holds Isabel and her lover now and 'tis certain they will be swiftly judged and hanged."

"Then why must ye linger here?"

"There is always the chance that the need of another witness might arise—one who isnae a Douglas leastwise."

"And would ye be that witness, kenning that your words will send her to the gallows?"

"Dinnae look so worried, Will," he said to his brother and, with one sweeping look, included his other kinsmen in that advice. "Aye, I feel some regret, but little else. She has killed or helped to kill five men and was willing, twice, to let me hang for her crimes. E'en if I felt more deeply than I do, I would still be willing to act as witness to her guilt. Honor demands it."

"Honor was one of the things that got ye into this mess," Will muttered, then crossed his arms over his broad chest, leaned against the post at the foot of the bed, and studied Cormac steadily for a moment. "Ye are cured."

"An odd way to put it."

"Nay." Alaister shook his head, his riotous bronze curls swishing over his shoulders. " 'Tis right. That woman was a sickness with you."

Cormac smiled faintly at his young, often too serious brother. "Aye, mayhap she was. But I had made a vow and my need to honor it had also become somewhat of a blind sickness. I clung to it and ignored all else."

"I would think that ye would be more upset then ye are."

"So would I, but it appears that the cure had already begun ere I learned the whole ugly truth. I was just too slow to recognize that. And if I had opened my eyes to the truth that was all around me, I would have been freed of my pledge long ago."

"Are we to believe that ye were drinking yourself blind in celebration then?" asked William.

Before Cormac could reply to William's sarcasm, Alaister demanded, "Who is Elspeth?"

"The cure," Cormac replied softly, then tried to pour himself a tankard of water only to have William hurry to take over the chore. " 'Twas strange. Elspeth asked all the same questions the rest of ye have, made many of the same accusations, and yet she constantly raised my doubts. She somehow doggedly pushed me toward the truth I fought so hard to ignore for so long."

"Where is she? I should like to meet the lass who finally broke Isabel's spell o'er you."

"Gone." Cormac was not really surprised when just saying the truth hurt. "I feared I was still trying to understand what had changed, or e'en if it had, when I was forced into a corner. I had to make a choice. I chose to cling to that old vow, to my honor, nay realizing it was wasted on one like Isabel."

Alaister cursed, causing the others to stare at him in surprise. "Ye chose Isabel."

"In truth, I didnae really have the wit to make any real choice, but Elspeth felt I had. Worse, I didnae do anything to stop her. How could I? I still felt I was pledged. She is probably back at Donncoill now cursing the day she e'er met me."

"Donncoill?" Alaister frowned; then his eyes widened. "That Elspeth? The Murray lass? The wee lass who saved your life ten years ago? Jesu, Cormac, dinnae say that ye seduced her."

"Aye, that Elspeth, and I didnae seduce her. She seduced me." Cormac was not surprised to see the looks of scorn and disbelief on his kinsmen's faces. "I willnae say she had to do verra much to succeed, but I was trying to be an honorable mon and she wouldnae let me." He shrugged. " 'Tis hard to explain."

"Why dinnae ye try?" William drawled.

Cormac started to tell his brother that it was none of his business; then he sighed. In many ways it was. If Elspeth wanted to, she could bring a lot of trouble down on his head, and the heads of his family. There was also the matter of a debt owed. Ever since the Murrays had saved his life, Cormac and his kinsmen had sought some way to repay that. The honor of their whole small clan would be at risk if it was thought that he had insulted the Murrays through Elspeth. Such were the things that stirred long, bloody feuds. Although Cormac did not believe Elspeth was the sort of woman to stir up that sort of deadly trouble, he could not forget the look of pain and fury on her face.

"I will tell ye all of it, sad mess that it is, as I dress," he finally said as he got out of bed.

Although he was circumspect to some extent, Cormac was honest with his kinsmen. He told them everything, from the moment he found Sir Colin holding Elspeth against her will to the day Elspeth left. It was painful to do so, but he related every word and action of that fateful day. Cormac realized that he had some hope that they would not hear the same strong note of finality in Elspeth's words that he did.

"Ye did make a wretched muddle of it all, didnae ye?" said William, shaking his head.

"Love doesnae die in a winking," said David, his dark eyes fixed unwaveringly on Cormac.

"Ye be but sixteen. What do ye ken about it?" William snapped.

"Love doesnae die that fast. Ye dinnae have to be old or experienced to ken that. She said she loves him."

"Loved," Cormac corrected. "Did once. Doesnae now."

"I think that was just the anger talking. Weel, unless ye think her the sort to be fickle."

"Nay, not Elspeth."

"So woo her."

"I thought I had," Cormac said, remembering all too clearly the passion he and Elspeth had indulged in so greedily.

"Nay, ye bedded her as ye traveled to meet with another woman. And I would wager ye ne'er seriously considered breaking your pledge to Isabel e'en if ye wanted to. My sister says a woman who thinks a mon's passion goes any farther than his cullions is a fool. Is Elspeth a fool?"

"Nay." Cormac was a little surprised at the wisdom young David was revealing. "She may think she is, though. I hurt her verra badly. As she sees it, she gave me everything and I spit on it. She kenned what Isabel was and it must have made it hard for her to ken I would turn from her to honor a vow made to a whore."

"And the hurting will stay if ye leave her thinking 'twas only passion she wrung from you. Woo her. Let her ken she means more to ye than a warm nest for your rod. What do ye have to lose?"

Before Cormac could reply, a sharp rapping sounded at the door. Malcolm opened it to reveal a young lad. When Cormac recognized the clothes as those Isabel dressed her servants in, he tensed. Did the woman really believe that, after all he had learned, she could pull him back into her web?

"I have a message from Lady Isabel," the youth said.

Then he backed up when Cormac's four kinsmen all glared at him.

"What is it?" Cormac asked.

"M'lady says that ye must come and speak with her. She says she has something she must tell ye—a secret she has kept for years. Ye are to come with me. I ken where they have put her."

All four of Cormac's kinsmen loudly protested, but he silenced them with one sharp wave of his hand. There were some advantages to being laird, he decided. "She wouldnae tell ye what she wishes to talk about?"

"Nay, sir. Just that ye must come. If ye dinnae, ye will regret it all of your days."

"Wait for me downstairs."

The moment the door closed behind the boy, William said, "Ye cannae mean to go to her."

"Aye. I expected her to try to woo me into aiding her at least once. To try to turn my sense of honor against me just one more time. Dinnae fear it will work. I swear to ye, 'tis ended. And kenning how devious the woman is, how deeply sunk into murderous plots she is, it may serve to play the game if I can stomach it. If she still thinks that I am naught but a besotted fool, that that old vow will still protect her, she may weel give me e'en more proof to set against her."

"True, and I suspect ye are a wee bit curious as weel," Will said.

Cormac grinned. "Aye. Wouldnae ye be if someone told ye to come heed their words or ye would regret it for all of your days?"


As Cormac followed the young page into the bowels of the gaol he began to feel uneasy. It struck him as odd that, after ten years of approaching Isabel with only eager anticipation and lust, he should now see any summons from her as a threat. The fact that the Douglases had locked her away in such a deep, dark place only enhanced that feeling.

The same two men who had guarded her chamber door as he, Ranald, and James had listened to her confession now guarded her cell. Sir Ranald clearly trusted only his own men near Isabel. Cormac stood in front of Isabel's cell and studied her new quarters as she rose from her bed to approach him with measured wariness. Although it was chilly, damp, and lit only by torchlight, her cell was the most comfortable he had ever seen. The narrow bed was covered with soft furs and pillows. Tapestries hung on the walls—one was even draped to hide the necessary bucket. And there were rugs on the floor. It was very clean, as was Isabel. She had obviously been allowed both bathwater for washing and new clothes. Cormac suspected she was allowed regular visits from her maids. Such courtesy and gentle treatment must surely give her the confidence to believe that she would be able to escape justice if she could just find the right ploy to use. Isabel, Cormac decided, was not going to accept her fate until the bitter end. She simply could not conceive that, this time, she was not going to be able to lie or seduce her way out of trouble.

"Cormac, my love, I was afraid ye wouldnae come," she said as she reached through the bars, frowning when he clasped his hands behind his back so that she could not hold them.

"If naught else, Isabel, ye have stirred my curiousity," he said, deciding that he did not have the stamina to even pretend that he still cared. "What do ye think I must hear?"

"Ye are so cold to me," she whispered in an unsteady voice. "How can ye so quickly forget all we have meant to each other?"

" 'Tis hard to recall much more than ye trying to decide

how ye could make me hang for yet another murder ye committed. That sort of thing tends to cool a mon's ardor." Cormac smiled faintly when the guards snickered.

"Sir Kenneth forced me to do those things." She faltered into silence beneath the look of utter contempt Cormac gave her. Then she started to get angry. "So ye side with Sir Ranald. I ne'er thought ye would fail me, Cormac. Ye have let them turn ye against me with their lies."

"Ye did it all by yourself. I but listened to your own words and watched how deftly ye used your whore's skills." If she could get free, he thought as he watched her grip tighten on the bars, she would rip my eyes out.

"It matters not what ye think. Ye will still help me."

"Nay, I think not."

"Aye, I think so—that is, if ye e'er wish to see your son alive."

Cormac was faintly aware of the gasped curses of the guards as he stared at Isabel. A slow, smug grin started to curve her full mouth and he ached to slap it away. It took several moments to rein in the confusing array of emotions that had assaulted him when he had heard and understood her words. A son? With Isabel? It was something he was finding impossible to grasp. And why, if she had borne him a son, had he never seen or been told of the boy? He realized he had asked that question aloud when Isabel chuckled.

"Did ye think I would take the little bastard with me when I got married or when I traveled? Jesu, I tried to rid myself of him the moment I realized your seed had taken root in my womb, but unlike the others, I couldnae shake free of him. So I have had the burden of the brat for nearly seven years."

Her words chilled him to the bone. "So ye should have told me. I believe ye were widowed then. We could have been wed. Or I could have taken the bairn and raised him myself."

"I ken it, but I decided he might prove useful at some time. A time such as now," she said brightly. "So ye help me and I shall give ye the boy. He isnae far away."

"Nay, he certainly isnae," drawled Sir Ranald as he stepped up to the bars. "Ah, my sweet betrothed, it truly astounds me that no one has yet wrung your bonny neck. Howbeit, we will soon rectify that problem."

"Go away, Ranald," Isabel snapped. "I am trying to talk to Cormac."

"Ye are trying to bribe the poor mon with something ye ken every mon wants. I suspected ye would."

"How verra clever of you."

"I am a verra clever mon. Did ye nay ken that I have suspected ye of murdering my kinsmen for years? I began to watch you closely, verra closely, several years ago." He smiled slowly as he tugged a slender boy out from behind his back and watched Isabel pale, her expression a mixture of fury and fear. "Christopher, meet your father." Never taking his gaze from Isabel, Ranald nudged the boy closer to Cormac. "Armstrong, your son, Christopher."

"Ye cannae just grab the boy and drag him here," shrieked Isabel.

"I believe I did just that."

"And how do ye ken that the lad is mine? Mayhap I was just lying to Cormac."

" 'Tis certain that ye have done that a lot, but this lad is your son. Did ye think ye could hide him away for his whole life? Aye, ye dinnae have much to do with the lad, but ye do struggle to visit him now and again to see if he still lives. The old nursemaid was ready to talk to me. Ye dinnae inspire much loyalty in your servants, ye ken. And, m'lady, one needs to see the lad but the once to ken whose fruit ye bore."

Cormac paid little heed to the argument between Ranald and Isabel. His full attention was on the boy, who stared at him as intensely as he suspected he was staring back. Eyes very like his own and hair much like his brother Alaister's proclaimed the child his. There seemed to be little of Isabel in the child. A hint around the mouth and, Cormac suspected, a stronger influence in the delicate perfection of the child's features.

"Hello, Christopher," he said quietly, the wealth of emotion he fought to control making his voice hoarse.

"Hello, sir," the boy replied. "Are ye truly my father?"

"Aye, I am. Ye have come as a wee bit of a surprise to me."

"I ken it, sir. Lady Isabel didnae tell ye about me, so how could ye have kenned I was born? Nurse Agnes says Lady Isabel was keeping me tucked away until she thought ye might need your chain yanked taut again. Nurse Agnes says I should wait until ye ken that I am alive and see what ye do then ere I decide if ye are a good mon or nay."

" 'Tis my hope that ye will decide in my favor. How old are ye, laddie?"

"I will be seven in a month."

Cormac took a deep breath to try to push aside the fury welling up inside of him. All those years, and Isabel had not once mentioned a child. He had missed years of the boy's growth, from his first smile to his first full sentence. Yet another thing Isabel had stolen from him. Cormac knew that, if he did not leave, he would soon thrust his hands through those bars, wrap them around Isabel's slender throat, and end all need of a hangman.

"Would ye like to come with me, laddie? To stay with me?"

"Can I bring Nurse Agnes?"

"If she wishes to come along, aye, although I think

ye may be getting a wee bit old for a nurse. But she is welcome."

Christopher glanced nervously at his mother. "Does Lady Isabel come, too?"

"Nay." Cormac realized that it was going to be difficult to explain matters to the child. "I dinnae think ye will see your mother again, so ye had best say your fareweels now." His eyes widened slightly when the child visibly relaxed, shyly slipped his small hand into Cormac's, then looked at Isabel.

"Fareweel, Lady Isabel," Christopher said and bowed slightly. "I will live with my father now."

"Nay," Isabel screamed. "Ye havenae agreed to help me, Cormac. Look at the boy. I have given ye a fine son. Ye owe me. Curse ye. Do something about this. Can ye truly turn your back, walk away, and let the mother of your child hang?"

"I owe ye nothing," Cormac replied, "save the promise that I will care for Christopher." He glanced down at the child, who appeared to be unaffected by Isabel's tirade. Then he looked back at Isabel. "And better than ye e'er have, I am thinking, *Lady Isabel.* I suggest ye cease plotting ways to escape justice and call for a priest." Cormac nodded his farewell to the Douglases and walked away.


"Jesu, I still cannae believe ye have a son," William muttered, sitting on Christopher's bed next to Cormac and watching their three kinsmen try to teach the boy how to play dice. "Still, there is nay doubt in my mind that the lad is yours. That old woman could see it, too, though 'tis clear she doubted Isabel was capable of kenning for certain what mon fathered any child of hers."

Cormac smiled as he thought on stout, middle-aged Agnes. The woman had not hesitated to agree to go wherever Christopher went. After one long look at Cormac, she had told him and his relatives to move into the small cottage Isabel had settled her in. Although Agnes carefully measured her words whenever Christopher was near, she made it very clear that she thought Isabel to be unfit as a mother, that Isabel's complete lack of interest in the boy had actually been in his favor. It was plain to see that Agnes was the boy's true mother and Cormac was pleased that the two did not have to be separated.

" 'Tis a shame Isabel let him be born a bastard," William continued.

"Aye, but I will see him settled as weel as I can."

"Did ye think on what David said ere ye went to see that bitch? Will ye now woo your Elspeth?"

"I had thought to do so, but how can I now? I now have a son by the verra woman who came between us."

"Is Elspeth nay the one who fought to save a tattered, ugly cat? The same lass who took in a child no one else wanted? Do ye truly think your wee Elspeth will fault the lad because he was born of Isabel? If so, 'tis probably best if ye just forget her."

"Ye have ne'er even met Elspeth."

"Dinnae have to. She freed ye from Isabel. All that vow and honor business just meant ye were a little slow to accept your freedom. For that I am willing to kiss her wee feet."

"Ah, now, to see that I am willing to risk a lot. So a-wooing I shall go."

# Chapter Seventeen

"Isabel has been imprisoned for the murder of precisely *all* of her husbands."

Elspeth stared at Payton, stunned to hear that someone else had not only shared her suspicions, but acted upon them. She sank down in the chair opposite Payton at the head table in the great hall. There had been whispers about the woman since the death of her first husband, but very few had ever even suggested that she was responsible for the death of them all. Then Elspeth frowned. Payton had returned to court right after bringing her home, but now that she considered it, he must have stayed only long enough to gather this news. While it was pleasing to hear that Isabel might actually be made to pay for her crimes, Elspeth suspected there was more news to come. And that more had to be dramatic if it prompted Payton to ride immediately back to Donncoill to tell her.

"Who has imprisoned her?" she asked as a page poured them each a full goblet of wine.

"Sir Ranald Douglas—her betrothed," Payton replied and then took a long drink of wine.

"She was to be married *again?*"

"Aye. And he, too, was supposed to die. It seems Isabel has had yet another Douglas as her lover from the very beginning. 'Tis said that she and Sir Kenneth were patiently killing off everyone who stood between him and the lands he wished to be laird of. Sir Ranald was the last. He was a reluctant groom."

"That is evident. But Isabel could yet pull him beneath her spell."

"Nay. I spoke to the mon when the betrothal was agreed to. He is a good mon. A little hard, but quick of wit and honorable. I told him a few cold truths about his bride, including the fact that I, too, had been her lover once."

"Payton, he could have killed you," she said, her voice weakened and made hoarse with shock over his recklessness.

"He could have, but I felt certain he wouldnae e'en try. He was interested in all I had to tell him and assured me that he had no intention of marrying Isabel. The mon told me that he kenned exactly what Isabel was, that he had been watching her closely since her third husband died. He was gathering all the information he could and felt he was finally uncovering the truth. 'Tis clear that he finally did."

Elspeth sipped at her wine and murmured, "I wonder what happened that gave him the power to act against her."

"It seems that he and a few others had their ears pressed to the right door at just the right time."

"And they actually heard her confess?"

"Aye, that as weel as proof that Sir Kenneth was her lover, that the pair of them plotted together, that Sir Ranald wouldnae survive his marriage, and that they had already selected the mon who would take the blame for the death."

The way Payton watched her so closely made Elspeth's blood chill. It was not hard to guess which poor fool had been chosen to be accused of Isabel's crime. Just the thought of Cormac's name was enough to make her wince, which was why she had forced herself to think of the man as little as possible. In the ten days since she had left him, she had wept herself dry, cursed Cormac and his honor, longed for him, cursed him again, then tried to work herself into such a constant exhausted stupor she could think of little, save for getting some sleep. Her parents were watching her so closely she knew that soon they would cease waiting for her to tell them what was wrong and demand some answers. Elspeth was dreading the inevitable confrontation.

And now, just as she had obtained an almost perfect state of unthinking numbness, Payton returned with news that brought all the pain and confusion rushing back. Isabel would actually pay for her crimes now and Cormac was about to face a scarring heartbreak. The fact that she found herself worried about him infuriated Elspeth. When a small part of her began to wonder if Cormac would turn to her when Isabel was gone, when his pledge was severed by her death, Elspeth almost screamed. She did not want to think she could be such a priceless fool.

"Has Cormac learned of any of this?" she asked, hating the weakness that prompted the question.

"He was there."

"Oh, sweet Jesu." Elspeth was shocked, but she found the strength to quell the urge to go to Cormac, to try to help him overcome what had to be a devastating revelation. "Do ye ken what he has done or is going to do?"

"He lingers at court in case he is needed as a witness. Since Sir Ranald made it verra weel kenned that he did

not want Isabel as a bride, and the other witnesses are all
his kinsmen, that verra weel may be necessary. Sir Ranald
clearly wants her and Sir Kenneth to meet justice at the
end of a rope. He works diligently to gather together all
who have any knowledge of Isabel's or Kenneth's crimes,
no matter how small. I think he also wishes to make it
clear that Isabel and her lover were not simply brushed
aside because they had annoyed a Douglas. He wants there
to be no doubt about their guilt.''

"The fact that he could simply use the power of the
Douglases, but willnae, does seem to show that he is a
good, honest mon.''

"And one who kens weel how to survive. There is trouble
brewing, lass. The Douglases grow too powerful and far
too arrogant. There will be blood spilled soon, lands lost
and gained, and a shifting of power. Sir Ranald intends
to survive that, lands and power intact. I think he has the
wit to do just that. We shall see. What of Cormac?''

Payton said the name without warning and Elspeth could
not completely hide her reaction to it. It was a sad thing,
she mused, when the mere mention of a man's name could
so pain her, could make her flinch as if struck. Aside
from all of the news Payton had brought her, he had also
revealed to her that she had to work a lot harder to bury
her feelings about Sir Cormac Armstrong. She knew it
could be years before those feelings died, but she was
determined that they would stay entombed within her until
that time when they had the grace to wither away.

"What of him?" she replied. "He has seen what Isabel
is and that is good. Now he is free—free of whate'er he
may have still felt for her and free of that cursed vow.
Naught else matters.''

"Ah, Elspeth, do ye really believe that?''

"I must.'' She sighed, resigned to the fact that she would
have to talk about Cormac and praying that she could do

so without weeping. "I gambled and I lost. I havenae the heart left to try it again. Mayhap I have become a coward. It hurt more than I could have imagined when he chose Isabel and I dinnae wish to inflict that upon myself again."

"He is a fool."

"Weel, aye." She smiled faintly, her heart pounding from the strain of keeping her emotions reined in. "But mayhap I am a bigger one for thinking that I could end ten years of blind, ill-placed devotion with just a few weeks of honest loving, that somehow I could be the one to make him see that he could end his pledge to her and still keep his honor."

"And if he comes after you?"

"I dinnae ken. Beneath my pain I am still verra angry and, I beg ye, dinnae stir a hope in my heart. 'Twould be too easy for it to take root and I shudder to think what I would feel when it never bore fruit."

"Fair enough."

"Elspeth," her father called as he and her mother entered the great hall, "a messenger has brought ye something."

"Ye havenae told them, have ye?" Payton whispered as he watched his aunt and uncle approach.

"Nay," Elspeth replied, "but I believe my period of grace is over." She smiled at her father, but could tell by the way his dark eyes narrowed that it had been a sad effort gone to waste. "Who would send me something?" she asked as he handed her a small package wrapped in a bright piece of silk.

"I dinnae ken," Balfour replied as he sprawled in his chair at the head of the table and watched his daughter closely. "The lad who brought it wouldnae say. He waits for a reply."

Elspeth was not surprised to see her hands shaking as she opened the package. The moment it had been placed in her hands she had felt Cormac's presence so strongly she was surprised he did not walk into the hall. A brooch pinned to a small piece of parchment was revealed, a beautiful brooch of a heavy silver decorated with dark, blood red garnets. Below it, scrawled on the parchment in a broad, masculine hand were the words:

*Forgive me. Cormac.*

At the edges of the emotional maelstrom she had been plunged into, she sensed her father and mother studying the brooch, the note, and then her.

"Forgive him for what?" Balfour demanded.

"Nothing of any great importance," Elspeth answered as she staggered to her feet, desperately needing to retreat, needing some privacy in which to pull her shattered insides back together.

"The lad awaits a reply."

"Tell him thank you." Elspeth walked away, fighting the urge to run out of the great hall.

"No more?"

"Nay. No more."

The moment his daughter left, Balfour looked at Payton. "Something is breaking my lass apart."

"Aye," Maldie agreed as she sat down opposite Payton and fixed him with a stern gaze. "It has gone on long enough. What happened between her and the Armstrong lad?"

"And why does he ask for forgiveness?" Balfour added.

Payton sighed and dragged his fingers through his hair. "It isnae my place to tell you. Ye must speak with Elspeth."

"Oh, I intend to," Balfour said. "I would just like some wee hint of what quagmire I may be stepping into. He has hurt her."

"Aye, but she willnae let ye punish him for it. Weel, nay

let ye kill him leastwise. And in truth, he doesnae deserve killing. In many ways, Elspeth brought this upon herself. She gambled. She lost. Or so she believes.''

"Ye think otherwise?" asked Maldie, absently stroking Balfour's clenched fist where it rested upon the table in an attempt to soothe his rising temper. "Ye think it will all right itself in the end?"

"I do," Payton replied, "yet Elspeth is right to say it would be cruel to stir any hope in her breast. I dinnae really think she has lost her gamble. 'Tis simply that the prize she sought didnae come to her as quick and clean as she thought it would. Then again, I am nay sure I understand how she could have lost even for a little while. 'Tis a verra complicated situation."

"Obviously," Balfour drawled, "for ye have left me more confused than I was when ye started talking."

Maldie stood up, grabbed Balfour's hand, and tugged him to his feet. "So now we talk to Elspeth. Get some sleep, Payton. Ye are looking almost plain," she said and winked at her nephew.

Balfour followed his wife out of the great hall and paused when he saw the young messenger still waiting. "The lass says thank you." Nodding at the boy's frown, he said, "Aye, 'tis a puzzle, but 'tis all she said. Howbeit, ye may take that young fool another message. Tell him that he has broken something precious to me, and if he doesnae fix it soon, I will be paying him back in kind."

"Balfour!" Maldie protested, pausing on the steps to frown at him.

He shrugged and started to follow her again. " 'Twill do the mon good to ken that his idiocy isnae a secret kept between only him and Elspeth."

"We dinnae ken yet if it was *his* idiocy."

"Weel, we will soon," he said as he strode toward his

daughter's bedchamber, moving so fast that Maldie was soon following him.


Elspeth sat on her bed and stared blindly at the brooch she still held in her hands. Muddy curled up at her side, stroking her hip with his head as though he knew she was in dire need of some comfort. She reached down to idly stroke him back, that soothing motion and his loud purr soon taking the sharp edge off her pain. There was no doubt in her mind that her parents would soon arrive and she wanted to be calm enough to answer all the questions they were sure to ask.

*Forgive me,* he had written. For what? was the question. For hurting her? For not wanting her anymore? For not knowing what he did want? For wasting his honor on a woman who did not deserve it and being too blind to see that? Perhaps for not having the strength to resist the passion they shared. There were too many possibilities and few of them gave her any hope that Cormac himself would soon follow his gift. At the moment, she was not even sure she wanted him to. She had wanted him to choose her over Isabel because he wanted her more, loved her more. She did not want him turning to her because Isabel was dead, hanged for her crimes, and forever out of his reach. Or because, now that the one he had pledged himself to was gone, he could trot into her arms with his precious honor intact. Her pride rebelled at the mere thought of that and so did her heart. To know that she was merely his second choice would be like a slow poison to her spirit. Eventually, she could grow to hate him, could even grow to hate herself.

After a brief, sharp knock on her door, her parents entered. Her father shut the door, leaned against it, and crossed his arms over his broad chest. There was anger hardening his fine brown eyes and Elspeth knew he had already guessed at some of her secrets. There was sympathy there, too. When her mother sat down next to her on her bed and took her hand between hers, Elspeth felt her sympathy, too, and prayed she had the strength to resist it. She was a woman grown now and should be beyond crying on her parents' shoulders. That might ease some of her hurt, but it would not cure it.

"Elspeth, we have watched ye struggle not to fall apart for ten long days," her mother said. "We cannae just stand and watch any longer. Tell us what has wounded ye so verra badly. Let us help."

"Ah, Mither, I fear ye dinnae have a poultice that will cure this wound," Elspeth murmured. "I believe a shattered heart will bleed until it decides it has bled enough and no salve or bandage will change that."

"So I was right," said Balfour, his deep voice rough with anger. "The bastard used ye and then tossed ye aside." He grimaced when his wife and his daughter scowled at him, their matching green eyes sparkling with matching annoyance.

"Ye could have said that more kindly, husband," Maldie said.

"Aye," Elspeth agreed, "and 'tis nay the way of it. Truly."

"Ye mean he didnae bed ye?" her father asked bluntly.

Elspeth felt herself blush. "I am sorry to disappoint you so, but, aye, I am no longer a maid. Howbeit, 'tis unfair to say that Cormac is at fault. He didnae take my innocence. I gave it to him. Ye see, I have loved him since the day I found him wounded on Donncoill lands."

"A child's infatuation."

"Aye, then it was. But it grew with me, matured with me. When Cormac came to my rescue at Sir Colin's, I took one look at him, and I kenned that he was my mate." She looked at her mother and half smiled. "I should have heeded ye more closely, Mither. Ye were right. I kissed him minutes after seeing him." She briefly glanced at her scowling father. " 'Twas a kiss I stole, thinking that I could always excuse it as a rash act born of gratitude. And, aye, Mither, I tasted his passion. His desire fed mine and I truly believe mine fed his. 'Twas then I realized why he had lingered in my mind and heart for so long and I decided I would have him."

"Couldnae ye have done that without bedding him?"

"Nay, Fither. Ye see, whilst I was growing to love him, he was in love with Lady Isabel Douglas. He had pledged himself to her ere he showed up bleeding on our lands." She saw her father's scowl deepen and asked, "Do ye ken the woman?"

"Only by sight and rumor. A beautiful whore who has buried four husbands."

"Weel, it looks as if she will soon hang for those deaths along with the lover who plotted with her. Nay, not Cormac," she hastened to say when she saw the looks of alarm on her parents' faces. "He now kens that all the evil spoken of her was the truth. He was one of the men who overheard her confession. Aye, and heard her and her lover plot how they would be rid of her next husband and then have Cormac hanged for the murder. Payton can tell ye the whole of it."

"So the lad is free to come to you," said Maldie.

"Is he?" Elspeth shook her head and held her mother's gaze. "What if Fither had come to ye because the woman he truly wanted was now dead? Because the vow he had given her was ended by a hangmon's rope and nay by his own doing?" She nodded when her mother winced; then she proceeded to tell them everything that had happened from the moment Cormac had entered her room at Sir Colin's keep, careful not to mention how often or how vigorously she and Cormac had indulged their passion for each other.

"Ye told him he would have to crawl?" Maldie said, her voice unsteady with a mixture of laughter and shock.

Balfour laughed softly. "There's my lass."

Maldie tsked and shook her head at him. " 'Tis nay funny, Balfour."

"Isnae it? Aye, her pain isnae funny at all, but what she left him with has a touch of humor in it." He looked at Elspeth. "Ye salvaged whate'er pride ye think ye lost with those words, little one. I dinnae think ye lost your pride, but I ken that it will be a while ere ye can believe that. I am still nay sure why ye felt ye had to toss him your chastity, however."

"Fither, he was, or believed he was, in love with another woman," Elspeth said. "For ten years he had loved her, believed her a poor lass wronged and misused by her kinsmen, stood by her, felt himself bound by honor and vows, and had run to her side each time she called for him. He was almost completely faithful to her despite kenning that she was sharing the beds of her husbands."

"And near every mon who went to the king's court."

"Aye, but Cormac didnae ken that. I think she was also his first woman. And, he was in love and entrapped when he was still a lad, and my brothers have shown me how hot passions and other feelings are at that age. How deep. Isabel wove her web around him then, and there he dangled. She always gave him just enough to keep him there. Any hint of wavering and she reminded him of his pledge, kenning how much he wanted, e'en needed to hold fast to his word and his honor. Ye cannae fight ten years of such blind devotion with smiles, soft words, or coy looks. I had to give him all she did and more. I am sorry if I have caused ye to lose faith in me," she began.

"Nay, lass, ne'er that. Ye were fighting a battle against

an older, more experienced foe, one with nary a scruple
or a moral to hinder her. Ye had to use every weapon ye
could. I understand. I may wish that one of the weapons
ye chose wasnae your maidenhead, but I do understand.
I am but troubled that ye paid a high price, that ye are
here alone and hurt, mayhap by the fact that ye chose to
barter that bounty on a mon too stupid to ken what he
held—and that ye willnae let me kill him.''

Even though there was the bite of anger behind his
last words, Elspeth knew that he did not truly wish to kill
Cormac. By telling her tale as truthfully as modesty allowed,
she had soothed away a murderous fury against her lover.
She did notice, however, that her father made no promise
not to hurt Cormac. Despite her own anger at the man,
she hoped Cormac had the good sense to stay out of the
reach of her father.

They talked for a little while longer, but there was really
not much more to say on the matter. Elspeth noticed how
carefully her parents tried not to give her even the faintest
glimmer of hope. When they finally left, she sprawled on
her back on her bed, staring blindly at the ceiling, Muddy
settling himself comfortably at her side.

On the one hand, she felt a lot better now that the truth
was out. On the other, she felt wretched because there was
one possible truth she had kept to herself. The time for
her menses had come and gone. It was still too early to
be certain, but she could be carrying Cormac's child. If
she was, nothing, not even the reminder that she had
chosen this path for herself, would ease her father's anger.

After sending his messenger away, Cormac sank into a
chair near the fire and sighed. ''She is going to make me
fight.''

William handed his brother a drink of wine, then sat down in a chair opposite him. "And will you?"

"I must." He took a long drink of wine. "Still, something a little more than a simple thank-you could have helped me to decide just how to fight. The lad said she went marching out of the hall shortly after her father gave her my gift, then ran up the stairs as if the devil himself was tugging at her skirts. At least she reacted in some way, but was it from anger or confusion or . . ." He shrugged.

"If 'twas me, I would worry more on the message her father sent you."

"Oh, aye." Cormac winced. "I would rather not think on that."

"I wonder what precious thing of yours he wants to break."

Cormac gave his brother a look of pure disgust. "Dinnae play sweet and dumb. It truly doesnae suit you. I just wonder why he hasnae already appeared at my door, sword in hand, ready to separate me from my cullions."

"Maybe the lass asked him not to?" William frowned. "Nay, that wouldnae matter."

"It would in that family. True, he may have had to have been held down ere they could get him to listen, but Elspeth's father would at least consider her wishes. Mayhap I should take that as a good sign. If she hated me, she would tell him to have at me."

"I suppose." William smiled at Christopher as the boy edged close to his father's chair. "How are ye, laddie?"

"Fine, Uncle Will," the boy replied; then he looked at Cormac. "Did your lady like the present?"

"She said thank ye," Cormac replied, ruffling the boy's bright curls.

"Am I going to meet her? Are ye going to marry her?"

"I dinnae ken yet, laddie. She is verra angry with me."

"If we do see her, do ye think she will like me?"

Cormac hesitated only a moment. He saw Elspeth as a child refusing to leave him hurt and alone. He could see her raging at the village lads who had tormented that cat, then tenderly caring for the animal. He saw her shock, anger, and dismay when she found little Alan cast aside and left to die, emotions only enhanced when not one of the villagers would name or take in the child. And so she had taken the child herself. He looked at Christopher and smiled.

"Aye, she will like ye, Christopher. I have no doubt about that at all. 'Tis just me we have to get her to feel kindly toward."

"Will Lady Isabel go with us?"

The boy stood tense, wide-eyed, and unsmiling. Yet again, Cormac saw silent proof that Isabel shared no bond with their child. Christopher acted afraid of his mother and Cormac wondered what she had done to the child the few times she had had anything to do with him. He actually hoped that there was no love or longing for his mother in Christopher, that Agnes had given the boy all he required, or the truth about his mother could leave him badly scarred.

"Nay. I told ye, son, ye will ne'er be seeing her again." Since it was becoming more certain each day that Lady Isabel would be going to the gallows for her crimes, Cormac decided to touch on the matter a little now. "I fear she has made some verra bad mistakes, lad, and the ones she has wronged intend to make her pay for them. That is why ye will ne'er see her again—unless, weel, ye wish to visit her."

"Nay," Christopher replied quickly. "Nay, sir. She ne'er liked me. Nurse Agnes told me that it wasnae my fault, that there wasnae something wrong with me. Nurse Agnes said some people just dinnae have much heart in them, just dinnae ken how to care for another. Lady Isabel just doesnae have a big heart. Does your new lady have a big heart?"

"Oh, aye, a verra big one. I just have to make her let me back in."

"Ye will, sir. Nurse Agnes says ye arenae too bad, for a mon. She says ye will eventually ken what must be said to mend things."

As the days slipped by, Cormac began to think he ought to ask Nurse Agnes what to do. Elspeth continued to receive his gifts and messages with a cool courtesy at best and curt refusal at worst. His wooing of Elspeth appeared to be a dismal failure. More of his kinsmen arrived, including his brother Dougal who was barely a year younger than he. Cormac began to think that, if and when he did go after Elspeth, he would be dragging most of his family along with him.

Despite the protests of his family, Cormac attended the hanging. Someday his son might ask about his mother, and Cormac wished to be able to tell him the truth. It was also for the sake of his son that he collected Isabel's body and saw to her burial when it became clear that her kinsmen would not. Alone at her graveside, he stared at the newly turned dirt and wondered yet again how she had managed to fool him so completely for so very long. When he turned to leave, he was surprised to find Dougal waiting for him.

"Do we return home or do we ride to Donncoill?" Dougal asked.

Cormac sighed as they started to walk back to the cottage. "She hasnae asked me to come to her."

"She hasnae told ye not to, either."

"Nay, and I have to go. At least once, I must face her. She told me what I would have to do to win her back, but I had hoped to avoid it. It seems Elspeth meant every word she said that day." He smiled when Dougal cursed. "I ken ye dinnae want me to do this."

"Do ye expect me to encourage ye to humiliate yourself? Has this business with Isabel taught ye nothing?"

"Oh, aye, it taught me a lot. It taught me that, if a woman like Elspeth wants some sign, no matter how humiliating, that she means as much to me as Isabel did, I would be mad indeed not to give it to her."

# Chapter Eighteen

"This is going to hurt," Cormac said quietly as he stared down at the rock-strewn path that led through the gates of Donncoill.

He sighed and stared at the keep, where Elspeth hid from him. In the last two months, even as he had helped to bring Isabel and her lover to justice, he had continued to ply Elspeth with messages and gifts. Cautiously at first and then with an ever growing frequency as he continued to receive back only brief words of thanks for his gifts and hard-wrung words of passion. A few gifts had even been returned as items a gentleman should not send to *an aquaintance.* That stung. Elspeth had even thrown some of his own foolish words back in his face. This was his last chance.

Cormac had hoped, right up to the last minute, that it would not come to this, that pretty words and gifts would be enough. He should have known better. Elspeth had her pride and he had ground it into the dust. If anyone should understand how that felt, it was he. She had given him everything she had to give and he had treated it callously. He had done to Elspeth what Isabel had done to him. It was somewhat galling to know that Elspeth had the strength and wisdom to step out of such a trap, something he had never found. If it took such a grand gesture to win her back, that was what she would have.

"Are ye sure ye wish to do this?" asked his brother Dougal for what had to be the hundredth time.

Glancing back at Christopher, Agnes, and the six brothers and seven cousins who had trailed along with him, Cormac smiled faintly. "Nay, but I will." He briefly looked at a solemn Payton, who still stood holding the reins of the mare Cormac had brought for Elspeth, another gift she had politely refused. "Aye, I must."

"I would have thought ye had had more than enough of tossing your pride at the feet of some lass."

"Oh, aye, more than enough. However, unlike Isabel, Elspeth tossed her pride at my feet and I was too stupid to see what a precious gift that was. So 'tis time I repaid that in kind. I just pray that she doesnae make me do it for verra long, that, despite how poorly I treated her, she still feels a kindness toward me."

Payton glanced at Christopher, who stood next to Dougal and watched Cormac with wide eyes. "It may have been wise to tell her about the lad ere ye set him afore her."

"I thought it would best be done face-to-face," Cormac said. "A woman can sometimes think a child is proof of deep feelings between the two who created it. I want Elspeth to be able to look into my eyes and see that that isnae true." Cormac shrugged. "I also thought that, if she could just see the boy, she wouldnae mix him up in her mind with Isabel."

"Aye, now that I think on it, that may actually be the wiser way."

"Ye need not act so surprised. I can show a flicker of wit from time to time." He smiled faintly when Payton laughed. "I was surprised when none of you came after me."

"It was tempting at first, but once it was clear ye were trying to woo the lass, tempers eased." Payton glanced toward the keep. "Weel, at least the men's did. Are ye really going to do this?" he asked, looking back at Cormac.

"Aye, it seems I must."

"I cannae believe Elspeth is going to make ye do this. 'Tis nay like her to be so mean-spirited, so unforgiving."

"Have ye e'er been in love, Payton? Have ye e'er given someone all ye have and had them toss it back in your face?"

"Nay," Payton replied quietly. "Is that what ye did?"

"Feel like killing me now, do ye?"

"Pondering it. So is that really what ye did?"

" 'Tis what she says I did and who would ken it better than she? And who would ken better than I just how that feels? I dinnae want to do this. A part of me is choking on the verra thought of enduring the humiliation. Ah, but then I recall the emptiness that has rested inside me since she walked away. Anger will pass, humiliation will ease, but I ken without doubt that, if I dinnae get her back, the emptiness will set there all the rest of my days."

"Weel, get on with it then," snapped Dougal, "and ignore me if I weep o'er the shame of it all."

" 'Tis good for a mon to have the support of his family," drawled Payton, and he grinned when Cormac laughed. "If it is any consolation," he said more seriously as Cormac slowly knelt down on the ground, "when my aunt sees what ye are doing, even if Elspeth hesitates, she willnae allow it to go on. At least ye will get the chance to meet with the lass and talk to her."

"Aye, that does help some," said Cormac.

It took every ounce of will he possessed to start along the path on his hands and knees. He had to bludgeon his pride into submission and blind himself to the fact that far too many people watched him. Cormac prayed that Payton was right in saying it would not be allowed to continue for very long. He was more than willing to make the gesture, but he was not sure how long he could endure this blow to his pride. Right or wrong, it would begin to choke him until he and Elspeth found themselves with yet another obstacle to overcome.

"She sent the mare back to him," said Maldie as she strode into the bedchamber she shared with her husband

"Now that is a shame. 'Twas a fine horse," murmured Balfour as he stared out the window at the large group of young men just outside his gates.

Maldie joined her husband at the window and frowned. "She kens he is out there, but says naught. She is a stubborn lass. I understand her hurt and anger, but she needs to relent some or she could end up cutting off her own nose just to spite her face."

" 'Tis early in the game yet, love. Aye, she shouldnae let him ride away, but seeing as he shows no sign of doing so, let it rest. The lass may just be feeling wary and needs to take a breath or two to clear her head. I dinnae think she believed he would come."

"She wouldnae allow herself to even think it." She frowned at the small crowd outside the gates. "What is he doing now?"

Balfour cursed in surprise, then laughed softly. "He is crawling."

"Oh, nay. Nay." Maldie started toward the door. "That cannae happen. She will go to him now e'en if I must drag her there myself by the hair."

"Are ye certain ye should interfere?"

"Aye. For one thing, she cannae see his grand gesture from her bedchamber. For another, if 'tis allowed to go much beyond a gesture, 'twill sit in his innards like a poison. Elspeth will suffer, too, for she would ne'er truly wish him to humble himself completely."

"A shame," Balfour muttered as his wife ran out of the room. "He probably willnae be down there long enough to even mar his fine hose." He started to follow his wife. Then he realized that she would be returning in a minute or two, so he hurried back to the window. "Ye won, lassie," he said and wondered just how and when he should do a little interfering of his own.

Elspeth stared at the short note that had come with the mare.

> *I have come for you, my heart.*
> *Cormac*

*What arrogance,* she thought, even as her traitorous heart beat with anticipation. He was so close. He said he wanted her. Why, she wondered, was she not racing out there to hurl herself into his arms?

"Because I am terrified," she admitted aloud and was disgusted with herself.

For two long months she had lived a perfectly hellish existence. When she was not numb with exhaustion, she was crippled with pain. A thousand times she had found herself wondering what else she could have done to make Cormac love her. Good sense told her she had done all any woman could, but her emotions did not respond well to good sense.

He had hurt her so. Some of it was her own fault. She

had expected too much, too soon. The truth did not lessen her pain, however. In none of his notes did he declare that he loved her. He asked forgiveness, called her sweet, loving names, spoke of his need for her and his want, and wooed her in the sweetest way. If there had never been an Isabel, she would have been won over. Now, even though he had begun wooing her before Isabel had been executed, she was left to wonder if she was just a second choice. After all, he had learned the truth about Isabel before he had begun to send his gifts and love notes. He had not willingly left the woman to come to her.

When the door to her bedroom was flung open, Elspeth stared at her mother in shock. "Is something wrong?"

"Ye will come with me, Elspeth Murray," Maldie said as she grabbed her daughter's hand and dragged her out of her room. "There is something ye have to see. I pray ye dinnae disappoint me in how ye react when ye see it."

Elspeth hurried to keep pace with her mother, who was practically running down the hall. When they entered her parents' bedchamber, she saw her father standing at the window and smiling faintly. A moment later her mother pushed her in front of the same window.

"Look there, Elspeth," Maldie ordered, pointing toward the gates.

At first, Elspeth was not sure what she was supposed to be looking at. Then her gaze fell upon the man crawling along the path that led to the gates. She gasped and gripped the edge of the narrow window, unable to believe her eyes. Then she became utterly horrified by what was happening. For all of her angry words when she and Cormac had parted, this was not what she wanted. Softly crying out a denial, she hiked up her skirts and raced out of her parents' room, heedless of everything and everyone, save for the need to get to Cormac as fast as she could.

"I thought that was what she would do," Maldie said,

the satisfaction clear to hear in her sultry voice as she hooked her arm through Balfour's. "Shall we go?"

"I suppose it is for the best that it was stopped," agreed Balfour as he began to escort her to the front gates at a leisurely pace.

"It was. I dinnae think she e'er truly meant for him to do it anyway."

"Probably not. Why do ye think she was hesitant to go to him?"

"Fear, my love. He hurt her verra deeply. What woman wishes to chance such pain again? Aye, he wooed her, but I think, for all his pretty words and fine tokens, he ne'er said what she needed to hear to soothe her fear."

"So matters are not yet settled completely."

"Nay, but they will be soon."

"Are ye certain?"

"Balfour, the mon was on his hands and knees before his kinsmen, our kinsmen, our men-at-arms, and anyone else close enough to see our gates. What do ye think?" She smiled when he laughed and kissed her cheek.

"I think ye will be verra busy for the next few days planning a wedding."

"Is that your Elspeth?"

At Dougal's question, Cormac rose, sitting back on his heels and looking toward the gates. He caught his breath when he saw Elspeth. Her thick hair was loose, swirling around her like an angry storm cloud, and her skirts were hitched up to her knees as she ran toward him. She made him ache.

"Aye, 'tis my Elspeth."

"Keep crawling," Dougal said, roughly pushing him back down.

Cormac was just sitting back up to succinctly tell Dougal

what he thought of him when Elspeth reached him. He barely kept himself from falling backward when she bumped into him as she stumbled to a halt. Then, as she grabbed his arm, he saw that she was weeping and felt his heart clench with fear. Tears were not the sign he had been looking for.

Elspeth yanked on Cormac's arm, trying to pull him to his feet. "Dinnae do this," she said, her voice soft and hoarse with tears. "Please dinnae to this. I am sorry. I was just so verra angry."

Realizing that she wept for him, he tugged her down until she knelt on the ground in front of him. He smiled faintly as, still weeping, she almost frantically brushed the dirt from his hands. When she started to do the same to his hose, he quickly took her hand in his. He was so starved for her that the slightest brush of her hand on his leg was almost enough to break his control. A soft grunt escaped him when she flung herself against his chest, wrapping her arms tightly around his waist. Elspeth obviously did not recognize the danger she was in, and for once, she was too upset to sense the desire rapidly flooding his body.

"I am sorry," she mumbled into his doublet, still crying softly. "I ne'er meant for ye to actually do it. I swear I didnae."

He put his hands on her damp cheeks, pulled her face back until he could look her full in the eyes, and brushed a kiss over her mouth. "Ye shouldnae be apologizing to me, angel. A wee bit of groveling willnae kill me, although I am glad ye didnae make me go too far. These rocks are verra hard on a mon's knees." He had to kiss her again when she smiled. "To see ye smile again, I would be tempted to crawl through fire."

She reached out one trembling hand to stroke his cheek. "Isabel?" she asked even though just saying the woman's name threatened to choke her.

"They sent her and her lover to the gallows. And if ye are searching my eyes for her ghost, ye willnae find it. I swear to ye, I kenned my mistake ere the door finished closing behind you. It but took this poor fool a wee bit of time to clear his muddled brain of ten years' worth of lies. What I learned of her but confirmed and clarified what I felt."

A curse escaped him as a strong hand abruptly grasped him tightly by an arm and yanked him to his feet. Cormac got one brief glimpse of Elspeth tumbling back to sprawl in the dirt before he was crushed against a broad chest. The hold and the slap on the back were both far too painful to be completely friendly. When he was released and saw that the man still gripping him by the arm was Elspeth's father, he understood.

"Good to see ye, lad," Balfour said. "Glad to see that ye brought some of your kinsmen to attend your wedding."

"Fither," Elspeth protested as a young man who hastily introduced himself as Cormac's brother Dougal helped her to her feet. "Cormac hasnae asked me to marry him."

"Nay?" Balfour looked at Cormac. "Interrupted ye a moment too soon, did I?"

The voice was calm, almost friendly. The smile was an easy one, amiable and welcoming. In the eyes, however, was hard command. Balfour Murray may have been understanding enough not to hunt him down, but now that he was here, he would be held until he married Elspeth. Since that was exactly what Cormac wished to do, he just smiled and nodded.

"Angel, will ye wed with me?" he asked, biting back a grin as she angrily pushed her tousled hair out of her face and glared at her widely grinning father.

"Fither, I willnae allow ye to force him," Elspeth said, although she did think that Cormac looked a little too happy for a man who was being forced to do something he did not wish to do.

"I am nay forcing the lad," Balfour said, "and who is the laird here, eh?" He looked at Cormac. "The lass says aye. Introduce me to your kin then."

"Fither!" When her mother stepped up beside her and calmly brushed off her skirts as she lowered them, Elspeth said, "Can ye nay stop him?"

"Any other father would have either killed the lad or dragged him before a priest two months ago," Maldie said as she nodded a greeting to each new Armstrong she was introduced to. "A handsome lot, these Armstrongs."

"I dinnae want him forced to marry me," Elspeth muttered, hoping that, despite her distraction, she would be able to recall the names of all the handsome young men who stepped forward to kiss her hand.

"Lass, do ye think the mon was crawling to our gates just to tell ye that it was nice to see ye again?"

Before she could respond to that sarcasm, Cormac brought a young boy and a plump older woman to stand before her. Shock pushed aside every thought and concern from her mind. One look was all that was needed to know that this was Cormac's son. Cormac had told her that there were no ghosts, that Isabel was gone, but he had lied. Her ghost rested there in the perfect features of the son she had given Cormac.

"This is my son, Christopher, and his nurse, Agnes," Cormac said, not surprised to hear Sir Balfour softly curse, although hearing Lady Maldie do the same did startle him a little.

It was not easy but, refusing to make the innocent boy pay in even the smallest way for the sins of his parents, Elspeth greeted him and then Agnes with all the charm and courtesy she could drag out of herself. Agnes gave her an approving smile, but her gray eyes were sharp as they studied her face and those of her family. Christopher was sweet, obviously shy, and well mannered, making it easy for Elspeth to keep control of her emotions. She straightened up and looked at Cormac, pleased to see that he had the good sense to be uneasy.

"Christopher and I are still coming to ken each other," Cormac said, holding Elspeth's gaze with his own.

"Aye," said Christopher. "Papa met me but two months ago. I lived with Nurse Agnes till then."

*God bless you, Christopher,* Cormac thought as he watched some of the anger leave Elspeth and her family, their scowls and tense stances easing a little. A small frown touched the full mouth he ached to kiss. As long as the child was near, however, he could not give Elspeth the fuller explanation needed to soothe away those very unkind thoughts she was so clearly having about him. A moment later, he decided, yet again, that Nurse Agnes was a very wise woman.

"Come, lad. We shall go to the keep." Agnes looked at Maldie, bobbed a curtsy, and said, "If that is acceptable, m'lady."

"Of course," replied Maldie. "Go right along, all of you. Ye will be shown where to freshen yourselves, where ye can sleep, and anything else ye may wish. We will be along in a minute."

The moment Agnes, Christopher, and the others with Cormac walked away, Elspeth demanded, "Isabel?"

"Aye. She kept him hidden from me for all of his seven years. If ye can recall, we once puzzled o'er her apparent barrenness. Weel, she wasnae barren. From what she said, Christopher is here simply because she couldnae rid her body of him as she had the others." He nodded when both Elspeth and her mother gasped in horror. "I ne'er had the heart to ask if any of those others were mine, too."

"So when she kenned she was going to die, she finally told ye about the child?" Elspeth asked.

"Nay, I think she would have gone to her grave with her secret, but she thought she had finally found a use for the boy. She said she would give him to me if I helped her get free. She said that, if I didnae, I would ne'er see my son alive. God help me, I might have done it just to get the boy, e'en though I wondered if she was lying yet again."

Elspeth could tell by the look on his face that he was still very angry about that. "But ye didnae do it."

"Nay, I was saved from making that choice by the keen eyes and wits of Sir Ranald. He had been watching Isabel since the death of her third husband, and so he kenned about the child despite how rarely Isabel went to see her own son. The moment she was captured, I think he suspected how she would try to use the boy and brought him to me." Although it was evident that Elspeth was no longer angry, he was not sure what she thought or felt and did not want to ask while her family stood there.

"Come," Maldie said as she slipped her arm through Cormac's. "We will join the others now."

"Does Christopher ken the truth about Isabel?" Elspeth asked as she fell into step on the other side of Cormac, her hands clenched into tight fists at her side as she resisted the strong urge to touch him.

"As much as a child that young can," replied Cormac. "He called her Lady Isabel and actually seemed pleased that he could go with me and ne'er have to see her again. Both Agnes and I have told him that she is dead and why, although we ne'er told him exactly what crimes she had committed. He sometimes mentions her in his bedtime prayers, but otherwise, ne'er asks of her or speaks of her. To Christopher, Agnes is his mother, and Lady Isabel is the woman who made him verra unhappy during her rare visits."

" 'Tis verra sad, but in this case that may be for the

best," said Maldie. "Be grateful that he was blessed with Agnes."

While her mother asked Cormac questions about Christopher, obviously trying to see if there were any wounds of the heart or spirit that might need tending, Elspeth tried to decide how she felt about it all. She felt no anger or dislike of the child, knew she would have no trouble loving him as all children deserved and needed to be loved. What she was not sure of was what Cormac felt about it all. Men often felt something for the mother of their child, and considering what Cormac had always felt for Isabel, such a bond should be even greater. Yet she sensed little more than disgust and anger in him whenever he mentioned Isabel. It was hard to believe he could have changed toward the woman so completely. Somehow she was going to have to get him to talk about it.

There was no doubt in her mind that she would soon be married to Cormac. Her father wanted it and Cormac appeared to want it as well. Part of her was elated, yet another part was deeply afraid. She would be married to the father of her child, to the mate of her heart and soul, to the man who could make her burn with just a look. There would be no more lonely nights, no more aching for his touch or the sound of his voice. Her fear was bred of the fact that he had not openly chosen her over Isabel, that he had come to her only after Isabel was dead. Despite the gifts, the sweet words, and even his grand gesture in front of Donncoill's gates, she did not know what was in his heart. It was just another thing they needed to talk about. Cormac might be telling the truth when he said there were no more ghosts inside of him, but Elspeth suddenly realized that she had a few.

By the time the evening meal was done, Elspeth realized that she was not going to have a chance to talk to Cormac until after they were married. The wedding was to be held in three days and she suspected that Cormac was going to be heartily sick of her family's company by then. Everyone was friendly and annoyingly cheerful, but she quickly saw how one or more of the men in her family constantly and closely shadowed Cormac. Someone also shadowed her at all times. The longest time she was able to stand alone with Cormac was barely long enough to ask him how he fared before Payton and her brother Connor arrived to lead him away. Elspeth cursed, leaned against the wall with her arms crossed, and glared at the crowded hall, most especially her family.

"They willnae allow ye two within feet of each other until ye kneel afore that priest," Cormac's brother William said as he slouched against the wall on her right.

"In three days ye will have him all to yourself," said his brother Dougal as he slouched against the wall on her left. " 'Tisnae so verra long."

"Mayhap I wish to speak privately with the mon my fither is dragging to the altar," she said, her glare doing nothing to vanquish their identical looks of amusement.

"Now, lass," said William, "does our brother look verra troubled by all of this? Why did ye think he came here?"

"And just mayhap it isnae the *why* of his arrival that troubles me. Mayhap 'tis the *when*."

"The *when?*"

"Aye, *after* Isabel is dead and gone."

"Ah," William murmured as he watched her walk away. "So that is the way of it."

"Do ye think we should warn Cormac?" asked Dougal.

"Warn our brother the idiot who let that bonny lass leave his bed? Our brother who, in three short days, will be curled up between the sheets with a lass who, in his own words, has a voice that could melt rock? Our brother who could revel in the love and passion of that wee lass

with but the muttering of a few sweet words?'' He looked
at Dougal and cocked one brow.

"Ye are right. The bastard is already too cursed lucky
for words. Let him figure it out for himself."

Cormac watched Elspeth leave the great hall and sighed.
Her father was obviously willing to forgive and forget. He
should be grateful and he was. Her family was welcoming
him with open arms, and considering all he had done, he
knew he was very fortunate in that. In three days he would
be married to Elspeth; he would be able to love her and
hold her close throughout the night. He should be in the
chapel on his knees thanking God for that. However, her
family, smiling and friendly as they were, clearly meant to
keep him and Elspeth completely separated for every hour
of the day and night between now and the wedding. It was
going to be a very long three days.

# Chapter Nineteen

"And just where might ye be going, lass?"

Elspeth squeaked in alarm and stumbled as her mother's voice came sharply to her through the shadows. She struggled to think of something to allay the suspicion she could see on her mother's face when she turned toward her. The way her mother stood in the doorway of her bedchamber—her arms crossed and one small, slippered foot tapping—made Elspeth feel like a small child caught out in some mischief again.

"I was feeling a wee bit hungry," Elspeth said.

"Ah, I see," her mother murmured. "It must be the excitement of your wedding on the morrow that has caused ye such a strange confusion."

"What confusion?"

"The confusion that has ye tiptoeing in the wrong direction in the verra keep ye grew up in." Maldie shook her head when her daughter blushed; then she grabbed Elspeth by the arm and tugged her into the room. "I have some food in here."

"I just wished to speak with him," Elspeth muttered as her mother dragged her into a small room just off her bedchamber and pushed her into a seat before a small table. "Dinnae ye think he and I should talk a little ere we are set before a priest?" she asked, looking over the selection of bread, cheese, fruit, and tarts on the table and helping herself to an apple tart.

"Do ye mean to tell him about the child?" Maldie asked.

Elspeth choked on her tart, but then winced as her mother slapped her on the back a little too sharply before handing her a soothing glass of wine. "How long have ye kenned the truth?" she finally rasped.

Maldie shook her head again and sat down opposite Elspeth. "I guessed it shortly after ye came home. I kenned it for certain a few weeks later. Elspeth, my child, did ye really think I wouldnae see it?"

"Nay," she said, a little disgusted with herself. "In truth, I didnae think on it too often except to mark when my first menses didnae arrive when it should and then my second didnae, either. Then I would fret a while o'er how to tell ye and Fither and what would happen. Then there would be a few visions of Fither dragging a gaunt, still grieving Cormac from the shrine he had built to Isabel and forcing him to kneel with me afore a priest." She was not surprised to hear her mother badly stifle a giggle, for it was a truly preposterous imagining. "Then I would be right back to trying verra hard not to think of the mon at all. And if I couldnae think of the mon, I couldnae let my thoughts dwell on the child I carried, either, could I?"

"Of course not. Weel, were ye going to tell Cormac about the child?"

"Nay, that wasnae my plan. I just wished to talk to him. We didnae get to say much ere he was surrounded by my kinsmen. Somehow I thought talking to him might ease some of my concerns. I dinnae feel all that sure that Isabel is truly gone from our lives."

"Because of the boy?"

"A wee bit. If I can see his mother in him, surely Cormac can as weel. And I dinnae ken if I should worry on that or nay."

"The woman treated the child most unkindly and I believe Cormac kens that, if nay the how of it. One thing she seemed most fond of doing was complaining about how he didnae have the grace to die like the others." Maldie nodded, her expression grim, when Elspeth gasped in shock. "I dinnae think the woman beat the child or hurt him physically, aside from being to quick to slap, but what little I have found out indicates that she did her best to make him feel unloved, unwanted, and mayhap, unloveable. Agnes told me that once, shortly after the lad turned six, Lady Isabel arrived while the boy was finishing his bath. Nothing happened, and Agnes feels nothing e'er did, for she kept a close guard, but something in the way Isabel looked at the child and insisted upon drying him made Agnes sick with fear for the boy. I did hear a rumor or two at court that said Lady Isabel liked the verra young lads, the beardless boys who hadnae yet had a woman." Maldie shrugged. "Still, I can sense no deep scars in the boy, although there are some wounds. He will need a lot of nurturing."

"Are ye saying that I should set aside my own concerns for the sake of that poor, sad boy?"

"I am saying that, aye. Sort out your troubles, for an unhappy union will do the lad no good at all. Now isnae the time, however. And to be quite blunt, child, ye will still be wed on the morrow no matter how much ye grumble. Your father is adament and Cormac seems just as set on the business. Ye carry the mon's child. He has brought his son to you and clearly wishes the three of ye to be a family. And there is wee Alan to consider as weel. There is also the fact that ye love that mon, and if ye are as much like me as I suspect ye are, ye will ne'er love anyone else as completely, as deeply, or as passionately. Dinnae toss it all aside because ye fear a dead woman or fret o'er a vow made by a lad of little more than sixteen."

Elspeth saw no point in relating any more of her concerns. Her mother had made her position quite clear and her final words made Elspeth feel as if she was being foolish or weak. As Elspeth ate, they talked about who was going to attend the wedding in the morning. Then her mother escorted her back to her bedchamber and left her there with a kiss on the cheek that silently offered encouragement.

Her mother's words were still haunting Elspeth in the morning as she slipped away to the nursery to visit with little Alan and Christopher. She knew it would soon be too chaotic to do so, for with her family would come a great many children. Christopher sat on the floor, piling up blocks for Alan to knock down, smiling when the tiny boy giggled madly as the blocks tumbled loudly to the floor. Christopher had taken to Alan very quickly and Elspeth wondered if he felt some bond with the child, who had been so cruelly cast aside. Agnes gave her a brief smile and a wink as Elspeth sat down with the boys; then she returned to sewing a little shirt for Alan.

"He does enjoy that," Elspeth murmured as Alan knocked another pile of blocks over, giggled merrily, and then crawled over to sit in her lap.

"He is a good bairn," Christopher said, briefly and shyly touching Alan's dark curls. "His mother didnae have much heart, either, just like mine. I will let him ken that it isnae his fault that she didnae keep him."

"And I think 'tis advice he will heed much more closely if it comes from you."

"He will come to live with us, willnae he?"

Elspeth had the feeling that Christopher would fight her with every possible weapon a clever child of seven could muster if she said nay. "Aye, that was my plan. I think your father will allow it."

"Oh, aye." Christopher gave her a smile that made her heart ache because it so strongly resembled his father's. "He told me all about wee Alan. He said he missed the bairn almost as much as he missed you. He said he missed waking up and hearing the bairn sucking on his toes and babbling at the cat. Muddy is a verra good cat," Christopher added, glancing toward Muddy, who was sprawled near Alan's crib, watching them all closely.

Flung into a mixture of delight and confusion over what Christopher had told her his father had said, Elspeth took a moment to gather her wits before she said, "He is. A verra good cat indeed. Now, lad"—she looked right at Christopher—"I came to ask ye if it is acceptable to ye that I marry your father." Out of the corner of her eye she saw Agnes nod with approval and Elspeth wondered why that should make her feel so absurdly pleased.

"Aye, Lady Elspeth," Christopher replied, his pretty face solemn. "I asked my father if ye had a heart and he said ye had a verra big one. I can see that he was right. He also said he hopes ye will let him back in."

"Just between us, laddie, I ne'er cast him out. I just got a wee bit angry, and I will tell ye true: He still has some explaining to do."

Christopher nodded. "Ye want to ken that ye are in his heart, too."

"Aye, my bonny boy, that I do." *Or at least know that someone else is not still lurking there,* she mused.

For a little while longer, she played with the children;

then she started to leave. Agnes rose and walked her to just outside the nursery door. It was clear that Agnes wanted to say something, and Elspeth tried to wait patiently for the woman to begin.

"Young Sir Cormac is a good mon, m'lady," Agnes finally said. "The moment that bi—her ladyship's secret was uncovered, he took on the care of his laddie. He and that lot of handsome kinsmen of his filled my wee cottage near to bursting, but it did my bairn more good than I can say. Ye see, he was finally accepted. The only one of his blood he had kenned of before they all arrived—weel, she made it verra clear that he wasnae wanted. Those big lads treated him like one of their own, teasing him, playing with him, and sometimes teaching him things I had to box their ears for."

It was hard, but Elspeth bit back a smile at the image of Agnes sternly ruling over a small horde of full-grown Armstrong men. Although Agnes was Christopher's nurse, it was clear she meant to mother the whole lot. Elspeth wondered if any of the Armstrongs understood that yet.

"What I am trying to say, m'lady, is that all the lad needs is to be accepted," Agnes continued, "to have himself a true home."

"I will have nay trouble doing that," Elspeth assured her.

"I ken it, and when done with my rambling, I was going to bless ye for it. And 'tis good of ye to keep that wee bairn. Christopher has grown most fond of the bonny wee lad."

"Oh, aye, 'tis easy to see. But they have a bond, dinnae they? They were both cast aside and both had unnatural mothers who wished them dead and gone."

Agnes shook her head. "I ken it happens, but I have ne'er understood it or been able to forgive it. Weel, ye had best go and prepare for the wedding. I have said all

I meant to say. I just wished to thank ye for giving the poor lad a home."

"Ah, Agnes," Elspeth kissed the older woman's cheek and then started to walk back to her bedchamber. "Christopher has always had that because God blessed him and gave him you."

The moment Elspeth entered her bedchamber she was set upon by her cousins Avery, Bega and little Gillyanne, as well as her sister Morna and several maids. Elspeth protested at so much help, but she was ruthlessly ignored. She was undressed, bathed, and dressed, and her hair was washed, brushed dry, and decorated with bright green ribbons. By the time they were done and she was left alone with just Avery and young Gillyanne, Elspeth was exhausted, but she had to admit that she felt pretty. The green of her gown suited her. Thinking that was a little vain, she blushed.

"Blushing?" teased her cousin Avery, who looked particularly catlike as she stretched on Elspeth's bed, her golden eyes alight with laughter. "Dinnae tell me ye have forgotten what to do?"

"Young ears," Elspeth muttered, glancing at Gillyanne, who promised to be as beautiful as her elder sister Sorcha.

Gillyanne snorted indelicately. "Nay that young. Nay with brothers and cousins like mine."

"Just why have the two of ye lingered here?" Elspeth nervously toyed with a lock of her hair.

"Gillyanne is to hold the wedding cup and I am to make sure that ye dinnae trip on your gown and fall on your face," Avery answered cheerfully. "And we wished to visit, though 'twill be a short one, for Gillyanne and I are soon off to France to visit my cousins."

"Truly? I am surprised Aunt Bethia will allow it."

"I think she feels she has near to caged the lass since

what happened to Sorcha. We hope to be gone ere she grows too fretful again and snatches Gilly back.''

"Is Sorcha to be here, too?''

"Nay,'' Gilly replied. "She couldnae leave the convent on such short notice, but she vows to attend you when ye have your first bairn.'' Gilly laughed when Elspeth instinctively rested her hand on her stomach. "Aye, she said that she doubted it would be verra long before ye sent her word that a bairn was due.''

"Wretched brat,'' Elspeth teased, then took a deep breath to steady herself. "Weel, let us go and get this o'er with.''

"Such romance,'' drawled Avery as she scrambled off the bed with a grace Elspeth envied. "He is a bonny lad, Cousin, and I think he is most eager to claim you. And, his son is verra sweet.''

"When did ye meet Christopher?'' she asked as they started out of her room.

"Late last night. We arrived after ye had already retreated to your chambers. Between the journey and meeting so many bonny Armstrongs, I found that I couldnae sleep. I crept down to the kitchens, hoping to find some warm, spiced wine. Agnes was there feeding wee Alan some porridge and a sleepy Christopher was watching her verra carefully. She kindly made me some hot, spiced wine and we all had a nice visit as I drank it.'' Avery winked at Elspeth as they entered the great hall. "Agnes wants your first bairn to be a lass. She says there are already too many male Armstrongs.'' Looking at the crowd gathered in the great hall, Avery laughed softly. "She may be right.''

Elspeth smiled in reply to Avery's good humor, but her attention was on Cormac. He stood with her father, talking quietly to the young priest. The way his tall, lean body looked in the black and silver doublet and hose he wore made her insides ache. Off to his side were several of his brothers and young Christopher, dressed in plaids and crisp white shirts. Her father still looked tall and fit in his equally black doublet and hose and Elspeth smiled faintly as she recalled how often her mother had tried and failed to get her *big brown mon* to wear anything colorful. To her father's side were her brothers Connor, Ewan, and Liam all handsomely arrayed in their plaids. It was a sight, she mused, to linger in a young lass's mind.

As if he sensed she was looking at him, Cormac turned. He searched her face intently, as if trying to judge what she was feeling. Then he smiled. Her breath caught in her throat and she heard both of her cousins sigh in appreciation.

It was an effort, but Elspeth inwardly pulled herself together. There was no stopping the marriage and she was not even sure she would do so if there was, but she and Cormac had a few problems to sort through yet. That would never happen if she let him addle her wits with smiles and warm looks. Even if the answers she got did not completely please her, Elspeth was determined not to begin their marriage with questions unanswered, explanations ungiven, and doubts unassuaged.

Taking a deep breath to steady herself, she walked toward him. She suspected every bride felt a little nervous, though probably with not as much reason as she had. What she needed was his love and she did not know if she had it or ever would. Once she had allowed herself to think she had reached his heart, and then he had turned to Isabel. She could not bear such hurt a second time. There would be no more assumptions made on her part.

"Ye are looking verra solemn, lass," Cormac said as she stepped up to his side.

"Marriage is a solemn business," she said haughtily, but she ruined her pose by glaring at her father and adding,

"Especially when one of the participants ne'er got a chance to say aye or nay."

Balfour clasped his hands behind his back and gazed at the ceiling, sighing as if with infinite patience. " 'Tis a wee bit late to be complaining about that."

"If I could have found a certain fither alone for one tiny moment in the last three days, I might not have had to wait till now."

Fixing a stern gaze upon the nervous priest, Balfour ordered, "Get on with it."

"Weel," the priest shakily cleared his throat, "both parties must be willing."

When both her father and Cormac looked at her, Elspeth crossed her arms and began to hum softly. Although she had every intention of proceeding, she decided it would not hurt to make then sweat just a little. She heard the men curse, her mother and aunts groan with a mixture of amusement and mild despair, and behind her, her two cousins doing a very poor job of stifling their giggles. Elspeth was curious as to how her father and Cormac would solve this little problem she had just presented them.

"This isnae funny, lass," snapped Balfour. "Ye will do as ye are told." When his daughter just hummed a little louder, Balfour cursed and dragged his fingers through his lightly graying hair. "Ye are as stubborn as your mother."

Elspeth stopped humming long enough to murmur, "Thank ye."

"It wasnae a compliment."

"Balfour," Maldie warned as, flanked by Elspeth's aunts Bethia and Giselle, she moved to stand beside him. "Ye are swimming in some verra dangerous waters."

When his wife did no more than stand there watching her daughter with a half smile on her face, Balfour asked, "Are ye nay going to help?"

" 'Tis your mess. Ye made it. Ye clean it up."

Cormac was torn between amusement and dismay. He noticed that their kin, after the first shock had passed, were all openly amused. Balfour even had a glint of it in his eyes. Ordering Elspeth was obviously not going to work, but Cormac did not feel completely helpless. He had a way he could persuade her. After a heated kiss or two, Elspeth was usually so muddled that he could probably tell her that the moon was green and she would agree with him. At least that used to be the case. For one brief moment, he hesitated, not sure he wanted to put it to the test. Then he decided that, if he could no longer affect her like that, it might well be a good idea to halt the wedding. Being tied for life to Elspeth when she no longer felt that deep, rich passion for him that she had before would be hell on earth.

"Sir Balfour, if I may ... ?" Cormac asked, bowing slightly.

"Ye think ye can make the lass see reason?" asked Balfour.

His plan was to make Elspeth lose all reason, at least long enough to get them married, but he could not say so. If nothing else, he did not want Elspeth warned. " 'Tis worth a try."

"Weel, do your best."

"Oh, I intend to," Cormac drawled and yanked Elspeth into his arms.

Elspeth's humming stopped on a squeak as Cormac covered her mouth with his. He was vaguely aware of the hoots of approval from the men and the cries of dismay from the women, but most of his attention was fixed upon the slender woman in his arms. Her body was stiff, her lips pressed tightly together, and Cormac feared that he had killed all the passion inside her. Then she softened with a sigh. He trembled and felt her echo it as he plunged his tongue into her mouth. He kissed her long and hard, breaking off only long enough for them both to catch their breath. Then he kissed her again.

When he ended the second kiss, he looked at her. Her lips were soft and wet, her cheeks flushed, and when she opened her beautiful eyes, he nearly groaned aloud. There was the look he had missed so desperately. For a moment, he was so aroused, so moved he almost forgot what he was doing. He kissed the hollow by her ear, then lightly nibbled on her earlobe.

"Say, aye, my angel," he whispered as he heard the priest, nudged out of his shock by Balfour, ask again if Elspeth was a willing bride.

"To what, Cormac?" she asked, clinging tightly to him.

"To the priest. Tell him aye, loving." As a *coup de grâce* he stuck his tongue in her ear.

"Oh, aye," Elspeth said and wondered why she should be hearing laughter.

Prompted yet again by a nudge from Balfour, the priest began to read the vows. Cormac kept Elspeth close by his side as he urged her to kneel with him. Every time he thought she might be coming to her senses, he toyed with her ear or kissed her outright. When the priest pronounced them man and wife, Cormac sprang to his feet and pulled Elspeth up. He kissed her soundly, then leaned away a little and grinned at her as they drank from the wedding cup Gillyanne hurriedly gave them.

"Ah, my Lady Armstrong, no mon could have a bonnier wife," he said, then waited a little tensely for realization to hit her.

Elspeth blinked, then looked around. Although she had been vaguely aware of where she was, little else had been clear besides the feel of Cormac's mouth on hers. It took only a moment for the sensual haze he had put her in to clear her mind. With a soft curse, she pulled away from Cormac.

"That was verra sneaky, Cormac," she said as, her fists planted on her slender hips, she glared up at him.

She was furious. Not only had he used her passion against her, but he had let both of their families see him do it. The only thing that kept her from hitting him, very hard and frequently, was that he was as aroused as she was. She could almost smell his desire. He was undoubtedly aching as much as she was. She, however, could wait and not suffer quite as much discomfort as he did.

"Now, Elspeth," Cormac began as he watched her lovely eyes narrow.

"Nay, 'tis done. No sense in arguing the matter."

He frowned, not trusting her blithe acceptance of his trickery. "That is verra gracious of ye."

"Thank ye. And now, 'tis time for the feast." She leaned close to Cormac and kissed his cheek, giving him such a sweet smile that his frown immediately deepened. "A verra long wedding feast," she said precisely as she hooked her arms through those of her cousins. "Why, with so much food and drink, and all the entertainments planned, it could easily go on till dawn."

Cormac cursed and watched her stroll away, her female relatives hurrying after her and every one of them not making any attempt at all to hide their amusement. She had found a way to make him pay for his trick. He already ached for her almost more than he could endure. If she was going to make him wait until dawn before sharing his bed, he would undoubtedly be found huddled in a corner, gibbering like an idiot.

A light slap on the back brought him out of his dark musings. He turned to look at a grinning Sir Balfour. Cormac noticed that neither her kinsmen nor his own, all gathered round him, showed the least bit of sympathy for his obvious state of discomfort or the torment his new bride had just promised to put him through.

"She is all yours now, laddie," Balfour said and laughed softly.

"I thought fathers were supposed to dislike handing their daughters o'er to another mon," Cormac said.

"I have had two months to get used to the idea."

"Ye believed I would come for her?"

"Most days, aye. I am married to one just like her. Let my Maldie walk away from me because I was being a fool. Took me nearly as long as ye to go after her. I found I really had no choice in the end."

"Nay, no choice at all," Cormac agreed softly. "Still, 'twould be better if all was right and settled between us."

"Cannae be as bad as ye think. She married you and the way ye could get her to say aye tells me a great deal and should tell ye something as weel."

"She didnae really wish to marry me."

"Lad, 'tis clear ye dinnae ken the lass as weel as ye should yet. If my wee Elspeth truly didnae want ye, there would have been a bloody war needed to get her to kneel beside ye before that priest. Aye, and most of the Murray women plus nay too few of the lads would be standing firm at her side. Now, I am going to tell ye something that might help ye."

Connor hooted. "Run, Cormac. He is about to give ye advice on women. Oof!" Connor both laughed and grimaced when his father elbowed him in the stomach.

"I speak as a mon who has long walked the rockiest, most trecherous path any mon can—marriage." Although his eyes danced with laughter, Balfour scowled at his sons when they all said the last word at the same time he did. Then he turned back to Cormac and continued. "The lass is like her mother, and if my brothers dinnae lie, her aunts, too, are much the same. If ye have some confessing to do, take the lass to bed first and love her hard. When she gives ye that look that makes your innards clench, tell all."

"Weel, I dinnae have any confessions to make," Cormac said, "but some explantions are due."

" 'Twill still work."

"Strange advice for a father to give."

Balfour shrugged. "As I said, I have had time to become accustomed to the fact that my wee lass is a woman grown."

"Weel, 'tis good advice, but I fear 'twill be many long hours ere I can put it to any use."

"Aye? Ye are wed now. No one will be keeping ye and the lass apart." Balfour laughed when Cormac's eyes widened. Then the younger man grinned and strode purposefully toward his new bride.

# Chapter Twenty

"The cursed sun hasnae even finished setting," Elspeth grumbled as she stared out the window.

Her bedchamber was to be the wedding night chamber and she was in it far earlier than she had intended to be. For a little while Avery and Gillyanne, along with her sisters and a few other of her female cousins, had helped her avoid being cornered by Cormac. Then the younger girls had been sent to bed and the older girls had been carefully extracted from Elspeth's side by their mothers. Cormac had wasted no time in taking full advantage of that. The next thing Elspeth knew she was in the cleaned, scented, and decorated bridal chamber. She had been undressed, washed, lightly scented, and dressed in a nightgown whose only purpose was seduction.

As if Cormac needed such inducement, she thought. Half her trouble in trying to resist him was that she could sense Cormac's desire every time he drew near to her. It had been even more powerful when he had touched her, which the rogue had done every chance he could. He had not tried to sway her with heated kisses again, but he had not needed to. After far too short a time, she had been more than willing to be led away to begin the wedding night. It was embarrassing to be so easily routed, especially by her own desires.

The sound of the door opening and closing drew her attention and she turned to face her new husband. Elspeth was pleased to see that he had the good sense to look uncertain, even a little contrite. She was not pleased to see that the only thing between her and the feel of his warm skin appeared to be a loosely tied robe. The way he was looking at her, his beautiful blue eyes darkening with need, was making her blood heat. It was not going to be easy to rein in all that hunger long enough to talk. Elspeth hurriedly poured them each a goblet of spiced wine.

Cormac took one look at Elspeth and felt as if he had been kicked in the chest. The thin silken gown she wore was a soft rose color and so thin she might as well have been naked. Even more tempting was the way it was secured from neck to hem with lightly tied bows. It would be so easy to undo, so easy to reveal all those now shadowed curves he ached to kiss. When she handed him a goblet of wine, he stared at it blindly for a minute, so dazed with lust he had to pause and think about what it was he was suddenly holding.

"I think we need to talk," Elspeth said. Then she hastily took a sip of her wine when she heard the husky note of desire in her voice.

"I ken it." Cormac downed his wine, tossed his goblet aside, and pulled her into his arms.

"This isnae talking."

"Lass, I ken verra weel that there is a lot we must say to each other, that I need to explain a verra great deal."

In a vain attempt to cool the heat caused by his closeness

and the touch of his hands, Elspeth drank the rest of her wine. It did not work. With each stroke of his hands on her back, she wanted to press closer to him.

"So start talking," she said, her voice too thick and unsteady to manage any more words than that.

"Cannae." He began to brush soft, nibbling kisses over her face. "Ah, my wee angel, I ache for ye. My need is so strong, so overwhelming that soon I doubt I will be able to recall my own name."

"We cannae ignore what is wrong between us," she protested, but she did not stop him as he slowly undid each bow, softly kissing each new patch of skin the slowly parting gown revealed.

"Nay, and I dinnae mean to ignore it. Just set it aside for a wee while."

Elspeth shuddered as he fell to his knees in front of her and finished untying her gown. She clutched his shoulders and cried out softly as he caressed the backs of her thighs with his long fingers and covered her still flat stomach with heated kisses. When he slipped his hands up the inside of her thighs and gently nudged them apart, she could not offer him any resistance. She clung to him, almost frantically stroking his shoulders, arms, and head as he loved her with his mouth. It did not take long for her to shatter from the strength of her release.

Cormac caught her in his arms as she started to collapse, her legs too weak and trembling to fully support her. He carried her to her bed, gently laid her down, and yanked off his robe. Elspeth only got a brief glimpse of his gloriously aroused form before he nearly fell into her open arms.

She cried out softly when he plunged into her. The feel of their bodies united again soothed a few of her emotional wounds. She wrapped her body around his, welcoming the near desperation of his possession, for she shared it. Although too caught up in her own passion to understand the heated words he whispered against her skin, she cherished them. Elspeth fought to hold on to the moment, but then, with a soft growl that told her Cormac knew what she was doing, he took her aching nipple deep into his mouth and suckled, hard. Every meager restraint she had put on herself disappeared. She cried out his name as he yet again took her to passion's heights. Even as she sank into that sweet bliss, she felt Cormac drive deep into her body and shudder with the force of his own release, and then he sweetly called her name.

It was several moments before Cormac came to his senses. The way Elspeth was stroking him with her small, soft hands and feet was not making it easy for him to remain sensible, however. Nor was the feel of her tight heat surrounding his swiftly recovering manhood. Kissing her gently, he eased the intimacy of their embrace. He also raised himself up on his forearms to ease some of the temptation of being flesh to flesh with her.

Then he looked into her eyes. The green was still dark with lingering passion. She was looking at him as if he was everything that was important to her. Sir Balfour was right. That look made a man's innards clench. Cormac admitted to himself that one of his greatest fears had been that he would never see that look in her eyes again.

The thought of Sir Balfour made Cormac remember the man's advice. The warmth she felt for him right now might not last long. If he got her started discussing things now, began all of his explanations now, matters might be nearly smoothed over before her hurt and anger had a chance to return. It would certainly all go along much more easily if those fierce emotions did not tangle everything up.

"Angel, ye are a mon's dream," he said, brushing a kiss over her lips. "I kenned it when ye were with me and within moments after ye left me."

Elspeth felt some of her lingering pleasure fade away,

but she did not try to leave Cormac's arms. If he was going to be honest with her, she might find she either needed or wanted him close. If not, she might as well enjoy their closeness for a little while longer before hurt and anger again pulled them apart.

"Yet ye didnae come after me," she said quietly. "Ye didnae stop me."

"Weel, I fear I couldnae have no matter what I felt like doing. Despite having made love all night long—something sure to steal a mon's strength—I had spent the morning walking. I think it all helped bring my strength back, but not for a while. At that moment, I could barely cross the room without my legs buckling beneath me. I was as weak as a newborn."

"Oh." And that meant that a kiss was all he and Isabel could have shared, despite what the woman had tried to imply with all of her frettish tidying, Elspeth thought crossly. "I think ye hesitated for more reasons than your weakness."

"Some, but if I could have that day, I would ne'er have let ye leave me. Confused though I was, I was verra certain about that, about wanting ye to stay with me."

"For this," she whispered, indicating their lightly entwined bodies with one brief wave of her hand. "Ye wanted me to stay for this."

"Would ye believe me if I said nay? What mon wouldnae hold fast to something as fine as what we share? From the beginning I kenned that it was as fine as any I had e'er had, that none had e'er been or e'er would be so fine." He half smiled and kissed the faint frown curving her full lips, easily guessing her thoughts. "Aye, in all ways I kenned it was the best and that deeply troubled me. How could it be, I asked myself, when I—" He choked to a halt when he realized what he was about to say and to whom.

Elspeth almost smiled at the look of consternation on

Cormac's face. "Nay, dinnae stop. We are wed now. There is nay turning back." She brushed the back of her hand over his cheek. "I may flinch, but pay it no heed. Ye may say things I dinnae like or dinnae want to hear, but I have just spent two long months filled with questions I had no answers for. I dinnae want to spend the rest of my life that way."

He took a deep breath and continued. "How could what ye and I shared be the best when I was supposed to be in love with Isabel? And I cannae describe what I felt when I realized that Isabel hadnae been the virgin she had claimed to be. That was the first lie I discovered. And as always, I struggled to ignore it."

"Ye loved the woman for ten years, Cormac."

"I was her toy for ten years—the wee pup too young and too stupid to see anything but Isabel's beauty. A fool who was so worried about breaking a boyhood vow, so concerned about losing e'en a scrap of honor, that he ne'er looked close enough to see that the woman he honored wasnae worth it."

There was a lot of anger behind his words. He had a right to it, but Elspeth wondered how deep it went and what the true cause of it was. Was it just a man's anger over being played for a fool or the pain of a betrayed heart?

"Many men were fooled by her, blinded by her beauty and their lust," she said, watching him closely.

"For as long as I?" He grimaced with self-disgust when she said nothing; then he rolled on his side to face her and dragged his fingers through his hair. "Weel, there was her lover Sir Kenneth, but 'tis uncertain who used whom the most between them. He at least had the wit to see Isabel for what she was and put it to use for him."

"Which got them both a trip to the gallows."

"True. What I am trying to say is that, from the verra

beginning, ye made me doubt and question the path I had chosen, the truth of my feelings for the woman I had trotted after for so long. Everything ye and I did together— from simply talking to making love—left me with even more doubts, more confusion, and more questions. At times, I foolishly blamed you for my muddled state. Then I would blame myself. My mistake was that I ne'er paused to blame Isabel." He muttered a soft curse and got out of bed. "Some more wine. This talking dries the throat and I babble so. 'Tis clear I will be at it for a while."

Elspeth's eyes widened as he strode over to the table where she had set the wine. He poured them each a goblet full. The man did not know the meaning of the word modesty. How could he expect any woman to be sensible and talk when he was flaunting himself like that? When he turned to walk back to the bed, she took one long look at his trim, muscular form, groaned, and pulled the covers over her head.

"If ye mean to keep talking, Sir Cormac, either get dressed or get back under the blanket," she grumbled.

Cormac grinned as he set her goblet of wine down on the little table by her side of the bed, then slipped beneath the covers while still holding his own. "Stirred by me beauty, are ye, lass? *Wheesht,* ye need to learn some control."

"Control, is it? Shall we see how much ye feel like talking if I get up and prance about naked?" She sat up and picked up her goblet of wine.

"Oh, please, angel," he said, his voice shaking with laughter, "do it. I am willing to be tested."

"Were we nay having a discussion?" Elspeth asked, eyeing him with a hint of annoyance as she sipped her wine.

"That we were, and as I was prancing o'er to get our wine, I had a thought." He decided it would be best to ignore her soft clapping. "I ken what mistakes I have made, but I dinnae ken exactly what troubles you. Mayhap if ye just ask me what ye wish to learn, ask me some of those questions that have troubled ye for months.''

"Why did ye choose her?" she asked bluntly, her voice roughened by the remembered pain. "After all we had shared, why didnae ye e'en hesitate?"

"Ah, but I did, my love." He put his arm around her shoulders and tugged her close to his side. "All the time she was there I was in such a state of confusion I doubt I could have recalled my own name if anyone asked. I felt as if I was in some play, merely belching out words—the same words that had been said time and time and time again. Then I said what I felt she needed to hear so that she would leave. I wanted her gone because I was terrified that ye might come back and see us together and because I felt as if everything was suddenly wrong, verra wrong, and I desperately needed to think."

"And then I arrived."

"Just so. E'en when Isabel left and ye started talking, most of the words tumbling out of my mouth were ones of habit. *Isabel has had a sad life. Isabel needs me. I have made a vow to the woman and I must hold fast to it.* I have realized o'er the last few months of soul-searching that I had been verra weel trained. She caught me when I was young and innocent of women and has led me about by my boyish image of her e'er since."

"Actually, I thought she led ye about by something a wee bit lower," drawled Elspeth.

"Aye, mayhap, but isnae that where all the dreams of lusty young lads begin?" He set down his goblet, saw that hers was empty, and tossed it aside before pulling her firmly into his arms. "I didnae want her, Elspeth, but I didnae understand how that had happened, what had changed, or why. I needed to see Isabel and then calmly think o'er all that had happened during our long-awaited meeting. I needed time to realize that everything I had kenned for so long was no longer true. For the first time since I swore that I would ne'er break my word, that I would show the world not all Armstrongs were like my notorious parents, I found myself wondering how to get free of that vow I had given Isabel. I wanted to slap her for insulting you. I was annoyed by her demands, and I desperately wanted her to just go away for any number of reasons. Now, fool I might be, but I kenned there was something deeply wrong with that.''

There certainly was and Elspeth barely kept her hope and delight hidden. Cormac spoke as if he had been inconvenienced by his former lover. He did not sound like a lover at all, but simply like any irritated male. To realize that he was feeling that way, had felt that way before she had walked away, and toward the woman he had adored, honored, and chased after for ten years had to have been a great shock to him. It was no wonder he had not been able to think clearly.

"I just wish ye could have decided all this *before* ye heard her confession and could have come to me *before* she was dead.''

"I wish I could have, too, angel mine," he said softly, brushing light kisses over her face. "All I can do is swear to ye that I was already seeing the truth about her, looking clearly at all that had passed between her and me, and beginning to feel that I had trapped myself with that cursed pledge. I couldnae talk away the doubt any longer. After ye left, I was angry with Isabel for making such a mess of it all then disappearing, but I longed for you. Lying alone in that bed, I wasnae thinking of Isabel, but aching for you. I e'en realized that ye and I had made love more often during our short time together than Isabel and I had in all the years I had kenned her. By the time I joined the Douglases in hearing the woman's confession, I kenned it was done, over, but I couldnae get those words out of my mouth. That would be admitting that I was a complete fool, that I had wasted all of those years.

"There was simply nothing left. I felt no jealousy as I heard her loudly rut with Sir Kenneth. I felt only anger and disgust when I heard her and her lover talk of the murders they had committed already and the ones they planned. I cannae e'en begin to describe what I felt when I discovered she had hidden my child from me and now tried to use the lad to bring me to heel."

"He is a verra good lad," Elspeth said, smoothing her hand over his broad chest and savoring the feel of his warm skin.

"I do see a hint of Isabel in his face, but it doesnae move me."

"I was a wee bit concerned about that," she confessed. "And ye need nay fear that I would e'er blame him for his mother's crimes."

Cormac framed her small face with his hands and gently turned it up to his. "I ken that. My only fear in bringing him to you was that ye might see him as proof of some lingering bond between Isabel and me. There is none. There hasnae been since I first looked into your eyes at Sir Colin's. Forgive me for being too stubborn and blind to see what was in my own heart, for being afraid to admit that I had been wrong and had been played for the fool for so verra long. I hurt ye for the sake of a woman who wasnae fit to clean your wee slippers.

"Ye gave me so much, Elspeth. Aye, and I fed on it like some greedy bairn, yet gave nothing back. Ye gave me my life back," he whispered and touched a reverent kiss against her mouth.

"That old debt has been verra weel paid for," Elspeth said, nearly moved to tears by the sweetness in his gentle kiss.

"I dinnae mean the time ye found me bleeding into your father's dirt. Ye saved me from Isabel. With each touch, each kiss, ye pushed her out of my foolish, stubborn heart. Ye showed me what loving was meant to be and it revealed the ugliness of my relationship with Isabel. She was sent to the gallows, but in truth, she was dead to me ere she climbed the ladder to the gallows, ere I watched her executed."

"Ye watched her die?" Despite her feelings about the woman, and Cormac's long affair with her, Elspeth found some small hint of sympathy in her heart for all that Cormac had endured.

He nodded. "I wanted to for Christopher's sake. Someday he might ask about her. And when it became clear that all of her kinsmen had deserted her, I also saw to her burial. I was a witness against her, as weel. That is why I didnae come for ye for so long. I had to see it all through till the end."

"'Tis best. Ye needed to see that it was really finished."

"So, answer me this, my heart: Have I destroyed all ye felt for me?"

"Nay," she replied softly, knowing that she owed him the same amount of honesty he had given her, even if he had not said the three little words she so hungered for. "The words I spat out that day were but words born of my anger and pain. I did try, ye ken. As I watched the days slip by, I tried verra hard to kill all feeling for you. 'Tis just that I didnae want to hurt anymore. I tried even harder when Payton brought the news about Isabel, for that made me feel a flicker of hope that ye might yet turn to me, and I feared I was weak enough to allow myself to be your second choice. Nothing worked. Ye are set deep in my heart and soul, Cormac Armstrong. I couldnae push ye out. Aye, I still love ye."

Cormac held her tightly, feeling such a strong sense of

relief he shuddered from the force of it. "Ah, lass, I was so afraid that I had done more than ye could forgive, that I had killed your love, and now ye could ne'er return mine."

It took Elspeth a moment to understand the import of his words. "Ye love me?" she asked, her voice softened by shock as she pulled away just far enough to see his face clearly.

"Of course. I have told ye so."

"Ye *never*, not once, have said that ye love me."

"What did ye think all those notes I sent to ye were saying?"

"They didnae say that ye loved me. If ye dinnae believe me, I shall get them and show them to you." Out of the corner of her eye, she saw him grin, so she sent him a stern frown. 'What are ye grinning about?"

"Ye saved my notes."

"The backs werenae written on. I thought I could use them for my own scribblings." Her sarcasm took the smile from his face, but she could see it lingering in his eyes. "Believe me, Cormac, not one of them carries the words *I love ye, Elspeth*. I believe I would have noticed that."

He pulled her close and licked the hollow by her right ear, delighting in the shiver of desire that rippled through her slim body. "Yet again, I ask your forgiveness. I poured my heart into those notes. Foolish, but I think I felt ye would be able to read it there, even if I wasnae verra direct." He kissed her after each word as he said, loud and clear, "I love ye, Lady Elspeth Armstrong."

For a little while, Elspeth gave herself over to his intoxicating kisses. His touch was even more thrilling to her now that she knew there was love as well as passion behind each caress. When he covered her breasts with his hands, rubbing his thumbs over her nipples until they were hard and aching, she decided that she had to put a halt to the

sensuous play. It was time to tell him her secret. She soon
discovered that freeing herself from the hold of an amorous Cormac was not easy. Finally, she pinched the tender
skin beneath his arm. He cursed and rubbed the spot,
allowing her the chance to wriggle out from under him
and sit up.

"What was that for?" he asked, frowning at her and
suddenly afraid that he had heard only what he wanted to
hear, that everything was not all right yet.

"I need to tell ye something and ye were distracting
me," Elspeth said.

" 'Tis our wedding night. I am supposed to distract you
until neither of us has the strength to walk." He reached
for her.

Elspeth lightly slapped his hands away. "Ye can do that
in a moment."

That sounded hopeful, but Cormac still felt uneasy. Elspeth looked a little nervous about what she was about to
tell him. When she had left him she had been hurt, angry,
and undoubtedly feeling that she had somehow failed as
a woman or as a lover. He knew all too well the sort of
doubts one could wrestle with when believing oneself set
aside for another. Had she turned to someone else for
comfort? Elspeth was a passionate woman. It was all too easy
to envision what form that comfort might take. Cormac
clenched his hands into tight fists, discovering that the
mere thought of another man holding his Elspeth stirred
more anger, jealousy, and hurt inside of him than Isabel
ever had. Elspeth had thought herself cast aside and Cormac knew he had no right to complain about what she
might have done during that time. He desperately wanted
to be understanding, but he knew, in his heart, that it
would be the hardest thing he had ever done. He also
knew that she had better not tell him the name of her
lover, not if she had any affection for the man. He would,

without hesitation, kill the fool, and that would certainly not help his marriage get off to a very good start.

"Ye are looking verra fierce, Cormac," Elspeth said, a little startled by the hard expression on his face. "It isnae a bad secret."

"Dinnae pay any heed to me," he said, struggling for an even tone of voice and knowing by her increasingly wary look that he was failing. " 'Tis just that I have had a bellyful of secrets, none of them good, and the mere hint of one now sets my teeth on edge."

"Ah, of course. I dinnae usually keep secrets, Cormac, and have no intention of doing so with ye. At least, not any that concern the two of us. My family—the younger ones—might need one kept from time to time. I would have told ye this sooner, but just as I didnae want ye to come to me simply because ye couldnae have Isabel or because ye felt honor bound to wed the virgin ye had bedded, neither did I wish ye to come to me because of this."

"Elspeth, just spit it out."

She blinked in surprise at his curt tone, then admitted to herself that she had been babbling a little bit. Elspeth took a deep breath and, in as calm a voice as she could muster, said, "I am nearly three months gone with your child." When all the tension left his body and he flopped on his back, laughing softly, she frowned. "Of all the reactions I imagined ye having to this news, I must confess that that wasnae one of them. I rather hoped ye would be pleased," she added, cursing the tremor of tears in her voice.

"Oh, angel, I am, but if ye kenned what I had imagined your secret was . . ." He chuckled and shook his head.

"Just what did ye think I was going to say?"

"That ye had taken a lover whilst we were apart."

Cormac heard her gasp of outrage and grabbed hold of

her when she started to get out of bed. He grunted under the pummeling she gave him until he got her firmly pinned beneath his body. The extent of her outrage only cheered him more. Here was a woman who obviously believed in fidelity, saw it as a matter of honor.

"How could ye think that of me?" she asked, a sense of insult and hurt pushing aside her anger.

"Nay for any of the insulting reasons ye are thinking. I hurt you and, as far as ye kenned, had set ye aside for another. Ye are a passionate woman, Elspeth. I but feared ye might have blindly sought some comfort and it had become something more. I was telling myself that I had no right to object and that I would be understanding."

He said those last words as if they were going to choke him, and Elspeth grinned. "Was it working?"

Cormac sighed and rested his forehead against hers. "Nay. I was hoping ye wouldnae tell me the mon's name, for I would surely kill him."

She touched a kiss to his lips. "There were a few nights when the aching was so sharp I did wonder on the easing of it."

"I ken that feeling all too weel." He grinned when her eyes narrowed. "I endured—alone. Verra, verra alone."

"So did I, for I kenned it would but ease it for a few moments." She reached up to stroke his cheek. "And what of our bairn?"

He knelt between her legs, kissed her still flat stomach, then rested his hand there as he looked at her. "I am too full of joy to give ye any fine words, angel mine."

"Those are fine enough."

"Does your mother ken?"

"Aye, and she sees naught wrong with me." When he placed his hands on her hips, stretching his thumbs out across the space in between, Elspeth sat up and kissed him. "I am made in my mother's image, my heart, and look at the brood she produced. My family is bursting with women who have a skill in healing and they will all be there."

Cormac closed his eyes and held her close, finding comfort in her words, but knowing that comfort would not last long and would have to be repeated often. "I love ye, Elspeth."

"And I love ye," she whispered and kissed him. "Now, didnae ye say something about distracting me until neither of us could walk?"

Cormac laughed and tumbled her back down on the bed.

# Epilogue

"Push. That's the lass. Push hard."

Elspeth lifted her sweat-soaked head from the pillow and glared at her mother. "I *am* pushing."

"I can see the head, lass," Agnes said and patted Elspeth's upraised knee. "He is almost out."

"I cannae understand why it should take so cursed long," Elspeth panted. " 'Tisnae as if he has verra far to go." She faintly heard Agnes, her mother, and Sorcha laugh even as she obeyed her body's and the women's commands to push.

Sorcha wiped the sweat from Elspeth's face with a cool cloth. "Ye will be done soon, Cousin. I ken ye dinnae think so just now, but ye have been blessed with an easy birth."

"Easy?" Elspeth rasped.

"Aye. For one thing, ye still have the wit to talk."

"Oh, aye? Then bring Cormac here. There are a few things I should like to say to him."

The laughter of the women was the last thing Elspeth

heard before the demands of her body grasped hold of
all of her strength and attention. Soft voices, encouraging
words, and her own unattractive grunting were the only
things she heard. Then, suddenly, there was an overwhelming pain and she screamed.

It was only when the pain ceased that Elspeth began to
slowly become aware of herself and everything around her
again. Her body ached and she realized with a start that
it was all over. Then, just as her weary mind noted the
silence and her fears mounted, she heard the wail of a
child.

"My bairn?" Her voice was so hoarse she barely recognized it.

"Alive," said her mother. "Agnes is cleaning the bairn
and Sorcha and I will now clean you."

"But . . ."

"In a moment ye and the beautiful new life ye created
will meet. Ye waited nine months. Ye can wait a few more
minutes until the both of ye are cleaned up."

Elspeth resigned herself to waiting, although she tried
hard to get a look at Agnes and the child she held. Sorcha
and her mother were swift and efficient, rolling her back
and forth on the bed as they changed the linen, sponging
her down, tidying her hair, and getting her dressed in a
fresh night rail. Elspeth began to feel as much an infant
as the one she had just birthed. She did feel better, however, by the time they had her propped up against an array
of pillows and set her child in her arms. Elspeth noted
with approval that Agnes did not swaddle the baby too
tightly even as the woman slowly unwrapped the child.

"Ten wee fingers, ten wee toes, and no . . ." Elspeth's
eyes widened. " 'Tis a lass."

Agnes could not hide her delight. "Aye, a lass. A wee,
bonny lass with your black hair. Oh, she is so verra bonny."

With her mother's subtle aid, Elspeth gave suckle to her

child. There was not much milk yet, but the brief nursing would help bring it forth and teach her child where her food was to be found. It hurt a little but her mother had warned her about that, so Elspeth concentrated on the joy of holding her first child.

"Did ye want a lad?" asked Sorcha.

"Nay, I just expected one," replied Elspeth. "Between the Murrays and the Armstrongs there is a surfeit of laddies born." She smiled at Agnes. "We all ken what ye have prayed for these last months. Best ye go and fetch Cormac."

"Let me take the bairn, lass," Agnes said, reaching for the child. "Cormac will bring her back to you, but if she is shown about, however briefly, then ye willnae have the whole lot of them stomping up here to have a peek."

Agnes left, cooing to the baby every step of the way. After a little more fussing and a few kisses, her mother and Sorcha left as well. Elspeth yawned and hoped Cormac did not take long to come to see her or she would be sound asleep.

Cormac tensed when he saw Agnes enter the great hall. He had leapt to his feet when Elspeth's scream had echoed through the halls, but his brothers had finally wrestled him back into his seat. Since then, there had been silence, and each painfully long minute spent without sound or word of Elspeth had increased his fears. As Agnes approached him, he told himself that she would not look so cheerful if anything was wrong with Elspeth, but his fear refused to heed that wisdom.

"Elspeth?" he croaked when Agnes stopped by his chair.

"Fine," replied Agnes. "Just weary. Ye would ne'er ken it to look at her, but she is made to give ye many bairns."

"She screamed."

"Aye. So would ye if ye were pushing this out of your

body." Agnes slowly unwrapped the child and held it lower so that Cormac could see clearly. "See? Lots of black hair, ten wee fingers, and ten wee toes, and no pintle!"

"A lass. We had a lass." Cormac touched the baby's soft hair with one unsteady finger, then watched his child disappear into a circle of his three sisters and Agnes.

Dougal frowned at the four cooing women. "Agnes is a wee bit too pleased at the lack of a certain appendage on your bairn."

Cormac laughed shakily, downed the last of his ale, and stood up. "Agnes, can I see Elspeth now?"

"Aye." She wrapped the baby back up and set her in Cormac's arms, ignoring his look of alarm. "Take the wee lass back to her mother," she said as she tugged him away from his kin and pulled him toward the door. "Lad, your wee wife had an easy birth though 'twas her first and 'tis clear the two of ye are a fertile mix. Though Elspeth seems formed to breed, too many bairns too fast isnae good for any woman. 'Twill nay surprise ye, considering whose servant I was, but I ken a few ways ye can slow the growth of your family."

He kissed Agnes on the cheek. "So does Lady Maldie. She spoke to us as weel. I want bairns, but I need Elspeth. Children are a blessing I will always welcome, but Elspeth—weel, Elspeth is my life. I willnae waste her life on a birthing bed." He warily eyed the tiny baby he held. "Are ye sure I willnae drop her?"

"I am sure. Now, I will go and tell Christopher and wee Alan the good news. Ye go and see your wife ere she falls asleep."


Elspeth blinked when she felt the bed move. She realized she had fallen asleep and opened her eyes to see Cormac at her side. When he smiled at her and set their daughter in her arms, she felt some small part of her relax. The look on his face told her that he did not mind at all that she had not borne him a son.

"Agnes is beside herself with joy," he said and brushed a kiss over her smiling lips. "So are my sisters."

"This has evened the numbers a wee bit," Elspeth said.

"Are ye all right?" He sat beside her, eased his arm around her shoulders, and gently tucked her up against his side.

"Just verra tired and a little sore." Elspeth looked down at their sleeping child. "But she is worth every twinge."

Cormac stroked the baby's cheek with one long finger. "Aye, she is. She is worth all the agony and fear I have suffered through these last hours, too. I was torn between staying in the hall and praying until I was hoarse and running up here to be at your side, as if I could help in some way."

"I am glad ye stayed in the hall. Birthing is a messy, immodest business. And"—she grinned up at him—"a few times I had the strong urge to call ye a lot of verra unpleasant names." She laughed with him.

"Weel, do we call her Keira or Ilsabeth?"

"Ilsabeth."

He kissed the child's soft cheek. "Welcome, Ilsabeth Armstrong."

"If I ken men, our kinsmen are down there celebrating as if they did all the work. Ye can join them. I dinnae mind."

"Nay, I will stay and celebrate with you."

"I think ye will soon be doing nay more than watching me sleep."

Cormac put his hand beneath her chin and turned her face up to his, kissing her tenderly. " 'Tis all I need. I celebrate each time I see you, each time I hear ye speak, each time I touch you. Ye are my heart, my soul, the verra breath I need to live. I love ye, Elspeth Armstrong, my wee green-eyed angel. I vow I shall love ye until I am but dust in the ground."

"And I vow I do love ye, Cormac." She smiled sleepily against his mouth as he lightly kissed her. "And shall. Longer."

"Is that a challenge I hear?"

"Aye, I believe it is. Care to meet it?"

"With all my heart, angel. With all my heart."

Please turn the page for an exciting sneak peek of

Hannah Howell's newest Highland romance

HIGHLAND LOVER

coming in June 2006!

*Scotland, Spring 1475*

"Oof!"

*Oof!?* Dazed and struggling to catch her breath, Alana decided she must have made that noise herself. Hard dirt floors did not say *oof.* It was odd, however, how the rough stone walls of the oubliette made her voice sound so deep, almost manly. Just as she began to be able to breathe again, the hard dirt floor shifted beneath her.

It took Alana a moment to fully grasp the fact that she had not landed on the floor. She had landed on a person. That person had a deep, manly voice. It was not dirt or stone beneath her cheek, but cloth. There was also the steady throb of a heartbeat in the ear she had pressed against that cloth. Her fingers were hanging down a little and touching cool, slightly damp earth. She was sprawled on top of a man like a wanton.

Alana scrambled off the man, apologizing for some awkward placement of her knees and elbows as she did so. The man certainly knew how to curse. She stood and stared up at the three men looking down at her, the light from the lantern they held doing little more than illuminating their grinning, hairy faces.

"Ye cannae put me in here with a mon," she said.

"Got no place else to put ye," said the tallest of the three, a man called Clyde, whom she was fairly sure was the laird.

"I am a lady," she began.

"Ye are a wee, impudent child. Now, are ye going to tell us who ye are?"

"So ye can rob my people? Nay, I dinnae think so."

"Then ye stay where ye are."

She did not even have time to stutter out a protest. The grate was shut, and that faint source of light quickly disappeared as the Gowans walked away. Alana stared into the dark and wondered how everything had gone so wrong. All she had wanted to do was to help find her sister Keira, but none of her family had heeded her pleas or her insistence that she could truly help to find her twin. It had seemed such a clever idea to disguise herself as a young girl and follow her brothers, waiting for just the right moment to reveal herself. How she had enjoyed those little dreams of walking up to her poor, confused brothers and leading them straight to their sister. That had kept a smile upon her face and a jaunty spring in her step right up until the moment she had realized that not only had she lost her brothers' trail, but she also had absolutely no idea of where she was.

Feeling very sorry for herself and wondering why her gifts had so abruptly failed her just when she needed them the most, she had been cooking a rabbit and sulking when the Gowans had found her. Alana grimaced as she remembered how she had acted. Perhaps if she had been sweet and acted help-

less, she would not be stuck in a hole in the ground
with a man who was apparently relieving himself in a
bucket. Maybe it would be wise to tell the Gowans
who she was so that they could get some ransom for
her and she could get out of here. Appalled by that
moment of weakness, Alana proceeded to lecture
herself in the hope of stiffening her resolve.

Gregor inwardly cursed as he finished relieving
himself. It was not the best way to introduce himself
to his fellow prisoner, but he really had had little
choice. Having a body dropped on top of him and
then being jabbed by elbows and knees had made ignoring his body's needs impossible. At least the dark
provided a semblance of privacy.

He was just trying to figure out where she was
when he realized she was muttering to herself. Clyde
Gowan had called her an impudent child, but there
was something in that low, husky voice that made
him think of a woman. After she had landed on him
and he had caught his breath, there had also been
something about that soft, warm body that had also
made him think of a woman despite the lack of fulsome curves. He shook his head as he cautiously
stepped toward that voice.

Despite his caution, he took one step too many
and came up hard against her back. She screeched
softly and jumped, banging the top of her head
against his chin. Gregor cursed softly as his teeth
slammed together, sending a sharp, stinging pain
through his head. He was a little surprised to hear
her softly curse as well.

"Jesu, lass," he muttered, "ye have inflicted more

bruises on me than those fools did when they grabbed me."

"Who are you?" Alana asked, wincing and rubbing at the painful spot on the top of her head, certain she could feel a lump rising.

"Gregor. And ye are?"

"Alana."

"Just Alana?"

"Just Gregor?"

"I will tell ye my full name if ye tell me yours."

"Nay, I dinnae think so. Someone could be listening, hoping we will do just that."

"And ye dinnae trust me as far as ye can spit, do ye?"

"Why should I? I dinnae ken who ye are. I cannae e'en see you." She looked around and then wondered why she bothered, since it was so dark she could not even see her own hand if she held it right in front of her face. "What did they put ye in here for?"

Alana suddenly feared she had been confined with a true criminal, perhaps even a rapist or murderer. She smothered that brief surge of panic by telling herself sharply not to be such an idiot. The Gowans wanted to ransom her. Even they were not stupid enough to risk losing that purse by setting her too close to a truly dangerous man.

"Ransom," he replied.

"Ah, me too. Are they roaming about the country plucking up people like daisies?"

Gregor chuckled and shook his head. "Only those who look as if they or their kinsmen might have a few coins weighting their purse. A mon was being ransomed e'en as they dragged me in. He was dressed fine, although his bonnie clothes were somewhat filthy from spending time in this hole. I was wearing my finest. I suspect your gown told them your kinsmen might have some coin. Did they kill your guards?"

Alana felt a blush heat her cheeks. "Nay, I was alone. I got a little lost."

She was lying, Gregor thought. Either she was a very poor liar, or the dark had made his senses keener, allowing him to hear the lie in her voice. "I hope your kinsmen punish the men weel for such carelessness."

*Oh, someone would most certainly be punished,* Alana thought. There was no doubt in her mind about that. This was one of those times when she wished her parents believed in beating a child. A few painful strokes of a rod would be far easier to endure than the lecture she would be given and, even worse, the confused disappointment her parents would reveal concerning her idiocy and disobedience.

"How long have ye been down here?" she asked, hoping to divert his attention from how and why she had been caught.

"Two days, I think. 'Tis difficult to know for certain. They gave me quite a few blankets; a privy bucket, which they pull up and empty each day; and food and water twice a day. What troubles me is who will win this game of ye stay there until ye tell me what I want to know. My clan isnae really poor, but they dinnae have coin to spare for a big ransom. Nay when they dinnae e'en ken what the money will be used for."

"Oh, didnae they tell ye?"

"I was unconscious for most of the time it took to get to this keep and be tossed in here. All I have heard since then is the thrice daily question about who I am. And I am assuming all these things happen daily, not just whene'er they feel inclined. There does seem to be a, weel, rhythm to it all. 'Tis how I decided I have been here for two days." He thought back over the past few days, too much of it spent in the dark with his own thoughts. "If I judge it aright, this may actually be the end of the third day, for I fell unconscious again when they threw me in here. I woke up to someone bellowing that it was time to sup, I got my food and water, and was told about the privy bucket and, that blankets had been thrown down here."

"And 'tis night now. The moon was rising as we rode through the gates. So, three days in the dark. In a hole in the ground," she murmured, shivering at the thought of having to endure the same. "What did ye do?"

"Thought."

"Oh, dear. I think *that* would soon drive me quite mad."

"It wasnae a pleasant interlude."

"It certainly isnae. I am nay too fond of the dark," she added softly and jumped slightly when a long arm was somewhat awkwardly wrapped around her shoulders.

"No one is, especially not the unrelenting dark of a place like this. So, ye were all alone when they caught ye. They didnae harm ye, did they?"

The soft, gentle tone of his question made Alana

realize what he meant by *harm*. It struck her as odd that not once had she feared rape, yet her disguise as a child was certainly not enough to save her from that. "Nay, they just grabbed me, cursed me a lot for being impudent, and tossed me over a saddle."

Gregor smiled. "Impudent were ye?"

"That is as good a word for it as any other. There I was sitting quietly by a fire, cooking a rabbit I had been lucky enough to catch, and up ride five men who inform me that I am now their prisoner and that I had best tell them who I am so that they can send the ransom demand to my kinsmen. I told them that I had had a very upsetting day and the last thing I wished to deal with was smelly, hairy men telling me what to do, so they could just ride back to the rock they had crawled out from under. Or words to that effect," she added quietly.

In truth, she thought as she listened to Gregor chuckle, she had completely lost her temper. It was not something she often did, and she suspected some of her family would have been astonished. The Gowans had been. All five men had stared at her as if a dormouse had suddenly leapt at their throats. It had been rather invigorating until the Gowans had realized they were being held in place by insults from someone they could snap in half.

It was a little puzzling that she had not eluded capture. She was very fast, something often marveled at by her family; she could run for a very long way without tiring; and she could hide in the faintest of shadows. Yet mishap after mishap had plagued her as she had fled from the men, and they had barely raised a sweat in pursuing and capturing her. If she were a superstitious person, she would think some unseen hand of fate had been doing its best to make sure she was caught.

"Did they tell ye why they are grabbing so many for ransom?" Gregor asked.

"Oh, aye they did." Of course, one reason they had told her was because of all the things she had accused them of wanting the money for, such as useless debauchery and not something they badly needed like soap. "Defenses."

"What?"

"They have decided that this hovel requires stronger defenses. That requires coin or some fine goods to barter with, neither of which they possess. I gather they have heard of some troubles not so far away, and it has made them decide that they are too vulnerable. From what little I could see whilst hanging over Clyde's saddle, this is a very old tower house, one that was either neglected or damaged once, or both. It appears to have been repaired enough to be livable, but I did glimpse many things either missing or in need of repair. From what Clyde's wife said, this small holding was her dowry."

"Ye spoke to his wife?"

"Weel, nay. She was lecturing him from the moment he stepped inside all the way to the door leading down here. She doesnae approve of this. Told him that since he has begun this folly, he had best do a verra good job of it and gather a veritable fortune, for they will need some formidable defenses to protect them from all the enemies he is making."

Alana knew she ought to move away from him. When he had first draped his arm around her, she had welcomed what she saw as a gesture intended to comfort her, perhaps even an attempt to ease the fear of the dark she had confessed to. He still had his arm around her, and she had slowly edged closer to his warmth until she was now pressed hard up against his side.

He was a very tall man. Probably a bit taller than her overgrown brothers, she mused. Judging from where her cheek rested so nicely, she barely reached his breastbone. Since she was five feet tall, that made him several inches over six feet. Huddled up against him as she was, she could feel the strength in his body, despite what she felt like a lean build. Considering the fact that he had been held in this pit for almost three days, he smelled remarkably clean as well.

And the fact that she was noticing how good he smelled told her she really should move away from him, Alana thought. The problem was he felt good, very good. He felt warm, strong, and calming, all things she was sorely in need of at the moment. She started to console herself with the thought that she was not actually embracing him, only to realize that she had curled her arm around like a very trim waist.

She sighed inwardly, ruefully admitting that she liked where she was and that she had no inclination to leave his side. He thought she was a young girl, so she did not have to fear him thinking she was inviting him to take advantage of her. Alone with him in the dark, there was a comforting anonymity as well. Alana decided there was no harm in it all. In truth, she would not be surprised to discover that he found comfort in it, too, after days of being all alone in the dark.

"Where were ye headed, lass? Is there someone aside from the men ye were with who will start searching for ye?" Gregor asked, a little concerned

about how good it felt to hold her, even though every
instinct he had told him that Alana was not the child
she pretended to be.

"Quite possibly." She doubted that the note she
had left behind would do much to comfort her parents. "I was going to my sister."

"Ah, weel, then, I fear the Gowans may soon ken
who ye are e'en if ye dinnae tell them."

"Oh, of course. What about you? Will anyone wonder where ye have gone?"

"Nay for a while yet."

They all thought he was still wooing his well-dowered bride. Gregor had had far too much time to think
about that, about all of his reasons for searching for a
well-dowered bride and about the one he had chosen. Mavis was a good woman, passably pretty, and
she had both land and some coin to offer a husband.
He had left her feeling almost victorious, the betrothal as good as settled, yet each hour he had sat
here in the dark, alone with his thoughts, he had felt
less and less pleased with himself. It did not feel *right*.
He hated to think that his cousin Sigimor made sense
about anything, yet it was that man's opinion that
kept creeping through his mind. Mavis did not really
feel *right*. She did not really *fit*.

He silently cursed. What did it matter? He was almost thirty years of age, and he had never found a
woman who felt *right* or *fit*. Mavis gave him the chance
to be his own man, to be laird of his own keep, and to
have control over his own lands. Mavis was a sensible
choice. He did not love her, but after so many years
and so many women without feeling even a tickle of
that, he doubted he was capable of loving any woman.
Passion could be stirred with the right touch, and

compatibility could be achieved with a little work. It would serve.

He was just about to ask Alana how extensive a search her kinsmen would mount for her when he heard the sound of someone approaching above them. "Stand o'er there, lass," he said as he nudged her to the left. "'Tis time for the bucket to be emptied and food and water lowered down to us. I dinnae want to be bumping into ye."

Alana immediately felt chilled as she left his side. She kept inching backward until she stumbled and fell onto a pile of blankets. She moved around until she was seated on them, her back against the cold stone wall. The grate was opened, and a rope with a hook at the end of it was lowered through the opening. The lantern this man carried produced enough light to at least allow them to see that rope. Gregor moved around as if he could see, and Alana suspected he had carefully mapped out his prison in his mind. She watched the bucket being raised up and another being lowered down. As Gregor reached for that bucket, she caught a faint glimpse of his form. He was indeed very tall and very lean. She cursed the darkness for hiding all else from her.

"We will need two buckets of water for washing in the morn," Gregor called up to the man, watching him as he carefully lowered the now empty privy bucket.

"Two?" the man snapped. "Why two?"

"One for me and one for the lass."

"Ye can both wash from the same one."

"A night down here leaves one verra dirty. A wee bucket of water is barely enough to get one person clean, ne'er mind two."

"I will see what the laird says."

Alana winced as the grate was slammed shut and that faint shaft of light disappeared. She tried to judge where Gregor was, listening carefully to his movements, but she was still a little startled when he sat down by her side. Then she caught the scent of cheese and still-warm bread, and her stomach growled a welcome.

Gregor laughed as he set the food out between them. "Careful how ye move, lass. The food rests between us. The Gowans do provide enough to eat, though 'tis plain fare."

"Better than none. Perhaps ye had better hand me things. I think I shall need a wee bit of time to become accustomed to moving about in this thick dark."

She tensed when she felt a hand pat her leg, but then something fell into her lap. Reaching down, she found a chunk of bread, which she immediately began to eat it. Gregor was obviously just trying to be certain of where she sat as he shared out the food. She did wonder why a small part of her was disappointed by that.

"Best ye eat it all, lass. I havenae been troubled by vermin, but I have heard a few sounds that make me think they are near. Leaving food about will only bring them right to us."

Alana shivered. "I hate rats."

"As do I, which is why I fight the temptation to hoard food."

She nodded even though she knew he could not see her, and for a while, they silently ate. Once her stomach was full, Alana began to feel very tired, the rigors of the day catching up to her. Her eyes widened as she realized there was no place to make up her own bed; and she doubted there were enough blankets to do so anyway.

"Where do I sleep?" she asked, briefly glad of the dark, for it hid her blushes.

"Here with me," replied Gregor. "I will sleep next to the wall." He smiled, almost able to feel her tension. "Dinnae fret, lass. I willnae harm ye. I have ne'er harmed a child."

*Of course*, Alana thought and she relaxed. He thought she was a child. She had briefly forgotten her disguise. The thought of having to keep her binding on for days was not comforting, but it was for the best. Thinking her a child, Gregor treated her as he would a sister or his own child. If he knew she was a woman, he might well treat her as a convenient bedmate or try to make her one. She brutally silenced the part of her that whispered its disappointment, reminding it that she had no idea of what this man even looked like.

Once the food was gone, Gregor set the bucket aside. Alana heard him removing some clothing and then felt him crawl beneath the blankets. She quickly moved out of the way when she felt his feet nudge her hip. After a moment's thought, she loosened the laces on her gown and removed her boots before crawling under the blankets by his side. The chill of the place disappeared again, and she swallowed a sigh. Something about Gregor soothed her, made her able to face this imprisonment with some calm and courage, and she was simply too tired to try and figure out what that something was.

"On the morrow, we will begin to plan our escape," Gregor said.

"Ye have thought of a way out of here?"

"Only a small possibility. Sleep. Ye will need it."

*That did not sound promising,* Alana mused as she closed her eyes.

## ABOUT THE AUTHOR

Hannah Howell is an award-winning author who lives with her family in Massachusetts. She is the author of nineteen Zebra historical romances and is currently working on a new Highland historical romance, *Highland Lover*, which will be published in June 2006. Hannah loves hearing from readers, and you may visit her website: *www.hannah howell.com.* Or write to her c/o Zebra Books. Please include a self-addressed, stamped envelope if you wish a response.

# Discover the Romances of
# **Hannah Howell**

# Complete Your Collection Today
# Janelle Taylor